Some
Can
Whistle

Also available in Large Print
by Larry McMurtry:

Anything for Billy

Some Can Whistle

A NOVEL

Larry McMurtry

G.K.HALL&CO.
Boston, Massachusetts
1990

Published in Large Print by arrangement with
Simon and Schuster, Inc.

British Commonwealth rights courtesy of The Random
Century Group.

G. K. Hall Large Print Book Series.

Set in 16pt. Plantin.

Library of Congress Cataloging-in-Publication Data

McMurtry, Larry.
   Some can whistle / Larry McMurtry.
     p.   cm. — (G.K. Hall large print book series)
   ISBN 0-8161-4987-9. — ISBN 0-8161-5010-9 (pbk.)
   1. Large type books. I. Title. II. Series.
[PS3563.A319S58   1990]
811'.54—dc20   90-39452

For Jeanie

I

"Mister Deck, are you my stinkin' Daddy?" a youthful, female, furious voice said into the phone.

I could not have been more startled if I had looked up into the blue Texas sky and seen a nuclear bomb on its way down. I was on my south patio, having breakfast with Godwin, watching the fine peachy light of an early summer morning spread over the prairies; I had assumed the call was from my agent, who was in Paris and would soon be swimming up the time zones, hoping to spawn a few deals.

"I don't think I stink," I said politely. The remark caused Godwin to look up from his Cheerios.

"Stinkin's what I call it, never speaking to me in my whole life and leavin' me down here with two babies, only gettin' minimum wage," the young voice said, even angrier. "I seen it in *Parade* that you're the richest writer in the world. Is that the truth or is that a lie?"

"I probably am among the richest but I'm not exactly a writer," I said, even more politely.

The profuse ambiguities of my career held no

interest for the blazing young person on the other end of the phone.

"I don't give that much of a shit what you are exactly," she said. "If you're rich and I'm workin' in this Mr. Burger supportin' two babies, then I hope Jesus puts you right where you belong, which is in hell."

I heard the wail of an infant, and she hung up.

2

Godwin had been patiently watching his last six Cheerios float around in their milk. In his old age he had acquired mystic pretensions; he claimed to see things in the float patterns of Cheerios. Some days he would rattle off to Dallas in his ancient Volkswagen, where he would procure exotic milks (goat, camel—even, he claimed, yak) to float the Cheerios in.

The phone rang again. The previous call had been so brief, violent, and surreal that I almost felt I had dreamed it. Here was another chance; the morning might yet veer onto a normal course. Probably my agent had just finished his lunch at one of the internationally prominent watering holes he favored, in which case he might now have our European syndication in his pocket.

I picked up the phone a little gingerly under Godwin's newly watchful eye.

"This husband of mine's got his creepy side,"

Nema said. "On the other hand he's already ready. That's something, agreed?"

"Agreed," I intoned cautiously. Over the years I had learned to resist too-hasty agreement with Nema in her musing about her various husbands and even more various lovers. I was the scale she weighed them on, but often the scale took a lot of balancing. A given guy might tip up or down for an hour or more as Nema—a tiny, hyper-energetic redhead—moved small pros and cons onto the trays of the scale.

"Even if we got divorced we could still fuck a good bit, I just wouldn't have to let him use the kitchen," Nema reasoned. "One of his creepiest habits is that he never cleans the blender."

"A bad sign," I ventured. I was already wishing Nema would hang up and that my angry daughter—if it *was* my daughter—would call back.

"What's the matter with you?" Nema asked, annoyed. "You're not paying a bit of attention."

People who think TV stars are insensitive bimbos should have the experience of a few years of phone calls from Nema Remington. Talking to her took concentration, even if she was just idly musing over whether to sign her guy-of-the-year for a second season before dispatching him to the minors, as it were.

I had only uttered four words, but the fact that they had not exactly twanged with attentiveness registered in Nema's brain as evidence of an alarming *froideur*.

5

"Have you fallen in love or what, Danny?" she asked.

"Of course not, calm down," I said. "I think my daughter just called."

"Your daughter?" she said, surprised—and with reason; I had never seen my daughter and neither had any of my old friends.

"Well, is she all right?" Nema asked. "Where is she?"

"I don't know," I admitted. "She got mad and hung up. Maybe I better get off this phone, in case she changes her mind and calls again."

"I hope she does, what a great thing for you," Nema said. "Call me back later, I wanta know about this."

"I'll call you back," I promised.

"Bye," Nema said.

3

"As I was saying," Godwin said.

"You weren't saying," I countered. "You hadn't uttered a syllable."

"Quite incorrect," he insisted, concentrating his gaze on the Cheerios, which were still floating, though heavily milk-logged. "I was merely picking up the conversation where we left off yesterday. We were discussing the first sentences of novels, were we not?"

"Godwin, my daughter just called!" I said. "Who cares about first sentences of novels? That

6

was my daughter. Her voice sounded a lot like Sally's."

Just saying the word "daughter" filled me with a kind of excitement I had not felt in years—perhaps had never felt. I tried to call up for comparison Sally's voice, which I hadn't heard for more than twenty years; I tried to recall some throb or timbre that might connect it with the blistering young tones I had just heard.

The effort didn't really succeed, but it was considerably more compelling than the petulant debate Godwin and I had been having for several weeks about what constituted a good first sentence for a novel.

The debate had begun because—for the first time in many years—I had been trying to write a novel, and I was still hung up on the first sentence.

"The point I have been patiently trying to make," Godwin said impatiently, "is that you expect far too much of a first sentence. Think of it as analogous to a good country breakfast: what we want is something simple, but nourishing to the imagination. Hold the philosophy, hold the adjectives, just give us a plain subject and verb and perhaps a wholesome, nonfattening adverb or two."

"I hope the phone rings again soon," I said. "I hope she calls back. I'm almost positive that was my daughter."

The phone did ring and I grabbed it, but once again it was a movie star, and not my daughter. Jeanie Vertus's hopeful voice hit my ear.

"Hi, this is Jeanie," she said, as if I wouldn't know. Two Oscars had not brought Jeanie much self-assurance.

"Hey, aren't you the girl with the funny last name?" I said. "What's that last name again?"

"You gave it to me, Danny—you know it," Jeanie said, half reproachful, half abashed. I had found the name Des Vertus in a book on the history of the corset and persuaded Jeanie to use the Vertus part in a film I had produced. Up to then she had just been plain Jeanie Clark, a nice girl from Altadena, working mainly in commercials, touring companies, summer stock. The film was a modest hit, Jeanie got an Oscar nomination, and from then on she was Jeanie Vertus, though she never became comfortable with the implications of the name, virtue being the last thing Jeanie would have laid claim to.

Though I often teased her about it, I thought the name was a stroke of genius—Jeanie's own ambivalence toward it created an inner *frisson* that made her all the more appealing. It was in part her effort to grow into her own stage name that made Jeanie the great star she later became.

"Is the sun shining there?" she asked. "It's not peeping through in New York."

One of the many things we shared was a need for frequent sunlight.

"Guess what—my daughter just called," I said.

"Is that why you sound happy?" Jeanie asked.

"Do I sound happy?"

"I've never heard such in your voice, Danny,"

she said. "It's as good as the sun peeping through. What's her name?"

"I don't know," I admitted. "She didn't give me a chance to ask. But I'm hoping she'll call back."

"I'm getting off this phone, just in case," Jeanie said, hanging up.

4

At that point Gladys walked up to collect the breakfast dishes. Godwin had just opened his mouth to say something—no doubt he meant to expound on his theory of first sentences—but he noticed Gladys just in time and quickly shut up.

Gladys and Godwin were the same size—small—and they both had white hair, but there the resemblance ended. Godwin was English, Gladys was Texan, and a lot of twain lay in between.

"That phone's been ringing off the hook. Are all your girlfriends pregnant or what?"

She stood beside Godwin's chair and counted the Cheerios floating in his milk.

"Six again," she said. "What's so special about six? Are you into numerology or what?"

Neither Godwin nor I uttered a sound. We both knew all too well that the ever voluble Gladys was a veritable symphony of volubility at this hour of the day. The most casual word from either of us

would unleash an uncheckable stream of specu-
lation and commentary.

"Have you wrote down the first sentence of your
book yet?" Gladys asked, fixing me with a pale
blue eye.

"Yes, would you like to hear it?" I asked.

Godwin groaned and buried his head in his
hands.

"Oh, shut up, Godwin!" I said. "My tongue
gets tired of being held captive every morning."

Gladys pulled up a chair, made herself comfortable, and poured a half-inch layer of sugar on
a grapefruit I'd neglected. She looked cheerful.
Gladys knew perfectly well why Godwin and I
clammed up when she came around. She knew we
thought she talked too much.

"Yes, and my ears will get tired of hearing what
she says now," Godwin remarked, with some bitterness.

"I thought your hearing was shot anyway,"
Gladys retorted. "You're supposed to be deaf, so
what's it to you if a lonely old woman chatters at
you in the morning? You ought to be grateful for
the company. Reach me that spoon."

Godwin handed her a spoon, which was soon
plowing through the sugary grapefruit.

The phone rang again and I snatched it.

"Will you accept a call from T.R.?" an operator
asked.

"From whom?" I asked, surprised.

"From his daughter!" the hot young voice said
at once.

"Yes, yes," I said, suddenly frantic. "Of course I accept. I accept."

"Go ahead, miss," the operator said.

"I ain't talkin' if you're listenin'," my daughter said to the operator. "This is private between me and my daddy."

Then she began to cry. Loud jerky sobs came through the phone, shocking me so that I promptly dropped the receiver, which bounced off the table and hit Gladys on the foot. Though I had spent years of my life listening to women cry into telephones, none of the weepers had been my daughter. I was completely undone—nor was the steely-nerved Gladys exactly a model of calm. She kicked the receiver two or three times before finally catching it and handing it back to me.

Godwin watched us grope for the receiver with amused detachment. He might have been a critic enduring the rehearsal of a not particularly adept comedy act. He didn't say a word, but at least he'd stopped watching his Cheerios.

"I'm sorry, honey," I said. "I accidentally dropped the phone."

"A weird-looking Mexican came up and tried to sell me dope right here at this pay phone while your line was busy," my daughter said, calming a little. "He had one of them pit bulls and I was afraid it was gonna get my babies, plus I was afraid you wasn't ever going to believe it was me, anyway. I gave the dope dealer all my money just so he'd go away, that's why I had to call collect."

She sighed. I waited.

"The dream of my life is to have an inside phone someday," she said quietly. "I'd have a couch, and I could sit on my couch and talk as long as I wanted and not have to mess with no change or worry about dogs getting my babies."

She paused again. Godwin and Gladys were watching me closely.

"That's something that'd be nice," she said in a resigned tone—the very tone Jeanie Vertus sounded when she mentioned that the sun was not peeping through in New York City. What I heard in my daughter's voice was the brief, deep resignation of those who feel that their simplest, most normal hopes cannot possibly come true—not the hope of a ray of sunlight, nor of a couch and an inside phone.

"Honey, you can have an inside phone," I said.

"You're saying it but you ain't here," she said. "Bo, stop throwing dirt on your little sister."

"I like dirt," a faint voice said, the voice, presumably, of my grandson. I decided to try a two-handed grip on the receiver, lest I drop it again in some reflex of emotion.

This got the full attention of Godwin and Gladys. On the whole this was the most exciting breakfast any of us had experienced for ages.

"Tell me where you are and I'll be there," I said. "I'll charter a plane. I'll be there in an hour or two. I'll make it all up to you."

"Maybe you could," my daughter said thoughtfully. "But first I gotta decide if you deserve the chance."

Then she hung up again.

5

"You mean to say that child has called twice and you haven't yet managed to get her name?" Godwin said, once the situation had been explained to him.

"Or even what town she's in?" Gladys chimed in.

"Listen, I've only been an active parent for about ten minutes," I reminded them. "Plus I'm very nervous. Don't be so critical."

"She's probably in Miami," Gladys said. "There's nothing but Mexicans in Miami now, they say."

"She didn't sound that far away," I said, wishing the phone would ring again.

"I once received a call from Nepal," Godwin remarked. "The connection was remarkable. My friend might have been in the next room."

Silence fell. I needed to piss, but didn't feel like leaving the phone, even for a second.

"In retrospect it's nice we had such a good connection that day," Godwin remarked. "A day or two later my friend fell into a crevasse and that was the end of him."

"Should have watched his step," Gladys observed.

"Wait a minute," I said. "The operator asked if I would accept a call from T.R. Her name must be T.R."

"Nonsense, T.R. stands for Teddy Roosevelt," Godwin said. "Who would name a girl Teddy Roosevelt?"

"She was raised by savages, remember," I reminded him. I had only met my wife's parents once—the night they blocked me from the hospital where my infant daughter had been born—but my memories were vivid.

"Savages? You mean you got a half-breed daughter?" Gladys asked. "I thought you told me your wife's folks were Church of Christ."

"I think that's it," I said. "Some savage poor white fundamentalist sect. I didn't mean to insult native Americans."

"Well, I'm a native American and you've insulted me a million times whether you meant to or not," Gladys said. "Even so, I don't want no pit bulls getting your grand-babies. Why don't you trace the call?"

"No, that might upset her," I said. "She called twice, she'll call again."

"I wonder if she's as beautiful as her mother," Godwin said. "Imagine a young Sally in our midst, here in this pastoral Eden. I could teach her to swim if she doesn't happen to know how."

"Go write your book, Godwin," I said. "I'm sure my daughter knows how to swim."

The drift of his thoughts was obvious. Godwin was remembering Sally, my former wife, whose

14

lover he had once been in the days when he was a respected sociology professor at the University of Texas. In middle age he had adroitly crossed the disciplines to classics, and for a time had held a chair in Greek. Now he was retired and living in my guest house, writing a book on Euripidean elements in the music of the Rolling Stones. Godwin was nothing if not mod.

"You can't be sure until you ask her," he said. "I have few peers when it comes to teaching the crawl. She might need to improve her crawl."

"They say that people who keep on having fantasies live the longest," Gladys observed.

"*Don't* tell him that!" I protested. "I don't want him having fantasies about my daughter."

"How about *your* fantasies, my dear?" Godwin asked. He was not above trying a little Oxbridge charm on Gladys from time to time. "Perhaps you'd like to regale us with a few of them when you finish your grapefruit," he said.

"Mine involve things that go on while you're having a bubble bath," Gladys informed him. "You can't see much because of the bubbles."

I was beginning to worry about the pit bulls. Perhaps my daughter really was in Miami. She'd said she'd given all her money to the dope dealer. For all I knew the situation could be deteriorating fast. I had suddenly been brought to grips with the fact that I had three descendants—a daughter and two grandchildren—and I didn't know their names or locations. Godwin and Gladys's idle banter, which normally I enjoyed, began to irritate me.

"You two aren't taking this very seriously," I said. "My daughter's called twice. What do you think I ought to do?"

Before they could answer, two training jets from the air force base in nearby Wichita Falls roared overhead—"roared" was not too strong a word, either. They crossed the hill where my house sat at an altitude of about fifty feet, followed by a tidal wave of sound. When the trainer jets came over, there was no point in even trying to talk. The sound they brought with them had an almost paralyzing force; one just endured it, thoughtless, blank, and a little resentful at having the peace of the morning shattered.

The dark green fighter jets sped like darts toward the western horizon; the waves of sound that swept over us began to recede, and as it did we all heard another sound, a minute tinkle that had been completely smothered by the surf of jet noise: the phone was ringing. I grabbed for it instantly, but just as I did the ringing stopped.

6

"Oh, shit!" I said. "Oh, no!"

To their credit Godwin and Gladys were as horrified as I was.

"Sue the air force!" Godwin said, shaking his fist at the departing planes. "Get the Secretary of

Defense on the phone. This outrage has gone on long enough!"

"That was probably just one of your girlfriends anyway," Gladys said soothingly. "That Italian girl usually calls about this time of day."

She was referring to Marella Miracola—the Miracle, to her worshiping public. Marella was a great star and a good friend, but it was no longer exactly accurate to call her a girl, and in any case she had fallen in love with a man half her age and hadn't called for months.

"Now what'll she think?" I said, fearing it had been my daughter. "She'll think I don't want to have anything to do with her. I'll never meet my grandkids."

"Might be a blessing," Gladys said, reverting to form. "I've met mine, and it's my guess we'll be lucky if half of 'em even manage to stay out of jail.

"The person who said children are a curse wasn't far wrong," she added. "Look at how cute puppies are when they're young, but then they grow up to be dogs."

"Well put," Godwin said. "My own children seldom offer me the slightest assistance."

I was well aware that I was not taking breakfast with two of life's great successes in the parenthood stakes. Godwin's attitude was frankly Casanovian: for him conception meant goodbye. In his wanderings as a young classicist he had fathered children in most of the places where the British flag had once flown: Cairo, Hong Kong, New Delhi,

Cyprus, Kenya, all turned up regularly on my long-distance bill, but it was not clear to me that Godwin had ever actually *seen* any of his children. The only language he shared with them all was French.

Gladys had five girls, all clustered in a tight, bleak corner of the oil patch near Abilene, Texas. Their lives were a constant shuffle of divorcings, remarryings, new loves that soon seemed indistinguishable from old loves. The only thing more constant than this shuffle was the production of offspring; Gladys already had twenty grandchildren, and none of her daughters had yet reached her thirtieth year.

"Haven't any of your girls heard of contraception?" I asked once.

"It don't work in our family because of metabolism," Gladys informed me with a straight face.

Godwin heard her say it and bounced around in his chair for five minutes, making the strange gargling sounds that passed for laughter with him.

"Perhaps you and I have more in common than I supposed," he said to Gladys, when the gargling stopped. "Metabolism has always been my problem too. I expect it explains why Daniel—who doesn't seem to *have* a metabolism—will never understand the common lot.

"Not a bad title for a book," he added, smiling brightly at me. "Why don't you call your new opus 'The Common Lot'?"

"Thanks, I have an excellent title already," I

reminded him. "I have a metabolism too, for your information."

"What are you calling that book?" Gladys asked. "I know you told me, but my memory leaks."

" 'My Girlfriends' Boyfriends,' " I told her. "I think it's a brilliant title."

"It might appeal to the French," Godwin sniffed. "Hearty folk, of which Gladys and I are two, won't go for it, though."

"Too subtle for you?" I suggested.

"Too corrupt," Godwin replied. "The suggestion implicit in your title, that you permit your girlfriends to have as many boyfriends as they want, bespeaks an unhealthy complaisance."

"That's what I think too, and I come down with complaisance once and know exactly what I'm talking about," Gladys informed me.

"You came down with *complaisance?*" I asked, twirling my finger around my ear in the universally accepted sign of insanity.

"Yeah, it was right after I had that bad bladder infection," Gladys said. "Antibiotics didn't do no good because it's a virus."

Shortly after that the conversation stalled. There were mornings when Godwin and I could team-tackle Gladys and force her back a few yards, and then there were mornings when it seemed pointless to try. If she wanted to believe she had once suffered from viral complaisance, why not let her?

I was more irritated with Godwin, anyway. In

the twenty and more years I'd known him, his own girlfriends *and* boyfriends must have accumulated thousands of lovers—a Breughelian triptych would hardly have been sufficient to catalogue the writhings and squirmings he had been witness to. How dare he sit there and accuse me of complaisance!

Meanwhile the sun was well up, the day's heat was coming, and I had missed my daughter's call.

7

"There's nothin' I hate worse than waiting for the phone to ring," Gladys said. She stood up as if to clear the table, and then sat back down and stared into space.

"How old would she be?" Godwin asked.

"Who?"

"Your daughter," he said. "The young nymph with the two cherubs."

"She's twenty-two," I said. "Twenty-three her next birthday. I just hope my agent doesn't call. It won't matter to him if I have fifty daughters—I'll never be able to get him off the phone."

The phone rang. I grabbed it so quickly it squirted out of my hand and popped up in the air, like a frog. Godwin began to gargle. I caught the receiver on its descent; to my immense relief it was the operator, asking if I would accept another collect call from T.R.

"Certainly, of course," I said.

"Howdy," my daughter said. She sounded slightly amused.

"Hi," I said.

"I'm gettin' the hang of this collect calling," she said. "Shoot, if I'd known it was this easy I'd have been calling people all over the place and making them pay for it."

"I'm sorry if that was you who called a minute ago," I said. "Two jet fighters were going over and I didn't hear the phone until it was too late."

She didn't reply. A pause lengthened, during which I became nervous. She might be getting ready to hang up on me again.

"Is something wrong?" I asked. "Did I offend you?"

"Un-uh," she said. "I was just watching Bo."

"What's he doing?"

"He's trying to pee on a cat," she said. "He's at that tender age where he tries to pee on things. I feel a little sorry for the cat, but then a cat that can't outrun Bo don't stand much of a chance, in this part of town anyway. Bo ain't quite three."

Then her mood darkened.

"If them fighter planes you mentioned ain't got nothing else to do they could come down here and bomb this part of town, for all I care," she said. "I hate it."

"Can I just make one request?" I asked.

"I guess, it's your nickel," she said.

I was beginning to love her voice. If I'm a connoisseur of anything, it's the female voice. Through the years—fifty-one of them now—the

21

voices of women have been my wine: my claret, my Chardonnay, my Chablis. And now I had found a new wine, one with depth and color, bite, clarity, body. I was lapping it up, ready to get drunk on it.

"Just tell me your name and what town you're in," I asked.

"My name's T.R.," she said.

"Which stands for what?"

"It stands for Tyler Rose," she said. "What else would it stand for?"

"Well, it could stand for Teddy Roosevelt," I said.

There was another pause. I had the sense that I didn't quite have her attention.

"Oops, now he's trying to hit the kitty with a brick," T.R. said. "I'm gonna have to let this phone dangle for a minute, we don't want no squashed kitties today."

Godwin and Gladys were staring at me. They loved watching me talk on the phone. The concept of privacy held little meaning for either of them. Sometimes I got the sense that the romantic per-egrinations of my far-flung lady friends were the only thing keeping them alive.

"My grandson's trying to hit a cat with a brick," I informed them. "He *was* merely trying to pee on it, but he seems to have become homicidal."

"All kids are murderers," Gladys remarked.

"All kids are murderers," Godwin repeated. "Write that down. It's another good title—rather Euripidean, wouldn't you agree?"

Wails began to come through the phone. More than one voice could be heard wailing.

"What are you crying about?" T.R. said. "Your brother's the one who got the spanking.

"Now both these babies are crying," she said to me. "Jesse don't like me to spank her brother, even when he's being a dick."

The wails of my grandchildren grew louder.

"I hate trying to talk on the phone with them squalling," T.R. said. "That dope dealer's still around, too. He's standing across the street trying to get his pit bull to bite a turtle."

"You didn't tell me what town you're in," I reminded her.

"I sure didn't," she said crisply. "Why would you even want to know, after all these years?"

"So I can come and see you," I said.

The wails seemed to be diminishing, but T.R. was silent.

"It wouldn't be Houston, would it?" I asked, making a wild guess.

"Mister, I don't know a thing about you," she said, her voice suddenly blistering again. "You could be an old scumbag, for all I know. You could have AIDS and give it to my babies."

"I don't have AIDS, are you in Houston?" I asked. "I wish you'd just tell me that much."

"Wish all you want to," she said more quietly. "Wish for me like I used to wish for you. I ain't tellin' you nothing. If you're such a smart old fart, maybe you can figure it out. There's two people waiting to use this phone, and anyway I got to get

23

these kids out of this sun or they'll be red as lobsters."

She hung up with some force.

"I think she's in Houston," I said to Godwin and Gladys.

<hr>

8

"So are you gonna pull yourself together and put some clothes on and go get her, or what?" Gladys wanted to know.

"Gladys, I've got clothes on," I said. "A caftan is clothes. Millions of people in Africa wear them every day of their lives."

"Maybe so, but this ain't Africa," Gladys said. "If you show up at some Dairy Queen in Houston looking like you look now, your daughter's gonna take one look and run the other direction, that's my frank opinion."

I had picked up some caftans in Tunis several years ago, meaning to use them as crew presents for people who worked on my television show. But it was hot when I got back to Texas, so one day I tried one on, to see if what worked for North African heat worked for Texas heat, too. Pretty soon I was wearing caftans day and night, week in and week out. I don't know that they made me cooler, particularly—what they did was eliminate the problem of thinking about clothes at all. I just wore my caftans; they were perfect for the reclusive life I started leading right after I sold my production company and departed Culver City forever.

Gladys undoubtedly had a point, though. Caftans would not be ideal garb for my first visit to my daughter. Unfortunately I'd become neurotically attached to them; the thought of having to change to normal American clothes produced a certain dissonance in my thoughts. The dissonance made me grumpy.

"She doesn't work in a Dairy Queen, she works in a Mr. Burger," I pointed out, well aware that I was making a picayune objection.

"She'll still freak out if you show up in a caftan," Gladys insisted.

"I'm afraid this means you're finally going to have to get dressed," Godwin said in a gloating tone.

I gave them both a defiant glare.

The once-respected classicist sitting opposite me had just unscrewed the top from a bottle of suntan lotion and was casually pouring the liquid over his chest and shoulders. His clothes at the moment consisted of a towel across his lap, put there in deference to Gladys's sensibilities.

"If you think she'll run for the hills when she sees me, think what she'll do when she sees you," I said. "You're sitting there naked and you look at least a hundred years old."

"Two hundred," Gladys said. "He's the oldest-looking thing I ever laid eyes on, and both my grandpas lived to be over ninety."

"Sour grapes from two sourpusses," Godwin

said. "I'm frequently complimented for my youthful deportment."

The top of Godwin's head was completely bald; a few tufts of long, wispy white hair clung to the underside of his skull. In the summertime he rarely wore anything more formal than a swimsuit; with Godwin nudism was not so much a philosophy as a convenience. Three of his front teeth were missing, courtesy of a love affair with a biker of unstable temperament. Efforts to get him to replace them had so far been greeted with toothless sneers.

For a year or two, when he first conceived of the book about Euripides and the Rolling Stones, Godwin had staggered around my hill, doped to the gills with acid and other controlled substances, earphone clamped to his head, the Stones' music pouring into his ears for as much as eighteen hours at a stretch.

Gladys and I both felt that he had not really come back from that experience, though what "back" meant when you were talking about Godwin Lloyd-Jons was not easy to say.

"Anyway, why pick on me?" Godwin asked, pointing his bottle of suntan lotion at Gladys. "Gladys doesn't exactly dress her age, you know."

At the moment Gladys was wearing orange parachute pants, black Reeboks, and a yellow I Love New York T-shirt. Gladys had never been to New York and would not, in my opinion, love it if she happened to go there, but she was a frequent recipient of hand-me-downs and other surprising garments from various of the ladies I know. Gladys had somehow convinced them that she alone was keeping me sane and healthy, a task none of them had shown much interest in assuming; for this they rewarded her with wild-looking pants or strange baggy coats from places such as Parachute in L.A. or Comme Des Garcons in New York, paying God knows what sums so that my maid could flit around West Texas looking totally ridiculous. People in Thalia assumed that Gladys got the clothes from the Good-will store in Wichita Falls. She was probably the most expensively dressed woman in the county, but people still treated her like a clown.

And something sad in Gladys stood ready to believe that she *was* a clown, which is why I spoke up instantly when Godwin made his remark.

"Shut up, Gladys looks great!" I said. "She's the only one around here who dresses with esprit."

I rushed the comment out, hoping it would arrive in time to keep Gladys from bursting into tears, which she was wont to do if any reference was made of her appearance.

Quick as I was, I was still too late. Gladys burst into tears. Though Godwin and I had both seen this happen many times, we were still always stunned by the speed with which Gladys could move from equanimity, even pugnacity, to despair.

"I hope that poor little child of yours stays where she is," she said. Tears were streaming down her face, which was otherwise plain as a post.

"She'd be better off staying with the pit bulls than livin' in a hateful place like this," she said. As Godwin and I sat silent, she shuffled together a few of the dishes and headed for the house.

9

"I was merely defending myself," Godwin said meekly. "I didn't mean to hurt the poor thing's feelings."

"When are you going to learn that you can't kid Gladys about the way she looks?" I asked.

"The two of you insult me constantly," Godwin said. "But do I indulge my feelings? Do I burst into tears?"

Only yesterday he had stood by the phone in the kitchen and butted his head against the wall for five minutes, sobbing and wailing, because one of his boyfriends had refused to come over for a swim. Gladys and I had been forced to retreat to the front of the house, a considerable distance from the kitchen, in order not to be privy to some loud and messy recriminations.

"You don't behave any better than she does, if that's what you're claiming," I said. "She's got a point, you know. What *is* my daughter going to think when she sees this household?"

"What makes you think she'll come?" Godwin

asked. "So far she hasn't even given you her address."

That was true, but I still assumed that my daughter would be coming to stay with me now. I wanted to see her. I wanted to hear her voice some more—a lot more. I wanted to meet my grandchildren. I wanted them all to live with me. After all, I had a huge house, vast stretches of which had never been occupied. I had once envisioned various of my lady friends coming to visit for extended periods, so my architect had designed a series of luxurious semiprivate suites, with saunas and airy studio rooms flooded with fine Texas sunlight. The suites were tailored to the various proclivities of the ladies I thought might come and stay. I had laid in excellent wines, procured a video library of more than a thousand films. I had everything ready.

The house—I could see it as I sat, spreading over the long hill to the east of me—had been ready for nearly ten years, but none of the ladies had ever quite managed to get there. Something —romance or career—always intervened at the last minute. They never quite made it to Texas, never stayed in my house.

The thought that my daughter might come and live with me was the most exciting thought to strike me in at least a decade. What could possibly be better? There was room for several little families in my house; having my daughter and my grandchildren would be perfect. I would get to know my daughter at last. The fact that I even had grandchildren seemed like an incredible bonus.

But now, as I looked at Gladys's retreating figure weaving across my hill in her orange parachute pants, and at Godwin, a small, naked, virtually demented old man, stewing in his broth of suntan oil, a nervousness, even an apprehension, began to grow in me.

I was fifty-one years old. I thought I knew the difference between fantasy and reality, and I was well aware that the perfect domestic scenes my imagination had already begun to cast up would not likely be that perfect if they were ever actually lived. There might just be tension and anger instead of love and fun.

"What do you think my daughter would really make of all this, if I can persuade her to come?" I asked uneasily.

"She'll probably think she's enrolled in a lunatic asylum," Godwin said bluntly. "She'll think we're all crazy as loons."

"That's a stupid metaphor," I said. "Have you actually ever seen a crazy loon? Has anyone? Why would a bird be crazy?"

We were both writers, in a sense, and often criticized one another's figures of speech, particularly when we were nervous about impending change.

My daughter's arrival would certainly represent change: three young lives would suddenly have to try and mesh with three old lives. I wanted it, yet I could feel my apprehension rising. Godwin was

30

watching me closely; he knew I was nervous. He didn't seem disposed to be helpful, either.

"You know she's gonna think we're lunatics and you're scared shitless, aren't you?" he said.

"I'm a little nervous," I admitted. "She's twenty-two and I've never met her. But I still want her to come. We're not *really* lunatics, you know. We're just a little odd."

"Do you think a twenty-two-year-old can grasp the difference?" he asked.

"I've never met her," I repeated. "How would I know what difference she can grasp? Anyway, first things first."

"What does that mean?" Godwin asked. "What do you regard as a plausible first thing?"

"Seeing if the Mercedes will start," I said. "I haven't driven it in a while. It may not start."

10

Godwin looked smug, as if the fact that I hadn't driven my car in six months meant that I was hopelessly unfit to have a relationship with my daughter.

"Godwin, I'm not trying to pretend we're not odd," I said. "Of course we're odd. If she comes, we'll all have to do a little adjusting."

One big difference between me and Godwin was that he had always had complete disdain for what might be called normal behavior, whereas I had never entirely lost the habit of thinking of myself as a normal person, though of course I recognized that the concept of normalcy was comparative. If I had only Godwin and Gladys to compare myself to, I might easily convince myself that I was a pretty average guy.

But my daughter, an evidently healthy young woman who had two small children and worked at a Mr. Burger, might well not see it that way. To her I might just seem like an aging freak, slopping around my house in caftans, not leaving my hill for months on end, watching horrible European *policier* videos half the night, and talking on the phone hour after hour to a kind of aural harem of beautiful women scattered all over the world, most of whom I only saw for maybe an hour or two a year.

Indeed, thanks to the steady advance of technology, not only did I not *see* these women very often, I rarely even talked directly to them anymore.

Most of the time now I talked to their message machines, a new and seductive form of communication that most of us seemed to be coming to prefer. Already, in only a few months of practice, I had become a kind of Proust of the message machine, leaving elegant, finely modulated monologues on the message machines of distinguished, or at least distinctive, women in New York, California, Paris, Rome.

The women, in turn, left me rambling, chatty monologues of their own—little oral letters, in a sense. In only a few weeks we all established a rapport with our new machines; monologues were soon floating in daily from various of my far-flung chums.

"It's sort of like a new art form," Jeanie Vertus pointed out shortly after we developed a tendency to talk mainly to one another's machines.

Of all the minds I kept in contact with, Jeanie's was the quickest, the most likely to key in immediately to the human consequences of technological advance.

"It's kind of nice to know you don't necessarily have to deal with a real naked voice anymore when you dial the phone," Jeanie said. "Real naked voices have said some pretty fucking ugly things to me."

"Real voices have, but my voice hasn't," I pointed out. "I've never said ugly things to you, and I don't think it's likely to be destructive if we have a live conversation once in a while."

"Live conversations are kind of hit-or-miss though," Jeanie said pensively. "Monologues are more concentrated. I can dump out a lot of thoughts quickly and then you can sort of sift through them at your leisure."

Over the next months she delivered a series of dandy monologues, her speedy mind racing over a vast range of subjects.

Then one day she suddenly stopped calling. Worse, she turned off her message machine. I had to call seven or eight times before I got her.

"What's wrong?" I asked. "You suddenly stopped leaving monologues."

"I suddenly stopped leaving monologues, Danny," she said in a voice thick with sadness. When Jeanie descended into sadness, she descended to pure depths.

"I wish you hadn't stopped," I said cautiously—one didn't just wade out into one of Jeanie's sadnesses. "I miss your monologues."

"It's all getting too remote between us," Jeanie said. "The monologues are just taking us farther apart, and we're already too far apart."

I thought she might cry, but she didn't. She was resting on the bottom, well below the level of tears.

"At first it was kind of nice just to talk to machines," she said. "It eliminates the conflict, which saves energy. But the trouble is, it eliminates the person, too. We don't answer one another anymore, Danny. We just leave our views, separate but equal. Now I feel so separate I don't even know if I'm your friend."

"Of course you're my friend," I insisted, suddenly panicky at the thought that I might have lost her because of some stupid message machines.

"I'm getting gloomy about it," she said. "I think we were doing better before we got the machines."

Jeanie and I weathered that gloom, though—in the ensuing weeks I called her every day, missing her, getting her at bad times, waking her up. Several of the women I called woke up snarling, but Jeanie just woke up blank, puzzled that anyone had supposed she was worth a call. Despite several calls that were duds and a few that were actually setbacks, the sun finally peeped through, to shine on our friendship again; after that I made only modest and careful use of the message machine where Jeanie Vertus was concerned.

The episode came back to me as I sat at the breakfast table watching Godwin sulk, and wondering whether in fact my household was too odd to receive a normal young woman with two small children.

The thought that troubled me most was that when all was said and done I might *not* be the most normal member of my household, as I was wont to think. Even Godwin and Gladys might react to adult life more normally than I did.

Godwin at least still butted his head against the wall in despair when his boyfriend wouldn't come over for a swim.

Gladys still got purple with rage when Chuck, her long-suffering truck-driving husband, lingered in north Amarillo for a few extra days, enjoying a fling with a waitress at the stockyards café.

Neither Godwin nor Gladys seemed to be exactly happy, but neither were they conducting their lives via telephone, Federal Express package, and message machine.

I was the one doing *that*—which might mean that I was the craziest person in a crazy house.

11

"Even a sixty-thousand-dollar car needs to be driven once in a while," Godwin pointed out, once it had been determined that the Mercedes definitely had no intention of starting.

I sat in the driver's seat in a state of deep gloom. From time to time I turned the ignition key, hoping a miracle would happen. After all, it was a very expensive car; maybe it was just hibernating. At any moment the powerful German engine might roar into life.

Godwin and Gladys were pacing around the garage, smoking: Gladys smoked tobacco, Godwin marijuana. The more nervous they were, the more they smoked, and they were plenty nervous today, but at least they had transcended their immediate differences. Godwin apologized profusely for having hurt Gladys's feelings at breakfast. I don't think he was really contrite; he just feared Gladys's vengeance, which was apt to take bizarre forms. Once she had poured a jar of molasses into his sock drawer after a similar contretemps. Fifty pairs of socks had congealed into a giant sock ball. Godwin wasn't taking any chances on that happening again.

"You could use my Toyota," Gladys offered. "Your daughter probably ain't used to luxury anyway."

Her Toyota sat a few feet away, the moral equivalent of a battered spouse. Hardly an inch of its surface was not dented, rusted, or crumpled.

"It's because I like to let my mind roam free when I drive," Gladys explained. "My mind will be off somewhere, happy as a lark, and the next thing you know my car's smacked into something."

"The thought of driving your Toyota to Houston doesn't appeal to me," I said politely.

"Take my bug," Godwin offered.

"No, thanks," I said, trying the key again and getting nothing, not even a click.

"He's impossible when he's depressed," Godwin said to Gladys. "Have you noticed that? He won't take his car and he won't take mine or yours, although ours are in excellent mechanical condition and his won't start. I call that perversity."

"I call it prudence," I said. Godwin's Volkswagen was not as battered-looking as Gladys's Toyota, but enough drugs had been spilled into its floorboards to send me to prison for at least a decade. Also, in recent years, much of Godwin's love life had been conducted in the bug—the part involving hitchhikers, principally. Gladys and I had long since callously dubbed it the Aidsmobile, though we avoided the term when Godwin was around.

The fact that my Mercedes wouldn't start was horribly depressing. Indeed, it was destabilizing, though of course an element in my depression was the thought that I was allowing such a minute problem to destabilize me.

It was ridiculous to be even mildly depressed, and I *knew* it was ridiculous. After all, I had neglected the car for six months—it had a perfect right not to start. And also, of course, by any rational standard, it was an *extremely* minor problem. There was a filling station only seven miles away. If I called them they'd be at my house in ten minutes and the Mercedes would be purring like a tiger long before I could get myself shaved, bathed, dressed, packed, and in a fit state to proceed to Houston.

Unfortunately, knowledge that I was dealing with a problem that was very minor, circumstantial, and in no way life-threatening didn't make me feel a bit better. If anything, the very triviality of the problem contributed to the destabilization.

I was a very rich man. "Al and Sal," the sitcom I had created twelve years earlier, was the top-grossing TV sitcom *of all time*. Worldwide it had earned over a billion dollars, nearly a third of which was mine; "Al and Sal" was far and away the most popular show in syndication on the world market, with another billion dollars in earnings projected over the coming decade.

So, not only was I very successful, I also had a lot of money. In the particular world in which I became successful—the world of entertainment, or, to be precise, the world of television—no illusion is more crucial than the illusion that great success and huge money buy you immunity from the common ills of mankind, such as cars that won't start.

The maxim, the Golden Rule, the first motto of the world in which I achieved my success is: *All Things Are Supposed to Work Instantly.*

If they don't, then what's it all for? The fact that you might have to wait ten minutes to get your car jump-started, like any ordinary slob, calls a whole value system into question. *If you don't have total immunity, then why bother?*

"He's gonna have a fit," Gladys said. "I can tell by the way he's twitching."

Wearily I tried the ignition key one more time. There was no click.

"I'm not twitching and I've never had a fit in my life," I said honestly. "I produced that stupid sitcom for almost nine years, and no one who worked on it can claim they ever saw me have a fit. I don't know how to have fits, Gladys. I often wish I did."

"I know, but there's always a first time," Gladys said. "You've been saving up fits all your life, if you ask me. I just hope I'm on vacation when you finally have one."

"Perhaps we'd best just call the filling station," Godwin said. "They're quite efficient. I'm sure they'll get over here fast."

"No, thanks," I said. "I'm going to call Wichita Falls and have them bring me a Cadillac. They should be able to get one here while I'm shaving. I don't like my Mercedes anymore."

"You're not serious," Godwin said. "It's almost brand-new. You just let it sit too long and the battery's down."

"I'm perfectly serious," I said. "You want to buy this car? It's yours for five thousand dollars. Buy it. Then you won't have to ride in that semen-encrusted Volkswagen anymore."

"If he don't want it can I buy it?" Gladys asked. She was quicker than Godwin to seize a good opportunity.

The thought of Gladys tootling around in a Mercedes almost cheered me up.

"Where would you get five thousand dollars?" I asked, amused. "Where would either of you get five thousand dollars, for that matter?"

"Spoiled, spoiled, spoiled!" Godwin said. "You aren't remotely ready to go to Houston. You're still in your caftan. You look like Yves Saint Laurent might look if he were fat. Why not just let the filling station come and start the car while you attempt to make yourself presentable for your daughter?"

"So who gets the car?" Gladys asked, her eyes firmly fixed on the main chance. "I could take over the yard work and pay it off in a summer or two. That old Mexican don't have no business doing yard work at his age."

She was referring to old Pedro, an ancient person who lived in a little adobe hut he had built for himself on the western edge of my hill. Pedro was the oldest person any of us had ever known. I had found him standing by the road near Deming, New Mexico, several years earlier, on one of my drives from California. I had passed him without thought and driven for another ten miles be-

40

fore it occurred to me that I had just passed a very, very old, very small man. Pedro was about the height of a large sheepdog.

I rarely pick up hitchhikers—that's Godwin's sport—but after some thought I turned, went back, and picked up Pedro, a tiny man who looked as ancient as the rocks. He had no possessions at all, just himself. He spoke a little English, but the drift of his thoughts was cryptic, to say the least.

"I am just traveling along now," he said, when I asked him where he wanted to be taken. "My family died before I did. Just take me where you want to go."

So I took him home and never regretted it. The fact that my huge house was made of adobe pleased him, although he was highly critical of the workmanship itself and spent his first year or two with us correcting a number of major flaws.

Then he built his own little hut on the edge of my hill. Every day he would walk up and do a little yard work; we got our water from a windmill, which Pedro kept in fine repair. There was an old barn on the property, filled with dusty, rat-nibbled saddlery and harness. Pedro killed the rats, and, over the years, repaired and polished the saddles and the harness.

"I believe he eats them rats," Gladys reported one day, nearly in shock at the thought. "I seen him carrying five or six dead ones down to that hut of his."

Whatever the truth of that, Pedro mainly lived on frijoles, tortillas, and Budweiser beer. He was very fond of Budweiser and would appear in the kitchen once a day to appropriate a six-pack.

"Okay, the Mercedes is yours," I said to Gladys. "Godwin doesn't seem to want it."

"I don't want it," Godwin said petulantly. "I don't want your absurd favors."

"Does that mean I start doing the yard work?" Gladys asked.

"No, Pedro likes to do the yard work," I said. "When my grandkids get here you can pay out the Mercedes by being their nanny."

"Their nanny? Her?" Godwin said. He gargled hysterically for several minutes under our disapproving eyes. I got out of the Mercedes for the last time and slammed its expensive door.

"That's like a baby-sitter, right?" Gladys asked.

"No," Godwin said. "Not at all. A nanny is responsible for her young charges' moral instruction. Nannies should be women of impeccable character."

"That's why I'm giving the job to Gladys," I said. "Her character's perfect."

It wasn't, but what the hell. Gladys could rip around Thalia telling everyone she had been promoted to nanny. Her status, already high, might rise even higher.

"I had a very proper nanny myself—her name was Mrs. Frazier," Godwin said. I could tell by his voice that he was about to make one of his abrupt dives into sentiment. If we weren't careful he would soon be in tears. The thought of her appearance made Gladys cry; memories of his very proper Yorkshire childhood had the same effect on Godwin.

"The sainted Mrs. Frazier, whatever I've become I owe to her," he said in thickening tones.

The man, after all, was an old friend. I should have been more tolerant; I should have bitten my tongue. But the sight of him standing there, hairless, toothless, spavined, wearing only an old green bathing suit and a pair of Nepalese sandals that his mountain-climbing friend had sent him a day or two before dropping into the crevasse, smoking marijuana as a prelude to his daily intake of methamphetamines, cocaine, hash, or anything he could get, and sure to set off in an hour or two in pursuit of comely young hitchhikers, while building up to a cry about his old nanny, was too much for my resistance.

"If the sainted Mrs. Frazier could see you now, I'm not sure she'd want you on her resumé," I said with surprising forbearance. After all, the man was an idiot, a drug addict, and an orgiast. What self-respecting nanny would want to claim him as her best work?

Gladys headed for the house. "If you two are going to start saying ugly things to one another I'm leaving," she said.

Godwin maintained an air of studied calm. "The pot should think twice before addressing the kettle," he said.

"The pot did think twice," I assured him.

"That's a terrible first sentence you've written,"

he said. "It's as bad a first sentence as I've ever heard."

This thrust took me slightly off guard.

"Godwin, it hasn't taken its final form," I said, before trudging into the house to order a Cadillac.

12

The sentence Godwin didn't like—the first sentence of my new novel—read something like this:

"True maturity is only reached when a man realizes he has become a father figure to his girl-friends' boyfriends—and he accepts it."

I had been tinkering with the sentence for nearly three months. A character, as yet unnamed but not unlike me, speaks it to another character, also unnamed but somewhat resembling Godwin Lloyd-Jons.

I had never been pleased with the sentence. The sentiment, or opinion, it expressed was perfect for the novel I planned to write, but the words had not yet been put in a satisfying or compelling order. I had written the sentence at least two hundred times, rearranging the words, and sometimes the punctuation. For instance, I tried using a semicolon rather than a dash; but after a few dozen tries with the semicolon I went back to the more emphatic dash.

For, after all, the sentence contained two assertions, both of which were sure to be questioned: that a man would at some point become a father figure to his girlfriends' boyfriends; and that emotional maturity is only reached when the man accepts this development.

In the course of the three months I had read many variants of the sentence to Godwin, and he had sneered at them all.

"What a ridiculous utterance," he scoffed. "I certainly have no intention of being a father figure to *my* girlfriends' boyfriends.

"Of course, I might be prepared to be a *boyfriend* to some of them," he added. "Although, to be frank, myself excepted, my girlfriends have not exactly been distinguished for their taste in males."

"Godwin, it's the first sentence of a novel," I said. "For all I know the novel will refute the sentence. I was just trying to start with a broad generality. Think of the first sentence of *Pride and Prejudice*, or the first sentence of *Anna Karenina*."

"Never read either of them," he said in an ill-tempered tone. "You might recall that I had a classical education."

Gladys had heard my first sentence a few times too. Her reaction was if anything more discouraging than Godwin's.

"I get downhearted every time I hear it," she said. "What makes you want to write books anyway? You're rich enough."

"Gladys, I just want to," I said. "I was a writer, you know, before I got into television."

"That was a long time ago, maybe you ain't one anymore," she said unsentimentally.

45

"It's just a sentence," I said. "Why does it make you downhearted?"

"'Cause it makes me realize I wasted my best years," Gladys said. "I ain't never had no boyfriends—just Chuck, and he's a heel."

"Chuck is not a heel," I said. "He may slip from the narrow path of virtue once in a while, but we all do that."

"I don't, because who would want to slip with an old hag like me?" Gladys said.

"Well, Frank would want to slip with you," I reminded her.

Frank was the mailman; my house was the last stop on his route. He arrived about noon every day, his tiny pickup laden with magazines, newspapers, videos, and books, all for me. I subscribed to thirty or forty continental magazines, which I hunted through obsessively, hoping to find pictures of various aging actresses who had once sort of been my girlfriends—I had had a long Grade B continental period before I hit it big with "Al and Sal."

Any mention of Yorkshire made Godwin nostalgic for his old nanny; in the same way the slick, shiny European magazines made me nostalgic for the Mediterranean littoral, along much of which I had traveled in the late sixties and early seventies, accompanied by a sprightly and vivid string of minor European actresses, Italian, French, and German, many of them vulgar and tacky on the screen, but alert, fastidious, and exacting in real life. How I missed them!

46

Frank Lucketts, the mailman, couldn't believe any one person read so many magazines and newspapers.

"My eyes would wear out from all that reading, if it was me," he said, dropping a bale of magazines on my table.

Then, since his working day had just officially ended, he would retire to the kitchen, have a beer, and flirt with Gladys, with whom he had been hopelessly in love for several years.

"Frank's sweet, but he's a loser," Gladys said when I made inquiries about their nascent romance. "I don't need to get mixed up with no more losers, I already got Chuck."

"I could be considered a loser myself," I said. "I've worked for three months on one sentence and neither of my housemates likes it. I think I'll go read it to Pedro, maybe he'll like it."

"That old man's lost in his own thoughts," Gladys said. "He don't say two words a month. At least Frank talks. He don't make sense, but he does make noise. Chuck used to buy me flowers, but he don't no more. He and that old Mexican could trade places and I'd never know the difference."

"I may have to give up on this first sentence," I admitted. "I don't really like it myself."

47

13

My Cadillac turned out to be maroon. It was the size of a young whale. At the sight of it my spirits rose, and when I sat in it they rose even further. The seats, also in a soft maroon leather, smelled good—new and expensive and good.

Godwin, still in his green bathing trunks, and still smoking dope, sneered at me when I got behind the wheel, but I didn't care.

"I should have bought a Cadillac long ago," I said. "I'm a Texan, after all. I like big cars. Why was I driving a Mercedes anyway? Am I a European?"

"No, but at least you were trying to be one," he said. "Now you've reverted to barbarism, just as I always knew you would."

"You're a boring little dope addict, leave me alone," I said. "I doubt if you can even read Greek anymore."

The salesman who brought the Cadillac was what is now called a hunk. He was in his mid-twenties, not very good-looking but still a hunk. Godwin offered him several varieties of drugs, all of which he refused. Godwin stared at him appraisingly, but the young man was rather stolid and may not have realized he was being appraised. A bored mechanic in a pickup was waiting to take the young salesman back to the Cadillac agency.

It was clear he didn't like Godwin, who hadn't offered *him* any drugs.

I gave the young man a check, he gave me a receipt, and the good-smelling car was mine.

"Have a good day," the young man said as he left. Godwin had tried to make eye contact with him but the young man wasn't into eye contact.

"You're as spoiled as a pig," Godwin said to me. "Besides that, you're irresponsible. Gladys will probably kill herself in that Mercedes."

A dust cloud came pouring up the road from the south. At the head of it was Gladys; she had called the filling station, got the Mercedes started, and was now practicing driving in her new car. She sped by the house, going about eighty; the dust cloud engulfed Godwin before following Gladys on north.

"She seems to have got the hang of it," I said. "As for you, you're lucky that mechanic didn't run over you. I don't think your charm worked on that mechanic."

"I rarely waste my charm on aging laborers," he said archly. "Perhaps I should accompany you on this fatherly errand. I might overlook your rudeness and accompany you. It could well be that you'll need my charm when you locate the young lady."

"Why would I? She's *my* daughter," I said. "Anyway your appearance more than offsets your charm. One look at you and she'd probably want a restraining order of some kind to keep me away from my own grandkids."

Actually, I was tempted to take him. I was still pretty apprehensive at the thought of meeting my daughter. Godwin was strange, but on the other hand a known quantity. Having him along to bicker with might keep me from getting too nervous on the drive down.

Then, abruptly, I rejected the notion—a gutless notion at best. She was *my* daughter—I had spent many miserable years hoping against hope that I'd someday get a chance to meet her. Now the chance had come. Providing myself with a buffer before I even laid eyes on her would be the act of an emotional coward.

I *was* an emotional coward, more or less, but in this case, if ever, I knew that I had better try to transcend my cowardly instincts. I wanted that girl to like *me*, not Godwin.

"You better stay here and look after Gladys," I said. "What if she did have a wreck?"

"You're just greedy," he said. "You don't want to share your daughter with me. You probably won't even bring her home. Pig that you are, you'll take her somewhere where you can have her all to yourself."

"The thought hadn't occurred to me," I said. "But now that you mention it, maybe I will. I wonder if she has a passport."

I was getting a little tired of the reclusive life in Hardtop County, if the truth were known. I had begun to dream Mediterranean dreams, and to miss the girls of those golden shores: Claudia Cardinale and Melissa Mell, Ingrid Pitt, Senta

50

Berger, Françoise Dorléac, Romy Schneider—all my continental dreamgirls. Maybe I'd take a house in Rome, get to know my daughter in a European setting—the grandkids could grow up bilingual.

Godwin had known me long enough to quickly sniff the drift of my thoughts.

"She works in a Dairy Queen," he reminded me. "I hardly think she'd have a passport."

"A Mr. Burger," I corrected. "A Mr. Burger, not a Dairy Queen."

"There may be a difference," Godwin said, "but I doubt if that means she's much of an internationalist."

I got out of the Cadillac and went to get my bags.

"God, you're tiresome," I said. "If I don't leave, I'll be too tired to drive, just from arguing with you."

"Look, I'm an experienced dad," he said. "I've got nine children to your one. You may well find yourself in need of my expertise."

"Godwin, not this time," I said, stiffening my spine. "This is something I want to do alone."

_____**14**_____

"Self-parody is the first portent of age," I said to myself as I cruised through Jacksboro, the first town on my route south. Jacksboro was distinguished among the small towns of the region for having kept intact a block of old limestone buildings; the buildings were in no way appealing, but they *were* consistent in an area where few things were, architecturally speaking. The stone buildings of Jacksboro looked as if they'd all crack to bits and fall down if you whacked them a time or two with a big sledgehammer.

I drove on to Decatur, reflecting cheerfully that there wasn't a single man-made structure within one hundred miles of my house that wasn't ugly. The Kimball Museum in Fort Worth, which happens to be precisely one hundred miles from my front door, is the first appealing building one can hope to encounter in any direction, if one starts from my house.

"Self-parody is the first portent of age" was not some little personal warning I was issuing to myself; it was an alternative first sentence to my novel.

"The first portent of age is self-parody," I said, to see if changing the word order would help things along. It seemed to me from what I could remember of novel writing, an activity I had unfortunately let lapse for nearly twenty years, that the first sentence of a book was of critical, even crucial, importance. If you could think of a good one, all the other sentences might follow after it obediently. They might just come marching briskly out of your brain, like well-drilled soldiers.

It was apparent to me that my girlfriends' boyfriends sentence wasn't working, although I had set my heart on it. Certainly it was an accurate reflection of my life, and though I'm odd, in the end I may not be all that odd. Several of my girl-friends now had boyfriends who looked to me for fatherly counsel. I spent a good many hours each week dispensing advice to the bewildered young men who—often to their intense surprise—had been adopted as the boyfriends of my older, but still perplexing, girlfriends. It was ironic, of course, that fatherly counsel was what I had been called on to provide—after all, I had never even seen my own child, and as yet had given her *no* counsel—but, if ironic, it might also be paradig-matic.

More odd, if possible, was the fact that I rarely spoke directly to these lucky young men. I relayed my counsel through the often cloudy medium of the girlfriends. I might say to Jeanie Vertus, "Why don't you tell Carver this? You could just mention that I mentioned it."

Or I might say to Nema Remington, "I think A.B. ought to consider such-and-such." Nema, never one to let the grass grow under a useful thought, would promptly call her husband and demand that he consider such-and-such.

In that way, life proceeded. The process re-minded me a little of a teen-age party game, pop-ular in the fifties, of passing Life Savers from boy to girl on the ends of toothpicks. It was a game that suggested kissing, yet a sharp object stood between you and the kiss. Sharp objects also stood between the boyfriends and me—i.e., the girl-friends. That the girlfriends were sharp was fine with me. Their sharp behavior was what had got me interested in the girlfriends in the first place; life is too short to waste on dull women, of which there are far too many—most of them employed in the television industry, or so I had once thought.

One or two of my girlfriends' boyfriends were actually young in age—Marella Miracola's, for example—but the ones who seemed to need the most counseling were merely young in mind.

"He's a child, you see," my girlfriends were always saying to me gravely in the wake of some particularly messy bit of behavior on the part of a boyfriend.

"He's never grown up," was another sentiment often heard in these conversations.

"He's like a giant four-year-old," Jeanie said of one lover. Jeanie often put things brilliantly.

By contrast with their lovers, I was, in the view of most of my old girlfriends, thoroughly grown up. The consensus was that I was not only grown up, I was *too* grown up. None of them had ever met Pedro, but they knew about him and seemed to feel that in ways that counted with them I was not much his junior. Chronologically I was three or four decades his junior, but chronology meant little to my girlfriends. All of them were firm subscribers to the nonsensical theory that you're only as old as you think you are.

My own position was more realistic. I think I'm as old as I am, and I am fifty-one. At forty-eight, I was a different man; at forty-five, I was more different still. But fifty-one seemed to be the age at which one was most likely to cross the threshold of self-parody—which is why I was thinking of changing my first sentence.

15

The courthouse in Decatur looked as if it belonged in Bavaria. It was built of red granite and was topped by a grotesque tower with a clock in it. The clock had been stopped for several years—and the same could be said for the town over which the courthouse towered. Decatur was a stopped clock of sorts, but its citizens were very proud of their courthouse and kept spotlights trained on it all night. To me it resembled one of the lesser castles of the mad King Ludwig II. If the Danube had been flowing past it, the courthouse might have looked appropriate, but unfortunately the only thing that flowed past it was Highway 287, a bleak asphalt river that carried one north to Amarillo and the drear Oklahoma panhandle.

I sometimes whiled away my drives by directing what I liked to think was a sharp eye at the many nondescript little communities through which I passed. There was obviously no guarantee I was going to make it as a novelist—I had left my imagination in mothballs too long. Travel writing might have to be my fallback position. My mind was not entirely gone, but it had acquired a tendency to drift. It seemed to me I might make a virtue of necessity and drift along with my mind.

I had a friend named Jack McGriff, an antiques scout. Jack spent his life on the highways of America finding wonderful things wherever he went. During the nine years when I had been chained to a sound stage in Culver City, I had envied no one so much as Jack. He seemed to have the perfect life, going where he pleased, and—more importantly from my immediate point of view—not going where he didn't please.

"I spend very little time in Gary, Indiana," he remarked to me once. In the trade he was known as "Cadillac Jack," due to his penchant for cars just like the one I was presently driving through Decatur.

While Jack McGriff was enjoying some of the best scenery in America, I was spending fourteen hours a day amid some of the worst, i.e., Culver City, the Gary of the entertainment industry. During my years there, I must have averaged at least two confrontations an hour. I had confrontations with writers, confrontations with actors, confrontations with light men, sound men, camera men, prop men, and—worst of all—network men.

Network men are a much-maligned species, and they deserve to be much maligned. They usually have glue for brains, and can only be communicated with through the medium of the screaming match. Day after day I screamed myself hoarse trying to stir their gluey thought processes a little; often I failed utterly, and it was on those days that I most envied Jack McGriff. Why was I wasting my life screaming at glue-brained shits in twelve-hundred-dollar suits?

The answer was that my show was Number One in the ratings: six years straight, Number One, an unprecedented thing. My inventions, Al and Sal, were a normal middle-class family living in Reseda, California, with their three normal middle-class kids, Bert, Betsy, and little Bobby. They experienced the normal strains, the normal delights, the normal tragedies of American life, and, to my surprise, eighty or ninety million Americans chose each week to experience these same strains, delights, and tragedies with Al and Sal and their children.

When I wrote the pilot for "Al and Sal" I was living in one room in a motel in Blythe, California. I was a loner and a loser who had pretty much failed at everything: at the novel, at screenwriting, at marriage, and, over and over again, at romance. I had never enjoyed one day of normal domestic life, and I knew perfectly well I probably never would. Then, inexplicably, as a last throw of the dice, I produced from my fantasies of what domestic life could be a sitcom that not only had held America in thrall for nine years, but that was even now causing people who actually *had* domestic lives in places as far flung as Pakistan, Finland, and Brazil to neglect their own perfectly normal domesticities in order to watch a series that had been born of my own despairing fantasies.

One doesn't easily stop being El Primo, even in television, where almost everyone's daily fantasy is that some happy morning he'll wake up and not be working in television anymore. I had hoped it every day for nine years, but Number One is not something you just casually walk away from; even in our last year, when the show was barely still in the top forty and I was worth hundreds of millions, I didn't find it easy to leave.

I departed in stately stages, first to a palace on the cliffs at Laguna, then across the hills to another palace in Rancho Mirage, then to a spacious hacienda in Patagonia, Arizona, where I had the distinction to be the first gringo millionaire to be robbed by the famous cross-border Robin Hood, Vega Vega, about whose career I produced a pilot for a series that died after four episodes: my public, if I still had one, wanted a newer, fresher, more yuppified Al and Sal, not some absurdist comedy about a Mexican bandit. "Cheech without Chong" was how one callous reviewer described it.

In removing myself in slow removes to Laguna Beach, Rancho Mirage, and Patagonia, I was duplicating, in high style, a self-removal I had undertaken in the sixties, in low style; in that instance I had drifted out of L.A., from cheap motel to cheap motel, East Hollywood to Azusa, Azusa to San Dimas, San Dimas to Calimesa, Calimesa to Banning, Banning to Indio, and, finally, Indio to Blythe, where, on the very edge of California, I wrote the immortal pilot to "Al and Sal."

Once, in early life—the day after my daughter was born, in fact—I had drowned the manuscript of my failed second novel in the muddy Rio Grande near Roma, Texas. I had been in the mood to drown myself with it, but that had only been a mood, and when I imagined how horrible it would be to actually have water in my lungs I changed my mind, walked out of the river, hitchhiked to L.A., and took the Hanna-Barbera test —first step on the ladder to screenwriting stardom—passed it, and spent three years writing dialogue for cartoons.

In Blythe, ten years after I walked out of the Rio Grande, I came to another borderland defined by a river—in this case the green Colorado. I arrived in a low, almost despairing, state. The Colorado soothed me, as the Rio Grande had soothed me long before. I felt horrible, but I didn't want to die, and I had no reason to think that I would feel any better if I crossed the flowing border into some kind of exile.

The Colorado, like all great rivers, has force as well as beauty. I walked beside it, watched it flow, skipped rocks in it, meanwhile fantasizing about recovering one or two of the relationships that I had fucked up during my decline.

The rest of my days and nights were spent in a dingy desert night stop called the Old Palm Inn, named for the one moldering old palm tree that stood in its courtyard. There I wrote the pilot which, a mere eight months later, soared into the entertainment empyrean, to become the highest flying eagle of the ratings. Once that happened I became far too busy to walk in sadness by rivers, though I lived for a time in a riverbank condo in Studio City and from my window could see the concrete viaduct through which the Los Angeles river flows, looking like an irrigation canal that had somehow strayed into a metroplex.

When the nine years passed and "Al and Sal" ceased production and I removed myself all the way to Patagonia, Arizona, I soon discovered that the town I had chosen was only the outermost suburb of L.A. Quite a number of the glue-brained executives I had once had screaming matches with, in my imperial days in Culver City, had spacious retreats in Patagonia, too. The more determined of them raised Arabian horses and mingled freely with the fascistic old Republicans who controlled southern Arizona.

Determined to go someplace where Culver City would not be tempted to follow, I moved all the way back to Hardtop County and built Los Dolores, my mansion on a hill. At that time it had just become possible to fly nonstop from Dallas to Paris or London or Frankfurt, and I often did just that, proceeding immediately by airbus to Rome or the Riviera. I went to China, I went to India, I went to Egypt, Argentina, Sweden. The one place I did not go was L.A.

I didn't go to Austin, Texas, either, but Austin came to me unbidden in the form of Godwin Lloyd-Jons—the university had finally managed to ease him out of the Greek chair. Godwin had never made any bones about the fact that he was in teaching for the fucking. "Boys for summer,

60

girls for winter," was his motto, as I well knew, my former wife having been one of his winter girls. The University of Texas, well aware that this was a litigious age, no doubt decided that a professor who held such beliefs—and *practiced* them—was a potential liability it could ill afford.

I hadn't seen or thought of Godwin for many years until I stumbled on him one day in the customs line at the Dallas/Fort Worth airport. Never one to conceal his emotions, he was weeping bitterly over the loss of a young man who had robbed him, beaten him up, and abandoned him in the airport parking lot in Rio, after having promised several times to accompany him back to Texas.

The other passengers in the customs line were horrified at the sight of a weeping man; but I had been twenty-three hours getting home from Cairo and it would have taken an outstanding massacre to raise much emotion in me.

"Godwin, is that you?" I asked—he had cried a lot in his days with Sally, I recalled.

"Why, Daniel, you're fat now," he said, wiping his eyes on the sleeve of his Burberry.

"I tend to gain weight when I travel," I said, though in fact I tend to lose it.

It was an unpromising reunion, but Godwin didn't notice. The customs line was long. Once Godwin had dried his eyes he launched into a long and detailed account of his lost Brazilian lover's endowments and proclivities. I wasn't really listening, but I must have been the only one who wasn't, because the line immediately grew shorter as people fled from his revelations, and before I knew it we were out into the bright Texas sunlight, blinking like owls.

The last part of any trip through the moonscape of DFW, as that airport is called, is a ride on the rumbling, computer-driven airtrans that takes passengers from terminal to terminal. It also takes returning passengers to remote parking lots, so remote that they seem to be in north Waxahachie, a town some thirty miles south of the airport.

On the lengthy airtrans ride we shared I became slightly paranoid about Godwin's intentions. I hadn't seen him in over twenty years, but he followed me in puppylike fashion, as if there were no question but that now we were together. He got in the same airtrans with me, though I doubted very much that he had a vehicle waiting in north Waxahachie.

During the long bumpy ride he regaled me with the sexual highlights of his trip to Rio and Buenos Aires. A hardened priest who had heard a million confessions might still have blanched or blushed at hearing the things Godwin told me. Godwin, the renowned classicist, made no distinction between sexual and textual; he spoke of butt-fucking as lengthily and casually as he might have discussed some emendation of Euripides. I was too tired to mind particularly, but many of the passengers traveling with us had not been deadened by twenty-three hours in an airplane; when the doors of the little train opened at each stop, passengers bolted like rats. After six or eight stops Godwin finally noticed.

"What's wrong with these people?" he asked. "You'd think we were contagious."

"Well, Godwin, after what you've just been describing, maybe you are," I suggested, as gently as possible.

"Oh, rot, perfect rot!" he said, glaring at the remaining passengers, all of whom were huddled warily at the far end of the car. At the next stop, South Remote Parking A and Auto Rental, they all converged on the door, obviously planning to bolt the second it opened.

The sight enraged Godwin; he had always had a short fuse. Just before the train stopped he leaped up and began to jerk and twitch, as if he had Saint Vitus' dance. Then he lurched into the passengers and began to pant in their faces.

"I have a new disease," he shouted suddenly. "It's called omniplague. It's a fungoid disease which combines the worst features of leprosy and lupus. It's transmitted by human breath—soon whole populations will be wiped out by it. I caught it in the jungles of the Amazon while fucking a monkey."

He panted at them some more.

"Terribly sorry but we're all doomed now," he said, just as the doors opened, allowing the terrified passengers to spill out.

One burly passenger, who was wearing Levi's and a dozer cap and looked as if he had just come off rig duty in the Gulf or perhaps Alaska, didn't take his doom casually: he swatted Godwin in the face with a small tote bag. The tote bag must have had rolls of silver dollars in it, because it knocked Godwin down and broke his nose. He sprawled on the floor at my feet, bleeding like a stuck hog.

"Omniplague! Omniplague!" Godwin yelled, just as the doors closed. The passengers were safe, but what about me?

"I hope you were just making that up," I said, offering a handkerchief. "I hope you didn't really fuck a monkey."

The whole front of his suit was covered with blood, but his mood was much improved.

"Wouldn't attempt it, they bite," Godwin said.

16

Eventually we got to my car. Godwin's nose was still bleeding freely; his condition was beginning to alarm me. He was weaving around the parking lot in a glassy-eyed fashion, but his mood was euphoric.

"Odd how the flow of blood energizes a man," he said. "It must have to do with evolution."

"I think it has to do with insanity," I said. "I think you'd better take it easy. You're losing significant amounts of blood."

"Nonsense, I have quarts and quarts of it," he said. "Would you like to go to a bar? It's been decades since we talked."

Ten seconds later he collapsed on the asphalt.

I began to hyperventilate—Godwin always had that effect on me. My memories of first aid methods were sketchy, but I knew I had to do something. Fortunately he was a tiny man, easy to drag. I stretched him out on the little sidewalk in front of my Mercedes and dug a dirty T-shirt out of my luggage. I used the T-shirt to attempt to stanch the flow of blood.

Then, when it seemed to be slowing a little, I raced over to the rent-car counters, which proved to be farther away than they looked. By the time I actually reached them I had slowed to a walk and was so out of breath I could hardly stammer.

"Hey, you're a little out of shape, ain't you, mister?" said the bright young girl at the Budget counter. "Have you had that cholesterol level checked out lately?"

After flying all the way from Cairo, the last thing I wanted to deal with was a health freak. Unfortunately, all my women friends were health freaks; the day scarcely passed without criticism of my cholesterol level, my indifference to exercise, green vegetables, and other presumably healthy things. Thousands of times I had pointed out to women that medicine—not to mention nutrition —is a soft science, and that things such as vitamins and cholesterol are merely the reigning health myths of our age, no more scientific than the theory of humors that prevailed during the late Renaissance.

None of my women friends enjoyed hearing my little speech about health fads; they believed that

65

the current orthodoxies exalting exercise, vitamins, and the like were unassailable truths. Health theories (and I insisted that all statements about health were no more than theories) were a permanent bone of contention between me and several women, and *I* certainly didn't enjoy having to deal with health issues at a rent-car counter while for all I knew Godwin Lloyd-Jons's lifeblood was draining away in the parking lot.

"There's an injured man in Remote Parking B," I gasped. "He may be bleeding to death."

"Oops, better get that ambulance right over there," the young lady said, grabbing a phone.

By the time I managed to stumble back across several acres of asphalt to where Godwin lay, the ambulance was there, red lights whirling, and Godwin was having what could only be described as a seductive conversation with the two young attendants who were trying to strap him onto a stretcher. Both of the young men looked as countrified as the young woman at the rent-car counter; I doubt either of them realized that the diminutive, demented Englishman drenched in his own blood was making a pass at them.

"It's rather like bondage," he said happily when they finally got him tied to the stretcher.

"I guess I better follow you to the emergency room," I said. "You may be sicker than you think."

In the emergency room, somewhere in the hideous labyrinth of subdivisions and amusement parks that constitute Arlington, Texas, the blasé emergency-room staff soon made it clear that they didn't consider Godwin sick enough to treat.

"It's a slow night, though—I guess we'll condescend to stop your nosebleed," a cool young intern said condescendingly.

They brusquely sponged him off, stuck a bandage on his nose, and relieved me of one hundred and fifty dollars. Godwin, of course, had arrived back from Brazil without a cent, a fact that didn't dampen his spirits at all. The young nurse who sponged him off caught his fancy to such an extent that he began to try to impress her with his scholarly accomplishments.

"Look, I've done a little book on Catullus that you might enjoy," he told her. "It's a trifle, but it might amuse you for an hour or two. If you'll just give me your address I'll send it to you at once."

"Is he the one who wrote *Jonathan Livingston Seagull?*" she asked.

I didn't think Godwin had ever heard of *Jonathan Livingston Seagull*. He looked bewildered.

"No, the man he's talking about was a poet," I said.

"Oh," the girl said. She wore a good deal more eye makeup than you usually see on nurses. Hers was silverish and was probably meant to coordinate with her frosted blond hair.

"I write poetry sometimes," she said. "I don't read much, though—I doubt you ought to waste your little book on me."

Godwin was not quite ready to give up on the

notion, absurd on the face of it, that reading his book on Catullus would cause the young lady to plop right into his arms.

"It's really a very quick read," he said hopefully.

"Naw, mostly when I read I just get a kind of depressed feeling, you know," the girl said. "It's that feeling you get when you realize you're kinda missing out on life."

"I often get that feeling," I admitted. I was beginning to like the young nurse, but Godwin merely looked perplexed. I don't think he could imagine missing out on life.

"A little book on Catullus can't hurt you," he insisted. "It received excellent reviews."

"Naw, you keep it," the girl said, squinting briefly up his nose. "I'm gonna give you some cotton to take with you, but I don't think you'll need it. You ought to be coagulatin' any time."

17

"You haven't changed a bit," I said to Godwin as we drove hopelessly around Arlington—hopelessly because municipal Arlington contains one of the largest numbers of suburban cul-de-sacs west of the Mississippi. Once you penetrated far enough into that city it was almost impossible to find your way out without a native guide: cul-de-sac followed culd-de-sac in an intricate but discouraging procession.

The detached part of me that hoped to become a meticulous travel writer some day made itself a mental note to write a travel article called "Arlington: City of Cul-de-Sacs"; meanwhile the fatigued part of me that had been twenty-three (now twenty-five) hours getting home from Cairo grew depressed at the thought that I had flown around the world only to get profoundly lost one hundred miles from my home. Fort Worth lay only fifteen miles to the west, Dallas fifteen to the east. If I could catch a glimpse of either skyline I felt sure I could rapidly extricate myself from the maze I was in, but I couldn't see a building in any direction taller than the millions of ugly two-story houses that fill greater Arlington. Night had fallen while we were in the hospital, and at night everything in Arlington looked alike.

Another cul-de-sac I was failing to extricate myself from—a moral one, in this instance—was the presence of Godwin Lloyd-Jons. He had coagulated, just as the young nurse predicted, but he showed no sign of being the least bit interested in fending for himself. He also showed no sign of having changed a bit in the twenty-two years since I'd last seen him.

"Why are we driving around this ugly town?" he asked, somewhat insolently. "I'd like to go to a bar. I need a drink. That young nurse was extraordinarily rude to me."

"She wasn't rude, she just didn't find you attractive," I said. My fatigue was beginning to open a tunnel deep into my memory—many horrible things that this same little man had done, mostly things involving my then wife, were beginning to hop around like crickets at the bottom of the tunnel.

"I feel sure she would have liked my book, though," Godwin said wistfully. "It might have disposed her to be kind to me."

"You're far too old for her, and anyway your chances of seducing her were nil," I pointed out unkindly, as we emerged from about the eightieth cul-de-sac of the night.

Then a glimmer of hope appeared, in the form of lights in the sky. The lights belonged to airplanes, descending in graceful sequence into the great airport we had just left.

"Look, the airport's over there," I said. "If I just go toward the planes we'll eventually get out of here."

"I'm sure she would have been kind to me in time," Godwin said, his mind still on the nurse with the silver eyelids. "It was your presence that threw things off. You're very sulky now, Daniel, quite sulky. I suppose it's because you've grown fat."

"Where's your car, Godwin?" I asked. "I want to take you to your car."

"I'm afraid I lent it to a friend," he said. "I think he planned on touring Seattle, or some place near Alaska."

It was exactly what I didn't want to hear.

"So where were you planning to go?" I asked.

"I never plan, it's so middle class," he said. "Why won't you take me to a bar?"

"Godwin, I just flew in from Cairo," I said. "I want to go home. In fact, I'd be home now if it wasn't for you."

"You can't be much of a world traveler," he said. "Look at you. You're not even able to find your way out of Arlington."

Godwin and I had never complemented one another that well. His fevor only seemed to activate my passivity. The minute he came around, my hands slipped right off the steering wheel of my own fate, to put it grandly.

It happened that night, too. I did finally find my way out of Arlington, but instead of driving straight home to Los Dolores I let myself be talked into stopping at a honky-tonk in the stockyards area of Fort Worth.

Actually, I had a dark motive in stopping at the honky-tonk. So far, Godwin had tried to seduce virtually everyone we'd met since leaving the airport. Undoubtedly he would continue to try, and maybe he would actually succeed. Maybe he'd find a horny barmaid or a gay cowboy—anyone to take him off my hands. He did, apparently, manage to seduce a good many people; possibly he'd get lucky in north Forth Worth.

Nothing of the sort happened, of course. The cowboys in the honky-tonk interested Godwin more than the barmaids, but the cowboys, most of whom were probably carpet salesmen or dry-wallers anyway, seemed not to be gay. None of them appreciated Godwin's forthright suggestions, and one or two seemed inclined to give him a thorough stomping. As he got drunker and drunker, his suggestions became more and more forthright.

Finally I gave up. Much as I didn't want to take him home, even less did I want to get into a fight, and a fight was looming. Godwin had never won a fight in his life, and neither had I. In a literary bar we might have stood some chance, but Peppy Lou's Lounge in north Fort Worth was not exactly Elaine's. When you got stomped in north Fort Worth you knew you'd been stomped.

"Godwin, let's go," I said.

"Why?" he asked. "I'm not even very drunk."

"I don't like the ambiance here," I said. "It's a violent ambiance, if you ask me."

"But that's the fun of it," Godwin said, his eyes shining. "I've been knocked about in far worse places than this, I assure you. It might be stimulating."

"Also, it might be fatal," I said. "I just flew home from Egypt. I'm really not in the mood for any more emergency rooms."

"Oh, stop harping on Egypt and enjoy yourself," he said. "Are these real cowboys or are they the pharmacy variety?"

"Drugstore, not pharmacy," I said. "Listen, I'm serious. I'm getting out of here. I don't feel like getting beaten up. I'm not a masochist."

"Possibly not," he said, looking at me coolly. "You don't seem to be anything, really—just fat."

"Let me point out that I'm not responsible for you, sir," I said formally. "It's not my fault your car's in Alaska. I'm willing to put you up for a few days, though it's against my better judgment. But the offer expires in three minutes. I'm leaving, and if you don't come I may never see you again."

Godwin fell silent. He looked wistfully at one of the carpet salesmen, two or three of whom were glaring at him.

"Oh, well, they're probably only pharmacy cowboys anyway," he said, draining his Scotch.

We arrived at Los Dolores two hours later. Since Cairo, I had been awake for twenty-four hours, but it was Godwin who was asleep—so soundly that I had to leave him in the car. The next morning I heard the unfamiliar sound of whistling from the kitchen and came in to find him scrambling eggs. Gladys was squeezing oranges. She seemed to take Godwin's presence for granted, and she might as well have—that was five years ago, and he had been with us ever since.

18

The drive to Houston did little to awaken the nascent travel writer that I hoped was slumbering within me. The Decatur courthouse was the last sight on the whole trip that could fairly be described as picturesque.

Once the Fort Worth courthouse had also been picturesque, but the thing that rendered it picturesque—a neon American flag with forty-eight neon stars—had been removed. Both Fort Worth and America had outgrown the flag. America had summarily added Alaska and Hawaii, and Fort Worth had added a veneer of big-cityness. Now the old courthouse, shorn of its wonderful, bright flag, was just an ugly pile of granite on the Trinity bluffs.

I had once liked Fort Worth. I never loved it as I loved Houston, but I did enjoy its hicky vigor, of which the neon flag had been a perfect symbol. Dallas would never be original enough to stick a neon flag on a public building; Dallas remained what it had long been: a mediocre big city, growing larger, but never growing interesting.

I passed through Fort Worth like an arrow and then deflected the arrow slightly eastward until it pierced I-45, the interstate connecting Houston and Dallas. Once on that interstate it was smooth but boring sailing. The black land south of Dallas receded, the horizon began to thicken with trees, but the change was undramatic; the next real sight was the huge prison at Huntsville, two hours south.

I was glad I had bought the Cadillac; it passed scores of Datsuns and Toyotas as easily as a powerboat passes canoes. Just driving it made me feel almost stable, a feeling I rarely enjoyed.

But even a brand spanking new Cadillac couldn't make me feel stable for long. Soon I was in the pine trees, which meant that Houston couldn't be far. Even if I crept along at the legal speed limit, instead of doubling it as was my habit, I was sure to be on the banks of Buffalo Bayou within an hour or so.

Then what?

Although I had traveled much in the twenty-two years since my daughter's birth, I had never been back to Houston. Many times, the city had tried to entice me back; in the years of my success, when I was the reigning genius of American television, Houston had attempted to claim me. I had been educated there—why shouldn't it claim me? I was offered banquets, honorary degrees, a Danny Deck day, the keys to the city, etc., all of which I sadly declined.

Sadly because Houston had been, among cities, my first love. In my failed second novel, the one I had wisely drowned, the only parts that might have deserved to survive were paeans to Houston, to the city's misty beauty and sweaty power, to its funkiness and its energy. I had come to it at the right time, as a young man sometimes comes to his ideal city. In Houston I began to write, formed my first young sentences. Its energies awakened mine; the ramshackle laziness of some of its forgotten neighborhoods delighted me. I walked happily in it for years, smelling its lowland smells. It was my Paris, my Rome, my Alexandria—a generous city, perfect home for a young talent.

But that time ended. Disorder and early sorrow, of a very average kind, thrust me out and propelled me westward where for many years I failed at

75

everything. All that time I missed Houston and missed it keenly. When I would happen on an article about the city in a newspaper I would hastily turn the page; just seeing the name Houston in a newspaper made me miss the place so much that I ached.

I missed it as much as I've missed certain women—and there are women I've missed so much that I've become afraid to see them again: it becomes too big a risk, because if you miss them that much and then see them and they turn out not to like you anymore—or, worse, you turn out not to like *them* anymore—then something important to you is forever lost.

Once I got famous and began to fall in love with famous women, queens of the screen and the tube, I came to understand why I preferred to skirt all mention of Houston. I soon started trying to avoid all public mention of my famous loves as well.

Perhaps in some respects all love may have common elements, but it can also have striking differences, and attempting to love famous women, women whose pictures appear regularly in newspapers and on the covers of magazines, involves dangers that don't arise in loving obscure women. The dangers don't lie within the women, of course—any suburban housewife can stab you with a paring knife just as quickly and as fatally as the most high-strung movie star.

The danger develops in that brightly lit, well-patrolled area called publicity. Loving women who merit more or less continuous publicity is a specialized pursuit, rife with little dangers. The innocent and common act of going into a 7-Eleven to buy a gallon of milk acquires a new tonality if you happen to be in love with someone whose face is apt to appear regularly in *USA Today* or the *National Enquirer*. There she'll be—Jeanie, Nema, Marella—with a new or a fading husband, or a rumored new boyfriend. In all likelihood I would already know that the husband was being phased out or the boyfriend phased in, but such knowledge did little to cushion the shock. There was always a moment of unease as I fumbled for change; sometimes I marched stoutly out without buying the tabloid, only to stop and buy it at the next 7-Eleven down the road.

As much as I hated encountering my girlfriends' pictures in one of those publications, I was apparently not equipped to resist even the most absurd and fallacious mention of them, or the hastiest and most unflattering paparazzi picture. In fact, the more unflattering the picture, the worse the temptation: the sight of one of them looking wildly unkempt, hair a mess, ridiculously dressed, some lout on her arm, undid me more than the glamour shots that were always turning up on the covers of *People, Paris-Match*, or *Vanity Fair*. In the glamour shots, staged with a full complement of hair, makeup, and costume personnel, you got more or less the woman the world wanted to love; the work of the paparazzi, disgusting as it was, nonetheless gave you something more true—the woman herself, in all her bewilderment, vivacity and élan undimmed, messiness unreduced, gloriously or ingloriously female, and always, to me, deeply affecting: the woman, in short, that I *did* love.

For decades I had been a haunter of newsstands the world over, but as the years passed I gradually began to avoid them, along with drugstores, 7-Elevens, any place where I might see a picture of one of my girlfriends on a magazine cover. I didn't want to have to handle the emotional electricity such little shocks produced—and it was for more or less the same reasons that I had flipped past hundreds of mentions of Houston in the years since I left her. Houston, too, was sexy, glitzy, high-profile, her green trees and shining glass buildings a temptation to photographers of all levels of skill. Even a slick shot in an airline magazine, glimpsed high above the Pacific, sometimes made me deeply homesick for Houston, for the weedy neighborhood, the pulsing freeways and cunty smells of the Houston that I still loved.

I yearned, but I didn't go back: Danny Deck Day never happened.

Now I was definitely going back, in fact, was almost there. Huntsville and its prison were already behind me. Apprehension, which had been flitting across my nerve ends since my daughter's first call, flitted ever more rapidly. Not only would I soon have to reckon with a child I had never seen; I would also have to reckon with a city I had once loved deeply but had neglected for twenty-two years.

The women I knew always exacted an immediate price for the most minor neglect; even Gladys was not above giving me margarine rather than butter on my pancakes, though I had repeatedly forbidden her even to *buy* margarine—if she thought I was inattentive to what she called her "situation" for a few days—her "situation" being her evershifting relations with Chuck, who had lately shown an increasing tendency to absent himself to places as far afield as Tucumcari.

If Gladys, my faithful cook, repaid my neglect with margarine, what would a female entity as powerful as Houston do? Would she forgive all and draw me back to her bosom? Or forgive nothing and suck me off the freeway into a bad neighborhood, where I would be shot down by a young crack dealer with an Uzi before I even got my bearings.

Twenty-two years is a long time; more than a generation, as generations are now reckoned. Even though I averted my eyes at newsstands and flipped past articles in *The Times*, I had not missed the fact that Houston had grown; huge when I left, it was now much more huge. I was scarcely past the town of Conroe when plinthlike glass buildings began to appear, at first singly, then in clusters. To the east, near the airport, a kind of minicity seemed to have risen.

I had gotten a late start; the day was ebbing and the pastels of a summer evening colored the sky above and behind the downtown skyline when I came in sight of it. A stately white battleship of a cloud was crossing the ship channel toward Galveston.

I began to relax a little; though most of the downtown had not been there when I left, the clouds, the pastel sunset, and the sky itself had a familiar and reassuring beauty.

Just as the freeway passed over Buffalo Bayou a pickup passed me on the right—a little surprising, since I was still slicing along at a comfortable eighty-five. I glanced over in time to catch a glimpse of the driver, a big, raunchy-looking girl with long hair flying. She was putting on her eye makeup while rocketing over downtown Houston at roughly ninety-five miles an hour. The hand that had been assigned to the steering wheel was also finger-tapping in rhythm with a song I couldn't hear.

The girl must have sensed my glance; she looked over and gave me a big toothy grin, eyebrow brush still poised; she honked loudly, as if to say, Let's go, then she was past. On the curve ahead I was still close enough to see her open a lipstick.

I slowed down and drifted off the freeway at the next exit, relaxed and feeling fine. I *was* fine; moreover, I was home. The spirit of Houston might have assigned that girl to pass me just when she did; where else do girls drive pickups at ninety-five while doing their eye makeup? Besides that, driving so well that you don't even have the sense that anything reckless is happening? The

80

main thing, obviously, is getting to the party while the party's fresh.

I touched a button and my window went down, letting in the old fishy smell of Houston, moist and warm, a smell composed of many textures. I stopped at a 7-Eleven on West Dallas Street, already back in love with the place. Now all I had to do was consult a phone book, make a list of Mr. Burgers, and go meet my daughter.

19

Mr. Burger was not yet a threat to McDonald's —not in Houston at least. There were only three locations listed in the phone book: Airline Road, Telephone Road, and Dismuke Street. Airline lay to the north—I had missed it coming in. The address on Telephone Road had such a high street number it could almost have been in the Gulf of Mexico.

"I bet she works in the one on Dismuke Street," I said out loud.

"They don't call it Dismuke Street no more," a man said.

I looked around but didn't immediately spot the source of the voice.

"Now they call it Pit Bull Avenue," the voice said.

The voice seemed to come from above me, and in fact did come from above me. An old man wearing tennis shoes and cutoffs sat on the rim of a giant blue dumpster.

"I think my daughter works on Dismuke Street," I said by way of explanation.

"She's lucky she ain't had a leg chewed off, if that's the case," the man said. "I'd call this a friendly town but I wouldn't call Dismuke Street a friendly street. I'm from the Panhandle myself, but the fact is I hate the goddamn Panhandle. Got any change?"

In fact, I didn't. I had only hundred-dollar bills. For the last few months Gladys had taken care of all my petty expenses. Change wouldn't have worked in a caftan, anyway.

"I'm sorry, I only have large bills," I said.

"I can spend them too," the man said, easing down from his perch. "I'm Kendall."

"Hi, Kendall," I said. "Thanks for warning me about the pit bulls."

"I'd rather live in a dumpster in the great city of Houston than to own the best wheat farm in the Panhandle," Kendall said. "I hate wheat and I hate farming and I hate the goddamn Panhandle. Do you own a machine gun?"

"No, why?" I asked.

"They're about the only weapon that's effective against the common pit bull," Kendall said.

20

Dismuke Street, as I recalled, was in the Lawndale area—an area between the Gulf Freeway and the ship channel that was the home of many warehouses. I could not recall that Dismuke was much of a street, and my memory was accurate not only as to its location but also as to its not being much of a street.

The mere fact that I still had such a good memory for even relatively minor Houston streets—those, that is, with no mythology—struck me as a good sign, in terms of my aesthetic future. Perhaps I could yet manage to become the city's Balzac.

On the other hand, my brief encounter with Kendall, a well-spoken man who lived in a dumpster, seemed like a bad sign. Why was I fated to keep running into eccentrics on the order of Godwin, Kendall, and the several hundred others I had run into through the years? Was the whole human race eccentric, or was there something within me that drew eccentrics to me like filings to a magnet?

In fact, the constant presence of eccentrics was the one constant factor in my life. Even a reclusive strategy didn't really save me from them, for if I wasn't still meeting them on the street or in hotel lobbies or airports, my imagination was spewing them up in an unending, disquieting stream.

Even "Al and Sal," my one hundred-and-ninety-eight-episode hymn to normal American domestic life, had its share of eccentrics, including Al, the most normal male I had ever been able to imagine. An automobile salesman by day, Al became a lawn fanatic at night. One of the staple comedy lines in the series, sure to be worked in at least every third episode, was Al's penchant for mowing his lawn at one in the morning. He had equipped his power mower with automobile headlights so he could do a neat job of mowing. Naturally Sal, the kids, and the neighbors all objected to this particular, sleep-disturbing eccentricity of Al's. The kids sometimes ran away from home rather than go to school and face the taunts of their peers, taunts all directed at their father's eccentricity. Sal constantly threatened to leave if he didn't promise to mow the lawn only in the daytime, and the neighbors tried everything from lawsuits to sabotage to stop him.

Al, a stubborn man, held his own with them all, sometimes operating his lawn mower and his power hedgetrimmer until three in the morning. He refused to yield. "Leave!" he told Sal (she didn't). "Leave!" he told his children (they left but soon came back). The neighbors he told a great variety of things, edging as close to "Fuck you" as we could get on a national network.

"I'm proud of my lawn," Al said. "Due to the fact that I have to make a living for a bunch of ingrates, I can't devote the daylight hours to taking care of it properly to the extent that it deserves, you know. So I devote the nighttime hours to taking care of it properly. You want me to neglect my lawn? Are you communists or what? I'll never neglect my lawn. Not unless they bury me beneath it will I neglect my lawn. All of you whom don't like it, get blanked."

At first the network refused to allow Al to say "Get blanked"—several screaming-match meetings were devoted entirely to the subject—but finally they let us try it and it worked so well that within a month millions of Americans who habitually said "Get fucked" were saying "Get blanked" instead.

Al, my lawn eccentric, not only managed to clean up the language slightly; he also convinced the country that mowing the lawn in the middle of the night was a normal American thing, a right among other classic American rights. Many polls were taken—even the *Washington Post* took one—and in all of them Al gained at least a 90 percent approval rate. True, the American Lawn Care Association, fearing a grass-roots revolt of some sort, issued a statement deploring the after-hours use of power mowers, but nobody paid any attention to them.

The confusing thing about *that* uproar was that Al Stoppard was not supposed to be the eccentric on the show. The eccentric was a neighbor named Jenny, three houses down from Al and Sal. Jenny was a bird freak, with more than one hundred birdhouses on her property. Jenny plus Al made for a noisy neighborhood; by day the block was filled with the chirping of hundreds of birds, by night it resonated with Al's mowing. Jenny was one of Al's bitterest foes, too, claiming that his mowing caused her birds to suffer from sleep deprivation.

"One of my pigeons got so sleepy while flying it fell to its death," a grieving Jenny told Al in one memorable confrontation.

"Who's gonna miss one pigeon?" Al responded, a bit defensively—secretly he was a little sweet on Jenny.

"Me, that's who, you pigeon murderer!" Jenny screamed, swatting him with a bag of birdseed.

The episode had national repercussions, pitting as it did the pigeon lovers against the lawn fanatics; I issued several statements in an attempt to calm the waters, meanwhile laughing all the way to my broker's office.

As the years passed, Al stayed normal but for his one little eccentricity, whereas poor Jenny got crazier; her lover, Joe, a TV repairman much respected in the neighborhood, got in his TV truck one day and drove away.

"I love you, Jenny, but I can't take any more birds," Joe said, tears in his eyes.

His departure broke America's heart; Joe was a popular character. Actually, his contract was up and he was angling for a series of his own, otherwise I would have seen to it that he hung in there with Jenny a few more seasons. Joe, in real life a horrible little actor named Leland, who spent his spare time parked across from North Hollywood

High trying to pick up high school girls, was not one of my favorite people, and I was delighted when the series he secured for himself failed well before mid-season.

Jenny, however, kind of went to pieces once Joe left. She took to cruising the freeways at all hours of the night and day, trying to rescue wounded birds; soon her backyard was full of bedraggled hawks with broken wings. The neighborhood, previously tolerant of Jenny, began to have its doubts. Several housewives who had been sweet on Joe soon turned against her. Even Sal, a generous woman, turned against her.

"Joe was the best thing that ever happened to Jenny," Sal declared. "So look what she did. She drove him off for a hundred million birds."

"Please don't exaggerate," Al pleaded. Sal's *modus operandi* was exaggeration, and Al hated it. "She doesn't have a hundred million birds," he said. "I doubt if she's even got twenty million."

"Do you want a divorce so you can move in with her, is that what this conversation's all about?" Sal asked, her eyes blazing.

One of my personal misfortunes is that I can still remember every scene and every line of dialogue in all one hundred and ninety-eight episodes of "Al and Sal." Wake me from a sound sleep— if you can ever catch me in a sound sleep—and ask me what Al said to Sal in a particular episode and I'll mumble it at once. For a decade that show was my life—my only life; if I live to be a hundred

I doubt I'll ever forget a single one of Sal's many stinging retorts.

Al didn't move in with Jenny, but he was, to the end, her most loyal supporter. The end was not pretty, either. One day Jenny brought home a young buzzard that had not risen from its meal of road kill quite fast enough. A car clipped it, dealing it a hard bump (sensing that America had about had its fill of birds with broken wings, I was never very specific about the buzzard's injuries). Jenny soon found it, brought it home with her, and fell in love with it.

From then on her decline was swift. Her other birds ceased to interest her: she had only eyes for her buzzard. Soon she found another, and then another, as more and more buzzards failed to leave their meals of dead rabbit and skunk quickly enough. Jenny brought them all home. Then one day, despairing of ever having a normal love life again, she awoke with a grand vision: she would turn her backyard into a buzzard aviary. She envisioned a great canopy of some sort under which hundreds of buzzards would lead secure lives, no longer having to snatch a bite of skunk here and there as the traffic of the freeways thundered down upon them. Jenny herself would go out at night and collect the road kill; when the buzzards hopped off their perches in the morning their breakfasts would be waiting.

As more and more buzzards began to fill Jenny's backyard, and as news of her plans for a buzzard aviary leaked to the whole neighborhood, the neighbors, patient for so long, finally revolted. Nobody wanted a buzzard aviary in the neighborhood. Some were of the opinion that buzzards carried the AIDS virus; others pointed out that property values were sure to plummet.

To make matters worse, Jenny, once Sal's only rival as a neighborhood beauty, began to neglect her appearance. Birds—in particular, buzzards—were all she cared about. Once a highly respected, even proper woman, Jenny became a kind of bag lady, right under the neighborhood's (and America's) eyes.

In the many debates that followed, Al was the voice of moderation, the voice of sanity. He defended Jenny endlessly, pointing out that many neighborhoods, some not far away, had worse things to contend with than buzzards—crack, for instance, and street gangs. Realizing that he was her only ally, Jenny forgave Al the death of her pigeon; the two inevitably grew closer, watched by a suspicious Sal.

The neighbors weren't impressed with Al's sanity. He was, after all, the man who mowed his lawn at one in the morning. Soon anti-buzzard sentiment flared into the open. Some of the angrier mothers sent their kids up and down the street carrying signs that said things like "Keep Out Carrion-Eaters," or "Buzzards Eat Skunks!"

Poor Jenny, never a strong character, wilted under the neighborhood's pressure. Little children for whom Jenny had once baked cookies paraded past her house with ugly signs. Jenny didn't fight; the Dian Fossey of buzzards she was not. Sadly she dismantled her hundred birdhouses, took her beloved buzzards back to advantageous spots in the wild, far from the murderous freeways. One day she surprised Al in one of his nocturnal mowings. Her station wagon was packed with what was left of her belongings; all that was left of her thousands of birds was one parakeet.

Jenny stepped out of her station wagon, kissed Al with tears in her eyes, left Sal her favorite cookie recipe, and prepared to drive away.

"But, Jenny, who'll look after you?" Al asked, horrified. "Where'll I go when Sal is mean to me?" (For nine years he had taken refuge from the snarling Sal in Jenny's house.)

"I never thought Sal deserved you," Jenny said tenderly.

"But who'll look after you?" Al repeated. "You know nobody really meant for you to leave; it was just the buzzards that were a little much. We all really love you, honey. Who'll look after you?"

"Nobody," Jenny said. "I'll just be a loony old woman with a parakeet."

Al, usually so quick with a retort, made no retort in this instance—he just fiddled with the ignition key of his riding mower, and looked sad.

"I love you, Al, you've been a good neighbor to me," Jenny said, as she got in her cramped station wagon.

"But who'll look after you, Jenny?" Al asked again, dismally.

Jenny just shrugged and drove away. She

looked almost thirty years older than she had looked only nine years earlier when America had first made her acquaintance.

Al and America were horrified. Jenny's parting words were nothing anyone in America wanted to hear, at least not in prime time. The thought that Jenny Sondstrom, a lovely, spirited woman, the Mother Teresa of birds, more or less, was now an aging bag lady, left to wander the streets with her one parakeet, was a thought that no one welcomed. The network certainly didn't welcome it; they pleaded with me for weeks to let Joe return, sweep Jenny off her feet, and make her secure in her old age. Sal didn't welcome it, either; she spent almost a whole episode staring into her mirror, wondering if such a sad fate would overtake her too. Sal, whose eloquent soliloquies with her mirror—about Al, about sex, about the pangs of marriage, marriage and children rearing—entertained the whole civilized world, delivered the most famous TV soliloquy of all, in which she envisioned her own slow decline into bag-ladyism.

The next week "Al and Sal" fell out of the top forty for the first time since it had premiered; six episodes later it closed for good.

21

I didn't really want to talk to Kendall, the man who hated the Panhandle, nor did I feel like giving him one of my hundred-dollar bills, so I merely copied down the addresses of the three Mr. Burgers, got back in my Cadillac, and drifted north on Heights Boulevard, known simply as "the Boulevard" to people who had grown up in Houston in the thirties and forties.

Then, the Heights had been the fashionable part of town—the fact that it was six or eight feet above sea level, rather than a foot or two below it like most of the city, gave it a certain distinction. Once the Heights had been filled with rather elegantly wrought two-story frame houses with graceful second-floor porches suggestive of New Orleans or Mobile.

Now the area was slowly becoming a barrio; time had brought down the old houses as remorselessly as the Spanish had brought down the Maya and the Inca.

I didn't seem to be quite in the mood to rush over to Dismuke Street and see if my daughter was at work dishing out burgers. For one thing, it was dark, though not really late. It seemed to me it might be more sensible to approach her during the day, when there was less likelihood she would be irritable from overwork.

At bottom, I just felt silly, and very afraid. I had no real reason to suppose that my daughter was in Houston; the fact that she hadn't actually denied being here wasn't really much to go on.

She hadn't placed herself in Houston, though —my imagination had placed her there, the same imagination that had charted the sad decline of Jenny Sondstrom, mother to a thousand birds.

Somehow, since being lifted by the sight of the big Houston girl putting on her makeup while driving ninety-five, my spirits had lost altitude.

Hoping to arrest their descent, I stopped at a taco stand on Twentieth Street, next door to a dental college; there I purchased a couple of excellent tacos while pondering the downturn my spirits had taken.

The dental college, housed in a moldering green building, was brightly lit; through its big windows I could see a number of would-be dentists, all of them either Asian or Hispanic, practicing drilling techniques on a group of volunteers. Many of the volunteers, who were writhing horribly, probably now regretted volunteering. What must have once seemed a golden opportunity to get some dental work done free was not working out exactly as they had imagined.

Excellent though the tacos were—I went back and purchased two more—their excellence couldn't quite banish from my thoughts an issue that had been looming larger and larger in my life of late: the issue of self-parody.

Already, in the half hour I had been back, Houston had thrust the issue directly under my nose. If the big girl doing her makeup on the freeway represented Houston exactly as I wanted it to be, Kendall, the man who lived in the dumpster, was all too clearly a parody of what I wanted Houston to be; his appearance had only served to remind me of the decline of Jenny, which in turn

93

made me remember what a parody of its best self "Al and Sal" had become in its final season.

In that season it was as if my imagination had acquired metal fatigue. All that had once been winning and lighthearted about the show became mean-spirited and charmless. Al and Sal's fights, once so wacky and inventive, became as vicious and bitter as the fights between real husbands and wives; in fact, they became *worse* than the fights between real husbands and wives. They were just close enough to being parodies of the earlier fights that you remembered the charm of what was gone while wondering where it went.

The thought that was making me gloomy was that the self-parodic not only was beginning to infest my life, it *was* my life. Day after day, month after month, everything that I did, said, or thought seemed to be a parody of something that I had once done, said, or thought more vigorously and better.

Now here I was in Houston, city of my youth, a place that had never failed me. I had left it just in time, before our love turned to viciousness, as had Al's and Sal's. In my thoughts Houston was still a golden town, and the best of all places in which to accomplish the task I was faced with, which was to start a father-daughter relationship twenty-two years late. When the big girl passed me on the freeway, I felt I was right to come; I felt I was still capable of good, nonparodic choices; but when Kendall, a parody of a Houston eccentric if there ever was one, began to talk to me from the rim of the dumpster, my confidence began to ebb away.

What if Houston, too, was now merely a parody of the city I had once known? What if my daughter really was in Miami, far across the salty Gulf, and across the state of Florida as well? What if she had merely been torturing me with phone calls and had no intention of actually letting me find her? What if she had packed her kids on a bus that very afternoon and headed for New York or L.A.? What if I had missed her by an hour, stupidly driving down in my Cadillac rather than chartering a plane, as I had offered to do? What if she never called again and I searched for the rest of my life and never found her?

Being parked in front of a dental college did nothing to check my mood's descent. Several of the apprentice dentists were having trouble with their volunteers, some of whom had clearly had enough of volunteering. One small Asian man managed to squirm out of the dentist's grasp; he was out the door and off down the street in a flash, still wearing a blood-splattered dental apron.

The little man's escape inspired me. After all, the ache I felt inside was a kind of cavity too—a cavity only the sight of my daughter could fill. I started the car, rushed to the freeway, and in minutes had found Dismuke Street, just where I expected it to be.

There, too, was the Mr. Burger, only a few doors from Lawndale; it was brightly lit, and had a number of Mexican teen-agers, some of them with babies toddling at their feet, lounging in front of it.

Slowly, very slowly, I eased the Cadillac past the Mr. Burger. My heart was beating as fast as it had ever beat in my life; I had not been so apprehensive since the night they premiered the pilot of "Al and Sal."

But T.R. was not there. A skinny black girl was working the cash register and a tiny Asian girl was cleaning tables. The Mexican teen-agers began to ogle my car. I eased up to the drive-in window and buzzed my window down. The black girl finished counting a handful of pennies before traipsing over.

When she saw the Cadillac her face lit up. "Look at that car," she said. "If I had me a car like that I'd leave right now and go to the beach."

"Excuse me, miss," I said. "Can you tell me if a young lady named T.R. works here?"

"'Course she works here, why you want to know?" the girl asked, with a look of suspicion.

"I don't suppose you know where she lives, do you?" I asked, for some reason reluctant to answer the girl's question directly.

"I know, but I sho' ain't telling you," the girl said. "Why you want to know?"

"I'm her father," I said. Just saying it made me feel a little giddy. "At least I think I'm her father," I amended. I was on new and shaky ground.

"Oh, yeah, you Mister *Deck!*" the girl said, the big grin coming back. "T.R. said you'd be showing up in an airplane, but I *knew* that was wrong, unless it was a helicopter. There ain't no place to land an airplane over here by Lawndale that I know of."

"I decided to come in the car," I said meekly.

"Don't blame you, I don't like them old whirly helicopters myself, less it's an emergency or something," the girl said.

"Where is T.R.?" I asked.

"Oh, goodness, I ain't got the answer to *that*," she said, waving the tiny Asian girl over.

"That's T.R.'s daddy," she said, pointing at me. "He left his plane at the house and come in his car."

"Hello, Mr. Deck," the Asian girl said. "You want fried shrimp? T.R. said you get a discount."

"Where'd she say she was goin'?" the black girl asked the Asian, who gave a polite shrug.

"She may be dancing," she ventured.

"Oh, I *know* she's dancin'," the black girl said. "If it's night and she ain't workin', she's dancin'. T.R. likes to be out kickin' up her heels."

That was cheering—at least it meant my daughter's spirit hadn't been destroyed by my neglect.

"What does she do with the babies while she's dancing?" I wondered. Actually I was curious as to whether there might be some sort of husband in the picture—or at least a beau.

"Oh, they all go," the Asian said. "The babies go where T.R. go."

"That little Jesse be dancin' herself soon as she can walk better," the black girl said. "You see the

97

way she swings her arms? She's already got the rhythm."

"I didn't know they allowed children in dance halls," I said.

Both the young women giggled.

"Round here folks allow pretty much what T.R. wants them to allow," the young black woman said. "She just sticks them babies on a pallet under the table, then when they get sleepy all they gotta do is go to sleep."

"T.R. very good mother, Mr. Deck," the Asian said, as if she felt I might be having worries on that score.

I may have looked strange, but I wasn't having any worries just at that moment. What I felt was immense, adrenaline-soaked relief that my guess had been right. T.R. was in Houston—in fact she was near, kicking up her heels. I wasn't necessarily going to be faced with a life of hopeless regret.

"It's nice of you to tell me that," I said. I wished suddenly to do something to help the young women who had brought me such sweet relief. I had an impulse to hand them all my hundred-dollar bills. But I checked the impulse, which a number of psychiatrically well-informed friends had assured me was no more than a misguided attempt to buy approval.

"Could I just ask your names?" I asked.

"Oh, she didn't tell you about us?" the black girl said. "I guess she was just too busy meeting her daddy. I'm Dew, 'cause I'm so fresh all the time."

"Sue Lin," the Asian girl said, with a smile.

"I'm Danny," I said, reaching through the carry-out window to shake both their hands. "Dew's a nice name," I added somewhat pointlessly. "They're both nice names."

I was suddenly feeling pretty tired.

"I've had a long drive," I said. "I think I better get some sleep and meet T.R. tomorrow. If you see her will you tell her I'm at the Warwick?"

"Maybe we can come visit?" Sue Lin said, shyly.

"Oh, sure, come visit," I said. "And tell T.R. to call me anytime. If she doesn't call I'll just drop by tomorrow."

"You can sleep late," Dew said. "T.R. don't go on till noon tomorrow."

"You know, Dew, I may just sleep late," I said.

22

I was deep in sleep, indeed deep in dream, when T.R. called.

"How come you decided not to bring the airplane?" she asked.

"What airplane?" I asked, for a moment completely disoriented.

"The airplane you said you was gonna come in," she said testily. It obviously was not bothering her that I had been asleep.

"Oh, that one," I said.

"Was that just one of your lies?" she asked.

99

"No," I said. "What do you mean, one of my lies? I've only known you a day. I haven't had time to think up any lies."

"It don't take long to think up lies," she said, unimpressed. "I've known people who could think up about a hundred a second."

"I could do that at one point, but now I'm old," I said. "I'm slowing down. My lie machine's a little rusty."

There was a pause.

"Are you old?" she asked in a softer tone. "I don't think of you that way."

That was interesting—my daughter thought of me.

"How did you have me pictured?" I inquired. I was beginning to feel a little more wakeful.

"Young and handsome and rich," she said.

"I was never handsome, and I was young only briefly," I said. "After all, I'm your father—that implies a certain age. But I am rich."

"I wish you'd brought the airplane," she said. "I told the kids about it. They're gonna be disappointed. They ain't never even rode in an airplane."

"Have you ridden in one?" I asked.

"What do you care, you never even come to see me!" she said with a flash of anger. Then she hung up.

23

The dream I had been having when T.R. woke me up was a typical fight-on-the-set dream from the days of "Al and Sal." Nema Remington had been erupting—volcanic imagery was the only imagery that adequately described one of Nema's fits. Nema's worst enemy would not have denied that she was a force of nature; though she was a tiny woman, cyclonic imagery was still invariably used to describe the kind of destructive force she could focus on a sitcom set when she chose to.

Fortunately she didn't unleash her full power very often. If she had, the show would not have lasted a year. Nema was, in fact, easy to get along with as long as certain conditions were respected. Food, sleep, and sex were three things she required in abundance, but if she even got any one of the three in abundance, the weather on the set was usually sunny. On the whole it didn't do to starve her in any of the primary areas. A good deal of the time she had spent as an actress had been spent at the bottom of the heap as the cheapest of cheap cuts in the meat market that is Hollywood. For years she had had to scramble even to land a commercial; some years she *couldn't* land a commercial and made ends meet waiting tables.

Stardom, therefore, had not given Nema the illusion that life is perfect; she didn't expect every minute of every day to go her way, but she was sensitive to insult and was often thrown into violent conflict with her costar, Morgan Underwood, the actor who played Al. Unkind items about Nema's highhanded behavior on the set were always appearing in the gutter press, all of them planted, in Nema's opinion, by Morgan Underwood.

Morgan Underwood was no angel—the word "chauvinist" might have been coined expressly to describe his behavior—but as the producer-creator of the show I took a more complex view of the matter, which was that most of the tawdry items that so infuriated Nema were actually planted by Morgan Underwood's *secretary*, without his knowledge. Not a few tawdry items about Morgan himself had also found their way into the gutter press—*all* TV press is gutter press—and these, I knew for a fact, were planted by Nema's secretary, also without her knowledge.

I could write a book—someday I may—about personality disorders in stars' secretaries, based on my experience with the forty or fifty Nema and Morgan went through in the nine years of "Al and Sal." The secretarial disorder most likely to drive producers into early coronaries is a secretary's tendency to identify too closely with the star she or he works for. Inevitably, secretaries derive their sense of status from the status of the star; just as inevitably they come to believe that they *are* the star—many stars' secretaries I've known acquire more airs than three-time Oscar winners.

So in my dream Morgan Underwood's secretary

had planted an item in the *Enquirer* claiming that Nema was fucking a prop man, an item which so infuriated Nema that she started her day by walking into the makeup trailer and squirting Morgan Underwood in the face with Mace, a squirter of which she always kept in her purse for defensive purposes.

This dream was a replay of a real scene: Nema did once Mace Morgan. Headlines the world over read: "Sal Maces Al!"

In the dream I was standing outside Morgan Underwood's trailer, watching him gag and vomit; I had a stopwatch in my hand, as if I were clocking a gag-and-vomit contest. I was probably just trying to calculate how soon a man who had just been Maced could reasonably be expected to trot back on the set and begin rehearsal.

Then T.R. woke me up. Once she hung up, I felt vaguely uncomfortable, but it was not because I had accidentally provoked my daughter; it was because I needed to know if Morgan had actually recovered and done the scene. In real life a whole day had once been lost, most of it spent trying to persuade Morgan not to sue Nema. It was ridiculous that I should need to know how much time was lost in the dream replay, but I did. The fact that the show had been closed for four years made no difference. Virtually my entire dream life still took place on the set of "Al and Sal." My dream strata were not deep; I never dreamed of my childhood, of my marriage; only rarely did I get a flicker from my European years, and those flickers tended to be heart-disturbing: a glimpse of Romy Schneider's face the last time I saw her, or Françoise Dorléac dancing at a party the very week of her accident. But most of my dreams were American, and firmly anchored in Culver City, on a sound stage so filthy it was the equivalent of a running sore. All my dreams were tension-laden; even the few that were sexual weren't very exciting; my dream sex was the sex-born-of-boredom variety—the kind of sex Nema might descend to with a fairly nice A.D. if one happened to step into her trailer at an opportune moment.

Why was I always dreaming of that set? I had had a life before "Al and Sal"—I had even had a life after it, insofar as continuing to breathe constitutes a life. How come Culver City got to hog my dreams?

I didn't know, but I switched on my bedlight, hoping T.R. would call again. I didn't feel like going back to sleep if the best I could look forward to was a dream about an actor who had just been Maced.

Five minutes later the phone rang again and an operator asked if I would accept a collect call from T.R.

"With pleasure," I said.

24

"I don't think you even have an airplane," T.R. said. "You probably ain't half as rich as that magazine said you were."

In the background I could hear a baby crying; also I could hear salsa music and the sound of cars passing.

"Where are you?" I asked, feeling a touch of alarm.

"I'm out in front of the Circle K, talking on this stupid pay phone," she said.

It was 1 A.M., and the Lawndale area wasn't the safest part of Houston—if there was a safe part.

"T.R., are you safe?" I asked. "Would you like me to come and get you right now?"

"Come get me and do what with me?" she asked, after a pause.

"Bring you and the kids to the hotel," I said. "I could get you a nice suite."

"No," she said. "I been dancing. I ain't dressed right."

"It doesn't matter how you're dressed," I said. "It matters that you're safe."

"Why'd you ask me if I'd ever ridden on an airplane?" she asked, belligerence in her tone.

"Well, we were talking about airplanes," I said. "I didn't see anything wrong with asking."

"I ain't never ridden on one, if you must know,"

she said defiantly. "If that makes me low class I guess I'm low class."

"Honey, I never meant to imply that you were low class," I said gently. "You sound anything but low class. You sound wonderful to me."

She thought my compliment over for a minute.

"I don't know how you'd know if I'm wonderful or not, since you've never seen me," she said.

"I have heard your voice now, though," I reminded her.

"You've mostly heard it hang up on you," she pointed out.

"You are apt to hang up frequently," I admitted. "But your voice is very lovely. It's the kind of voice that could only belong to a wonderful person."

"Right now it's the voice of somebody who's danced herself sleepy," she said. "If I wasn't holding this phone I'd probably just sit down and go to sleep right here in front of the Circle K."

"Don't do that," I said. "I'm sure that wouldn't be safe. Why not let me come and get you?"

She didn't answer. For a moment I thought she was going to carry out her threat and go to sleep on the sidewalk.

"Where are the babies?" I asked.

"They're right here in their laundry basket," T.R. said. "I think Jesse just pooped. She just got that little look of concentration she mostly gets when she's wetting or pooping."

"If you don't mind my asking, what are they doing in a laundry basket?" I asked.

"I found the basket in the Goodwill," T.R. said in a voice that sounded sleepier and sleepier. "It's a mighty nice basket and it only cost seventy-five cents. I pack the kids in it while I'm dancing. Otherwise there's no telling where they'll wander off to. Once Jesse gets her speed up she can wander off real quick."

"I can't wait to meet them," I said. "They sound like wonderful children."

"I wish you'd stop talking about how wonderful we are," T.R. said. "You ain't even met us, and you may not have the slightest idea what to do with us when you finally do."

"I can't claim much experience, I admit that," I said. "But I'm willing to learn."

"I'm getting too sleepy to think about you," T.R. said. "Little Dwight just about danced my socks off tonight."

"Dare I ask who Little Dwight is?" I asked.

T.R. chuckled. "I don't know, Daddy," she said. "Dare you or don't you?"

"So who is he?" I asked.

"He's one of those people you might meet if you're really willing to learn," she said.

Then she seemed to wake up a bit.

"Yep, Jesse pooped," she said. "I can smell it. You better go back to sleep there in your fancy hotel, because once you meet up with this crowd of kids I got you're gonna need more than willingness—you're gonna need energy, and plenty of it."

"I'll be asleep in five minutes," I said.

25

I wasn't asleep in five minutes, or fifty minutes either. The thought that on that morrow I would finally be assuming not only parental but grandparental responsibilities made me wakeful. I spent an hour or two reading a wonderful book on Peru. It was called *Cut Stones and Cross Roads* and it convinced me that the Incas must have known more about the qualities of stone than any people who ever lived. One of the things I learned was that the Incas could lay stones together so skillfully and delicately that the stones could even pass the shock of earthquakes from one to another in such a way that the building they composed wouldn't fall down. Spanish buildings erected over Inca buildings fell down in seconds, but the Inca buildings remained.

It was a saddening fact, however, that the Incas themselves hadn't remained—just their superb stonework. They themselves had succumbed to Spanish diseases and Spanish greed. Their civilization proved fragile, and, on a vastly smaller scale, so did my mood. At reading of the sadness of Peru, I became depressed. Resolving never to go to Peru didn't help much, either. One reason I read so much travel literature is that it helps me avoid places where I might get too sad. This time, however, I got as sad as if I had actually been walking in the streets of Lima or Cuzco. Part of my sadness was the realization that I was getting a migraine. It seemed to me that the cells in my head were arranged more on the Spanish than the Inca model; instead of passing the shock of events or moods along from synapse to synapse, they allowed the shocks to fall with earthquake-like force right on my brain, whereupon my whole systemic mass began to shudder with migraine.

It shuddered with migraine for several hours at the Warwick. I knew that fear of meeting my daughter caused the earthquake that was pounding my brain cells to mush, but knowledge didn't help—it never helped. I turned on the TV but could scarcely see it—a certain amount of visual distortion is likely to accompany my migraine quakes. I thought I heard the voice of Don Ameche, though.

I got up, gobbled four amphetamines, filled a bathtub with very hot water, and sank into it. The speed and the heat of the water soon began to reduce the force of the tremors. I kept filling the tub, keeping the water as hot as I could stand it. Eventually my brain stopped quivering, the after-shocks subsided, and I was able to get back into bed. I felt a little spacy from the speed, but the main quake was over.

Since there was no likelihood of my going right off to sleep, with all that speed in me, I picked up the phone and called my message machine.

The first message was from Viveca Strindberg, another of my lost continental loves.

"Allo, this is Vi-ve-ca," she said, pronouncing

109

each syllable distinctly. "I love you. Call me sometime."

I could have called her right then; it was late morning in Paris, where Viveca lived. But Viveca had a certain Baltic heartiness that didn't fit well with my after-quake mood. She wasn't working too much these days, but she had married a rich Finn who let her bat about the world pretty much as she wanted to—last time we talked she had been to Bangkok and had taken opium. "What a hangover!" was her comment. "I am depressed ever since and I don't want sex either."

I decided I'd call and catch up with Viveca in a day or two, and took the next message, which was not a message but just one of the many occasions when Gladys and Godwin picked up phones at the same time, oblivious to the fact that the machine was recording.

"What do you want now?" Gladys demanded to know. "I'm on my coffee break."

"Your whole life is a coffee break," Godwin said irritably.

"How would you know, you ain't in this part of the house ten minutes a year," Gladys said. "I slave my life away, and who cares?"

"If Leroy calls while I'm in the shower please be polite to him," Godwin said. "He's rather shy, and easily frightened."

"If he's easily frightened, what's he doing running around with a sex maniac like you?" Gladys asked.

"Oh, do what you're told, you ugly slave!" Godwin said.

"You ain't paying my wages!" Gladys reminded him, at which point I fast-forwarded until I was well past their argument. I came in on a message from Jeanie and had to backtrack a few beats to get the beginning of it.

"Hi, Danny, was it your daughter?" she asked. "Are you there, are you there?

"I guess you're not there," she went on, a little sadly. "But maybe that's good, maybe that means you're with your child. That's gotta be good, if you're with your child. Look, I'm gonna get off."

There was a click, then, immediately, another message from Jeanie.

"Danny, I'm just gonna take a minute to describe this script," she said. "It's about this woman who devotes her life to birds. She's kind of a zoologist and has a lab in her garage. Now the thing that's not too good is that she lives in Nebraska, and I don't know if I could play a person who lives in Nebraska. I don't think it's very urban out there. Otherwise, though, I like the woman and I like the script. She's kind of like that woman you had in 'Al and Sal' who was crazy for buzzards, only this time it's sandhill cranes, which I guess are a troubled species or something. Her name is Nellie, which I also like—I could be a Nellie, probably—and she gets more and more obsessed with cranes and starts neglecting her husband and children and stuff, which I could also easily do if I had any to neglect. Also she offends a lot of people, the governor and people who make the rules about birds, and in the end she just sort of loses track of normal life completely and becomes a crazy bird woman."

There was silence as the tape ran on.

"Now that I've described it I think I'll just leave matters to you, Danny," she said. "If you think I ought to do it give me a call right away. I have to let them know Monday."

The next message was also from Jeanie.

"You know, you don't have to help me with that one, Danny," she said. "I'm sorry I bothered you—you've got your child to consider now—at least I hope you do. The only thing that really worries me is that it's Nebraska—I'm not sure I can be that rural. My hope would be that the writer can think of a troubled bird that lives a little closer to the city. If not, I guess I better just say no, I like her obsession and all but I'm just too worried about Nebraska. All things considered I think I better pass on this one, Danny."

There was a lengthy pause; I could almost hear Jeanie's spirits sinking.

"It's nice to get hired, though, you know," she said. "They came up with the bucks, that means they want to hire me. In this business you can just get forgotten—they hire you for a while and then pretty soon they just forget you're there and hire someone else. I've seen that happen. One of these days it's gonna happen to me."

She sighed; there was a final pause. "Maybe I could manage Nebraska," she said, her tone brightening a little. "I could pretend it was just the park, only bigger. I think I'm gonna go over to the park right now and see if I get any vibes that feel like Nebraska. That's it. That's what I'm gonna do. Thanks for listening."

I decided not to get the rest of my messages. I read a little more in my Peru book. It was still a few hours before dawn, though, and my headache was not really gone. It had subsided, but only as a retreating surf subsides. Any minute the surf might come crashing back.

To take my mind off this possibility I called the machine once more, and once more, as I had expected, got Jeanie.

"I took that picture about the woman in Nebraska," she said in a tone of rich unhappiness. "I figure, at my age, if they still wanta hire me, I better let them—maybe Nebraska will get changed, the writer kind of sounded surprised when I asked about it, but he didn't entirely rule it out. So that's what happened, Danny, the decision got made. Call me sometime and tell me what your daughter's like."

26

Jeanie Vertus was forty-one, which meant that each role she got offered was an invitation to walk along the knife blade that separates stars who are still bankable and sought after from aging actresses who will never be bankable or sought after

113

for star roles again. Over the years I had watched a number of talented, spirited women walk that knife blade. The most brilliant among them, with the broadest skills, the best instinctive choice-making apparatus, the most photogeniety, and some enduring energy and sexual radiance, might make it to forty-six, even forty-eight or fifty before making a fatal slip—and with aging actresses, two flops in a row generally constitute a fatal slip.

Others slipped at once and were reduced to playing small roles in PG comedies, or larger but more embarrassing roles in cheap European films, where often they would have to show a flash of tit but would at least keep their billing a year or two longer before slipping forever from the list of those stars producers automatically think of when they're casting their leads.

Jeanie, Nema, Marella were all dancing on that knife blade now, and Viveca Strindberg had already slipped fatally; it had been seven or eight years since she'd been in a film in which she got to keep her clothes on.

I hung up again, depressed, and spent most of the rest of the night trying to decide if Jeanie could keep herself upright on that thinnest of edges— a star career—by playing a Nebraskan version of Jenny Sondstrom, with sandhill cranes instead of buzzards.

I decided she couldn't and resolved to call her the first thing in the morning and tell her to try to back out of the deal. In my view the quickest way to get severed from stardom was to start taking jobs just because someone was still willing to offer them to you; for the most part those were roles that had already been rejected by the hot actresses of the day, and rejected for good reasons. Taking them on for no better reason than that they had been offered was no way to advance along the sword's edge.

I decided to call my machine once more, though so far it had not been contributing to the sort of calm mood that helps one get over a migraine.

"I've been reading this book," Nema said. "My masseuse gave it to me. It's called *Oral Sex*. It describes a couple of things I don't think I've ever done, but maybe I have done them, maybe I'm just confused by this writer's terminology. I wish you'd call so I could discuss some of these terms with you. It's kind of frustrating not to know whether you've done a particular sex act or not. You know me, always willing to give things a try, particularly new sex acts. It's kind of exciting to think there might be some new ones, at my age —I could get some nice fantasies out of it, even if it didn't turn out to be so great in practice, or even if I couldn't get A.B. to do it. He's pretty vanilla in his way of proceeding with sex, but he can be coaxed, and I could probably coax him."

There was a pause—I heard her turn a page of her book on oragenitalism.

"Hum," she said. "Irrumation. It doesn't sound familiar but I may have done it with Joe. Joe certainly wasn't vanilla to the extent that A.B.

is. It's making me horny just to read about it—I wish I were doing it right now."

There was another pause. I assumed Nema's imaginative temperature was rising, as it often did when her mind was alertly exploring the possibility of new sex acts, or old sex acts with new partners. But this time I was wrong; for once reality seemed to be winning the constant battle it fought with fantasy for the control of Nema's spirit.

"There's this young guy I'm gettin' interested in," she said. "He's younger—I see him around the lot once in a while. He's a driver, but not for me. Unbelievably cute, Danny, but not too good a brain, from what I can judge. He'd do this irrumation with me in a minute, or anything else, either. Every time I run into him I have fantasies about him for two or three days. But I don't know—suppose I grab him? It's not going to be as good as the fantasies, no way. Either he'll get scared and I'll have to chase him or he'll fall in love and I'll have trouble gettin' rid of him when things cool down.

"I don't know," she said. "I used to just grab these cute young guys and deal with the mess when the mess came along, but I guess I'm losing my nerve or something. More and more I don't grab them. I remind myself that the fantasies would undoubtedly be better than the realities, and I stop with the fantasies.

"I don't know," she said again in a discouraged tone. "I guess I don't respect my new approach.

I'd really just like to grab that kid and fuck him and sort things out later. That would seem more brave—besides, I bet it'd be fun."

She sighed. "But I don't know if I will," she said. "This one might stay a total fantasy. Do you think it's because I'm older?

"If you've got that business with your daughter straightened out I wish you'd call," she said. "There's irrumation and a few other terms I want to discuss with you. Bye."

The final two calls on the machine were both from Marella Miracola and were made from a car phone somewhere outside New York—she was there promoting a new film. Unfortunately my message machine didn't handle car phone calls very well—it interpreted little cellular signals, as hang-up signals, and it hung up, only allowing Marcella about five seconds each time.

"Hello, it's Marella, I'm driving around," she said; then the beep cut her off.

The second call was no less brief, but its few seconds were packed with Latin indignation.

"It cut me off, I hate your machine!" Marella yelled. "I hate it, it's giving me dread!" She got the word "dread" out just in front of the beep, after which no more was heard from her. It was too bad, but I'd told her a million times the machine was erratic with car phones.

After that I backed the tape up and played another snatch or two of Gladys's argument with Godwin, to see if it had gotten serious or had merely remained rhetorical. Fortunately the latter

117

seemed to be the case; the two would probably not come to blows for at least a day or two, so all I had to remember was to call Jeanie and advise her to get out of the bird-woman movie, then call Nema and encourage her to fuck the cute young driver. Probably she would never get around to it, but the encouragement alone would be a tonic. It seemed to me that Nema was a little too young to allow her sense of adventurousness to fade into the light of common caution.

Outside, the sky was lightening, finally. I went out on my little balcony and sniffed the misty, slightly fetid Houston dawn—the smell awakened old memories, not merely of the several years I had spent in earlier life, smelling the city's dawns; but memories even older, cellular memories, per-haps, of life in the primordial swamp, which Houston in some ways resembles.

Across town, toward the ship channel and the faint promise of sun, T.R. and my grandchildren were sleeping—in my mind's eye their sleep was Edenic, shadowed with good dreams; soon they would be awakening to the first day of their new life with me.

At the thought that I would meet the three of them soon, I suddenly felt flooded with energy—a thing once common but now rare. I never sup-posed I had a first-rate mind or a first-rate talent, but I *had*, for some years, been in possession of first-rate energies; no one who lacks them will go as far as I went in episodic TV, where you need both the speed of the sprinter and the endurance of the marathoner if you're to live and function through the forty-two weeks that comprise a season.

Once I had trusted my energies completely; they were as natural as sunlight and seemed sufficient to carry me through any task; but then, for no reason medical science could determine, they began to leave me, and their departure was as swift as a winter sunset.

Success, which had once energized me, began to enervate me instead. For months at a stretch I awoke lethargic, paralyzed by the knowledge that there was no longer any need to rise. There was no likelihood that I would be doing anything very interesting or very useful if I did rise, so often I just didn't bother. Gladys could usually be badgered into bringing me orange juice or hot chocolate; often I just slipped another *policier* flick into the VCR and watched Franco Nero or his equivalent chase sleazy Mediterranean dope dealers around Genoa, Naples, or Palermo.

Godwin and Gladys hated it when I stayed in bed all morning watching *policier* movies. They took it as a sign of moral collapse, a point I didn't argue.

"The only difference between you and King Farouk is that he was fatter," Godwin would announce, standing nervously in my bedroom door.

"Well, I may get just as fat before I'm through," I said. I always replied cheerfully to accusations of moral collapse.

"Your whole problem is that you never had to

119

do no regular work," Gladys informed me. "It's important to move around and get the blood circulating."

"I believe it circulates whether one moves or not," I said, with scientific dispassion.

"Pecking on a typewriter gets it moving in your fingers, I guess," Gladys said, intent on the theme of moving blood, "but I wouldn't call pecking on a typewriter regular work. You got five fireplaces in this house, why don't you pop out of bed in the morning and chop a few pieces of wood? That might do the trick."

"It might do the trick of me cutting my foot off. Is that what you want?" I asked her. I had never chopped wood in my life.

"It'd be better than wasting your whole life watching movies," Gladys replied stubbornly. She didn't easily give up her visions, and she returned to the theme of woodchopping many times in the next few months, inspired, no doubt, by President Reagan's example; Gladys was deeply devoted to President Reagan, though cool to the First Lady.

"Them movies you watch ain't even in English," she said. "I wouldn't see no point in watching a movie in one of them old languages."

This morning, though, my energy seemed to have returned from its long absence. I felt like doing something, and, considering the hour, walking seemed my best option. As the sun colored the thinning mists, I dressed and walked along South Main to Rice, among whose dreaming groves I had spent so many absorbed hours as a graduate student in my mid- and late twenties. Then, I wanted to learn all there was to know about literature, and I felt sure I could: I meant to read everything in English literature, from the first runic fragments to Iris Murdoch, before going on, like a grazing ruminant, to digest the literatures of the continent, the steppes, South America, Asia. I would read it all, and meanwhile I would write.

Standing once again amid the great trees of Rice, I felt the kind of bittersweet feelings that seemed to me entirely appropriate for a man of my age and station; I had traveled a long road, circling the decades and the continents not of literature but of emotion, to reach those groves once again; I had written a poor first novel (I burned every copy of it I could find), married and lost one woman, loved and lost many others, while keeping the affection, I hoped, of a few women of brilliance. I had produced one hundred and ninety-eight episodes of a sitcom, a life's work squeezed into nine years, though it had taken nearly forty years to get to it.

Though no life could have been much less like Rilke's than mine, I thought of him as I walked through the Moorish colonnades of the old Administration Building. He had taken all his life to get ready to write those *Elegies*, had written them in two great bursts, and, not too long after, died.

Well aware that a sitcom producer should not be comparing himself to a great European poet, nonetheless I was conscious of certain parallels in

121

our careers—Rilke dealt with women largely through letters, but no doubt he would have used message machines had they been available in his day; that was one parallel. Women who were rarely actually with him nonetheless sustained him; that was two. And I had stewed and fidgeted forty years before spewing out "Al and Sal," after which, if I could have managed it, I would have serenely died. For at least three of its nine years "Al and Sal" was really good, too—the sitcom equivalent of the *Duino Elegies*, the only thing I ever did or would ever do that got close to being art.

Some insects die when they mate; I've always admired those artists who did their art-mating and got gone—it seemed better than sticking around to become an old drone, as Wordsworth had.

During the years when I had been unable to find, much less see, my daughter, I told myself that an artist was better off merely being a parent to his art; but I never believed that. For one thing, I had no real conviction that I was an artist—calling oneself one didn't cut it; you had to make art to have a right to the name, and I hadn't made any. But when I finally did make a little, inventing lively, true-to-life children for Al and Sal, it never made up for the fact that I wasn't being a parent to the child I had actually fathered. The burdens and blessings of parenthood were a constant theme in Al and Sal's debates, fights, marital wrestlings. Sal was pro-baby; in her late thirties she saw no reason why she couldn't have just one more, and she was pissed off at Al for three whole seasons because he suggested she have her tubes tied after she had their last child. Al was anti-baby; he would rather work on his lawn, and would cheerfully have taken Sal to get her tubes tied, though he knew better than to suggest it again—the mere suggestion had made Sal angrier than he had ever seen her, before or since. "I have to live with you, can't I at least be fertile?" Sal had screamed, at the apex of that memorable fight, a fight which left millions of Americans shuddering—after all, it could happen to most of them.

But Sal's dreams of another baby came to naught—so completely to naught that she developed the fantasy that Al had had a secret vasectomy, just to thwart her. Her references to his vasectomy became so constant and so bitter that Al was driven to drink; the debate did nothing for his potency, which, as Sal bluntly informed all America, had been known to flag. Fear that it would flag yet more tortured Al during the two black seasons before the series closed. He spent more and more time on his lawn mower, avoiding Sal's bed; Sal, for her part, became increasingly blatant about her deprivation. She did the dishes in a negligee and lolled around in bed watching soft-core pornography on the Z channel. She held many anguished soliloquies with her mirror on the theme of why her husband didn't find her attractive anymore. Al, in self-defense, bought his own TV and installed it on the screened-in porch, where, more and more frequently, he retired to watch hockey matches and drink himself to sleep on his beloved couch. Sal pursued him even there. Once, fearing her approach, a drunken Al floundered out the door and took off down the street on his lawn mower, only to lose control of it before he got to the end of the block; to everyone's horror the mower veered through the impeccably tended flower beds of June, a sad little neighborhood spinster who lived only for her award winning flowers. June forgave Al, but Sal didn't. "I hope you're satisfied," Sal said icily. "You've ruined June's life, and all because you had to go get that stupid vasectomy. I only wanted one more baby."

Al never recovered from that tragic night. In losing control of his lawn mower he had in effect lost control of his life. He even came to believe that he *had* got a vasectomy. Sal became so vicious to him that even Nema, who played Sal, got worried and started trying to get me to tone down her anger a little, but I couldn't. As Al and Sal's marriage self-destructed, so did the show, plunging on toward a Götterdämmerung of marital resentment, frustration, confusion, weakness, dishonesty. I was on the very verge of having Sal seduce her next-door neighbor's beautiful teen-age son— a plot turn Nema was all for; she had long since gagged at having to appear to retain sexual interest in the pudgy Al, which is to say, her costar, Morgan Underwood—when the network, horrified at what America would think of *that*, finally pulled the plug.

Personally I considered that the nine years' debate on the qualities of parenthood, all conceived by a man who had never been an active parent, was the true secret of the show's success. It was soon clear to me, from the mail the show got, that millions of Americans, not to mention citizens of the wide world, were, like Al, of a somewhat divided mind on the subject of children. Were they worth it? the show asked. Not sure, the world replied.

As I plodded through the silent Rice campus, I wondered again about Rilke. Did he dream the great phrases of the *Elegies* after he had finished them, as I still dreamed scenes in "Al and Sal"?; or, once his work was done, did his sleep become a peaceful blank, peopled, if at all, by the elegant rich women who supported him? In other words, did art bring peace? Did the *Elegies* pay off, for their creator, the decades of brooding, fidgeting neurosis that preceded them?

I would never know; I just knew that "Al and Sal" hadn't helped my sleep one bit. I was happy to have the hundreds of millions, but I had no sense of resolution at all; nothing that had been unsettled in my future had been settled by that show.

Across Main Street from Rice was the great twenty-hospital Medical Center. I slipped across the still-empty street and probed among the hospitals until I came to the oldest among them, the hospital where T.R. had been born. I stood on the small lawn in front of it for several minutes, trying to call back the emotions of that hard night, twenty-two years before.

But my memories of those emotions, once as vivid as a burn, had faded and blurred, the skin grown back over them. It had been raining, I remembered, and I had been very tired, having driven all the way from San Francisco with only brief stops. My timing in those years was frequently disastrous, but never more so than that night, because I arrived at the hospital just as Sally's parents were coming out. Her terrible father, Mr. Bynum, hit me several times, knocking me into the squishy grass; Mrs. Bynum, her equally terrible mother, had cheered him on, telling me all the many reasons why I wasn't fit to be married to their daughter, or to raise their grandchild. Confused from the blows, very tired and very wet, I had finally put the Bynums to flight by chanting obscene words, or words that I knew they would consider obscene: fuck, prick, clitoris, nipple, etc. Then, torn with pain, I had accepted what I supposed was only temporary defeat; I left the hospital, visited my wonderful friend Emma Horton—long since dead of cancer—and drove south to the Rio Grande, where I drowned my feeble, brain-damaged second novel.

The defeat—that is to say, the delay in commencing my life as an active parent—had lasted longer than I could ever have supposed it would, that night at the hospital. It had lasted a surprising, and obviously an inexcusable, twenty-two years.

But now, finally, I was back, and what I hoped was that the old saying about better late than never was true. Somewhere in the Lawndale area, across the purring freeways, beyond the shacks and unpainted houses of the Third Ward, T.R. and her babies slept. When they awakened, my life as a parent would at last begin.

II

1

Back at the Warwick I immediately had an anxiety attack brought on by my obsession with first sentences, or beginnings of any sort. I was about to meet T.R. What first sentence ought I to say to her, my long-lost child? Wasn't that question ten times more important, and thus ten times more anxiety-producing, than the choice of a first sentence for my novel?

In the case of T.R., the consequences of the choices were so immense as to be paralyzing. In a sense we had already spoken our first sentences, but those were spoken over the phone and wouldn't have quite the same force as sentences spoken face to face. What if I began by ticking her off, as in fact I had already done several times? She had the impatience of youth, or, perhaps, just the impatience of herself. She might be more demanding than the most demanding reader; she might expect too much—for instance, that I somehow make up for twenty-two years of absence with a few choice words.

After a few minutes of dithering anxiety, during which I discovered that I had forgotten to bring any clothes except what I had on—I had packed a suitcase and left it sitting in my study—I decided to seek advice, and began by calling Jeanie. But Jeanie Vertus wasn't in; I got a guarded message, in neutral tones, giving the phone number I had just reached; nothing else.

"Listen, since I have you, I think you ought to get out of that bird-woman movie," I said. "There's something I found out as a result of having a crazed bird woman in 'Al and Sal' and that's that very few bird lovers ever neglect their families. Ninety-nine percent of them are excellent nest builders; they do absolutely everything they're supposed to do, just like birds themselves. Didn't I tell you how the Audubon Society and all those other bird organizations got all up in arms over that character? My advice to you is: *Don't take a role in which you neglect your family!*—unless you neglect them for a grand passion with Marcello Mastroianni or somebody, and even then it could be risky. Your millions of fans like to see you behave well, and you just better remember that.

"I'm very, very nervous about meeting my daughter, that's why I'm so emphatic," I said. "Now that it's probably too late, I'm more than ever aware of the importance of good family behavior.

"I miss you," I added forlornly. "I love you. Bye."

Then I called Nema, who was in her trailer having less-than-magnificent fantasies as she dawdled her way through the second season of a not very energetic series called "Ms," in which she

132

played the most powerful female executive in America, a kind of cross between Katharine Graham and Sherry Lansing, a coldly efficient woman whose after-hours behavior was anything but cold. Unfortunately, the men producing the series were not coldly efficient; they muddled through episode after episode, making costly production mistakes and wasting everyone's time, including their own.

"Porcupines move faster than these producers," Nema said.

"You sound pretty bored," I said.

"Beyond bored, stupefied," she said. "Right now I'd probably fuck anything that walked through the door. It'd be something to do for a few seconds, at least."

"I've been wondering what I should say to my daughter when we first meet," I said. "First impressions can be pretty important. I wouldn't want to make the wrong kind of first impression."

"You haven't even met her yet?" Nema said. "She called yesterday. What's taking so long?"

"It hasn't been *that* long," I protested. "I had to drive to Houston, and when I got here, she was out dancing. I'm going to see her in a few minutes but I'm worried about what to say."

"How about, 'Hi, I'm your dad,' " Nema said, a little caustically. "Get in the car and go see your child. Don't sit there brooding about what to say for three hours."

"You're right, I'll go right now," I said.

"I'm gettin' worried that I might be losing my

capacity for fantasies," Nema said. "What do you think I could do about it?"

"I don't know," I said. "Maybe you could take a course or something."

"A course in how to have fantasies?" she said, startled. "I've never heard of a course in how to have fantasies. A college course or what?"

"There could be a college course," I said vaguely. Actually the remark had just popped out; Nema without fantasies was like Laurel without Hardy. I had no idea if any college had yet sunk so low as to offer credits for a course in fantasies, but it was certainly possible; not Harvard or Yale, maybe, but a lot of colleges were not Harvard or Yale.

"Be more specific," Nema said. "This is important to me. Working on this stupid show is so boring it's causing my fantasy life to atrophy. It's getting where it's hard to imagine fucking somebody in a unusual way—I mainly just fantasize the missionary position now, and sometimes not even that."

"I'll try to check and see if there's anyone who gives a course in it," I promised, just as Nema got summoned to the set.

"Call me back when you find out something," she said. "A woman as experienced as I am ought to be able to imagine something a little more baroque than the missionary position."

When she hung up I sat on my bed feeling lonely. Nema had told me exactly what to do, of course: Hurry on over to Dismuke Street, find

T.R., and say, "Hi, I'm your dad." Nema had seven children and handled them expertly; I had no reason to doubt that her command of basic parental procedure was sound. She liked kids, she had given birth to kids, she raised kids, and those she raised were all healthy, lively, and appealing. She had both broad expertise and abundant common sense; her recommendation was the obvious one. I needed to get moving, display some willingness, even if the willingness involved some crude phrasing at first.

I couldn't help wishing, though, that the two calls had been reversed; that I'd got Nema's message machine and Jeanie in person. Jeanie had no children and wouldn't have given me any advice; but she would have seconded me in my indecision, my squirming over the right approach; she might have no idea what I should say to T.R., but she would have felt, as I did, the necessity for rehearsal.

Indeed, much of our time together, face to face or on the phone, had been spent in what we frankly called rehearsals; only we weren't rehearsing scenes in plays and movies, we were rehearsing scenes we thought might soon occur in life—scenes that would have to be played for real. Jeanie called frequently, hoping to get in a little rehearsal time on life events that she knew were coming up and hoped to shape successfully in scenic form. It might be a business meeting, a benefit, a confrontation with the maid, a first date, or a last date. We worked together to prepare for these real-life dramas as intently as Stanislavsky worked with Nemirovich Danchenko, probing the infinite subtleties of the thing that was about to happen.

Then the thing would happen and of course bear no resemblance to our rehearsals. If it was a romance that Jeanie was rather hoping would start slowly, then the guy would try to fuck her in the elevator two minutes after arriving for the first date; or, if she was hoping it would start fast, then he wouldn't. "I'm so good at auditions, why am I so bad at life?" Jeanie asked frequently. "I rehearse and rehearse and then it never comes out like I rehearse it." In fact, she *was* brilliant at auditions and less so at life, at least if you consider love affairs and confrontations with film directors life.

What I valued in Jeanie was that she respected the fear that the infinity of human options can produce in some people, herself and myself for two. We talked and talked, rehearsed and rehearsed, always ending where we began, in indecision; for indecision was the port (to steal from H. James) from which conversations between Jeanie and I always set out, and also the port to which they inevitably returned.

In twenty years of relating, involving almost daily conversations, Jeanie Vertus and I had never really even been able to decide if we were in love. Probably at some level we both thought we were, but we could never quite get it rehearsed to the point where we felt confident enough to stage it exactly. We couldn't decide how to play it, which was precisely the problem I now faced with my daughter.

I yearned for a talk with Jeanie, but Jeanie wasn't there to indulge me in a final postponement. I sighed a few times, dialed the garage, and ordered my car.

2

When I first saw T.R.—after reaching Dismuke Street by a circuitous but subtly soothing route that involved going out the East Tex Freeway for a while and then doubling back—she was sitting on an old wooden bench behind the Mr. Burger, eating a banana split. Bo and Jesse, my grandchildren, were whining, salivating, and stretching their little hands up to their mother piteously; while Jesse whined she also bounced up and down in her stroller on what seemed like sturdy little legs. The stroller looked older than Bo and Jesse put together; it was held together with masking tape. In her indignation at being denied part of the banana split Jesse was bouncing quite vigorously—it did not look to me as if the stroller could hold together much longer.

Most of the banana split had already been eaten when I arrived on the scene: its remains, a rich chocolaty goop streaked with strawberry, filled the customary little paper canoe. When not actually taking a bite, T.R. held the canoe high, far out of reach of her children's hands.

137

"You shouldn't have thrown down your all-day suckers," she told the children matter-of-factly. I was instantly struck by her matter-of-factness. The trait had to have come from Sally, because, despite a lifetime of striving, real matter-of-factness had always eluded me.

"Them suckers was supposed to last all day, that's why they call them all-day suckers," T.R. went on, lowering the brimming canoe a bit and delicately filling a plastic spoon with the chocolaty goop.

Bo, concluding that he was not going to get any of the goop, began to jump up and down, his countenance darkening.

"Pow pow pow!" he said, pointing his finger at his mother.

In a smooth movement that reminded me a bit of Gabriela Sabatini's graceful turns at the baseline, T.R. set the canoe on the bench beside her, caught the hand that Bo was shooting her with, lifted him briefly, turned him a half-turn, and delivered one smooth open-handed smack to his rear end. Then she turned him back a half-turn so that he was facing her and looked him square in the eye.

"Don't you shoot at me, even pretend," she said sternly. "Jesus don't like for little boys to shoot their mothers."

"Pow, Jesus," Bo said defiantly. The second T.R. set him down he turned and fled, firing imaginary shots behind him.

"Pow pow pow," he said from a safe distance.

"Pow," Jesse echoed uncertainly.

T.R. picked up her banana split again.

"Now you see," she said, looking at Bo. "You taught your own little sister to try and shoot Jesus and me both. It'll be a long time before you get your next chance at an all-day sucker."

Looking a little more closely, I noticed two lemon-colored all-day suckers lying in the dust not far from Jesse's stroller. Bo, who wore nothing but a tiny swimsuit, the same ugly color as Godwin's, reached under the swimsuit, found his bobbin of a penis, and pulled it out. After a few moments of intense concentration, he began to pee in the general vicinity of the all-day suckers, frowning at his mother as he did.

"Pow," Jesse said, more softly. She was standing up in the stroller but had stopped bouncing. She took her tiny finger out of the air and put it in her mouth as she watched her brother urinate.

T.R., casually dressed in a T-shirt, Levi's cutoffs, and sandals, took this development calmly.

"Them suckers was already ruined, who cares if you pee on them," she said to Bo. "You can't really solve many problems by yanking out your little peter and peeing on things, but if you want to try, go right ahead."

Then T.R. looked up at me. I had parked well down Dismuke Street and approached the group cautiously, as one might approach a pride of lions who were momentarily intent on family play.

The image was appropriate because T.R. was a large, casually graceful girl—the image that sprang naturally to mind was of a tolerant young lioness, finishing off a light snack, perhaps of antelope, while playing with her cubs. She had tawny hair, neither quite blond nor quite brunette, and fine features, with more of a girlish curve to her cheek and a much more generous mouth than her mother had had.

Even at a distance of twenty yards I had the sense that I was approaching a superior animal, very beautiful to look at, very unpredictable.

Until she looked up, she had been paying no attention at all to the portly figure approaching along the sidewalk—the portly figure, of course, was me. But then I edged into the circle of her awareness; that is, I got close enough to threaten her cubs. She didn't get up or prepare for attack—after she glanced at me she took another bite of the banana split—but that was because the glance satisfied her that I was no threat.

"T.R., I'm your dad," I said faintly, feeling that I had just uttered the most inadequate first sentence of my life.

3

"That Dew makes great banana splits," T.R. said. Despite her matter-of-factness, I believe she was slightly nonplused by my actuality—like Nema's lovers, I may have worked better as a fantasy.

"These kids would give their sharp little teeth

140

for a banana split," she added, looking at me hopefully.

"I'll buy them one if they're allowed to have banana splits," I offered, waving at Dew, who was grinning at me through the window of the Mr. Burger.

T.R. studied the matter for a moment—studied me, studied her children.

"I'm not sure a little boy who pees on his all-day sucker deserves a banana split," she said, looking at Bo. He had drained his small reservoir of urine but was still fingering his penis as if he expected more to spurt forth at any time.

So far he had taken no notice of me, but Jesse had. She had pale blue eyes, wispy blond hair, and a buttercup mouth. After only a momentary inspection, she held out her hands to me.

"See, Jesse's the friendly one," T.R. said. "She's into singing and dancing and hugging necks. Bo's into slugging people when he ain't trying to pee on something or squash cats. Bo's just your average guy."

Jesse was still holding out her hands to me, but she suddenly upped the ante by beginning to squeal.

"Pick her up quick, she's about to squeal," T.R. said. "It's blackmail, but anything's better than hearing Jesse squeal. Dew gets a sick headache every time Jesse squeals."

I lifted the little girl out of the stroller and held her awkwardly. I had only occasionally held small children before in my life, and it had been years since I had attempted such a feat. Jesse was staring at me solemnly, so solemnly that I felt like I was on trial. Bo suddenly walked over and kicked me. Apparently he didn't like it that I was holding his little sister. Since he was barefoot, the kick hurt him more than it did me. Jesse looked down at him smugly—I believe she was enjoying being safely out of reach.

"That's your grandpa you just kicked," T.R. informed him. "He's the man with the airplane, but I don't see why he'd want to take you on it if you're going to be so unfriendly. It serves you right if you hurt your toe."

At that point we were engulfed by Mexican teen-agers, the same Mexican teen-agers I had seen at the Mr. Burger the night before. One chubby girl tried to comfort Bo, who glared at me balefully, picked up his dirty all-day sucker, and walked off a few feet away with it.

A pregnant girl who looked to be about fifteen held out her hands to Jesse.

"Can I hold Jesse?" she asked. "I need to practice for when I have my baby."

Decisions seemed to come thick and fast for grandparents. I had just picked Jesse up; now I was being asked to surrender her to a pregnant Hispanic teen-ager. Was this appropriate? I didn't know.

"The big question is whether it's okay with Jesse," T.R. said. "Jesse's got a mind of her own. She's the smart one in the family."

"She knows me," the Mexican girl said. "I hold her all the time."

To the inexperienced eye, Jesse seemed willing—she was staring at the Mexican girl with a soft, benign expression. But the second I started to hand her over I found out just how inexperienced my eye was. Jesse had been sitting comfortably in the crook of my arm; the moment I started to lower her into the waiting brown hands, she transformed herself into a rigid column of resistant flesh, and the squeal she emitted was so loud that for a moment I had difficulty believing it came from the tiny girl I held. Jesse's squeal made an ambulance siren seem flutelike. T.R. and Bo both put their fingers in their ears; the little Mexican girl ran away. The other teen-agers laughed. I couldn't put my fingers in my ears without dropping Jesse. The sound was so piercing it disoriented me for a moment; it was as if I had strayed onto an airstrip just as the Concorde was taking off.

I knew it wouldn't do to drop my granddaughter though, so I hung on. Jesse stopped squealing as abruptly as she had started; her face had become a bright red, but the color soon began to fade and the rigid little body became soft again and settled happily back into the crook of my arm.

T.R. took her fingers out of her ears. "That's what it's like when Jesse squeals," she said.

4

Suddenly I felt a little weak—Jesse's squeal had set off a series of aftershocks in my nervous system. I was still within the aura of the night's migraine, and it didn't take much to make me tremble. For a moment I felt worse than weak; I had the horrible conviction that I was about to topple over; I felt vertigo coming on. Through the window of the Mr. Burger I could see Dew and Sue Lin grinning at me, but their faces wavered, in the manner of mirages on a highway. I felt terrified—the world, once so solid, was shaking like jelly; or perhaps it was just me that was shaking.

I knew that it would constitute a bad start to family life if I toppled over and crushed my little granddaughter. Desperate to avoid this calamity, I took two shaky steps and plopped heavily down by T.R. She had put her banana split on the bench beside her and barely had time to jerk it out of the way. Even so, some of the goop sloshed out.

"I'm sorry," I said. "I don't feel so good."

"You're lucky she didn't squeal her hardest," T.R. said. She put a hand on my arm sympathetically. "Last week she squealed her hardest at a cop who was trying to make friends when she didn't feel friendly, and he had to go lay down in his police car for half an hour. They say babies squeal like that to scare off tigers but I don't know if that's true. Jesse's never met a tiger."

"La," Jesse said, spying a fountain pen in my pocket. She plucked it out, studied it briefly, and held it up for her mother's inspection.

"Ball," she said emphatically.

T.R. shook her head. "It's time you learned you can't call everything in the world a ball, Jesse," she said. "I know it's an easy word to say but it don't apply to everything."

Jesse examined the fountain pen more closely. She waved it around a bit, put it in her mouth, took it out.

"Ball," she said again, as if she had given the matter fair consideration and reached an unassailable conclusion.

A second later I was blind-sided by my grandson, who came rushing out of nowhere and made a leap for the fountain pen. His surge carried him into my lap but fell just short of its goal. Jesse snatched the pen safely out of reach, whereupon Bo, ignoring me except insofar as I was a useful platform, began to hit her with the dust-encrusted all-day sucker he had picked up. Bo was not large, but, like Nema, he was a little cyclone of energy. Jesse held the pen out of reach, and I held Jesse out of reach, but in the first several seconds of the assault it seemed that Bo might prove more than a match for both of us.

"Pow dead, pow dead!" he yelled at Jesse. He didn't yell as loudly as Jesse squealed, but he was loud enough.

I had just begun to ease out of my vertigo and hadn't been expecting to have a small dirty boy squirming in my lap, trying to whack his sister with a dirty all-day sucker. The one thing that came to mind during the first seconds of Bo's assault was the Salt II Treaty—it seemed to me I was receiving a first strike, while having no deterrent capacity. I was driven back on first principles, and my first principle was not to drop Jesse, whose deterrent capacity was not entirely negligible; she managed to keep both feet in her little brother's face, kicking vigorously.

I wanted badly to grab Bo but didn't have a spare hand to grab him with; the notion struck me with stunning clarity that God and/or evolution had erred in leaving us primates with only two hands. What a design flaw! It was obvious that parents and grandparents needed a pair of hands for each child, otherwise, how to hold one while grabbing the other?

I also quickly gained an understanding of why clichés are able to retain their force in the language: the cliché "Time seemed to stand still" held considerable resonance for me while my two grandchildren engaged in all-out war over my fountain pen. The scuffle couldn't have lasted more than a few seconds, but to me, the epicenter of the assault, it seemed endless, a Six Day War, a Thirty Years' War almost—a war that might exhaust whole generations.

My one coherent resolve, while the battle raged, was never to keep a fountain pen in my pocket

146

again. That seemingly innocent act had had terrible and unforeseen consequences.

Then T.R. snatched Bo away and held him at arm's length; she seemed perfectly calm, but Bo continued to kick and struggle violently. Fortunately T.R. had long, strong arms—his kicks couldn't reach her, and when he tried to bite one wrist she flipped him over and held him upside down until his struggles subsided.

When she set him on his feet, he gulped for a minute, gave his sister a look of cold violence, and burst into tears. In seconds he was crying so hard he could scarcely get his breath. T.R. watched for a bit, and then picked up what remained of the banana split and offered him a bite. He was crying too hard to notice, and when he did notice, his little chest was heaving so violently that it took him a while to calm down enough to be able to accept her peace offering.

Watching this negotiation had caused me to forget about Jesse—I was still holding her shoulder-high.

"Wah!" she said loudly. Once again she became a resistant column, only this time it seemed to me she wanted to get away from me. I lowered her to my knee, trying to remember if she could walk. Still clutching the fountain pen, she immediately squirmed off my knee.

"Wah!" she said again, directing this angry statement at her mother.

She quickly worked her way along the bench to her mother and opened her mouth like a little bird, waiting for her mother to feed her some of the goopy banana split.

"I never said I wouldn't give you any," T.R. pointed out, giving her some.

"Gosh," I said, exhausted. "You really can't win, can you?"

T.R. laughed.

"You're catchin' on quick, Grandpa," she said.

<hr>

5

Never have I been more grateful for the simple support of a bench than I was for the one I sat on behind the Mr. Burger. I had been a family man for only about five minutes, but I was completely exhausted, a fact not lost on T.R.

"You look kinda pooped," she said. "Do you think you're having a heart attack, or what?"

"I don't think I'm having a heart attack," I said. The notion that I might have one had never before occurred to me. I knew abstractly that fifty-year-old males with type A personalities drop like flies from heart attacks; still, I felt no danger.

"Why do you ask?" I said. "Do I look as if I'm having a heart attack?"

"You're pretty red in the face," T.R. said. She was doling out the last of the goop, a spoonful to Bo, a spoonful to Jesse. Just as Bo took the last spoonful, he turned and pushed his little sister in the face, knocking her flat. Then he ran off to join the Mexican girls.

148

Jesse began to wail. I bent to pick her up, but T.R. was quicker. She picked the little girl up and set her in her lap; then, to my surprise, she lifted her T-shirt and expertly installed Jesse at her breast. Jesse's wails were immediately choked off, soon to be replaced by soft sucking sounds.

It seemed as if life had become one unexpected activity after another. My daughter was calmly nursing my granddaughter right at my elbow; Jesse rested one of her tiny bare heels against my leg.

The Mexican teen-agers soon began to drift over; they stood in front of us, chattering and chewing gum, while Jesse nursed. Bo was squatting in the dirt some distance away, eying us balefully, or so it seemed to me.

"I wish I could nurse her," the pregnant teen-ager said.

"You better just enjoy life while you can, Elena," T.R. said pleasantly. "You'll be nursing that one of yours any time. Ow, Jesse—please don't bite. That tit's not a cheeseburger."

I glanced over and saw that Jesse's pale blue eyes were watching me solemnly. She released T.R.'s large nipple for a moment and smiled at me. Then she greedily stuffed the nipple back in her mouth and resumed her nursing.

"Jesse don't usually bite," T.R. remarked. "She's just not payin' attention. Too interested in her new grandpa. Bo was a biter and still is—you watch, he'll come charging over and try to get the other tit. He ain't really interested in nursing, he just don't like for Jesse to get it and him not."

"He looks a little old to be nursing," I remarked.

T.R. looked at me coolly, as if to say, What do you know about it?

"But I'm no expert on the subject," I hastened to remark. "I probably shouldn't even venture an opinion."

She laughed. "You're a funny daddy," she said. "I thought you'd come over here all rich and famous and start right in pushing me around, like Big Pa did and every other man I've ever known. But you don't look like you could push Jesse around, much less me."

"I've never pushed a living soul around," I said. It was true, too.

Bo suddenly came racing over. He flung himself at T.R.'s lap, but T.R. had been watching, and she expertly stiffarmed him.

Jesse turned slightly so she could watch her brother's assault, but she did not release the nipple.

Bo kept trying, but T.R. just put her hand on his head and held him off.

"If you were a nice boy you could have some nursy," she informed him. "But you ain't been the least bit nice all day, so you'll just have to wait till you feel a little more polite."

Bo flung himself down in the dirt and began to kick and squeal. He was clearly a child with violent emotions. Two or three of the Mexican girls bent

150

over and began to tickle him. At first he kicked out at them viciously, but gradually his tears turned to laughter.

Jesse had finished nursing. She lolled in T.R.'s lap, a picture of contentment. Occasionally she kicked my leg with her heel.

"Somebody told me Bo might be hyperactive, but I don't know about that," T.R. said. "I think he's just mean, like his daddy. Bo may have got some wildness from that side of the family."

"Where is his daddy?" I asked.

Once again she looked at me coolly.

"I'm sorry," I said. "I didn't mean to pry. Don't tell me if you'd rather not."

"You sure back off a lot," she remarked. "I don't know how you're gonna survive in this rough crowd you're with now."

"I'm just not used to interacting much," I said. "But maybe I can learn."

"Maybe you can, maybe you can't," she said. "I don't know why you'd even want to interact with us."

Then she looked uncertain.

"I don't have too good a vocabulary," she admitted. "Does interact mean be part of the family?"

"That's what it means," I said.

6

Bo kicked, squealed, and sobbed in the dirt for several minutes. The sight made me nervous, but T.R., Jesse, and the Mexican girls ignored it and went on with their lives. Jesse burped delicately and drifted into a nap. The Mexican girls took seats on some old milk cartons piled behind the little building and held a lively discussion with T.R. about natural childbirth. All of them, it seemed, were either pregnant or intended to be soon; T.R., a matriarch at twenty-two, was a source of wisdom to them. While they chattered, Bo stopped sobbing and went to sleep in the dust.

T.R. proved to be no advocate of natural childbirth.

"However you do it, it gets a little too natural," she said. "Jesse wasn't too bad, but Bo hurt like shit. I was yelling at them to kill me before they finally got him out."

She handed Jesse, slumbering so deeply that she seemed to be boneless, over to me.

"The thing I like to top a banana split off with is some onion rings," she said. "They take that sweet taste out of your mouth. Want some, Daddy?"

"Maybe I'll just have one or two of yours," I said. T.R. was about five ten and had beautiful legs. I felt a little awed at the thought that I had such a vigorous young woman for a daughter. I wanted just to look at her for a long time, not because she was beautiful but because she was my relation—my daughter. Since the death of my grandparents, nearly forty years before, I had had many relationships but no *relations*. Even at the pinnacle of my fame, when I heard people talking about their families I felt left out.

Suddenly a member of my family stood in front of me, stretching; another slumbered in my lap. The plain of my middle age, empty only two days before, had taken on unexpected contours.

T.R. let herself in the back door of the Mr. Burger.

"How come you never met T.R. before?" Elena, the most inquisitive of the teen-agers, asked.

"Her mother and I separated," I said unhappily. "We just never met until today."

I knew it wasn't an adequate answer. What *did* explain twenty-two years of absence? My own fear of confrontation, increasing in increments every year that passed, explained it, but I didn't want to have to put that into words Elena could understand, or even into words I could understand.

Elena, skinny except for her expanding belly, seemed to sense that she had exposed a nerve.

"But now you're here so it's okay," she said, as T.R. came out the door with a heaping pile of onion rings on a paper plate.

"You can stick her in the stroller, if you want to," she said. "Once she's gone, she's gone. I can hold her upside down and she doesn't wake up.

"I'm the same way," she added. "Both times I've been robbed I was just laying there asleep. Muddy took everything I had, both times. It wasn't much, but it was all my little treasures."

"Muddy?" I asked. "Is that a person?"

"Well, he's sort of a person," T.R. said. "Person enough to get me pregnant, anyway."

"Oh, is he their father?" I asked.

T.R. was in the middle of an onion ring and didn't immediately answer. She held out the plate. Several of the teenagers took one, and finally I took one too; they were smelly and irresistible. Life at the Dismuke Street Mr. Burger had a balmy Neapolitan quality that I was beginning to like. One sat around dining al fresco on local delicacies while discussing the great tissues of life with optimistic, not to mention animated, young women. It was just the way I had always planned to live.

"Muddy ain't *their* father," T.R. corrected, giving me one of her semi-severe looks. "He's just Jesse's father—if this business about genes is true, then it explains why Jesse is so sweet, 'cause Muddy's basically sweet as pie himself, he just happens to be a burglar, and stealing's what he does. He'll tell you himself he'll steal from anybody."

"That's not too nice," I said. "Has he ever been caught?"

"Muddy?" she said, laughing. All the teenagers broke into giggles. "Of course he's been caught. He's caught right now. He's sweet and he's a crook, but nobody ever said he was smart. I doubt

154

if Muddy ever broke and entered more than once or twice in his life that he *wasn't* caught."

"The cops like him, though," she added. "Muddy can charm anybody, but the main reason the cops like him is because he's easy to catch. He gets a few months here and there, but Muddy's never done hard time like Earl Dee."

She stopped and waited, watching me. There was a certain testing quality in her look. Clearly she was ready to find out if I really wanted to know anything about her, or if I was just window-shopping in her life.

It was not the first such look I had ever seen in the eyes of a woman. Despite my many flaws, I was not window shopping.

"Who's Earl Dee?" I asked.

"Bo's Daddy," she said.

"Is he a criminal too?" I asked.

"Yeah, but I don't like you to lump 'em," T.R. said. "Muddy's just a little no-good lazy burglar who's too worthless to work. He don't mean no harm. Earl Dee's a criminal. He's up in Huntsville right now, doing five to fifteen for armed robbery, and it'd be worse if I hadn't worked three jobs at once to get him a lawyer who could plea-bargain off the assault charge."

"He doesn't sound very nice," I said.

"He ain't, and it's one reason I finally called you," T.R. said. "It's real crowded up in Huntsville. I think they may let Earl Dee out early, and if that happens I don't want to be here."

"You think he'd be a pest?"

T.R. chuckled, but it was not a merry chuckle.

"I think he'll kill me," she said in a flat tone. "He said he would if I ever went with another man, and now he's found out about Muddy and Jesse. I don't want to be where he can find me when he gets out."

"I want the three of you to pack up and come home with me," I said. "That's what I'd hoped you'd want to do anyway."

T.R. didn't seem as cheered by my invitation as I had hoped she would be. Her flat tone went with a flat look, and she directed the look at me.

"I just met you," she said. "I don't know a thing about you. For all I know you might be worse than Earl Dee. He 'bout ruined my life, but at least he didn't neglect me. You done that, and now you're wantin' me to think you'll just take all my troubles away."

"I don't think I can take all your troubles away," I said. "I don't think anyone can do that. But I could try to make you a home for as long as you might want to stay."

"I don't think you like Bo," she said, taking another tack.

"So far I can't claim to have warmed to him," I admitted. "He seems pretty fractious."

"He's a writer, that's why he uses them odd words," T.R. informed the girls, who had been listening closely to all this.

"On the other hand, I already love Jesse," I said. "And besides that, I already love you."

"Don't even mention it, you're way too late to

156

be bringing that up!" she said. "You never sent me a single birthday present."

"Oh, I sent them," I said truthfully. "Your mother just refused them. I sent them every year until she told me she'd start burning them if I didn't stop. After that I bought them but I didn't send them. I just put them in a closet."

"In a closet?" she asked. This revelation really surprised her.

"Yep," I said. "Twenty-two birthday presents and twenty-two Christmas presents too, plus a few Easter baskets and stuff. They're all in a closet at my house. You can see them when we get home."

T.R.'s face reddened. It was clear she was about to cry.

"Did you really do that—get me them presents?" she asked in a quivering voice.

I nodded; it was true. Every year I had gone ahead and got the presents, feeling hopeless but doing it anyway, always asking a salesclerk what a little girl, or in time a not-so-little girl, her age might want. They were all in a closet at Los Dolores: Barbie dolls, doll dishes, makeup kits, a ten-speed bike, etc.

"By the way, how is your mother?" I asked, to ease the moment.

"I thought you said you'd talked to her," she said. "I thought you said she told you she'd burn my presents."

"I did, but that was several years ago," I said. "I just wondered how she was."

"She died when I was twelve," T.R. said. "Cancer got her."

"Oh, dear," I said. "I guess it was longer than it seemed when we had our conversation. I'm sorry, T.R."

"My dad, he's got cancer now," Elena volunteered conversationally.

T.R. put her face in her hands and began to sob. Tentatively I put my arm around her. In a moment she turned and clung to me, sobbing. For the first time in my life I felt my daughter's tears on my neck. That was fine, but in shifting position slightly, I almost dislodged the slumbering Jesse; she began to slide out of my lap. I raised one knee a little and just managed to stop her. T.R. sobbed and sobbed, seeming to grow larger and wetter the more tightly she clung to me. I felt as though I were embracing a giant, while at the same time trying to keep a midget—Jesse—from falling to the ground. The leg that I used to stabilize Jesse soon began to cramp.

Also, Jesse kept sliding—her movement was almost imperceptible, but she was sliding. Fortunately, T.R. stopped sobbing just before Jesse went over the trembling precipice of my knee.

T.R. wiped her face on the bottom of her T-shirt.

"I wanta go to your house," she said. "I wanta see if you really got me all them presents."

"I got them, they're there," I assured her. "As far as I'm concerned, we can go right now."

7

"First I gotta finish my onion rings before they get cold, though," T.R. remarked. "That's one delay. Then we gotta go by the jail and see Muddy, he'd never forgive me if I moved away without lettin' him have one last glimpse of his baby girl. I know Dew will wanta come, Dew's always ready to go places, but Sue Lin's a different matter. Sue Lin may take a little persuading."

"They live with me, you know," she went on, offering me another onion ring, which I took—I was getting the sense that my new family life was going to require more fuel than my old lonely life.

"We're sharing the rent, I can't just run out on them," she added. "How big's your house?"

"Oh, it's quite large," I said gamely. "There's room for everyone."

"In that case you better come too, Elena," T.R. said. "You'll need some help with that kid, when it comes, and anyway Jesse loves you, she ain't gonna like going off and leavin' you."

"Okay, I can be the baby-sitter," Elena said happily.

The rest of the teen-agers had skipped off to talk to some somber young men who were bouncing a tire in the back of a pickup near by. If they had stayed around I felt sure T.R. would have asked them too.

"I'm gonna go ask Sue Lin," T.R. said. "It

would be pretty hard to do without Sue Lin. She's about the only person Bo likes."

"Bring her, by all means," I said. Bo was still asleep, but he was beginning to twitch. T.R. was right that I didn't like him, although I knew it was ridiculous to judge a grandchild on such short acquaintance. Perhaps he'd grow up to be a theologian rather than an armed robber, but I doubted it. At first blush the thought of taking Dew, Sue Lin, Elena, in addition to T.R. and the kids, had seemed a bit much, but a moment's reflection persuaded me there might be safety in numbers.

Besides, what a stunning surprise it would be for Godwin and Gladys when I drove up with four young women, one of them black, one of them yellow, one of them brown (not to mention pregnant), and one of them my daughter.

"The problem's Granny Lin," T.R. said, when she came out. "She's kind of fuzzy in the head from all them days floating around in a boat and starving and stuff. I think we better just take Granny Lin too, she's not much bigger than a chicken. Otherwise Sue Lin will never budge and Dew won't either. I sure ain't up to leavin' every single person I know, even if there is that closetful of presents. And if I stay down here, Earl Dee will kill me, or if he decided to hold off on killin' me he'd try to put the kids to work making child porn or something—that's the direction Earl Dee's mind runs when he ain't off beatin' the piss out of some poor turkey working in a 7-Eleven somewhere. Seems like we just oughta gather up

Granny Lin and go. It's a pretty good bunch of us—that's why I was hoping you'd bring the airplane."

By my count we were up to eight passengers, but Dew, Sue Lin, and Elena were skinny, and the kids were tots. Granny Lin was said to be no bigger than a chicken. Only T.R. and I were large. It seemed to me we might all fit in the Cadillac.

"We can fit," I said. "We just might have to send a moving van for your possessions."

"There ain't no possessions," T.R. said. "Muddy just stole everything we had three days ago. See that pickup where those kids are bouncing the tire? He hauled off the bed and the TV set in that—the bed his own child was sleeping in—that's how good a burglar Muddy is. He brought Jesse back, but not the bed. We're lucky he left us the clothes on our backs."

"This is the person you want to visit in jail?" I said.

"Sure, so what?" T.R. said. "He was just out of money and needed to buy some marijuana," she said. "Muddy gets real bad headaches if he don't smoke marijuana. Our old TV only got two channels anyway—it was all just junk, what he stole. So far I never owned nothing in my life that wasn't junk. If I didn't have Muddy to steal it, I'd have to pay somebody to haul it off, sooner or later."

"I guess that's a healthy attitude," I said.

"It's a don't-give-a-fuck attitude," T.R. said in her flat voice. "I got more to worry about than a

161

few crappy possessions. I got Earl Dee to worry about. I don't even want to work my shift, I'm gonna see if I can get one of the girls to take it. What if Earl Dee got out yesterday? He could come walking right up any time."

She reached down and scooped Bo out of the dirt, where he was napping. He began to whine and rub his eyes.

"Elena, you take Jesse, Daddy ain't learned how to hold her yet," T.R. said. "Dew and Sue Lin will be off in a minute—I'll go tell Maria and Josefina that they're the new crew at the Mr. Burger. What I'd like to do is mobilize before that cocksucking Earl Dee wiggles out of the woodwork."

"I like your command of the vernacular," I said—and I did. The way T.R. put things had charmed me from the first.

But T.R. was mobilizing; she scarcely gave me a glance.

"Where's your car?" she said.

_____ 8 _____

An hour later we were all mobilized. Dew and Sue Lin had taken off their aprons and cheerfully hitched their fates to T.R.'s star. The Dismuke Street Mr. Burger proved to be a spongelike entity; it absorbed the two Mexican teen-agers and remained a fully functioning cheeseburger outlet. Everyone waved as we drove away.

T.R. had been right to describe her possessions as minimal. She, Sue Lin, Dew, Granny Lin, and the kids had been living in two rooms over a pet store on Telephone Road. Their possessions consisted of a few secondhand toys, an army cot, two mattresses, a few skirts and blouses, and a wok. Granny Lin, a very tiny and very ancient Vietnamese woman, sat on one of the mattresses, squinting at an old issue of the *National Enquirer* when we trooped in.

"Granny never gives up, she's tryin' to learn English," Sue Lin explained.

"From that?" I said, horrified at the thought of the conclusions the old woman must be drawing about our culture if she was really managing to read the *Enquirer*.

"Now don't you be runnin' down our reading matter," T.R. said. "I found it in the trash, and it's better than nothing."

Packing consisted of T.R. and Dew staring at the closet for a few minutes as they tried to decide if any of their clothes were worth taking.

"I say we junk this shit," T.R. said. "Daddy can buy us all a lot better clothes than these. Let's just go."

"And leave my sequins?" Dew said, grabbing a pair of profusely sequined pants. "If we was to go dancing I'd feel naked without my sequins. Reckon they dance out in the Wild West?" she asked, looking at me.

"Oh, sure," I assured her. "People up my way dance constantly."

163

T.R. was for abandoning the toys, too, but the children screamed and turned red at the mere suggestion that we leave them behind. The wok, the clothes, and a collection of dingy toys took up most of the Cadillac's trunk space. Jesse retained a stained Cabbage Patch Doll, and Bo kept a small green truck, which he raced up and down the back of my neck as we drove through town.

"Vroom, vroom, vroom!" he yelled—at least it seemed to me he was yelling. No one else seemed to notice.

Granny Lin had been assigned the seat next to me. She still clutched her copy of the *Enquirer*— the fateful issue whose cover carried a famous picture of Nema Remington and her then beau, Pinky Collins, a diminutive Irish terrorist, embracing in the surf at Malibu. The embrace itself was an echo of the famous Burt Lancaster-Deborah Kerr surffuck in *From Here to Eternity*, except that Pinky Collins was only about one-third the size of Burt Lancaster.

At that, he was probably larger than Granny Lin, who was humming a haunting if almost inaudible tune. The sound she made when she hummed was as faint as memory, in this case Asian memory. It caused me to imagine a misty village in the delta in a peaceful era, with rice paddies and dutiful water buffalo—but while we were stopped at a light Sue Lin informed me that her granny had grown up in Paris and had only returned to Vietnam in the fifties, to run a travel service.

"My goodness," I said—one more bucolic fantasy shattered.

I parked about a block from the downtown jail. T.R. spit on her finger and created a couple of curls out of Jesse's wispy hair.

"Muddy likes to think he's got a little curly-headed angel," T.R. said. "That Muddy's a dreamer.

"You coming?" she asked, looking at me across the humming head of Granny Lin.

"Sure, if you want me to," I said gamely, though I hated going into jails. I had been in a number of them in the last few years, always to get Godwin released after some embarrassing and marginally criminal escapade.

"I thought we was in this together," T.R. said, a little belligerently. "I don't call it together if you're just gonna sit in the car. Them cops are horrible to me—they think I oughta be sleeping with one of them instead of a little crook like Muddy."

"I wasn't sure if I was supposed to come," I said, popping free of my seat belt.

From the backseat, Dew laughed.

"If you wasn't supposed to come, you wouldn't be here," she said. "From now on, you *always* supposed to come."

"That's right," T.R. said.

I got a little nervous going into the jail. My imagination, not active enough to get my new novel written, was active enough to imagine the life in jails. It was a ridiculously fastidious imagination, with a snobbish selectivity. Where jails were concerned, it skipped over the things you usually read about—gang rapes, knifings, suicide, beatings— and focused on the seemingly trivial matter of dirty hair.

I hate dirty hair. I wash mine constantly, sometimes twice a day. The state most likely to propel me into immediate insanity is a state of tonsorial filth. Clean hair is a bedrock condition for civilization, in my view—a view shared, of course, by shampoo manufacturers and many members of the classes among which I traveled in my years of celebrity.

It is not a view shared by the people who work in jails, much less by the incarcerees, if that's the word for the people whose fate it is to be locked up. Hair care is not a priority for most of them; obviously it's absurd of me to wish it were, but I wished it nonetheless. I no sooner enter a jail than I begin to imagine how horrible I would feel if my hair were as dirty as the hair of the people in the waiting room, not to mention the people in the cells.

This happened almost as soon as we entered the

Houston jail. The waiting room smelled of mildew and ammonia. The air conditioner was off and the outer doors open, so the mildew may have been Houston's contribution. Most of the women in the waiting room were black, but there were five or six Hispanics and one or two poor whites. Several children were waiting, most of them clutching toys at least as dingy as those my grandchildren owned. A lot of lank, discouraged, none too clean hair could be seen in the waiting room—the tonsorial equivalent of those pictures of ravaged gums particularly insensitive dentists sometimes put in their waiting rooms.

T.R. charged into the waiting room, Jesse in her arms, but by the time she actually reached the grille where visitors had to make obeisance to the law, her charge had lost a lot of its force.

"I need to see Muddy Box," she said to an officer who was reading an old issue of *Teen World* with a semiotician's concentration.

The officer glanced up resentfully.

"Muddy's mopping," he said. "He's cleaning up the drunk tanks—they're mostly knee-deep in puke. Muddy's our best mopper. If he'd quit stealing he could get on as a janitor any time."

"Hoorah for Muddy. Can I see him?" T.R. asked.

She sat Jesse on the little ledge in front of the grille, hoping that the sight of an angelic curly-headed child would soften the officer's heart, but it didn't. He was more interested in *Teen World*.

"Fill this out and take a seat," he said, pushing

167

a form toward her. "Muddy won't be available for a while."

"You ask," T.R. said, turning to me. "Otherwise we'll have to sit around here for three hours and we'll all get depressed."

Her look said okay, we're in this together, start being a daddy *right now*.

I'm as timid as most people when confronted with even the most low-level representative of the powers that be, but it was clear that I had better, for once, make an effort to be a little more bold.

"Officer, I'm sorry to trouble you, but we're in an unseemly hurry today," I said.

Fortunately, I had my passport with me: I always do. Better yet, I also had a ticket, an open first-class ticket, Dallas—Paris, for those times when Godwin, Gladys, Texas, and America simply became too much. I extracted my passport and my ticket from an inside coat pocket and thrust them through the grille. I also had a meaningless little honorific visa the French government had given me as a return for my once having chaired a jury at the Cannes Film Festival. It had no real diplomatic validity, but it looked impressive, particularly for a jail clerk whose reading skills barely sufficed for *Teen World*. I gave him the visa while trying to imagine that I was Charles de Gaulle.

"You see, we have an international flight to catch," I said. "We have to be in France tomorrow. My daughter's film starts production next week. I assure you we won't take Mr. Box away from his mopping for more than a few minutes, and we'd be immensely grateful if you could possibly facilitate this visit."

Not merely the officer but the whole room was stunned. Several other jail clerks, including two matrons who had been picking their noses and killing time behind the grille, came over to take a look. The sound of my voice seemed to send them all into mild shock. From the look on their faces as they examined my passport, it was clear that a passport from a Martian couldn't have surprised them much more.

The officer who had been so engrossed in *Teen World* seemed to have been struck dumb by my feeble Gaullism. He fingered my little French honor as gingerly as if it were a letter bomb.

"Uh, what relation are you to Mr. Box, sir?" he asked, after exchanging several glances with his colleagues.

"I'm his putative father-in-law," I said, gaining confidence. I was beginning to sense that I could win this one-sided contest on vocabulary alone.

"We want to arrange for him to come to France when he's released," I went on. "There are some technicalities to discuss—you know the French.

"We'll be staying in Cap d' Antibes," I added as a flourish.

I doubt that any of the people inspecting my meaningless documents really did know the French—it was not evident that they even knew one another—but the mere fact that I had offered the documents caused them to abandon all efforts to push T.R. around.

"Go get Muddy," the skinny officer said to one of the matrons. "He's got all day to mop them drunk tanks."

Then, as the matron shuffled off, he put his thumbs in his ears, wiggled his fingers, stuck out his tongue, and made a silly face at Jesse, who was not charmed. She responded by instantly emitting a squeal far more serious than any of her previous efforts in the squealing line. Everyone in the waiting room, visitors and jailers alike, clapped their hands over their ears in shock. Jesse held the squeal for perhaps ten seconds, by which time the unfortunate jail clerk had become the most hated man in the room. If there had suddenly been an uprising in the jail, his own colleagues would probably have strangled him.

"I was just trying to make a funny face," he said lamely, when Jesse stopped squealing.

"She hates people who stick out their tongues at her," T.R. said. "Looks like you'd learn—she does that every time we come in here."

"She looks so cute," the jail clerk said. "Look at them little spit curls. I was just trying to make friends."

"I told her it was your fault her daddy ain't livin' with us now," T.R. said. "She's gettin' revenge on you for breakin' up our family. I'll be glad when we get to France so I won't never have to come in this crummy jail again."

"Well, you wouldn't have to anyway if Muddy would just earn an honest trade, like being a janitor," the clerk said defensively. "Here he comes now."

At first glance the young man who came into the room looked like what Gladys and I called Godwin-bait. He was short, slight, and blond. He was pushing one of those mop buckets on wheels that janitors used, and he was no taller than the mop. He sported a wisp of blond mustache—the fact that his jail pajamas were several sizes too large only made him look smaller.

At the sight of him Jesse began to coo. She almost wiggled off the ledge she was seated on in her excitement. Her immediate happiness was infectious; the dulled faces of the people in the waiting room brightened for a moment at the sight of Jesse's pleasure.

"I thought I heard my little squealer and I *did* hear my little squealer," Muddy said, scooping Jesse off the ledge.

She immediately became shy, holding her face in her hands.

Muddy stood on tiptoe and tried to give T.R. a big kiss, but she looked aloof and only offered him a cheek.

"I need to talk to you," she said, "and I don't like having to do it in front of a million people."

After a glance at the clerk, who had lost interest, and at the matrons, who had never had any, she linked her arm in Muddy's and started for the open door.

"We're just gonna sit on the steps a minute so

we can have a little privacy," T.R. told the clerk, who was once again absorbed in *Teen World*.

"Okay, but leave the mop," he said, without looking up. "There's people in this town who'd steal a mop, and he's one of them."

"This is Daddy," T.R. said, brusquely, dragging Muddy past us. "If it hadn't been for him they'd have made us wait all day."

Muddy offered a small, limp hand. He had the kind of dreamy face that betrayed no energy of any kind.

It was hard to believe that such a slight man had had the strength to burgle a TV set, much less the energy to father a child on my large energetic daughter—but apparently he had. A squib from a famous poem came to mind, the one about fine women eating a crazy salad with their meat. Muddy Box was a human version of one of those limp little salads you get served in country cafés throughout the West and South—a few leaves of tired lettuce, a shred or two of radish, an exhausted tomato.

But then I knew well enough that it was impossible to account for the confusing chemistries that sometimes combine in this life. Boys who looked as harmless as Muddy had more than once beaten Godwin to within an inch of his life and left him penniless in airport parking lots or beside remote roads.

When we stepped out of the jail the warm Gulf sun was beaming down on an empty street. Bo had escaped from the Cadillac and was sitting on its roof. Elena stood by the car, trying to coax him down. Dew, Sue Lin, and Granny Lin were just waiting. Muddy sat on a step with Jesse in his lap and began to try to charm her out of her shyness—her hands still covered her eyes. He would carefully pry loose a finger or two and she would immediately put them back. He and Jesse seemed totally absorbed by this game, but T.R. wasn't. She was looking up and down the street, practically crackling with tension.

"This street's totally empty," she said. "There's not a soul in sight except us."

"Well, it's a jail," Muddy pointed out. "We don't get too many tourists passin' through."

T.R. snorted at him—sometimes she exhaled disgust and frustration in a kind of violent snort.

"He don't have no ambition," she said, looking at me but referring to Muddy.

Muddy looked helpless in the face of what seemed to be her rising fury. He gave a tired little shrug. "I only finished sixth grade," he said.

"Oh, bull, you went to vocational school after that!" T.R. said. "You told me you did, or was that just another of your lies?"

"Well, I went a few days," Muddy said. "I was gonna learn diesel mechanics and try to get on at the truck stop, but shoot, that stuff's hard. I can usually fix a regular engine but I ain't worth a shit with a diesel."

He had abandoned his efforts to pry Jesse's fingers off her eyes, whereupon she dropped her hands and flashed him a brilliant smile.

173

"Aw," Muddy said, overcome.

"If you had any ambition you'd escape right now," T.R. said. "Nobody would care. I doubt you'd even be missed for a week or two."

"That ain't so," Muddy said. "I'd be missed tomorrow when they need somebody to mop the drunk tanks."

"So is that all you want to do with your life, live in jail and mop drunk tanks?" T.R. asked.

"No, but it's better than a lot of things," Muddy replied, trying to be reasonable.

"Oh, come on," T.R. said, grabbing his arm. "Come on, let's just go. We could be halfway to France while we're standing here arguing."

Muddy looked horrified. "But I'm in jail, you swore out the complaint yourself," he said. "*You* had me arrested."

"I was pissed off," T.R. said. "You oughtn't to have sold the TV. At least the kids could watch cartoons on Saturday morning, it's the one time I get to sleep late. Okay, that's water under the bridge, let's go. I'll just have Daddy's lawyer write them a letter and say I dropped the charges."

"Yeah, but that ain't the whole problem," Muddy said. "They pulled up that time when I walked off the dope farm. I got six months to do on that one before they even get to this one."

"Come on, I wanta go while there's nobody in sight," she said, half-dragging him down the steps of the jailhouse. "Daddy's lawyer can get it all fixed once we're in France."

It was clear that Muddy's heart was not in escaping, but his resistance was halfhearted and it took more than half a heart to apply an effective brake to T.R.

I was as appalled at T.R. as he was, probably because in the short time that we'd been together T.R. had developed the habit of taking everything I said at face value. She had not grasped the fact that I was a novelist, at least to the degree that I constantly improved on reality by inventing little scenarios that, if enacted, would make life better. The unfortunate truth, though, was that few of them *were* enacted. It seemed to me that our sudden trip to France might fall into that capacious category.

Muddy still held Jesse, who was now flirting madly with her father, all shyness gone. T.R. soon had us on the sidewalk by the Cadillac.

"Get off that roof and into that car, we're leaving!" she said, snapping her fingers at Bo. Her finger snap was so emphatic that, after a quick glance to determine that she meant it, he obeyed, leaping off the car into Elena's arms.

"T.R., are you sure this is a good idea?" I asked. "Maybe Muddy and I would be better advised to wait a day or two until my lawyer can look into things and get him out on bail. That way he won't be making his legal problems worse."

"Shut up, who asked you?" she said, whirling on me. "If he sticks around they may discover six or eight more crimes he's committed—they got them computers now that keep track of millions of old crimes."

"For that matter, I could probably find a bail bondsman and get him out right now," I said. The whole block across from the jail consisted of bail-bond offices.

"Won't work, it ain't the new charge, it's the fact that I walked off the dope farm," Muddy said. "I'm servin' out a sentence at the moment, that's how it works."

"How it works is everybody shut your stupid mouths and get in that car!" T.R. said. "You don't stand around arguing when you're making a jail-break."

My imagination was making scenarios a mile a minute, none of them involving Cap d'Antibes. They involved smelly jails filled with sadistic deputies in places like Buffalo, Texas—my imagination calculated that would be about as far as we'd get before they caught us. A passport, an airline ticket, and a French visa might count for nothing in Buffalo, Texas.

But T.R. had already stuffed Bo and Elena in the backseat and was handing Jesse to Dew.

"We're up to nine," I remarked nervously. "It's gonna be pretty crowded."

"Muddy don't weigh nothing, he can sit on my lap," she informed me with a grin. The street was still empty, her jailbreak was working, and her mood had improved.

They squeezed in, Muddy indeed installed on her lap. The Cadillac was crammed, and when I finally got behind the wheel it was even more crammed. I felt pretty jumpy, expecting sirens to start sounding at any moment. Three or four tries failed to fit the key into the ignition—finally Granny Lin tapped my arm, took the keys, and fitted the right one into the elusive slot.

"See, Muddy fits fine on my lap," T.R. said, delighted with the success of her venture. She goosed Muddy a couple of times, causing him to grin with embarrassment.

"I've even sat in Muddy's lap once or twice," T.R. said, passing Dew a stick of gum. "That works pretty good too, otherwise there wouldn't be no Jesse."

"Oh, is *that* what happened?" Dew said, and she and T.R. laughed heartily, unwrapping their gum. Muddy looked even more embarrassed.

"Whee, let's go, this is like Bonnie and Clyde," T.R. said. Bo once again began to run his little truck up and down my neck, saying, "Vroom, vroom!"

I expected sirens, the SWAT team, handcuffs, headlines. We met three police cars between the jail and the freeway, but none of them paid the slightest attention.

"How about that, Muddy? You're a free man," T.R. said.

"Free till they catch me, then I won't be," Muddy said, a certain weariness in his tone.

T.R.'s spirits were rising higher and higher. She squeezed Muddy back against her and gave him three or four noisy kisses on the neck.

"You ain't the least bit free," she informed him. "You're outa jail, but now I got you, and you know what *that* means."

Muddy may have known, but he wasn't saying.

"It means we're gonna have some fun up at Daddy's place, or over in France or wherever Daddy wants to take us," she said.

"I hope you brought some dope," Muddy said. "There was plenty of it in jail but I couldn't afford the prices."

10

The most eventful thing that occurred early on in our drive was that Bo threw his truck out the window in a fit of pique. T.R. finally got tired of hearing him say "Vroom, vroom," which he said without interruption all the way from Houston to Madisonville. She ordered him to stop, he didn't stop; the backseat by this time resembled a battlefield, but T.R. managed to reach across the battlefield, grab her son, turn him around, and give him a brief but decisive spanking, whereupon he threw his truck out the window.

By this time I had learned to drive with one eye on the road and the other on the rearview mirror, though so far the only thing occurring was that T.R., Muddy, Dew, and Sue Lin were smoking marijuana, occasionally passing a joint forward to Elena and Granny Lin. Everyone seemed to be enjoying the ride—even I was sort of enjoying it though I still expected justice to catch up to us somewhere around Buffalo.

When I saw Bo throw the truck out the window I immediately braked, but T.R. wouldn't hear of stopping.

"He done it, let him live with it," she said. "I hate that truck anyway."

Bo's way of living with it was to emit a series of earsplitting screams.

"Just ignore him, all he wants is attention anyway," T.R. said.

The other residents of the car seemed to be practiced at ignoring him, but I wasn't. I began to get a sort of low, migrainous feeling—I felt as if a headache were waiting somewhere up the road. There wasn't much airspace in the car, and Bo's screaming made me realize what a crowded situation I had got myself into. There were eight humans in the car with me, all of them going about being human in their own separate ways. Not since the day I finally left the set of "Al and Sal" had I actually been in close proximity to eight other humans at one time. Mostly I had been in close proximity to no one—I breakfasted with Godwin and Gladys, it was true, but that usually took place outdoors, with the great space of the plains around us.

Not in a long time had I been so uninsulated from human contact as I was at that moment. Soon the human emanations all around me, of which the most extreme manifestation was Bo's screaming, began to make my temples throb alarmingly.

A headache was coming. I metaphorized it as a great black eighteen-wheeler. The ominous black truck was just now leaving Dallas; it was racing south, we were racing north; unless I was very lucky the migraine collision would occur somewhere near Corsicana. It felt as if it would be a terrible collision, too: the bodies of my recently acquired family might be scattered like matchsticks beside the road.

I hated to admit it, but I was about to get sick. Solitude had given way to crowdedness too suddenly: my synapses weren't adjusting rapidly enough. I began to feel shaky, and my temples throbbed more violently as the great black headache shifted into high gear.

"I don't feel so hot," I said, with what I hoped was admirable control. "I wonder if any of you would like to drive?"

"You bet, me!" T.R. said. "Stop, I need to change Jesse anyway, she always loses it when she gets around her daddy."

She changed Jesse and took the wheel. Elena moved back and sat on Muddy's lap, more or less, and I took her place on the other side of Granny Lin. I gulped a few pills, hoping to deflect the headache; instead of being a head-on collision, maybe it would just be a fender bender.

I shut my eyes for a few minutes, hoping to fool the migraine into thinking I was asleep. It was not a tactic likely to work, and it didn't; with my eyes shut I was even more conscious of the angry pulse in my temples. When I opened my eyes again, the thinning forests beside the road were being left behind very fast.

T.R. was not driving slow. Her eyes were alight and she looked happy, though. While I watched with fascination and horror, we sped up almost onto the bumper of a pickup that was idling along in the fast lane.

T.R. honked and flashed her lights at the pickup repeatedly, but the pickup didn't move over. I recalled that the same thing had happened to me several times on the drive to Houston; people in Texas hadn't acquired the good lane-switching manners one can usually count on in California. Many Texans seemed to feel they had a perfect right to drive in the fast lane even if they were only going a sedate seventy-five.

Like T.R., I was irritated when I had to check my speed because of a slow driver in the fast lane, but I suppressed my irritation and she didn't.

Seeing that the pickup wasn't going to budge, she whipped around it on the right. As we shot past it she stuck her head out the window and yelled at two startled cowboys.

"Get out of the way, you stupid fuckheads!" she yelled. She cut back sharply in front of the pickup and then gunned the Cadillac down the road at top speed, as if to illustrate how fast they ought to be moving if they insisted on using that lane.

The way she yelled at the cowboys amused me. "For a disciple of Jesus, you certainly do use strong language," I said.

T.R. just grinned. "Jesus don't care if I call a stupid fuckhead a stupid fuckhead," she said confidently.

"How do you know, have you talked to him lately?" Muddy inquired, passing T.R. the joint they were smoking.

"I doubt he'd have no sympathy for people too dumb to know which lane to drive in," T.R. said.

"Oops, Jesse just got a little carsick," Elena said.

"She always does, just point her toward the floor," T.R. said.

Bo began to scream at his little sister. "Yuk!" he screamed. "Yuk, yuk!"

"Hand him up to Daddy," T.R. said. "It's time he got to know his grandpa better."

"I'm not sure that's a great idea," I said. "I'm not feeling too hot myself."

Nevertheless several eager hands immediately grabbed Bo and thrust him over the seat headfirst—his popularity with the backseaters was understandably slight. I took him and sat him on my lap. I tried smiling at him and got a sullen look in return.

"You're a writer," T.R. said. "Tell him a story. Stories are about the only thing that'll keep Bo quiet for long."

I was remembering my solitude so carefully cultivated over the years. Once I'd probably felt that I was developing my solitude for the sake of my novel, or for some kind of art work, but in recent years I had come to realize that that wasn't really true. I had become solitary because I liked it and needed it. Aloneness, I had come to believe, did not need an art work to justify it; aloneness was self-justifying, valuable for its own sake.

But the fact was, my solitude was now gone. I was in a car with eight other human beings. I had traded solitude for a daughter who clearly had no wish to be alone. Perhaps she had never really been alone; with two children it was unlikely she would be for a while. I wasn't sad about my choice—T.R. was there, there at last, and it would have taken a colder man than myself not to yield up solitude in response to her energy, her aliveness, her guts. I was ready to yield everything instantly, only something deep within me did preserve a warm nostalgia for my old, deep, civilized solitude.

At the mention of a story, Bo became a little less sullen. He was looking at me neutrally, and he wasn't screaming. For an instant, he seemed almost likable.

"You better start a story," Elena warned. "He don't like it if there's no story."

At that point Jesse, smelling slightly of her car sickness, arrived in the front seat with the help of the same willing hands. She smiled lopsidedly and arranged herself on my other knee.

"All right, Grandpa," T.R. said. "The pressure's on. I sure hope you know a story."

What I knew, first and foremost, was that the black truck of the headache was somewhere ahead, speeding toward me. It wasn't there yet, but the collision was coming—if I was going to win my waiting grandchildren with a story I would have to be quick.

Once, many years ago in Paris, I had made up a story for Romy Schneider's little girl, whose baby-sitter had had a car wreck. The child had been dropped with me at the Plaza Athénée for thirty minutes while Romy did an interview. When I asked the child what sort of stories she liked best she said that she particularly enjoyed stories about vegetables that talked. I was in an inventive mood that afternoon and immediately reeled off a story about a carrot and a radish. It was a great success.

Romy's little girl had been about four at the time; neither Bo nor Jesse was yet four. Would either of them know what a radish was, or even a carrot?

"Have either of you ever met a radish?" I asked tentatively. Four unswerving eyes looked at me critically—if either child had ever made the acquaintance of a radish, they weren't saying.

In fact, the whole crowd in the car, so raucous only a moment ago, had fallen silent. Everyone, it seemed, was waiting for my story.

"This story takes place in the land of peas," I began, trying to remember how I'd gotten the story off the ground the first time I told it.

"Once in the corner of a big pea patch there lived a carrot named Jimmy. Jimmy's best friend was a radish named François"—that part, as I remembered, had caused Romy's little girl to crack up. It made no visible impression on Bo and Jesse. Of course, they weren't French.

"One day Jimmy and François went for a walk, and François, who was rather fat, stumbled over a pea vine and went tumbling down a hill into the road, just as a big truck from the vegetable market came rushing along."

Without warning Bo suddenly shifted his attention from my story and punched his little sister in the mouth, knocking her into the floorboards at Granny Lin's feet. Jesse, who had seemed to like my story, or at least the sound of my voice, began to wail. Granny Lin picked her up and shielded her from her brother, who seemed fully prepared to punch her again.

"Hulk!" Bo yelled, directing the yell at me.

"Bo just likes stories about monsters, only he calls them hulks," T.R. said. "He ain't too interested in carrots and peas that roll downhill. Know any stories about monsters?"

"No, but I will once I get to know Bo better," I said. "He has many of the attributes of a monster himself."

T.R.'s face fell. I knew immediately that I had said something very wrong—but then Bo had punched Jesse when she had merely been sitting there quietly, listening to my story. I felt she would have enjoyed the story even if she wasn't fully aware of what a radish was.

"I know, nobody likes Bo," T.R. said, sniffing back tears. "Everybody thinks he's horrible. I was

185

hoping at least his grandpa would like him, but I guess that's too much to ask."

"I'm sure I will like him in time," I said, but without conviction.

"No, nobody really likes Bo 'cept me and Elena," T.R. said. "Muddy hates him and now you hate him too."

"I don't *hate* him," I protested. "I just don't enjoy his behavior."

T.R. gave me her flat look. "He's sitting right in your fuckin' lap," she said. "You're his grandpa. Spank the shit out of him—he deserves it. Why should I have to do all the dirty work?"

To the surprise of everyone in the car, I *did* spank him. It was not what T.R. said that enabled me to do it—it was the fact that the child was looking at me with such cold insolence. Before he could move, I turned him on his stomach and gave him three quick splats with my open hand. They weren't hard but in the silent car they seemed louder than I expected.

Bo began to scream and wiggle. He managed to get loose and flung himself over the seat into Elena's arms, where he sobbed as if he had been tortured for hours.

T.R. looked surprised. The flat look left her face.

"I'm glad you done that," she said. "I didn't really think you had it in you. Maybe I finally found somebody who'll help me try and turn Bo into a nice person.

"I want him to be a nice person someday," she

said in an uncertain voice. "I don't want him to just be a criminal like his daddy."

"He won't be," I said, exhilarated by my own performance. "We'll soon shape him up."

"You ain't gonna change that kid," Muddy said bluntly. "If you ask me, our best bet would just be to leave him beside the road."

"Yeah, but nobody did ask you, dickhead!" T.R. said hotly. "You're the one who'll be left beside the road if you don't shut up. Better yet, I might turn this sucker around and take you back to jail."

Muddy shut up, I shut up, Bo sobbed. Jesse regained her good spirits and crawled back into my lap. T.R.'s mood was hard to judge—dangerous might have been the right word for it.

"I hate the way people talk about Bo," she said. "He's just a little boy. He ain't even three, and I been doing the best I could with him. But every single person except Elena talks hateful about him."

Nobody denied it. T.R. sighed heavily; she had not slowed down. We were passing trucks and cars as if they weren't moving.

"Don't worry about it, sweetie," I said. "Things are going to get better now."

But before they were better, they were going to be worse, I knew. We were almost to Corsicana, and, right on schedule, the great black truck of the migraine came roaring out of the north.

This migraine might have been Peterbilt, such was its power. My vision began to waver; the road ahead seemed a jerky mirage. Needlelike pains shot up my neck into the back of my skull, while every few seconds there would be an intense throb just above my eyes, as if someone were striking me there with a small cobbler's hammer.

I swallowed three more pills, seeking any magic that might deflect the headache before it attained its full force.

T.R. saw me swallow the pills. Even driving ninety, she didn't miss much. She favored me with two or three searching glances as she blazed up the road.

Jesse, not realizing the pain I was in, decided it was a good time to flirt. She settled herself carefully astride one of my legs and smiled at me even more lopsidedly than before—one result of Bo's punch was a puffy lower lip.

Even with the black truck grinding its gears in my head I couldn't entirely resist Jesse. She hid her eyes behind my hands, inviting me to play the game she had played with her father. Carefully I pried a couple of her fingers loose—I had to be especially careful because my hands were trembling, and I certainly didn't want to mar the promising relationship that was developing with my granddaughter by poking her in the eye.

"What's wrong with you?" T.R. asked. "You're white as a sheet and you look real shaky. I hope you haven't got some old disease you could give my babies."

"No, I just have a headache," I said. "I have migraines—fairly intense ones. If it gets much worse we may have to stop for a while until I get over it. We've still got a way to go before we get home and I'm not sure I can make it."

T.R. looked fretful.

"It must be like PMS," she said. "Dew gets real bad PMS. Sometimes when she's trying to work with PMS she can't tell a hot dog from a cheeseburger, she's that out of it."

"I can't tell nothin' from nothin'," Dew agreed. "I feel like a stupid old tick, so full of blood I just need to be squashed."

"We'll all need to be squashed if we have to sit around in a car with these kids, waiting for Daddy to get over a headache," T.R. said.

I was wiggling a finger at Jesse—it was the most flirtatious behavior I was capable of in my throbbing state. To my surprise she studied my finger for a moment, then grabbed it and yanked it up and down, smiling.

"Oh, you wouldn't have to wait in the car," I said. "I'd just get us all motel rooms. You and the kids could go swimming or do whatever you want to do. If I could just take a hot bath and a little nap I imagine I'd feel well enough to travel pretty soon."

My suggestion seemed to stun everyone in the

car, except Granny Lin, who remained unaffected not merely by my suggestion but by life itself. Granny Lin seemed to be focused far ahead, or perhaps far behind. Her eyes reminded me of the eyes of old dogs—she was looking beyond this place, to the other place. Car, motel, shabby apartment were of little moment to Granny Lin.

T.R., without slackening our speed, was looking at the folks in the backseat, checking out their responses. She was grinning from ear to ear.

"Do you mean that?" she said. "You mean we could all have motel rooms?"

"Sure," I said. "Just stop at the next big one you see. We'll all get rooms and take it easy for a few hours."

"I keep forgetting I got a rich daddy now," she said. "I ain't stopping at the next one I see, but I'll stop at the best one I see. Everybody watch —we're all gonna vote except Muddy."

"Why not me? You never want me to have no opinion," Muddy said, deeply aggrieved.

"People that steal their own wife's bed don't get to vote, why would they?" T.R. said cheerfully. "You can stay in the room with me though, once we choose. Does that make you horny or not?"

"Aw," Muddy said, evidently too embarrassed by her remark to comment further.

"Okay, choose a good one, but don't wait too long," I said. "I'm feeling a little carsick, and I make a bigger mess than Jesse made."

"Grandpa don't feel good, don't wiggle his finger so hard, honey," T.R. said to Jesse. "Why don't you just give him a big kiss? It might make him feel better."

Jesse obligingly crawled up and gave me a big kiss; then she flopped back against my chest and was asleep within seconds. The kiss warmed my heart but had no effect on the headache; power surge after power surge coursed through my temples. I became increasingly nauseous and had horrible visions of having to open the car door and throw up, in which case Jesse might fall out, or we both might fall out. I decided I'd better buckle my seat belt around Jesse, too, but the seat belt wasn't long enough to reach around both of us. I turned it loose for a moment and it was instantly sucked back down the seat-belt holder and wouldn't come out. Once again, in trying to do the right thing, I had only made matters worse. The realization, coming hand in hand with a fierce power surge from my headache, made me feel doomed, or, at least, cursed.

"I hope we find a suitable motel pretty soon," I said. "This headache's not getting any easier to live with."

"It's gotta be a big one, though," T.R. said. "There's a bunch of us."

The big one, when it finally appeared, was in Arlington, city of cul-de-sacs. I had resolutely kept my eyes closed for fifty miles or so; with my eyes closed I felt slightly less nauseous. When I opened them we were sitting in front of a neo-Gothic monstrosity, complete with turrets, spires,

191

and a moat, called Ye Olde Camelot Inn. Giant suits of armor—Brobdingnagian was the word for those suits of armor—bracketed the entrance.

"It looks big enough, at least," I said.

T.R. had pulled across the moat and was right in front of the entrance, but she made no move to get out and register us.

"I love ye olde stuff," she said. "There used to be this miniature golf course in Lufkin that was ye olde. On the last hole you had to hit your ball into the mouth of a firebreathing dragon. Earl Dee took me there on our first date. I guess that's what led to my downfall."

"Then suits of armor look kinda spooky," Dew said. "A rapist could hide in something like that."

T.R. surveyed the suits of armor calmly. "I bet they're empty," she said. "We could drop Bo down in one and let him scream his little lungs out sometime when we don't feel like listening."

"It looks like a fine place to finish off my migraine in," I said. "Why don't you go in and get us seven or eight rooms?"

T.R. looked subdued—the turrets and spires of Ye Olde Camelot Inn had caused some of the confidence to drain out of her. Drained, she looked like a nervous teen-ager instead of the brash young woman who had just engineered a jailbreak.

"I never stayed in a fancy motel before," she said. "I'd be scared to walk in by myself. Besides, I ain't got a cent."

No one else in the car seemed any more confident than T.R. They were all looking down at the floor, socially paralyzed by the magnificence of the motel.

I dug some money out of my pocket and handed it to T.R. I suppose it was two or three thousand dollars, in hundred-dollar bills.

"Offer them cash," I said. "They'll give you all the rooms you need."

Muddy whistled. "Look at that money," he said.

"Yeah, well, don't look at it too hard, Muddy, it ain't yours," T.R. said, snatching the bills as if she expected him to grab them and flee, though he was firmly wedged in the center of the backseat.

"I wish you'd go in with me," T.R. said plaintively. "They're just gonna think I stole this money if I come walking in with it. Where would a person like me get a bunch of hundred-dollar bills is what they're gonna think."

"I don't know if I can walk that far without getting sick," I said truthfully. "Besides, if I move, Jesse might wake up."

T.R. reached across and transferred Jesse from my lap to Granny Lin's. Jesse, wheezing slightly, slept on, undisturbed.

"Both my kids can sleep through car wrecks, if they have to," T.R. said. "You don't look as sick as you did. Come on in with me."

Gingerly I opened the door and stood up. My vision was swimming and my legs felt shaky, but T.R. took my arm and we managed to walk the hundred yards or so across King Arthur's Lobby, as it was called, to ye olde reception desk, where a clerk dressed like a Knight of the Garter accepted my credit card and booked us most of a wing of the motel—three connecting executive suites. The clerk recognized my name from the American Express card: I had once made one of their I-never-leave-home-without-it commercials. Karl Malden made the first one, I made the second.

"Goodness, we're pleased to have you, Mr. Deck," the clerk said. "We'll just put you in the King Arthur suite and your friends will be right next door in Lancelot and Guinevere."

"Fine," I said. "This is my daughter. Please see that she and her friends get anything they want in the way of refreshments."

"Yes, sir, we'll send up a hospitality tray right now," the clerk said. "Do you think they'd like a pitcher or two of margaritas?"

"Dew would," T.R. said. "Dew drinks 'em like water."

"We'll just make that three pitchers, then," the helpful clerk said. Without his ridiculous Knight-of-the-Garter garb he would probably have been a nice-looking young yuppie. From the sparkle in his bright blue eyes I judged that few of T.R.'s charms were lost on him.

"I think that clerk just fell in love with you," I said as we were sorting out the giant ye olde keys we had been given.

"Naw, that was just the hots," she said with an aloof look. "I don't like them ass-kissin' types. I'll bite his head off if he don't behave."

We went up to check out the suites, which were vast and ugly—large enough not only for the crowd in the car but for the car too, if it could have been fitted into an elevator. Each room had a Jacuzzi—T.R. immediately kicked off a sandal and stuck her foot in the one in hers. She looked excited but also a little apprehensive.

"I still got all that money you gave me," she said. "What do you want me to do with it?"

"Well, keep it," I said. "I may be zonked out for a few hours. Six Flags and several other amusement parks are right across the road. You could take the kids, if you want to—or go shopping. It wouldn't be a bad idea to buy Muddy some clothes—as it is, he looks like he just broke out of jail."

"I probably should have left him, he'll want to steal everything he sees here," she said. "He'll wanta haul off the TV sets and most of the furniture. He always did like to steal antiques."

"Buy him some clothes," I said. "Maybe that'll satisfy him."

"Are you gonna leave the door to your room open?" she asked, looking more and more nervous.

"Sure, if you'd like me to," I said. "What's the matter?"

"I never been in a big old motel like this," she said in a shaky voice. "I might get scared."

"You've been living in one of the rougher parts of Houston and you weren't scared," I pointed out. "Nobody's gonna bother you here."

"I ain't scared on the street," she said. "I can handle the streets. But I don't know if I can handle this."

I felt a little faint, but T.R. was looking at me insistently. Actually, the rooms *were* depressing, particularly with all the curtains closed. I opened the curtains and let the strong sunlight in. Our suites were on the top floor; below us, across a freeway, was a giant water amusement park, with thousands of tiny swimmers in it. There were giant slides that seemed to plummet sliders straight down from alpine heights, and huge winding tubular tunnels through which kids shot in inner tubes. There was a pool that even seemed to have waves. Man-made whitetops curled toward the buglike swimmers.

"Look at that!" T.R. said. "They got one of them outside Houston. Me and Muddy were always gonna take the kids, but we couldn't afford it."

"Take them now," I said. "You can afford it."

"You can, you mean," she said. "I don't have a cent to my name and Muddy don't neither."

She was holding the bills I had given her, looking at them hostilely, it seemed. Then she looked at me, also hostilely.

"This is so much money it ain't real," she said. "It's like it's play money to you."

"It's just money," I said. "Go spend a little of it—you'll find out that it's real, soon enough."

T.R. suddenly flung the bills onto the floor.

"Men have offered me hundred-dollar bills before, only not for nothing," she said. "Men come up to the Mr. Burger every day and offer me money. They all say they don't want nothing, they just want to help me, but I took it once or twice, and that ain't true. They always want something, and they don't wait very long to let you know what it is.

"So what are you gonna want, Mr. Deck?" she asked, her eyes furious.

"I want to take a very hot bath," I said. "Then I want to take a nap and get over my headache."

"I mean, what do you want for this money?" she said. "I don't care if you have a stupid headache."

"For the money, nothing," I said. "Don't take it if you don't trust me—just bring the gang in and watch television or something. But I am different from those other men who offered you money, you know."

"I doubt you are—all men say they're different, I've heard that a million times," she said, her eyes still blazing.

"Oh, I'm sure you have," I said. "And you'll hear it a million times more. But I'm still different."

She stared at me angrily and I tried to meet her eye, but the headache was pounding harder and the room had begun to wobble. I felt as if I might faint; at the very least I was soon going to be sick at my stomach.

"Maybe it's too late to matter," I said, "but I'm your father. I don't want to buy you, I just

197

want to know you. Take the money or leave it, I don't care. Right now I have to be sick."

I made my way shakily into my suite and began to undress. I wanted to sink into the Jacuzzi; I also wanted to pile a towel full of ice on my throbbing head. Fortunately the room had a little refrigerator—it wasn't even ye olde—and I was able to get the ice tray out, but my hands were shaking so badly that I knocked all the ice cubes off on the floor.

To my surprise, T.R. picked them up.

"You're shaking like a leaf," she said, the fury gone from her voice. "You look worse than Dew looks when she gets her PMS."

"I just wanted some ice for my head," I said. "What I really need to do is get in the water. I've had a million of these migraines. It'll pass."

T.R. made a nice poultice of ice cubes. I held it against my temple and stood where I was, weaving slightly.

"I thought you was gonna get in the water," T.R. reminded me.

"I am, but I can't undress with you in the room," I said. "Which is not to say I want you to leave."

"I'd want me to leave if I felt the way you look," T.R. said. "I'm going right now."

I could think of nothing but sinking into the hot water of the Jacuzzi. T.R. left and I undressed and did just that, holding the poultice of ice to my head.

"Daddy, it's okay, I didn't peek," she said from

198

the doorway to the next suite. "I just want you to know I think I'm gonna take that money. I think I'll take the kids and the girls on a little spree."

"Do that," I said. "A little spree might be just what you all need."

Again I thought she was gone; again, I was wrong.

"Daddy?" she asked.

"What?" I asked—I was scarcely conscious.

"I don't want you to lock your door, though," she said. "I might need to get back in."

"I won't, honey," I said.

12

We stayed in the Ye Olde Camelot Inn for three days. T.R., Muddy, the girls, and the kids had spree after spree, hordes of sprees, while I entertained my migraine in the King Arthur suite.

I knew even before I left Houston that this migraine was going to prove to have a lot of kick, and I was not wrong. Like an obnoxious relative, the migraine moved in for a lengthy stay. I had not invited it, but, on the other hand, neither had I taken the trouble to negotiate the terms of the visit—I had been too busy with T.R., the kids, the move, the jailbreak, etc. For several hours, when I should have been taking firm steps to limit the visit, I did nothing, and the migraine settled in.

Once there, it refused to leave: I took baths, I

took pills, I slept under an igloo of poultices, and these methods, in combination, gained me a measure of control over the headaches—but only a measure. I subdued the migraine, but I couldn't evict it. As long as I kept still, it behaved, retreating to the far corner of my consciousness—but the minute I got up, put on my clothes, and acted as if I meant to resume a normal life, it insinuated itself back into my presence, if only as a low, intermittent throb.

After two or three unsuccessful attempts to resume my life, I gave up, went back to bed, and waited as patiently as possible for the migraine to get bored and leave. I could tell that it enjoyed interrupting what few patterns I had; it seemed to me that the only way to get rid of it was to make myself as vacant and patternless as possible. After a while, if I did that, the migraine might go look for someone more interesting to torment.

Shockingly, for the whole three days I didn't call my message machine even once. Jeanie, Nema, Marella, Viveca, not to mention Godwin, Gladys, my agent, were temporarily abandoned to their fates. I knew if I called and got the messages I'd start to feel things; I'd want to respond to the chatter of the machines. Perhaps new boyfriends had appeared; perhaps old boyfriends had been behaving even more terribly than they had been behaving when the headaches moved in with me. Perhaps exciting or depressing career developments had taken place. Undoubtedly *something* had taken place; my lady friends were nothing if not active. Their volatility had provided the counterweight to my passivity for years and years.

"You're always the same," Jeanie said often. "You're *always* the same."

Sometimes she sounded glad about that, but in this instance it clearly annoyed her.

"Yep, that's why you call me," I said, just as she hung up in disgust.

But this time I didn't check the machine. When I felt well enough to be amused, I was mildly amused at the thought of the annoyance this might be causing in several interesting boudoirs. In less ebullient moments I could not but reflect that in all likelihood it was causing no annoyance at all; none of the women might have noticed that I'd beeped off the radar screen. They might all have fallen in love simultaneously, or decided to go to Venice or Hong Kong. Their message machines might be my anchor, but the reverse was far from true; those ladies were mostly unanchored, apt to take off for anywhere, at any time, with anybody.

Several times I was on the verge of calling my machine, but each time I drew back, given pause by a certain tight, low-barometer feeling in my head. I knew that getting reinvolved in the distant swirl of life was exactly what the migraine wanted me to do. We were playing a kind of cat-and-mouse game, the migraine and I, and the headache was the cat. I had to be a very cautious, very devious mouse if I were to outwit it and make my way back into life again.

Meanwhile, true to my word, I never shut the

door between my suite and the Guinevere suite, where T.R., Muddy, and the children had settled. Except when the gang were out on one of their sprees, a constant river of sound flowed through the open door, voices chattering or quarreling, children babbling or screaming, the sound of TV game shows, the sound of rock videos, the sound of people splashing in the Jacuzzi.

I liked hearing the sounds at all hours of the day and night—I was never tempted to close the door. The sounds were a kind of rope I could cling to in order not to sink too deeply into the quicksand of the headache—they didn't really pull me out of it, but they were cheering for me.

Once in a while I sensed that T.R. was in the room watching me. Once, when the headache had reclaimed the offensive and I was on the verge of nausea, I saw her standing just inside the door. I lifted my hand and waved weakly. She came a little closer.

"How do you feel?" she asked.

"Like blowing my head off," I said.

"You ain't got a gun, have you?" she asked, looking worried.

"Oh, no," I said. "I'm not really going to blow my head off. I just said that."

"You better not," she said nervously. "We're running up quite a hotel bill. I doubt we'd ever get it paid if you was to die."

Once when I was feeling a little better she peeked in, wearing a sequined pink baseball cap.

"I took your advice and bought everybody new

clothes," she said. "Wanta see a few of us dressed up?"

"Sure," I said. "Let's have a little fashion review."

Jesse led off. She seemed to have mastered walking, after a fashion, in the last two days. She wore a purple bathing suit, and she covered her eyes in shyness when she saw me looking at her.

"We've been swimming six times, now Jesse don't want to do nothing but swim," T.R. said.

She herself was resplendent in a yellow blouse and stonewashed cutoffs. Bo wore tiny camouflage pants; he immediately raced over and machine-gunned me with a tiny AK-47.

"Bambo," he said defiantly.

"Muddy got him that gun to keep him occupied," T.R. said a little defensively. She had to go back into the other suite and virtually drag Muddy in for his inspection. Once I saw him, I could understand his shyness. He wore bright red cowboy boots, new Levi's, and a rodeo cowboy shirt, but his hair had been dyed pink and cut in the latest Fort Worth punker mode. Unlike most punkers, he had a couple of Vegas-like gold chains around his neck.

"It was his birthday, that's why I got him the chains," T.R. said. "He wanted to be disguised as a cowboy, but you can take one look at Muddy and tell he ain't a cowboy, so I decided we'd just punk him out. The cops won't be looking for a punker with pink hair."

"I don't know," I said. "This county where

203

we're going is pretty conservative. Up there they'd probably arrest *me* if I had pink hair."

"I got a hat," Muddy said, brightening at the thought that it might be necessary to wear it.

He left and returned moments later, half hidden under a giant black cowboy hat.

"You look like a dipshit in that hat," T.R. informed him. "It spoils the whole effect of punking you out."

"If I was to get put back in the Houston jail with pink hair I hate to think what would happen to me," Muddy said. "I'd rather take my chances with this hat."

"You ain't as much fun as you used to be—you know that, don't you?" T.R. said. "Maybe I shoulda left you in jail—the pickings might be better up in this part of the country."

"Just 'cause all them lifeguards over at the splash park have the hots for you don't mean the pickings are that great," Muddy told her. "Most lifeguards I've known have teeny little dicks."

T.R. flushed and swatted his hat off.

"Watch your language, my daddy's sick," she said. "I don't know why I even brought you here. You ain't pretty and you ain't nice."

Muddy just smiled one of his faint, vacant smiles. Her obvious annoyance didn't disturb him much.

"Uh, uh, uh, uh," Jesse said. She was trying to crawl up on the bed. I reached over and lifted her up.

Dew wandered in at that point, flamboyantly

204

dressed in silver pants and a bikini top of some sort.

"Ain't you well yet?" she asked. "You're missing all the fun."

"Not anymore, I'm not," I said. "Jesse's here."

Jesse, once on the bed, had again been overcome with shyness, but not for long; soon a pale blue eye was peeking at me through a web of small fingers.

"Where's Sue Lin and Granny and Elena?" I asked.

"Sue Lin's down playing video games, that's all she likes to do now," T.R. said. "Elena got homesick for her sisters and took the bus back—she can't stand being away from her sisters. Granny Lin's still trying to read magazines."

Jesse crawled over my stomach and peered off the other side of the bed. Bo raced up and machine-gunned her loudly; he was about to brain her with the toy gun when I snatched her out of the way. She regarded her brother stoically, neither frightened nor amused.

"Cool it, Bo, you ain't Rambo," T.R. said. "I wish just once you'd make a good impression on somebody."

"He'd rather gun 'em down," Muddy observed.

"Well, you bought him the gun," T.R. said. "I was just gonna get him some balloons."

The low-barometer feeling came into my head again—the headache didn't welcome the rivalry it was getting. It wanted me for itself. Although I was sort of glad to see everyone, I really had already begun to wish they'd leave—some of them, at least, except T.R. and Jesse.

"We could give him some cocaine," Dew suggested, noticing that I looked dim. "Maybe he could snort that old headache away."

"I don't know if he even uses drugs," T.R. said. "He gets along with Jesse, though, and you don't see that too often. Jesse's particular."

"She ain't, she'll flirt with anybody," Muddy said.

"Daddy looks awful, let's go and leave him in peace," T.R. said. "Just looking at him makes me glad I don't have headaches."

She stooped to pick up Jesse, but Jesse immediately flung herself on the other side of my body.

"Wah!" she said angrily. She turned red in the face and seemed to be gathering herself together for a squeal.

"That's okay, just leave her," I said. "I like having Jesse around."

T.R. darted around the bed to try and catch her, but Jesse was just as quick, flopping over me again and squeezing herself between the pillow and my head.

"Wah!" she warned again, even louder.

"Hold your ears, she's gonna squeal when I catch her," T.R. warned.

"You don't have to catch her, just leave her," I said.

"Nope, she's too quick for you," T.R. said. "Next thing you know she'll slip off the bed and pop into that Jacuzzi to show off her swimmin'. I ain't riskin' no drownded babies."

She leaned across me and extracted a rigid little girl from behind my head. Jesse did indeed squeal. Before the sound receded to the depths of the adjoining suite the whole group had vanished, including Bo, who paused in the doorway and flung a few parting bursts of machine-gun fire my way.

The barometer in my head kept dropping; brief as the visit with T.R. and her gang had been, it had allowed the headache to regain quite a bit of lost ground. I lay very still with my eyes closed, hoping it would get bored soon. I may have slipped into a brief, oppressive sleep; then I felt the bed sag and I jerked awake.

T.R. was sitting there, wiping tears off her cheeks.

"Daddy, don't die," she said. She looked utterly miserable.

"I'm not dying," I said. "I just have a headache."

"You don't look like you even want to live," she said. I noticed she had a bit of a mouse beside one eye.

"What happened to your eye?" I asked.

"Muddy's fist happened to it—the little turd hit me," she said. "You sure don't look like you want to live. It's got me real nervous."

"Nobody with a bad migraine looks too eager to live," I said. "But in fact I am eager to live, now that I've met you."

"Baloney," T.R. said dejectedly. "Meeting

me'd probably make you want to die sooner. I'm nothing but problems."

I reached over and took her hand, which seemed to surprise her.

"Why'd he hit you?" I asked.

"'Cause I'm always saying horrible things to him. I don't even blame him," she said.

She lay down beside me and began to sob. I put my arms around her and let her cry. In time she stopped. I thought she might have slipped off to sleep, but then she lifted her head.

"I spent all that money of yours," she said. "It's ten times more money than I ever spent in my whole life put together. I don't know what happened. I just started spending it and pretty soon it was gone. I guess I can work for you and pay it back in a few years."

"T.R., you don't have to pay it back," I said. "I gave it to you. I'm not mad that you spent it. Money's only to buy fun, you know. I hope you bought a little fun for everybody."

"Well, Muddy had a nice birthday for once," she said. "Them boots cost six hundred dollars. I just thought, fuck, why not buy 'em? You spoiled me, or something. I would never have bought no six-hundred-dollar boots before I met you."

"Relax about the money," I said.

"How can I?" she asked. "Now you've started something. I never realized I had such greedy friends. Dew's bugging me to take her shopping right now."

"Look in my pants pocket," I said. "There should be at least another couple of thousand in there. Take them on one last spree. I should be okay by this afternoon, and we'll go home."

"I wish now I'd never brought any of them," she said. "I'm thinking of calling the cops and having them come pick Muddy up. At least we'd be rid of that little bum."

"Is he often violent?" I asked.

T.R. shook her head. "He ain't big enough to be violent," she said. "He just flies off the handle 'cause he don't know what to do about me."

"I'm afraid that's common male behavior," I said.

T.R. nodded. "If he ever hits me again I'll kill him," she said. "That'll be the end of one stinkin' little male."

"On the other hand, he's Jesse's father," I said.

T.R. looked at me neutrally. "He is, but it won't save him if he ever throws another fist at me."

Then she got up, rummaged in my pants, extracted my last wad of hundred-dollar bills, held them up for my inspection, and started for the door. I thought she was going to leave, but she changed direction and came and sat back down on the bed. She put the money on the bed table.

"There's no reason you should waste your money on those people," she said. "You don't even know them. You just let 'em come along to be polite. All you really wanted was me and the kids."

"That's true, but it's not particularly important," I said. "Your friends are very likable, and there's nothing wrong with being polite."

"There could be such a thing as too polite, though," she said. "It ain't my failing, but maybe it's yours."

"You wouldn't be the first to think so," I said. "All my women friends think I'm too polite. They think it's wimpish and it bores them shitless. They'd rather have men like Muddy who fly off the handle from time to time."

"What do you say to that?" T.R. asked. She looked surprised.

"I say help yourself," I said. "It's not hard to find men who'll fly off the handle." I briefly replayed, in memory, hundreds of conversations in which various women, exasperated by my politeness, tried to goad me into something a little more forceful, if only into an expression of pique.

"Do you have a lot of girlfriends?" T.R. asked. Her mood was lightening; she seemed relaxed and curious.

"In a sense I do and in a sense I don't," I said.

"No wonder they get mad at you, if that's the straightest answer you can give," she said. "Is there some woman waiting in this place we're going to if we ever get out of here?"

"There's Gladys, but she's not a girlfriend, she's a housekeeper," I said.

"In other words, you don't have a girlfriend, right?" she said.

"Not at the moment," I said. "Not precisely."

"I guess that's why you came down to Houston and got me," she said. "You just felt like having a woman around."

"I felt like having my daughter around," I corrected.

She looked out the window for a bit. Then she felt my forehead, glanced out the window, reached over and took a few of the one-hundred-dollar bills, and stood up.

"You might have bit off more than you can chew this time, Mr. Polite," she said as she was leaving.

13

While T.R. and her friends were out on a last little spree, my migraine finally left. Within the space of an hour, the barometer in the peculiar ecosystem of my skull began to rise; the pressure diminished, the thick, threatening cranial weather cleared, and I soon felt as light and fresh as if I had just stepped out into a fine spring morning.

The light feeling was partially deceptive—it had been a three-day visitation, and my hand still shook so that I could hardly get my socks on—but the headache, my demanding guest, was gone. As always, the first hour of release seemed like a miracle—almost a rebirth.

No one was there to share my return to life, so I picked up the telephone and made a few calls. The first was to my message machine. Calling it always involved a measure of apprehension, particularly when I'd been remiss and neglected strict message-machine discipline for three days. Lives can change completely in far less than three days, as I was well aware. By unilaterally absenting myself without consultation, I ran certain risks: friendships nurtured for years on the long, loose intimacies made possible by the telephone might, if a critical moment was missed through inattention, cease to be living friendships—the remoteness that Jeanie warned against might insinuate itself too deeply, turning something vital, if peculiar, into something formal.

So I shook from more than the aftershocks of migraine when I hit the code and waited for the message machine to reveal where we all were at with one another, so to speak. I was remembering that in another migraine-induced period of dereliction I had had to wince my way through more than twenty messages from Nema, who was experiencing rough weather, thanks to the violent mood swings of a manic-depressive firearms instructor she had fallen in love with at a shooting range. Nema was a good shot who practiced often, and she was quite prepared to gun down anyone who gave her serious trouble, but the canker in this particular fruit was the knowledge that the firearms instructor—Rick was his name—might well be an even better shot; Nema's imagination was nothing if not dramatic. Indeed, it was a Jungian goulash of warring archetypes seasoned with images from the lower depths of popular culture. In a sense, she saw life, particularly romantic life, as a series of shootouts in which the fastest gun survived. How she had evolved this crude dramatism puzzled me. No empress of old, not Theodora, not Cleopatra, not Catherine the Great, could have been more confident than Nema, but the confidence was based on the conviction that she would always be the fastest gun. In light of this, her dalliance with the firearms instructor was particularly unfortunate—somehow she had chosen to fuck the one gun who happened to be faster.

This resulted in a string of messages that quickly escalated from agitated to furious, the fury resulting from my failure to call her back. By the time I came out of that headache and did call her back the crisis was over and the firearms instructor in jail, not because he had tried to shoot Nema but because he had fallen for a sting operation and been arrested for selling fully automatic machine guns.

"I could have been killed," Nema insisted for the next few months. "He was a Green Beret."

"Did I tell you to get involved with a Green Beret?" I asked, taking what seemed to me a plausible line of defense.

"You didn't stop me," she said. In her book that amounted to the same thing. She was determined to wring an admission of remorse from me.

This time my tape was empty except for a three-second query from Jeanie.

"Are you there? Are you there? Bye," she said.

Following that was a polite, nervous call from the local fire department inviting me to its annual

213

picnic. As a big contributor, I always got invited to the annual picnic.

I toyed with the notion of calling Godwin and Gladys to inform them I was arriving with a considerable party, but I finally decided against it. Life held few surprises for Godwin and Gladys; their existences were complacent existences, essentially. All I had done for the last two years was lie around the house and watch European videos in the spaces between phone calls to women all over the world. In the past six months I had not even started my Mercedes, and they had not really started their cars either—if starting a car can be used as a metaphor for the active approach to life. In all that time Godwin had only written eight pages of his book on Euripides and the Rolling Stones; Gladys had not extended her reach much, either. She was nominally the cook, but instead of learning a new recipe once in a while, she had dropped most of what she did know from her repertoire, substituting a pantryful of cornflakes and a freezerful of frozen pizzas for the chicken-fried steaks, pinto beans, and cream gravy she had once produced with a certain flourish.

I could have picked up the phone and warned them that those languid days were over: T.R. and company were arriving. There were grandchildren to be raised, and a triracial assortment of permanent and semipermanent guests to absorb. Gladys might really have to cook again; Godwin would have to start wearing clothes, and exercise a little more discretion in the matter of whom he brought home.

I stood by the big picture window of the King Arthur suite, happy to be on my feet for the first time in days. I felt a little like King Arthur myself, or maybe like Richard the Lionhearted or some triumphant Crusader. The trip to Houston had been my Crusade. I had awakened from deep slumber—the slumber of emotional withdrawal—and fought that well-armed Saracen, indifference. Somewhere in the sun-splashed water park across the teeming freeway, my family were probably swimming or otherwise disporting themselves. They were the Grail I had recovered. Standing by the window, I shed a tear or two—self-congratulatory tears, I imagine, but real nonetheless. It's not every rich, middle-aged, totally self-indulgent man who suddenly gets the gift of human beings as unignorable as T.R. and Jesse.

I wandered over to the door between my suite and the Guinevere suite and peeked in; Froissart's description (was it Froissart?) of the sack of Aleppo came to mind, if only because Crusader imagery had me in its grip. Open boxes from various department stores were scattered everywhere; tissue paper that had once enclosed new garments was in piles everywhere; some of it had floated into the Jacuzzi. The new clothes themselves were draped on chairs and couches; collectively they seemed pretty garish. Toys had proliferated: there was a giant green turtle that a child Jesse's age could ride; there were heaps of half-assembled

rubber monsters; there was a red bike with training wheels. Propped by the bed was a real, as
opposed to a toy, AK-47; a case of ammunition
sat on the coffee table. Transistors, tiny TV sets,
and huge ghetto blasters were scattered around
the room. I peeked into the bathroom, which contained a vast array of makeup, shampoos, lotions,
oils, perfumes. T.R. had indeed learned to spend
money.

I went back to my own suite, ordered up a
couple of grilled cheese sandwiches and some lemonade. The two sandwiches tasted ambrosial. It
occurred to me as I ate them that I might be eating
my last orderly meal, or at least my last meal as
a solitary.

I had never before actually admitted to myself
that I was a solitary—perhaps it took the soaring
sense of clarity that one is given for an hour or
two after an intense migraine to bring that fact
home. No one is supposed to be solitary—much
less *a* solitary—in this relation-laden day and age.
The planet is blanketed now with the literature of
relationships, most of it middlebrow at best. But
there would seem to be no book for the solitary.
It was just such a book that I had been setting out
to write—a book about the splendors and miseries
of being alone and about what it takes to sustain
a cultivated and civilized aloneness.

It would be an irony, if a common one in literature, that I would be writing the book—*if* I
wrote it, managed to write it—just as I lost the
condition I aspired to describe. The deep har-

monies of silence would soon be replaced by the screech of family life—loud, sharp tones—the very tones that, in "Al and Sal," had made my fortune. Only this time I wouldn't be imagining domestic life; this time I'd be living it.

For a moment I felt the same panic I had felt the morning T.R. called; the apprehension that had been with me on my drive to Houston came back. It wasn't a simple fear of parental inadequacy, either; I wasn't that worried about my ability to get along with T.R. and the kids. Rather, the panic was literary: What if I forgot the texture of solitude so fast that I couldn't manage to write about it? Gaining my family at long last was great; what wasn't great was the thought that I might lose my book. Already I was losing the subtle insights and high clarities of the solitary. Five minutes with T.R. and Jesse in the room and their immediacy robbed me not only of my old state but of my memory of it. There I was, and happy to be there; but what had become of the other, older, more familiar lonely me? The me that didn't start his car for six months, the American Oblomov? What if that turned out to be not so much the real me—there could be several mes—as just the more fruitful me?

Such troubling questions could not be answered over a grilled cheese sandwich and a glass of lemonade in an Arthurian motel in Arlington. I resolved, however, to call up Blackwell's first thing in the morning and order all the books they had on hermits and hermitry. I could no longer be a hermit myself, but at least I could read about hermits: St. Anthony, St. Simon Stylites, and various others who had lived in caves or sat on pillars for forty years. I was not so much afraid of no longer being solitary as I was of not being able to remember what being solitary felt like. Maybe the books would help.

It was annoying that it was already night in England; otherwise I would have called Blackwell's right then; I still liked to act on my impulses immediately. Instead, I called Jeanie Vertus. I didn't get her but I got her machine and a toneless, totally noncommittal invitation to leave a message.

"Hi," I said. "I'll be home in three hours. I found my daughter. She's wonderful and so is my granddaughter. I'm taking eight people home with me, mainly her friends. My granddaughter's father's along too, we had to break him out of jail."

At that point in the message I stopped to think. News such as that would startle Jeanie a lot. I wondered if I should explain that Muddy was only a burglar and not really harmful or dangerous. But if I started explaining in depth, my message might run for several hours.

"I have a lot more to tell you," I said, deciding against extensive exposition, "but I can't talk too long on this phone. I love you, call me soon."

For some reason I didn't feel satisfied with my message—it did no justice to the transitional mood I was in, whereas Jeanie's brilliant messages always did justice to her transitions, which were frequent and in many cases extremely subtle. Just

218

changing her outfit could mark a significant transition for Jeanie, involving, as it did, a decision about who she wanted to be on a given occasion.

The transition I was making, from solitude to family life, was more complicated than changing an outfit; I was going to change a *life*, or at least I was going to try. It would be a big change, and if I left a coherent message about the change I would not only be preparing Jeanie for it, I would be preparing myself as well. My message would be the moral equivalent of the first sentence of a book—the book of my new life.

A few seconds ticked by; the more I contemplated the change the less I felt prepared to summarize my anticipations on a message machine, even Jeanie's, the machine of the person I felt the most compatible with.

"Things are going to be different now," I added, not at all sure what I meant by the statement. It seemed an inadequate statement, too, but a few more seconds ticked by and I could think of nothing more satisfactory to say—nothing that wouldn't take the equivalent of a chapter, at least. Finally, after another thoughtful pause, I just said "Bye," and hung up.

III

1

Godwin was wearing only his ratty old green bathing trunks when he opened the front door of Los Dolores and confronted the mob of us for the first time. He looked as if he might have been bingeing for a few days, taking drugs, and listening to the Rolling Stones through his earphones.

"Where's the yard?" T.R. asked, surveying my expensive adobe home. "This stupid house looks as if it was made of mud pies."

"It's nice inside," I said meekly.

T.R. and Muddy had quarreled all the way from Arlington, and T.R. was not in a good mood, to put it mildly. Before I could even help Granny Lin out of the Cadillac—she had stiffened alarmingly during her stay in Arlington—the delicious Jamesian moment occurred in which Godwin and T.R. first set eyes on one another: T.R., beautiful despite her terrible-taste new clothes, sailing up to the house with Jesse on her hip, the epitome of American youth, American good looks, American ignorance, American energy; and Godwin Lloyd-Jons, the ultimate Euro, drugged out, fucked out, arted out—nothing left but brain.

"Who are you? I bet I could get AIDS just from shaking your hand, don't you kiss my babies,"

223

T.R. said, momentarily taken aback by the skinny, toothless figure inside the door.

Actually, Godwin wasn't quite so far gone as he should have been to fit the Jamesian equation I was placing him in. An immediate gleam came into his eyes at the sight of such a splendid young woman. Seeing the gleam gave me a powerful sense of *déjà vu,* for he had had just the same gleam for Sally, T.R.'s mother, a quarter century earlier; Godwin, in his disgusting way, was a sort of survivor.

"My dear, I'm Godwin, and I assure you I've led a life of chastity and scholarship these last few years," he said suavely. "I knew your mother well, do come in, what beautiful children you have."

"I'm Gladys, I do the cooking," Gladys said, amazement in her eyes. T.R. set Jesse down and Jesse, glad to be out of the car, toddled over to Gladys at once, winning her wizened heart in half a second.

"Well, look at this precious girl," Gladys said. She hunched over like a shortstop and scooped Jesse up.

"You should get dressed, I don't want to have to stand here counting your ugly ribs," T.R. said to Godwin. "We've got a lot of stuff to bring in, you could help if you were dressed."

"Righto," Godwin said submissively and went to do as he was told. Gladys and I were both very surprised—we were constantly ordering him to get dressed, and he didn't.

Before introductions could proceed further, Bo

instigated the first crisis of our new lives by racing over to the swimming pool and installing himself with his AK-47 on the very end of the diving board. The problem with that was that the pool had been drained for cleaning; if he fell off it was a twelve-foot drop to the tile bottom.

"Muddy, get him!" T.R. commanded.

Muddy, carrying the real AK-47, was surveying his new surroundings apprehensively. Actually there was not much in the way of surroundings to see—the house sat on a bluff, with the great plains stretching away to the north, and a few blue knobby hills to the south. Mainly what there was to see was the deep western sky, a feature that apparently didn't appeal to Muddy Box. He exhibited not the slightest interest in rescuing Bo from the diving board.

"This place is way out in the country," he observed with surprise and dismay.

"That's right, Daddy picked it just to keep you out of trouble, Muddy," T.R. said. "No apartment houses for you to steal TVs out of, no malls for you to shoplift from. I don't know what you'll do for excitement."

"I don't know what any of us will do for excitement," Dew said. She too looked a little apprehensive at the thought that she was going to live amid such empty vistas.

"Well, there's lots to read," I said nervously, realizing even as I said it that this was not a crowd likely to be won by my ten thousand eclectically selected books. But maybe the thousands of records and hundreds of videos would keep their minds off where they were for a while.

Muddy, ignoring T.R.'s command to rescue Bo from the diving board, wandered off across the hill, his AK-47 slung across his shoulder.

T.R. looked disgusted, and her disgust was of a voltage to make everyone nervous. As soon as I helped Granny Lin into the house, T.R. turned her disgust on me.

"That's your grandson out there about to fall off a diving board and crack his skull," she said. "If he falls off and kills himself I'm gonna sue you for the whole three hundred million, I don't care if you are my daddy. Why don't you at least act like you can do something and get him off it? What do you mean leaving that swimming pool empty when there's kids around who can fall into it?"

"I didn't know they were cleaning the pool this week," I said. "I'll see what I can do."

I walked over to the pool. Bo was now lying on his stomach on the diving board and seemed to be in no immediate danger of falling off. He trained his toy machine gun on me as I approached.

"Hi, Bo, why don't you come and see what's in the house?" I said. "There might be something in there that you'd like to play with."

"Bambo," Bo said. Then he made his approximation of an AK-47 spitting out bullets—in this case spitting them out at me.

T.R. and the gang had vanished into Los Dolores; Muddy Box was already halfway across the long hill. I was alone with Bo for the first time in either of our lives. He showed no sign of wanting to leave the diving board.

Bribery occurred to me as a possible solution. Many times, wandering through the zoos and parks of the world, I had seen desperate parents trying to bribe their kids. The bribes weren't always in the form of cash; they might be in the form of ice cream, cotton candy, or another trip to the small-mammal house; but the fact that the parents had been driven to naked bribery was always evident from their guilty looks.

What was good enough for them was certainly good enough for me. I reached in my pocket, but all I had in my pocket was a wad of hundred-dollar bills. In an ideal world—that is, a world in which I didn't have to account for my actions to anyone else—I would have given Bo the wad of hundreds in a second if I'd thought there was the faintest chance it would induce him to come off the diving board.

But it wasn't an ideal world; it was a world in which complications multiplied like ragweed. Bo probably had no interest in one-hundred-dollar bills—after all, he was just three—and if he accepted them and transformed himself into an obedient little person, I would still have the problem of peer disapproval to contend with. I could just imagine the ridicule I would be in for if Bo marched into the house and let it be known that I had given him eighteen hundred dollars to come off a diving board. Everyone would think I was insane, not to mention inadequate, though in fact eighteen hundred dollars had no more meaning for me than it had for Bo, and any one of my critics might have done the same if they were as rich as I was and as hopeless with children.

"Please come back off the diving board," I pleaded. Forced to reject bribery due to a lack of small change I fell back on groveling.

Unfortunately, that didn't work. Bo continued to lie on his stomach, pointing the toy machine gun at me.

Then, to my surprise, I had a practical thought. Why not just fill the swimming pool? I had done that a few times and was pretty confident I could manage to get the water on. The swimming-pool man would show up and be annoyed, since it meant he would have to drain it again to finish the cleaning, but on balance I felt I would rather have him annoyed with me than T.R. I could just let three or four feet of water in, enough to prevent Bo from cracking his skull in case he fell.

I went over to the pumping apparatus and turned the big valve; to my delight water immediately began to gush into the pool. Having a practical thought and being able to put it into practice gave me a sudden flush of confidence. It seemed to me I was developing; far from being defeated by the exigencies of grandparenthood, I was stimulated by them.

My euphoria lasted only a moment. Bo looked over the edge of the diving board and saw the water rushing in beneath him. To my surprise he reacted with shock and horror. He immediately got to his feet, clutching his gun, and began to scream and dance around on the diving board. Several times he seemed in danger of dancing off the edge. Of course there was not yet even an inch of water in the deep end of the pool, so he was still in as much danger as he had ever been.

"It's okay, it's okay," I said. "I'm just filling up the pool. Don't you like to swim?"

Bo only screamed louder—he was hysterical with fear of the rushing water beneath him. I saw that in fact he *was* going to fall off because he was crying so hard he couldn't see. I hadn't been on the diving board in years, but I was on it in a second. I managed to grab Bo by one arm and pull him off it just in time; his gun fell in and was swept toward the shallow end of the pool. Bo continued to scream and punch and kick but I hardly noticed; I dragged him with me to a nearby chaise longue and sat down. He was in a blind fury, but he was also very small, and it was not that hard to hold him. I slipped into adrenaline shock so strong that I felt a little faint, but I still kept a good grip on Bo.

"Hey, Daddy, you're doin' better," T.R. said. She had arrived poolside without my noticing, looking radiant. Beside her stood Godwin, but a Godwin transformed; he wore a clean seersucker shirt and immaculate white pants; if I hadn't already been in shock, I would have gone into shock at the sight of him—in a matter of minutes he had transformed himself from a fading intellectual derelict into a model colonialist; he looked as if he could be running a teak plantation in Ceylon. Not only did he look better than he had looked since moving in with me, he had also quickly managed to make friends with T.R.—they were casually passing a joint from hand to hand.

"I take back what I said about your house," T.R. said. "It looks like mud pies from the outside but it's pretty nice on the inside—only a lot of them books need to go. Half the rooms have so many books in them you can't see the walls."

"I guess Bo's scared of water," I said, hoping to draw attention to my last-second rescue.

"I caught him just in time," I added, but neither T.R. nor Godwin were paying the slightest attention. They seemed to be discussing post-New Wave rock bands, and took the fact that Bo wasn't dead as a matter of course.

"I did have quite a few good heavy metal cassettes, but Muddy stole them," T.R. remarked. "Muddy'll steal anything that's not nailed down, and if you give him time he'll yank out the nails and steal them too."

"We'll have to watch him closely," Godwin said gravely. "He seems a rather pleasant boy."

"Pleasant unless you cross him," T.R. said. "Then he swells up like an old frog."

Bo tore loose from me and wrapped himself around one of his mother's legs. He continued to sob, now and then pausing to point tragically at his machine gun, which had floated back near the middle of the pool.

"Speaking of the devil, where is Muddy?" T.R. asked.

"I guess he's just taking a walk," I said. "He wandered off with his machine gun."

"Would you like a swim?" Godwin asked. "The pool will be full quite soon. I could make some Bloody Marys and we could have a swim."

"Make that margaritas and I might just take you up on it," T.R. said. "Me and Dew bought quite a few new bathing suits we need to try on."

At that moment we heard the AK-47 begin to chatter from under the hill. Burst followed burst—the sound was loud enough and unexpected enough to cause Bo to stop crying.

"That's Muddy," I said. "I wonder what he found to shoot at. There's not much below the hill except some oil tanks."

A moment after I spoke, sound hit us like a tremendous slap. The sound the training jets made was as nothing compared to this sound. "Slap" sounded right as a description of its sudden arrival, but slap hardly did justice to the force of the sound—even to call it "the sound" seemed wrong. Life, the world, were briefly nothing but sound—all other sensations were obliterated. We all instinctively turned our backs and hunched over, mute and hopeless before it. I closed my eyes, unable to think or move at all. When I opened them I felt detached from myself, as if I and my thoughts—if I had any—had been blown in opposite directions from one another. I noticed Bo clinging tightly to his mother's legs. T.R. had

231

her head in her arms. Godwin, hunched over, was still smiling insanely, not to mention toothlessly.

I saw T.R.'s lips moving, but the normal speed of sound seemed to have changed; it had slowed and been made deliberate by the force of the great sound.

"I think it's the end of the world, Daddy," T.R. said. "Don't tell me if that's what it is."

A huge, tar-black pillar of smoke foamed up from the plain below the hill. It shot straight into the sky as if fired from a gigantic smoke pistol.

"It's not the end of the world, T.R.," I said. "It's just the end of the oil tanks."

"You better be sure, I ain't opening my eyes unless you're sure," T.R. said, her eyes tightly closed.

I watched the black smoke pour into the sky; it rose over the hill like black foam.

"I'm sure, honey," I said.

2

It was definitely the end of my oil tanks and almost the end of Muddy Box as well. Fifty-eight thousand dollars' worth of West Texas Intermediate Crude, representing most of the monthly milking of my several little oil wells, went up in smoke— a lot of smoke. By the time Godwin and I had persuaded T.R. that the world had not come to an end, half the pumpers, cowboys, and fire companies from two or three surrounding counties had gathered in my lower pastures. There was little they could do but scratch their heads and look awestruck. Fortunately one of them found Muddy, unsinged but also unconscious, in a chaparral bush. Local efforts at resuscitation failed, so an ambulance helicopter was radioed for. T.R. refused to fly in it or to take any responsibility for the unconscious Muddy at all. Somehow she and Godwin persuaded me that I was the logical choice to accompany Muddy to Dallas, where better-equipped resuscitators waited. I didn't feel really right about going—I couldn't rid myself of the haunting sense that events were sweeping me far downstream from where I wanted to be—but for all I knew poor Muddy was dying; someone had to go, so I climbed into the helicopter and we swirled up into the sky.

Most of the next three days I spent in a little waiting lounge at Parkland Hospital in Dallas, waiting for Muddy Box to regain consciousness. He was not brain dead, I was assured. When I phoned home to pass this good news on to T.R., she snorted.

"You can't be brain dead if you don't have a brain," she remarked, "and nobody with a brain would shoot at an oil tank with a machine gun."

Behind her I could hear quite loudly the sound of post-New Wave rock and roll.

"How's everybody getting along up there?" I asked nervously. I felt depressed and left out.

"Well, it's a long story, I'll tell you when you get back," T.R. said.

"I don't have anything to do but wait," I pointed out. "Couldn't you tell me some of your story now?"

"Nope," she said, just before she hung up.

The lounge, being a hospital lounge, was full of gloomy, apprehensive people waiting to find out if their loved ones were living or dying. Muddy wasn't really a loved one; I didn't know him and really didn't have much of an emotional investment in his recovery; as one day wore into two and two into three I began to feel gloomy about my own lack of true gloom. No man is an island, according to Dr. Donne, but I felt very much like an island; the hospital lounge itself seemed like an island, midway between the continents of life and death, the archipelagos of hope and hopelessness. Some of us islanders would pass one way, some another.

After quickly working my way through the *National Geographics*, *Sports Afields*, and *Texas Monthlys* in the waiting room, I called a taxi and went to a bookstore. All during the ride I felt guilty; I felt I had left the island without permission; by the time I got to the bookstore I decided to keep the taxi waiting so it could ferry me immediately back to the island. I became too nervous and guilt-ridden really to think clearly about what I might want to read; I hastily scrambled together six books about Wittgenstein and a biography of Alexandra David-Neel and rushed back to the hospital.

It was an immense relief to discover that Muddy

had not died in my absence; he was still snug in his coma, his brain rhythms as strong as ever.

My relief was soon tempered by depression as I read, alternately, about Ludwig Wittgenstein and Alexandra David-Neel, two people capable of a purity and a concentration it was evident I would never attain. By comparison with either of them I was no more than a fumbling dilettante. On the other hand, reading about them in that hospital waiting room made me feel like a snobbish freak. Everyone else in the waiting room was either making do with the ragged magazines or reading Sidney Sheldon or Danielle Steel. Why was I reading about a tough mystic and an even tougher philosopher? I began to develop an urge to hide the books or to pretend I wasn't really reading them; at the same time I had a compulsive need to race through them, sucking up whatever clues I could find. The key to achievement was what I sought. Did it really require one to be so selfish? Or was it merely that being as smart as Wittgenstein or as obsessed as David-Neel produced a focus so intense that ordinary notions of selfishness and generosity no longer applied?

I didn't know, but I did have a need to know; reading the books made me nervous and discouraged, though I couldn't really define the nature of my discouragement. After all, I didn't want to be a philosopher or to travel in Tibet; I just wanted to write a book that I could feel represented *me*. "Al and Sal," for all its success, didn't seem to represent me. Maybe it represented the American family, in some sense—I had only had an American family for three or four days, and my modest beginnings as a paterfamilias bore no resemblance to anything that had happened in the series.

As always, when I reached a certain stratum of discouragement, somewhere around the Pleistocene stage, I went to a phone and called Jeanie Vertus. I had convinced myself, on no evidence whatsoever, that she was in Europe, and was expecting to get her machine. I had prepared a doleful monologue about my experiences, as well as my doubts and fears, and was startled when Jeanie herself answered before the phone even completed its first ring.

"Hi," she said. Moodwise she didn't sound far above the Pleistocene level herself.

"Why were you sitting so close to the phone?" I asked, my gloomy monologue forgotten in the delight of hearing her voice.

"Sometimes when I'm depressed I call, and if people don't get it on the first ring I change my mind and hang up," she said. "I figured you'd be depressed by now, and your mind works like my mind so I just stuck my porta-phone in my bathrobe pocket, just in case."

"So why are you in your bathrobe?" I asked. "It's not morning and it's not night."

It was a silly question—I was so startled by the fact that she was actually there that I hadn't quite regained a grip on myself.

"Is there a law against wearing your bathrobe at other times?" Jeanie asked apprehensively.

Jeanie was always hoping to do the right thing; even the slightest suggestion that she might be doing the wrong thing, or even just something slightly unorthodox, was often enough to dash her hopes. In fact she almost always *did* do the right thing, but no one, least of all me, had ever been able to convince her that that was true—even my stupid question about the bathrobe was enough to activate her doubts.

"Of course not, I was just being stupid, I didn't expect to get you," I said. "I was all set to leave a monologue."

"Oh," Jeanie said. "Well, you still could. I could hang up and go in the other room. You could do the monologue and I could come right back and listen to it."

"No, that's ridiculous," I said.

"It is ridiculous, but we could still do it that way if you prefer," Jeanie said, "You sound fragile. Maybe you'd feel stronger if you were just talking to the machine."

"No, that's absurd," I said. "The machine doesn't care anything about me, and you do."

"It's true, but it's not the whole story," Jeanie said. "Sometimes when I'm feeling fragile I'm just not up to anything as unpredictable as a human conversation. It's because I'm a coward. I guess you have as much right to be a coward as I do, although in my heart of hearts I'd rather you just did talk to me instead of the machine. If I have to hang up with you sounding like that, I'm gonna cry, and I've already been crying about this."

237

"About what?" I asked.

"You said there was a jailbreak, why wouldn't I cry?" Jeanie said in a shaky voice. "You didn't even tell me why you were in jail. I didn't even suspect you were a criminal. I got upset trying to imagine what kind of crime you committed. You could have just put it on the machine, you know, so I wouldn't have had all this suspense. I can imagine all kinds of crimes, I just couldn't imagine you committing any of them, unless you've gone crazy, and if you've gone crazy you might end up in a bin somewhere where I couldn't call you, or you could be arrested again, how would I know? You don't tell me anything but then you expect me to get out of my bathrobe and go on as if I had a normal life when I didn't even have a very normal one before you called me up and got me worried."

Then she began to cry. I was horrified. I tried to remember the exact words of the message I had left from Arlington—I had only left it a few hours earlier, not time enough for Jeanie to have become so haunted with worry. But I felt guilty anyway. I couldn't really remember the Arlington message clearly. Perhaps I had inadvertently implied that *I* was the one in jail; anyway, such a melodramatic message had been inexcusable, given the fact that Jeanie's emotions traveled at the speed of light, besides which she also had an imagination at least the equal of mine when it came to conjuring up improbable catastrophes.

"I'm sorry, I'm sorry, I'm sorry," I said, perhaps a dozen times, as her sobs became snuffles and finally faded into silence. When she was silent I explained that it was Muddy Box who had been in jail.

"You know how my imagination works, though," she said. "You shouldn't frighten me. Life's scary enough without *you* frightening me."

"I know it, I'm sorry, I promise absolutely I'll never do it again," I said.

Jeanie snorted—her sense of humor was awakening. "Baloney," she said. "You'll do it again this afternoon if you can think up a good story."

"Well, I'm just trying to make my life sound more interesting than it is," I said. "It's an old habit of mine."

"Yeah, but now you've found T.R. and you have grandkids," Jeanie pointed out. "Your life's gonna be really interesting anyway—you won't have to invent stuff."

"Even if it is interesting I may not be able to stop inventing stuff," I said. "It's a habit, like salting my eggs."

There was a sudden silence. I immediately realized I had made a misstep.

"Danny, I thought you were eating better," she said, shocked. "I didn't think you were even eating eggs, much less eating them with *salt!*"

"Jeanie, it's just a pinch of salt," I said. "It's not like it's opium."

"I don't know which is worse, the salt or the egg," she said, as her shock deepened.

"Neither's very bad," I said. "It's not as if I'm Hitler just because I eat eggs."

"Maybe you're not Hitler," she admitted grudgingly, "but this is definitely a negative turn of events. Distinctly negative. You're just gonna make me mad and then die."

"I'm not going to die," I said. "I'm in a hospital right now and I'm perfectly fine."

"You're in a hospital?" she said, her anxiety soaring again. "No wonder you're in a hospital if you've been eating salty eggs and concealing it from me."

"I mean I'm making the call from a hospital," I said, corrected. "I'm not the one who's sick."

Desperately I began to explain about Muddy, the AK-47, and the oil tanks. For several minutes Jeanie listened in sullen, skeptical silence—she knew I was just trying to distract her from my faux pas about the eggs. But gradually, by using all my dormant wiles as a storyteller, I got her interested. The turning point came when I mentioned the girls' shopping sprees—Jeanie was a devotee of the shopping spree herself. Her curiosity soon outpaced her skepticism and we relaxed into a long chat, in which I was prodded to try to remember exactly what clothes and radios and CDs the girls had bought.

While I was producing this catalogue, much of it fictitious, a young doctor tapped me on the shoulder.

"Your patient's waking up," he said.

240

"Did you hear that?" I asked her. "Muddy's waking up."

"Now why did they name him Muddy?" Jeanie asked.

"I imagine it's just a nickname," I said.

"I wonder if it's because he has a muddy character, or what," she mused.

"Well, you can come down and meet him if you want to," I said.

"I might," she said. "On the other hand I hate to think how mad I'd get if I actually saw you put salt on an egg."

"I doubt if I'd be rash enough to actually do that in your presence," I said.

"You better not be rash enough."

"It must be nice to be so nutritionally virtuous," I said, it being a subject about which I was very reluctant to yield the last word. "I guess it's taken the place sexual virtue once held."

"Yep, it has," Jeanie agreed. "You know why? Because it makes you feel immortal, and sexual virtue doesn't. Sexual virtue just makes you feel so bored you don't care about being immortal."

"That's an interesting thought. I'll sleep on it," I said.

"Don't you hang up, I have one final instruction," she said.

"Which is?"

"Forget the eggs," Jeanie said. "Also forget the salt, or forget it, period."

"Forget it?" I said. "Forget it as in what?"

"Forget it as in us," she said crisply.

"Oh, stop it," I said. "I don't think you should threaten me with dismissal just because I ate an egg."

"Now, now," she said happily. "Let's have no defiance. You've been trouble enough for one day. It wasn't just an egg, it was a *salty* egg. Unforgivable, almost. Bye."

3

The doctors insisted on keeping Muddy in the hospital for a week—the fact that he was awake did not mean that he was well, they explained. Complications might still develop.

I in turn explained this to T.R. in several brief conversations from the hospital pay phone. Her attitude was skeptical, to put it mildly.

"That lazy little fuckhead just likes to have people wait on him," she informed me impatiently. "If it ain't a hospital it's a jail. He don't like to do nothing he's supposed to do. Tell him to get out of that bed and get up here and help me raise his daughter, she's driving me crazy."

"How could Jesse drive anyone crazy?" I asked. "She's not even two."

"What do you know about it? Two-year-olds have driven millions of people crazy," T.R. asserted. "L.J. taught her to play checkers and now that's all she wants to do. She's wore us all out, playing checkers. Tell Muddy to get out of that hospital and come on home. I guess he ain't too brain damaged to man the checkerboard. Anyway, Jesse don't like to play unless she wins, and Muddy's one person she could beat. He's only got the mental powers of a one-year-old, anyway."

"Wait a minute, who's L.J.?" I asked.

"What do you mean? He's your friend," she said. "Your English friend."

"Godwin?" I asked.

"Yeah, but who wants to say a name like that?" T.R. said. "We're just calling him L.J. now. I like to try and be normal."

"Lots of luck, if it's Godwin you're trying with," I said meanly. Probably I was just jealous because he was with her and I wasn't.

"I know, but life ain't perfect," T.R. admitted. "You got to start somewhere, so we started by giving him a normal name."

I told Muddy T.R. wanted him to hurry home. I thought it might cheer him up but instead it prompted him to feign another coma. His amateurish efforts to pretend that he had returned to his coma amused the doctors and nurses—they responded by giving him shots every hour or so until he gave up and started watching television. Naturally the first thing he watched was a rerun of "Al and Sal," the famous episode in which Sal moves out of the conjugal bedroom and installs herself on the family diving board; she decides that since Al is a total dud as a lover she might as well get in the *Guinness Book of World Records* as the woman who lived the longest on a diving board. In fact, she only holds out on the diving board for one night, just long enough to make a hilarious episode. Muddy and half the nurses on his floor were laughing at it, but I left the room shortly after it started, depressed by the sense that my past was following me around. I went back to the waiting room and made an unsuccessful attempt, perhaps my tenth, to read the *Tractatus Logico-philosophicus*. This failure left me more discouraged than the previous nine failures; this one seemed tinged with hubris—ill-defined hubris, but hubris nonetheless. I decided that not having written "Al and Sal" was probably a precondition for being able to read Wittgenstein—even though the latter had had a fondness for silly movies and might himself have liked "Al and Sal."

I soon convinced myself I shouldn't even try to read Wittgenstein and went back to reading about him. While I was doing that I conceived the idea for a light book I might write. It would be called *Forty-two Weeks in the Gulag* and would be a rehash of my bitter experiences filming one season of "Al and Sal." I went to the pay phone, called my agent, told him the title of the projected work and requested that he sell it immediately; the icy draft of financial paranoia, of the sort multimillionaires often experience, had just whistled through my brain.

My agent got on the phone and promptly added a theoretical two million to my net worth; almost before he finished confirming the deal I felt my interest in the projected book declining. Why had I decided I wanted to write about that stupid television show? Why had I supposed anyone would want to read about my battles with executive retards of various descriptions?

Attempts to curry sympathy for my own rashness fell on stony ears—Jeanie's. She was still mad about the egg.

"I think you should donate your whole advance to research on cholesterol, " she said crisply.

"Cholesterol is just a myth," I assured her, whereupon she hung up.

The next light to shine in the waiting room, where it seemed to me I now lived, was the bright, almost blinding light of T.R., who arrived unexpectedly—copying Gladys, she had brought some orange parachute pants and a top to match. She was dragging Jesse, brilliant in Oshkosh-By-Gosh overalls, and the two of them were followed by a large, middle-aged man in the uniform of a Fort Worthbased security service, who led Bo by the hand.

"Where's Muddy? He's sluffed off long enough," T.R. said without preamble.

"In his room—I don't know if it's visiting hours," I said, thoroughly startled. Since I now felt I was living in the hospital, its routine had become mine—I never rocked the boat, since now it was my boat too.

T.R. smacked into this particular boat like a thirty-foot wave. "It's visiting hours now," she said. "Come on, Buddy."

Buddy was the large security guard; he looked a little abashed.

"Buddy Modine," he said.

"Hello," I said. "Are we in danger?"

"I am. Earl Dee's out," T.R. said, dragging Jesse down the hall, but not before Jesse had given me one of her famous grins. The fact that she even remembered me was heartwarming.

When I got to the room, T.R. had already shaken Muddy awake and was questioning him closely about the business of the oil tanks.

"I just shot at a rabbit," Muddy said meekly. "I didn't even know all them oil tanks was there."

"That's horrible," T.R. said. It was clear to me, and probably to Muddy, that one of the purposes of her visit was to make him feel as guilty as possible.

The reason it was clear to me is that I'm a man who has spent much of his life being made to feel guilty by women, in many cases women I had been on the whole pretty nice to. I knew all the approaches to a little guilt-inducing session. Lacking my experience, Muddy did not immediately become guilt-ridden, or even hangdog. He just looked as if he wished everyone would go away so he could continue to watch TV.

T.R. upped the ante by setting Jesse on the bed. Jesse hid her eyes behind her fingers.

"Jesse loves bunny rabbits," T.R. said coldly. "Why would you shoot at a bunny rabbit when you know your own daughter loves them? She's got a stuffed rabbit right out in the car."

"Well, I missed it anyway," Muddy replied. "It ain't the end of the world.

"That bunny rabbit's still running around down there somewhere," he added, to emphasize his point. Then he smiled at Jesse and carefully pried one of her fingers loose from one of her eyes.

"Uh, ma'am, do you want me in or do you want me out?" Buddy asked.

"Oh, just wait out in the hall, Buddy," T.R. said. "If Earl Dee shows up at the window I'll scream."

"Right, fine," Buddy said. "Me and little Bo will just wait out in the hall."

"Whose idea was Buddy?" I asked. "Do you think Earl Dee is really that big a threat?"

"In my book he is," T.R. said. "I'm the one he's promised to kill. L.J. decided to hire Buddy, at least till you got home, and so far it's worked fine. Even if he don't save me from Earl Dee, at least he's calmed Bo down. Bo worships Buddy."

"He did seem calmer," I admitted.

"Hurry up, Muddy, let's go—I'm parked in a no-parking zone," T.R. said.

"But I ain't supposed to go," Muddy said. "I'm in the hospital, sick."

"You're just loafing, hurry up," T.R. said. "I hate getting tickets."

"You ain't got no respect for nothing, T.R.," Muddy said, a little grimly. "First you yank me out of jail and now you're yanking me out of a hospital. I don't feel like I'm getting no say in my own life."

"Right, you ain't, I'm tired of sleeping by my-self," T.R. said.

Then her manner softened and she looked at him mischievously.

"Not that I don't mean to make it up to you, though," she said. "If you'll scamper out of here before I get a ticket, I might even make a little of it up to you tonight."

Muddy gave a wan grin before scooping up Jesse and kissing her several times on the neck, to her immense delight.

"A sick man might not be able to handle too much making up at one time," he said, winking at T.R. "We might have to kinda spread the fun over two or three nights."

T.R. was looking at me thoughtfully. Seeing me in the context of a hospital room, in the thoroughly rumpled state into which I had declined, seemed to have given her a new perspective on me—and, on the whole, it appeared to be a sympathetic perspective.

She was looking at me, but listening to Muddy. Jesse broke into giggles, and T.R. smiled.

"That's a man whose tongue can get him into ten times as much trouble as his dick can get him out of," she said. "Do you think most men are like that, Daddy?"

"Quite a few seem to be," I said.

4

My Cadillac, scarcely a week old, no longer looked like a new Cadillac. It looked like central Beirut, like *Dog Day Afternoon;* the Marx Brothers might have filmed the final scene of one of their wilder farces in it.

T.R. didn't ask me to drive. She took the wheel as if it were hers by right, and soon we were doing eighty-five, northbound on the Stemmons Freeway. Muddy Box had walked out of the hospital as easily as he had walked out of jail. He just walked out, still trying to get all Jesse's sugar, and everyone who saw them smiled. No one on the hospital staff took the slightest notice of Muddy's departure, but a nurse did try to stop me.

"Excuse me, sir, has your doctor dismissed you?" she asked.

"I'm not a patient here," I explained.

"Sir, have you paid?" the nurse asked, as if I hadn't spoken.

"I'm not a patient here," I repeated. "I've never been a patient here. I was just visiting someone."

"Well, you look like you should be a patient somewhere," the nurse said rather huffily.

T.R. thought that was funny.

"Fat people catch a lot of flack, I guess," she said. "If you got skinny, people would probably think you were healthy."

The car was full of new toys, most of which were already broken; cassettes of various New Wave and post-New Wave rock groups were scattered on the floorboards, where they mingled freely with half-eaten sacks of Dorito chips, Cheesix, and other delicacies. Also, everyone except Buddy seemed to have changed clothes two or three times during the trip, with diapers predominating in the mix of discarded clothes.

"This car looks as if a war was fought in it," I observed.

"That's because living people have been using it," T.R. said with a pointed look. "Living people have to fight the war of life. At least nobody's accused me of being a patient in a hospital."

"You'll be a patient in a morgue if Earl Dee finds you, and so will I," Muddy said. "I didn't bargain for that son of a bitch getting out. When are we going off to France?"

"I don't know; when are we going to France, Daddy?" T.R. asked. "Think we could make a plane tonight?"

"We could make a plane, but there's the problem of passports and visas," I said. "I've got one, but none of you probably have passports. If we all go to the passport office we might have them in about ten days—quicker if we tell them it's urgent."

"I guess not being murdered is urgent," Muddy said. Jesse was asleep in his lap.

"Now, ma'am, you're all worryin' too much about this Mr. Dee," Buddy Modine said rather formally. "I have no doubt that he's a pure criminal, but a lot of what your criminal element says they're gonna do is just mostly bluff. I've let the sheriffs of all these counties around here know about Mr. Dee, and I've let the Highway Patrol know, and I know. If he shows up actin' nasty I

250

guess we can corral him before he does much harm."

T.R.'s response was to increase her speed about ten miles an hour. It was clear she was not really reassured by Buddy's remark.

"How many criminals have you ever corralled?" Muddy asked bluntly. He had not warmed to Buddy, who looked mildly offended by this obvious challenge to his credibility.

"I ain't been countin', but it's a goodly few," he said stiffly. "I was a deputy over in Wichita Falls for about eight years. I was on the robbery squad. I admit I didn't have to get involved with too much of this aggravated assault, but we had a good record with the breakin'-and-entering element."

Muddy smiled his faint smile.

"Shut up, Muddy, and you, too, Buddy!" T.R. said. "I don't want to talk about this anymore at all, understand?" Let's just all enjoy this nice drive home."

"How is everyone at home?" I asked, thinking how nice it would be to take a bath and stretch out in my own bed. Several days of failing to read Wittgenstein in a hospital waiting room had worn me out. I tried to get a grip on the problem of Earl Dee. If it was problem enough for Godwin promptly to hire a security guard, it was surely something I ought to get a grip on, but somehow I couldn't. Earl Dee was a specter from T.R.'s past—a flesh-and-blood threat to her, but only a kind of philosophical abstraction to me, a proposition out of Wittgenstein or one of the many other philosophers I had been unable to read. Terms that seemed to convince everyone else, such as threats to kill people on sight, were no more than faint conceits to me, and in my tired state I couldn't focus on them.

"Well, Dew's gone back to Houston and Sue Lin, too," T.R. said. "Me and Dew drove around for two whole days in this part of the world and didn't see more than one or two black people. It made Dew homesick and she went right back to Houston. Sue Lin got homesick too and went with her."

Her voice had a little droop in it when she mentioned Houston; she looked like a young woman who was about to cry, and indeed a tear or two did spill out and make its way down her cheek.

"One thing about Houston, there's lots of good places to go dancing there," she said. "I might have gone back myself if it hadn't been for that fuckin' Earl Dee. I enjoy them old sleazy dance halls quite a bit."

"I'm sure we can find you some sleazy ones in Fort Worth," I said.

T.R. shook her head. "Already looked," she said. "Shoot, me and Dew went up to Oklahoma City two nights ago, looking. We didn't find a thing up there, so we came back and looked in Fort Worth, but the pickings were so slim we still got home just after breakfast. These towns are tame up this way. Too many cowboys. Nothing's more useless on a dance floor than a cowboy."

252

"If you don't like cowboys why'd you buy me them six-hundred-dollar boots?" Muddy asked.

"Because it was your birthday, dickface," T.R. said, offering him a stick of gum.

"You could have bought me a motorcycle," Muddy pointed out. "I'd be perfectly satisfied with a secondhand one."

"I bought you that machine gun you begged for and all you did with it was blow up fifty thousand dollars' worth of Daddy's oil," T.R. said.

"You ain't sympathetic to me no more, T.R.," Muddy said. "I also blew myself up, just about."

"Right, that's why we're on the way home from the hospital this very minute," T.R. said. "And that's the reason you ain't gettin' no motorcycle."

"What could I blow up with a motorcycle?" Muddy wondered.

"How about your ugly skull?" T.R. said. "You're Jesse's father, you got some responsibility now. It's your responsibility to stay alive."

"We better get over to France, then," Muddy said.

Then he had a thought. "Did they find my machine gun?" he asked. "If he finds out we got a machine gun Earl Dee might think twice."

T.R. laughed and flashed her lights seven or eight times at a slow-moving Corvette that had strayed into the fast lane.

"Before Earl Dee could think twice he'd have to think once," she said. "Thinking ain't exactly one of his skills. If it was, he wouldn't have a record as long as this car."

253

The Corvette quickly moved over and we shot past.

5

The most interesting thing that had happened at Los Dolores in my absence was that Granny Lin had formed a relationship with old Pedro and was living with him in his little house on the western hill. As usual, opinions varied as to what was really going on.

"What's the mystery? Them two are madly in love," Gladys maintained. "I wish it could happen to me."

"Gladys, you've got a perfectly nice husband," I said—I rarely missed a chance to extoll Chuck's virtues.

"Yuk, do you think Granny Lin and Pedro actually do it?" T.R. asked. The thought that they might do it seemed to have just crossed her mind and had given her an uncomfortable start.

"They probably do it," Godwin said, keenly interested in her reaction. He looked even more like a teak-plantation manager than he had when I left, and had even gotten a bridge for his missing front teeth. In some ways he now looked better than he had looked twenty years before, when he was courting T.R.'s mother. I regarded this long-delayed self-improvement as an ominous sign— the only conceivable reason he had cleaned up was that he hoped to do it with T.R. I meant to lose no time in informing him that that was an event that would only occur over my dead body.

"What's wrong with old people being horny?" Muddy asked. "It's a good thing to be if you can manage it."

"Not if you're *that* old!" T.R. said, still horrified. "If you're *that* old it's ridiculous. Look at Daddy. He's a lot younger than they are and he ain't horny. I think that's sweet."

Godwin gargled over that one, while I entertained dark thoughts involving the revival of thuggee. My imagination now had Godwin lodged somewhere on the Asian subcontinent—a long way from T.R. but well within the reach of thuggee.

"Well, if there's a wedding, you'll have to hire me some help," Gladys said. "I ain't up to no wedding; all I want to do for the rest of my life is play with Jesse."

Another home-front development was that Buddy seemed to be teaching Bo the gentle art of fishing. Buddy had a large rod and reel, Bo a tiny one; we had not been home twenty minutes before they set off with a tackle box for the nearest fishing hole.

"Catch Mommy a fish and we'll eat it," T.R. said.

"I'm going to look for my machine gun," Muddy said. "A lot of good that guard's gonna be if he's off fishin' when Earl Dee drives up."

"Buddy's nice to Bo, though," T.R. said.

"Good, maybe he'll adopt him after we're

255

dead," Muddy said. "I'm going to look for my machine gun. I hope some stupid roughneck ain't stole it by now."

My first task upon arriving home was to learn to play checkers by Jesse's rules. The games took place in the kitchen, with Jesse comfortably ensconced in her high chair. I sat on a bar stool. Whenever I jumped one of her checkers Jesse promptly threw my checker on the floor. If I merely advanced a square her approach was more subtle—she extended a finger and delicately pushed my checker three or four squares back from where it had been.

T.R. filled one of my large iced-tea glasses about half full of vodka and then topped it off with grapefruit juice. Godwin was pacing around nervously. Despite his dapper appearance he seemed a little on edge.

"Will you stop trotting around?" T.R. snapped. "Go outside if you need to trot."

"Sorry, sorry, sorry," Godwin said, three times. Like me, he occasionally made massive apologies for small offenses if confronted with a woman in a bad mood. It was clear that T.R. was in a bad mood, but for the moment I concentrated on my checker game and let him bear the brunt of it.

Then Granny Lin and Pedro came in. They seemed exactly as they had been, which is to say, silent and inscrutable, except that now they were clearly together. When Pedro got his six-pack of Budweiser out of the refrigerator he carefully opened the first can and handed it to Granny Lin.

Then he opened one for himself, and they sat at the table a few minutes, just to be polite, I suspect. They quietly sipped their beers.

"Hi!" Jesse said loudly—it was her new all-purpose word. But Pedro and Granny Lin were beyond the reach of even Jesse's charms, a fact that Jesse recognized quickly enough. She looked at them solemnly for a minute or two. While she was studying them I quietly advanced one of my checkers. As soon as she completed her scrutiny of the old couple she extended her finger and quietly pushed my checker back.

T.R. took her vodka and left the room without a word, trailing clouds of bad mood behind her.

"She does drink quite a lot of vodka," Godwin said.

"Well, so do you, L.J.," I said. "Are you trying to say she's an alcoholic or what?"

"Oh, no, she's a wonderful girl," Godwin said. "Truly wonderful. I find her a credit to the race. She has a heart, unlike her dreadful mother, and quite a good brain. Every time I venture some little observation about the human condition, I find that she's far ahead of me. She makes me feel rather shallow, I suppose."

I found what he said, and the tone in which he said it, quite moving. He was still nervously pacing back and forth across the floor.

"If you thought her mother was so dreadful, why did you try to take her away from me?" I asked.

"Who tried to take her away from you? Not

me," Godwin said, looking horrified. "From the moment I first bonked Sally I thought of nothing but escape."

"Bonked?" I said. "Bonked? When did we start saying bonked?"

"Oh, well, we can't very well just continue to say the F word in front of your grandchildren," he said. "You *do* recognize the impropriety of that, do you not?"

"I guess," I said. "I just never expected you, of all people, to help me clean up my language. Anyway, the word bonk reminds me of all those cartoon sound effects I used to write when I worked for Hanna-Barbera. For me it suggests the Flintstones, not a sex act."

"Hi," Jesse said, this time in a warning tone. Used thus, I think "Hi" meant that it was time to stop worrying about the F word and start worrying about checkers.

I looked back at the board, but my mind was elsewhere—it had followed T.R. out of the room, but she had outdistanced it. My mind was standing distractedly in the hall, more or less wondering what next.

This was not good enough for Jesse—she promptly threw a checker into the sink, and then another, looking at me coolly all the while.

"If you're going to play with Jesse, you have to play," Gladys said. "She don't care for opponents that just sit there looking dazed."

I *was* dazed, though. Godwin had made a moving statement about T.R., moving but troubling

258

—it seemed to suggest that I now had responsibilities that I wasn't being sensitive to. Before I could organize my thoughts and ask him what he thought I ought to do about T.R., or her drinking, or my responsibilities, Jesse began to throw all the checkers on the floor. It was a deliberate, willful act: how should I, as a grandparent, respond? Should I just smile at her whimsy or deliver a fond but stern statement in which I'd point out that good little girls didn't knock all their checkers onto the floor just because their grandpa was disheartened for a moment?

It seemed to me that suddenly all eyes were on me: Godwin's, Gladys's, Pedro's, Granny Lin's, and, of course, Jesse's. Was this the point at which I was supposed to start Jesse's moral education, or was flinging checkers around just a normal act for a little girl who wasn't even two? Not since the days when I had been the emperor of "Al and Sal," leading my reluctant army into battle every day, had I been the sinecure of so many watchful, not to say judgmental, eyes.

Unfortunately, a quick decision was called for. Jesse, after flinging half a dozen checkers, changed her tactic—now she began to sweep them off the checkerboard with her chubby little arm. In a very short order the checkerboard would be cleared, and I would have missed the great opportunity I felt I was being offered to become a force for moral good in my granddaughter's life.

The truth is, I missed my opportunity. I felt I should say something; I knew it was wrong, not to mention ridiculous, to let myself be dominated by an eighteen-month-old child, but that's exactly what happened.

"I guess that's the end of that checker game," I said lamely. "I wonder who won."

The adults in the room, myself included, knew perfectly well who had won, and so did Jesse. She smiled in triumph and held out her arms to Gladys.

"Hi," she said, as Gladys came to pick her up.

6

That night, worn out by my own indecision, my lack of confidence, my conviction that in my whole life I had never at any critical moment really known what to do, or managed to do what was in retrospect the obvious right thing, I went to bed early; but no sooner had I slipped into a doze than I felt an uneasy pulse in my head. A migraine was sneaking up. Sometimes I thought of it as a Comanche—once lord of these very plains where I lived, or failed to live, the Comanche-migraine hid quietly in the cave of my indecision, my fear, my fragmented conviction, sneaking out to attack whenever it saw its chance. Its approach, in this case, was stealthy, silent, intermittent, and might have gone undetected by anyone less experienced with sneak headaches than me.

I could not be fooled, though. Even when the migraine, a smart Comanche, crouched behind a bush for half an hour and restrained its torturous pulses, hoping to lull me into a deeper sleep, I wasn't fooled. I knew that if I allowed myself to be deceived, if I sank too deeply into sleep, the Comanche would pounce, his knife at my scalp.

Tired though I was, I didn't feel like being knifed by a migraine just then. Two can play the sneaking game, after all. I decided to get up and see if I could sneak past the headache, walk around it, as it were. Sometimes such a tactic worked, sometimes not. I had worn a caftan to bed, so I didn't have to dress—I just got up and slipped down the hall.

I thought I heard Elvis Presley music coming from the video room, and I was right. Muddy, Buddy, and Gladys were watching *Fun in Acapulco*—Elvis had just finished a song and was cavorting rather innocently with Ursula Andress. I watched only a minute or two, but seeing the two of them looking so young and innocent made me feel old and sad. Eras end every few years in Hollywood; *Fun in Acapulco* definitely called back an era that had ended. I had been there and lived through that era; I had seen Elvis a few times and Ursula Andress many times. Ursula was still going strong; but Elvis had not only faded, Elvis had died, and the Hollywood where they made pictures like *Fun in Acapulco* seemed quainter and more remote now than Belle Époque Paris.

"We're watching Elvis," Gladys informed me. Several more Elvis cassettes were scattered around.

"Where's T.R.?" I asked.

"She's pissed off," Muddy said, without explanation.

"Well, enjoy your film festival," I said.

I found T.R. on the porch after failing to find her in the rest of the house. I had insisted on a little porch—who would want a house without a porch?—much to my architect's disgust. I loved to sit on the porch on nice summer nights, especially if the moon was full; moonlight made the plains seem timeless, the pale grasslands beautiful. The stars, a show of their own on moonless nights, could not compete with the full lunar power on such nights; they shrank to faint specks.

The porch had immediately become popular with the kids. I had to pick my way through a minefield of toys to get to the couch where T.R. sat. She was still drinking.

From the road in front of the house I heard what sounded like the crackle of a police radio.

"Is that Buddy listening to the radio?" I asked.

"Nope, that's Gene," T.R. said. "Buddy's the day pig, Gene's the night pig. That's what Muddy calls them. Muddy hates cops."

Despite my caution, I sat on a toy—a plastic monster of some kind. Somehow its head snapped off.

"I'm afraid I decapitated a toy," I said.

T.R. just shrugged.

"Do you mind if I sit and talk?" I asked.

"You ain't shown me that closet full of presents yet," she said. "Was you lying about that?"

"No," I said. "I can show them to you right now, if you'd like."

She didn't answer for a bit. Far across the valley we saw the yellow lights of an oil derrick.

"I wonder if there's any nice roughnecks around here," T.R. said. "I've danced with a few roughnecks, but I ain't went out with one since high school, and then it was one of them offshore roughnecks. Johnny—I still remember him. Boy, was he sexy."

"What happened to him?"

"Alaska happened to him," T.R. said. "He wrote me two letters. We had a hot little time while it lasted. I was gonna go up and see him— he offered to pay my way—but it was just one of those things that never came about."

"Did Godwin leave?" I asked, remembering that I had not seen him during my recent house tour.

"Yeah, I bit his head off and he left," T.R. said. "I don't know how far he'll get without no head.

"Don't call him Godwin, either," she said. "It gives me the creeps to hear a name like that. Call him L.J., it's shorter and it's sort of his initials, anyway."

"I'll try to remember," I promised.

"I've known people like him down in Houston," T.R. said. Her mood seemed to be improving.

"They puzzle me," she said. "Why would any-

263

one want to fuck an asshole when they could be fucking a pussy? That just don't make sense."

I laughed, and T.R. chuckled too, as if it had just dawned on her that her own language might be considered a little inappropriate. I loved her candor, of course, but in this case she seemed a little embarrassed by it.

"Well, it don't make sense!" she said defiantly. "You think it's bad to talk about it?"

"Of course it's not bad to talk about it," I said. "It's not bad to talk about anything."

"Maybe not with somebody, but what about if it's with your daddy?" she said. "I never thought I'd be talking about pussies and stuff with my daddy. I don't know if that's too proper."

"Do you want to be proper, T.R.?" I asked.

"I might if I knew what it was, for sure," T.R. said. "Back when I was a teen-ager I wanted to be proper so much it hurt. I thought if I could just learn to be proper life would be perfect."

"I used to think that too," I said. "My metaphor for proper was a nice kitchen with a nice woman in it. I knew a very nice woman once, and she spent most of her life in her kitchen. I thought that if I could just marry someone like her and live in a kitchen something like hers, that would mean I was proper at last. And from then on, life would be perfect."

"What was her name?"

"Her name was Emma," I said.

T.R. looked at me a little sadly. I don't think

she approved of my caftan, but she refrained from comment.

"Maybe you can still try," she said.

"I can't try," I said. "Emma's dead."

T.R. was silent for a bit, thinking over the tormenting issue of propriety, or its lack.

"For me, it was just getting asked to one of the dances over at the country club, in Tyler," she said. "I wanted to dress up and go to one of them fancy dances so bad I could taste it."

"Did you ever get to?"

"I finally got to," she said. "A stupid little rich boy finally got up his nerve and asked me, even though his parents didn't approve. He took me but then he got ashamed of me and never came near me the whole night. One or two old sots danced with me, and some of the college boys.

"It was real boring," she said. "Just a big flop. I wouldn't even kiss my date when he took me home. He was real pissed.

"It was just a big flop," she said again. "It was the one thing I really wanted, and then when I got it I hated it. Right after that I quit school and left home. I guess I figured out that I was never gonna be proper as long as I lived. I figured I might as well just quit dreaming and throw in with the criminals."

Suddenly she threw her glass off the porch, then threw the vodka bottle after it and burst into tears, her face in her hands.

I waited a bit and scooted over toward her so I could put my arms around her. T.R. didn't resist.

265

"That's one trouble with life," I said. "Frequently when you do get something you want a lot, then you find out it wasn't worth wanting after all."

She took her wet face out of her hands.

"Is that how you feel about the woman's kitchen?" she asked.

"No, that's another problem," I said. "She was worth wanting, all right. The problem there is that I wouldn't have been able to live in that kitchen, even if I'd got to try. I wouldn't have been any good at it. It's not a way I could live."

T.R. watched me—she was sniffing, but her cry was over, basically.

"Why not?" she asked. "If she loved you and she wanted you to, why not?"

"I'm not sure I can answer that very clearly," I said. There was a hard throb in my temples as my headache gained a few yards. "I've been thinking about it for twenty years and I don't really have a good answer. I just doubt it would have worked out.

"I may just be a loner," I added, after a bit.

T.R. snorted. "If that's it, you're in trouble," she said. "You sure ain't alone now. You're looking at a crowded future unless you kick us all out."

"I won't be kicking you out," I assured her.

I wasn't alone now, and that was fine, but T.R.'s haunting desire to be proper enough to go to East Texas country club dances set off troubling reactions; it jarred with the view of her life I had been imagining for so many years. In my imagi-

266

nation T.R.'s life had always been proper, and this was not merely the wishful thinking of a sadly neglectful parent. Neglectful though I certainly had been, I had never entirely lost track of the fact that I had a child in the world. Many regrets haunted me as I fumbled through life—regrets about women won, lost, or just missed; regrets about art that got botched or never made at all—but nothing had haunted me so constantly as the fact of my missing child; I had long ago hired a detective and instructed him to make a discreet investigation. The detective had filed a convincing and reassuring report; I still had it. The one thing that seemed unarguable from the report was that T.R.—in the report she's called Rosemary—was enjoying an impeccably proper childhood. I had pictures of her on her bicycle, at about age nine; of the very normal-looking school she went to; of the proper two-story frame house where she lived; of her twirling a baton with other little girls on a well-kept lawn. From the report, it appeared clear that she was growing up as a member of the small-town East Texas gentry. The yard had huge trees in it and a picket fence around it. Any girl growing up in such a house in a small Texas town would automatically have been proper. She would have been quite welcome at country-club dances, would never have had to yearn for such a puny token of her acceptability.

But T.R. *had* yearned, yearned so much that she still couldn't talk about it in a steady voice. Something was wrong, and my knowledge of it wasn't likely to slow the advance of my migraine. A dark gap suddenly yawned between the life I had imagined T.R. having and the life she might actually have had.

I felt a tremendous need to close the gap at once.

"T.R., please don't get mad if I ask you questions," I said. She had settled back into my arms.

"You better ask them nice, then," she said tiredly.

"How come you weren't considered proper?" I asked.

"Why would I be?" she said. "I grew up with Big Pa and Big Ma."

"But I thought your grandfather had a successful car dealership," I said. "I thought your grandmother was the county clerk of the county you lived in. I was told that your mother worked in the bank."

"What made you think so?" T.R. asked, surprised. "Momma never worked in any bank. Big Pa didn't own no car dealership, either, unless you mean a *stolen* car dealership, and Big Ma wasn't no county clerk. She worked in the courthouse for a while, but that was just so she could steal old documents and stuff. Big Ma was in jail half the time. Big Pa always worked it so she was the one who had to go to jail when they got caught, and Big Ma was so simple-minded she let him get away with it. They had her in jail four times for stuff Big Pa actually stole."

"Is that true?" I asked, in shock. Inside me a long-held vision was collapsing, crumbling like an

ill-built house at the first shaking of an earthquake.

The ill-built house, of course, was my belief
that T.R. had had an irreproachably upper-mid-
dle-class American girlhood, complete with a
proper house, respectable, hardworking grandparents, a normal school, and proms at the country
club, at which she was by far the most popular
girl.

"What made you think stuff like that?" she
asked again.

"I wanted to be sure you were all right," I said.
"I hired a detective to come to Texas and find
you. I didn't have much money then, but I
thought he was a competent detective. I still have
the report. He took pictures of the house you lived
in and the school you went to. It all looked pretty
nice."

"Show me," T.R. said. "It sounds to me like
you got took."

Finding the file wasn't easy—what I fancifully
called my study was the least-used room in a house
where most of the rooms were rarely entered,
much less used. My professional life, such as it
was, had been compressed into one large filing
cabinet, almost all of it crammed with contracts
from the "Al and Sal" years. On a bookshelf beside the cabinet I had the scripts of the one
hundred ninety eight episodes, all bound in modest morocco.

For a moment, looking through the masses of
"Al and Sal" contracts, some of them the size of

a phone book, I felt panicky. Maybe I *didn't* still have the detective's report, in which case T.R. would think I'd been lying and had never tried to look for her at all.

Finally, in the bottom drawer, I found a few scraps from my own professional prehistory, years before "Al and Sal." There were my Hanna-Barbera contracts, as well as contracts for the two or three novels I'd started but never finished. Among them was the report from the A-Triple-AAA Detective Agency, the first one, as it happened, in the Los Angeles phone book. I well remembered the detective, a neat, middle-aged Hispanic named Jose Guerra—his secretary, an aging white woman, not so neat, referred to him as Jose Cuervo.

Jose had borne no resemblance to the gumshoes of myth, the Sam Spades, Philip Marlowes, Lew Archers. Jose had been an accountant in the office of a prominent L.A. divorce lawyer; the lawyer had even handled one of Nema's divorces, as I remembered. In fact, it was the lawyer who had referred me to Jose; at that time Jose dressed with all the sobriety of a submanagement-level accountant. At first I had some hesitation about sending a Hispanic to East Texas, but after a meeting or two I concluded that Jose Guerra really belonged to the nation of accountancy, not the nation of Mexico. It was all I could do to notice him even when I was sitting across the desk from him; he blended in so well that he was almost invisible.

I sent him to Texas, and a month later he filed

a meticulous report, complete with Polaroids of house, school, little girls twirling batons, etc. Those Polaroids, so reassuring in their middle-Americanness, had formed my vision of T.R.'s childhood all these years. When I handed them to T.R., she immediately began to shake her head.

"That's me with the baton," she said. "I did have a baton. It wasn't my bike, though, and that sure wasn't our house. That was Annie Elgin's house. We was best friends for a while—her daddy owned the bank. I went to lots of slumber parties in that house till I got a bad reputation and didn't get asked no more. Annie's folks weren't so bad. They knew Big Pa and Big Ma were crooks, but they let Annie have me over anyway, for a while."

"You didn't live in this house?" I asked, although she had just told me she hadn't.

T.R. shook her head. "We lived two blocks from nigger town," she said. "We were about as close to being niggers as you could get in Tyler, considering that we were white."

She looked at me with some concern to see how I was taking this news, and then began to read the report. She didn't hurry. I was beginning to feel horrible. I felt like apologizing over and over, although T.R. was reading the report calmly enough, occasionally stopping to take a thoughtful swallow of vodka. When she finished she closed the folder and handed it back to me.

"Isn't any of it true?" I asked.

"It's all true," T.R. said. "It's just a report on Annie Elgin's life, not mine. Big Pa ain't dumb

—that's why he's never been in jail, despite being a crook his whole life. He always expected you to come looking for me. He told me how horrible you were a million times—how you took dope and didn't believe in Jesus. He knows every cop and every little courthouse secretary in East Texas. He pays off cops—gives them free body work in one of them crooked body shops he works with. He gets them silly old women in the courthouse to believing he's about ready to divorce Big Ma and run off with them. He probably knew that detective was in Tyler before the man even found a parking place. I bet he bribed him before he even got unpacked."

"It never occurred to me," I said. That was the humbling truth.

"Oh, well," T.R. said, "I don't see that it matters a whole lot now. Big Pa just fixed it so you thought I was living like Annie Elgin. He's fooled smarter people than us, I guess."

"I only saw the man once," I said. "I never suspected he'd be that cagy."

We sat in silence for a bit. T.R. didn't seem either surprised or disturbed by the fraud we had just discovered. *I* was surprised and disturbed, though. I felt horrible.

"I haven't been thinking about Annie Elgin lately," T.R. said. "She was a real good friend to me. It's nice she got to have a good childhood. These pictures just reminded me of how nice she was."

"What happened to her?"

"She was killed in a car wreck last year, with both her little boys," T.R. said. "A truck just kinda drove over them—at least that's what I was told. So don't look so gloomy about that stupid detective. Annie had a nice childhood, and I didn't, particularly, but I'm alive and my kids are perfect, and she and her kids are dead. That's a lot sadder than what happened to us."

"You're right," I said. "But I still hate it that I was such a fool."

"Show me the presents," T.R. said. "If you've really got the presents, then maybe you weren't such a fool. Maybe you just didn't know what else to do."

That was certainly true—I hadn't known what else to do. For the first year or two after T.R. was born, when I was back in Hollywood and at my lowest ebb, I often called Sally, hoping she'd have softened toward me. She hadn't, though; at the sound of my voice she always immediately hung up. Then she began to get unlisted numbers. The first little presents I got T.R. were refused at the post office. I probably wouldn't even have known where the two of them were, had not Sally continued to expect me to pay for her life. She got my address off the packages I sent, and soon bills would arrive, mostly for car repair. She seemed to be continually wrecking cars; I always scrounged up the money and paid the bills because it was a way of keeping some kind of track of Sally and my child. I suppose I nourished the hope that someday Sally would come back to me, bringing our daughter. She didn't, but she sent the bills, and I was able to keep up with the two of them through several moves—Lake Charles to Lufkin, Lufkin to Sherman, Sherman to Tyler. Jose Guerra hadn't been forced to start from scratch. I had always known where to send T.R.'s presents.

I took her to the closet where I kept them. From time to time I had been tempted to throw them away or give them to the children of friends. The thought of them, unopened and unseen in their closet, more than forty of them now, seemed too weird, even for me. Its weirdness had become oppressive—sooner or later, I imagine, I *would* have just told Gladys to get rid of them, but fortunately that day didn't come. T.R. had come instead.

Buying those presents on her birthday and at Christmas every year was a ritual I couldn't let go of—it was the statement of my parenthood—though often I writhed inside when the saleswomen at the fancy toy stores I went to in Beverly Hills innocently asked me what my little girl liked. The worst part of buying the toys was having to deal with the salespersons' questions—that and having the presents arrive back in the mail. I sent each of them off with hope—surely sooner or later Sally would let her keep one—and received them back with despair, but I went on buying them.

I think T.R. hadn't really believed me—not until the moment when she stepped into the closet where the presents were. She was fairly drunk, but I think it wasn't vodka that caused her hands to tremble when she lifted the first present off the shelf. Except for the ten-speed bike, all the presents were still in their original gift wraps—some of which now looked as if they belonged in a museum of gift wrapping.

She looked at me, a kind of fright in her eyes.

"I never really thought this would happen, Daddy," she said. "I'm shaking like a fuckin' leaf. What am I supposed to do?"

"You're supposed to open your presents," I said. "Let me get you a chair."

I got two chairs—fortunately it was a large walk-in closet. I sat in one, T.R. in the other, and we had a combined birthday party and Christmas morning, deferred for twenty-two years. As the fetus recapitulates the history of the species, T.R. and I recapitulated her own history and mine, a history that had floated unborn in both our consciousnesses until that hour. We progressed from stuffed animals—raccoons, possums, a giant koala that filled half the closet, to Barbie dolls and doll-houses, doll dishes, toy phones, radios, makeup kits, a rabbit-fur coat suitable for a ten-year-old; we went from preteen to teen to young woman, as represented in the styles of the times: tote bags, Walkmen, leather jackets, necklaces, bracelets, watches, ending with garments of the sort my girlfriends sent Gladys from the most advanced boutiques in the world.

At first the unwrapping went solemnly, with very little talk. "Look at that sweet possum,"

T.R. said, without conviction; I think she still found the fact that the presents were there hard to believe. I felt awkward too: I had never developed much confidence in my choice of presents; having to be confronted with the wavery decisions of ten and twenty years ago did nothing to calm my cranial pulses. Probably we both felt somewhat awed, so awed that for a bit it looked as if the whole thing was backfiring. We spoke very formally; instead of bringing us close at last, the fact of the presents, or the lost life they represented, was making us feel hopelessly separate. I got more and more nervous; T.R. spent more and more time not looking at me; she meticulously untied the ribbons around each present.

Then who should wander up but Jesse, dragging her dirty old Cabbage Patch Doll. At the sight of the toys and stuffed animals her wide eyes widened further; she popped a thumb into her mouth. She stared with wonder at the koala for a moment, but concluded it was more than she could cope with. Instead, she dropped her Cabbage Patch Doll and grabbed the possum, bringing T.R. to life. For a moment motherhood was forgotten; she whirled on Jesse as if she were a sibling.

"You put that down and get out of here!" she snapped. "You got plenty of toys. That's my possum."

I was horrified—it was just a stuffed possum, the least of the presents—but no more horrified than Jesse, who dropped the possum as if it were hot and instantly took to her heels, wailing loudly as she ran to find Gladys, her bulwark.

"It was just a possum," I said, as mildly as possible.

T.R. looked confused by her overreaction.

"I don't know what's the matter with me, I must be drunk out of my mind," she said. "Now I've bit Jesse's head off too. See what you've done to me? It's all this stuff! It's this . . . stuff."

Before I could answer—I don't know what I would have answered—she buried her face in the giant koala bear's lap, sobbing loudly. When I put my hand on her shoulder she shrugged it off and clung more tightly to the koala. Her knee knocked over her drink and I had to snatch the rabbit coat off the floor to keep it from being soaked with vodka. At this point Bo appeared with his toy AK-47. He seemed to feel that the koala bear, not me, was the cause of the trouble; he began to pepper it with imaginary bullets. T.R. didn't let this interrupt her sobbing. Muddy Box, wherever he was, sensed that something was amiss. He came cautiously down the hall and peeked into the closet.

"Looks like what you all need is some paper towels," he said calmly, and went to the kitchen to get some. I stood up and helped him make a carpet of paper towels. They soaked up most of the vodka, but a little stream had run under the koala bear.

"Let me lift him up just a minute, T.R.,"

Muddy said. "We don't want this old bear to get his balls wet."

T.R. released the bear and grabbed Muddy, squeezing him tightly as the emotion broke out of her in gulps and snorts. Muddy calmly began to whisper to her, stroking her neck and back.

Then Gladys showed up, carrying a wet-faced Jesse, who looked ready to hide her face in Gladys's bosom if her mother yelled at her again. But T.R. didn't yell; under Muddy's patient ministrations she was calming down. Bo squeezed past me into the closet and began to inspect the loot, little of which held any interest for him. He leaned on my knee while he made his inspection; he even briefly handed me his machine gun while he tried out the toy phone. Seeing this, Jesse immediately wiggled out of Glady's arms and recaptured the possum. She tried to get the raccoon too, but Bo forestalled her by sitting on it. Jesse, keeping one eye on her mother, decided not to press her luck. Clutching the possum, she retreated to a safe position between Gladys's legs before giving the possum the careful inspection she felt it merited.

"Hi," she said, after a moment, holding the possum up for Gladys to see.

T.R. looked around at that moment, and Jesse froze.

"Hey, what does a possum do, Jesse?" T.R. asked, sounding tired but sane.

Jesse looked at the possum and shrugged, as if to say she had no idea what a possum did. "Hi," she repeated.

"A possum curls up and acts dead, so T.R. won't be tempted to beat the shit out of it," Muddy said. Then he proceeded to curl up on the floor of the closet in imitation of a possum.

"Get up, Muddy, you're gonna break my doll dishes," T.R. said, but Muddy, charmed by his own imitation of a possum, kept silent until T.R. began to tickle him, whereupon he wiggled and sat up.

"A possum can't afford to be as ticklish as you are," T.R. informed him. "Come on, I want to go in the bedroom and try on some of these weird clothes Daddy gave me. Some of them look like they were made to fit a boy—if you're good I might give you a few."

"I may not be good, though," Muddy reasoned.

Bo stood up, got his machine gun, and annihilated the raccoon loudly, from point-blank range.

"Wah!" Jesse said angrily, annoyed by this savagery.

"She's right, don't be shooting raccoons, they're cute," T.R. said.

She stood up and gathered up all the most recent presents, two or three of which were still unopened, stepping over Muddy and a mountain of wrapping paper on her way out of the closet.

"You come too, Gladys, Muddy don't know nothing about women's clothes," she said. "You better get some sleep, Daddy. You don't look so good."

"Some of this wrapping paper looks older than

me," Gladys said. "I don't usually see nothing that's older than me."

"I'm older than you," I reminded her, but I don't think anyone heard me. Just then, Bo tried to climb the koala bear, which fell over, causing him to split his lip. Gladys picked him up and carried him screaming to the kitchen to wash the blood off. Taking advantage of her brother's injury, Jesse quietly made off with her possum, plus the raccoon, and T.R. and Muddy departed for the bedroom, carrying large armfuls of clothes.

No further notice was taken of me. I turned off the light in the closet and sat in the chair for a few more minutes, while the backwash of the crisis subsided. Perhaps it had been no worse, or really any different—no more climactic or anticlimatic —from a normal birthday party or an ordinary Christmas morning. I had no way of judging; I was just glad we had all survived it.

Then I went to bed, and no sooner did I lie down than the migraine, that watchful Comanche, came screaming in the window.

7

I always sleep facing east: if you're likely to have a Comanche camped in your skull much of the night, the first hint and tint of light is important. The sun was the one power that could force the Comanche into retreat; the reddening horizon out my window seemed to infuse my cells with hope.

On the other hand, a gray dawn with clouds zipped to the horizon was bad news if I happened to be having a headache. Instead of the optimism sunlight brought, I wallowed in pessimism, depression, morbidity; I became like a sad Balt, as heavy with my headache as if I were living in Göttingen or Königsberg or someplace Kant or Hegel might have lived—somewhere in northern Europe where thought trod heavily under perennially leaden skies. My own thoughts hardly stirred at all on cloudy days.

Unfortunately the day dawned in the Baltic mode, squally and dark gray. I felt the Comanche settling in. He had not whooped and hollered too much during the night, had contented himself with a campfire near my right temple, but he showed no sign of being inclined to depart.

I kept my eyes shut for a while, hoping I had misread the morning. Perhaps when I opened my eyes again the sun would have made some headway; perhaps the clouds would have cracked, let a ray or two through.

The clouds stayed put, my headache stayed put; but fortunately T.R. and Jesse were up and moving around. T.R., holding Jesse, peeked in the door.

"Are you sick?" T.R. asked.

I gave a weak wave; I wasn't sure.

"Come on in," I said.

She sat down rather cautiously on my bed. Jesse, still clutching her possum, indifferent to me at the moment, was angling for a breast, and, after much wiggling and pawing at T.R.'s gown, she eventually got one. T.R. slumped against the headboard of the bed, while Jesse sucked greedily, waving one foot in the air.

"Slow down, I ain't a gas pump," T.R. said. She looked depressed—perhaps she had inherited my sun-dependency.

"Did the clothes fit, more or less?" I asked.

"Yeah, it's like a miracle," T.R. said. "All of a sudden I got a bunch of weird new clothes. Thank you."

She said it in a tone of such clear discontent that I winced, and she saw me wince.

"I guess saving the presents wasn't such a good idea after all, was it?" I said.

"No, but I can't figure out why not," T.R. said. "You didn't lie. You got me the presents. It makes me mad at Momma. She could have let me have one or two—then at least I would have known you were there, somewhere."

"She should have let you have all of them," I said. "But she didn't, and it was stupid of me to think they make up for anything. It's just stuff, like you said last night. There's no way it can be the same as having a father."

Jesse abruptly switched breasts, which took some rearranging of T.R.'s gown, my pillows, etc. I looked at Jesse and saw her watching me through half-closed lids. T.R. adjusted her automatically; her mind was still on the birthday presents. She idly brushed Jesse's light hair.

"Sometimes I wish I was Jesse," she said.

282

"There's a happy one. She's not thinking about nothing except titty. She don't waste a minute on all this depressing old stuff."

"Nobody's Jesse except Jesse, though," I said. "You and I can't help but think about depressing things. We'll never make up the time we missed, but on the other hand we're not very old—even I'm not *very* old—and we've got a lot of time ahead of us. I bet our future's going to be a lot happier than our past."

Jesse sat up, looked inward for a moment, and burped.

"Hi," she said, picking up her possum.

"Hi, Jesse," I said.

T.R. didn't look cheered by my optimistic prediction. She looked young, uncertain, and forlorn. I felt like taking her in my arms, but she didn't look like a woman who felt like being taken into any man's arms just then.

"Muddy thinks you're the weirdest man he's ever met," she said. "That don't mean he don't like you—he just says he never expected to meet anyone as weird as you. Have you still got that sick headache?"

"Oh, I've got it," I said.

"Rich as you are, looks like you could get some pills for it," she said.

"I have pills," I said. "But I don't like to just whop these headaches with drugs. Now and then I do, but it's not a smart idea. If you don't manage to kill the headache completely, it'll just wiggle off and hide until it can come back and bite you all the harder."

T.R.'s attention had wandered. She looked tired, but also restless.

"Muddy's right," I said. "I'm weird. I think it's mainly what blocked me from coming to see you. I convinced myself you were leading a happy, normal life in a nice town with nice friends. When you were little I had no friends and I had failed at everything, plus I knew I was weird. I wasn't really afraid of your mother or your grandparents—I was afraid of what you'd think if I suddenly showed up in your nice, normal life. You might have thought I was gross or yukky or something."

I paused. She wasn't looking at me, but she was listening.

"Maybe you think that anyway, now that you've seen my house, and the way I live," I said.

"It ain't the way you live, it's the way you don't live," T.R. said. "Shoot, I like to get out and buzz around. What do you and L.J. do out here all day? I know L.J. likes to get high, but what do you do all day?"

"Well, I'm writing a book," I said. "I can't run around much when I'm writing."

"I want to read it," T.R. said. "There's so many books in this house, I don't know where to start when it comes to reading. I'll just start with your book. When can I read it?"

I was flattered that she'd be interested, but painfully aware that I really had nothing to show. Even the first sentence of my new book was in doubt; since meeting T.R. I'd had no time even to muse about the various first sentences I'd once contemplated. Life had thrust art aside, but of course I didn't want to admit that to T.R.

"You can read it when I get a little farther along," I said. "I did publish a book about the time you were born. You could start with that one, if you like."

She was looking around my bedroom, which essentially consisted of three walls of floor-to-ceiling bookcases, all crammed, and a final south wall of glass, a kind of cinema screen for the brilliant sunlight to project itself on. In front of some of the books were pictures of the five or six women who had been most important to me. Jeanie was there, a lovely snapshot of her at her most winning, taken by a street photographer in Paris. Jeanie was so stern about her pictures, she might well have censored this one right out of my bedroom if she had ever come to visit and noticed that I had it. "I prefer just to be lodged in your mind," she had once said gravely when the subject of pictures had come up.

There were Marella Miracola and Antonella Napthi, the most dazzling and most constant of my various Italian loves. I also had a few pictures of women who had never been girlfriends, but who nonetheless loomed large in my memories of Europe—Pier Angeli, Françoise Dorléac, Romy Schneider; they flashed in my imagination whenever I thought of Paris or Rome. I didn't treasure them as I treasured Jeanie Vertus, a lifelong love, but they had all been glorious young women and were vivid threads in the tapestry of my past. I kept their pictures, and now T.R., my daughter, was looking them over; it seemed to me there was a kind of jealously in her look.

How could she, a girl from a little oil town in the west, compete with these great world beauties? That was what I read in her look.

"Are you fucking any of these women?" she asked in the flat tone into which she seemed to mix both anger and resignation.

"Nope," I said. "Why do you ask?"

"I just want to know if some movie star is going to show up down here and move in with you and start ordering me around," she said.

"It won't happen," I said. "I just moved in the only woman I'm likely to move in."

"I ain't no star," T.R. said. "I ain't much of nothing."

She seemed to be sliding into the yawning pit of unconfidence that looms beneath most, if not all women—even monoliths of female arrogance, of which I've known several, slide into that pit from time to time.

"T.R., this is a trite thing that parents are always saying to their children, but I'm going to say it to you anyway, since this is my first chance," I said. "You're just starting out in adult life. You're twenty-two and healthy. You can be as beautiful as any of these women, or as well-educated, or as famous, if fame interests you. You aren't nothing, and you can make yourself into whatever you want to be. You can go to college, you can study acting, or anything you want to study, we can travel for a year or two and see some of the world. I don't really have a thing I need to do except make up as best I can for all that time I lost with you."

T.R. ignored my pitch—she was studying the pictures.

"Who's that?" she asked, pointing to a severe little photograph of Jill Peel. Jill was sitting alone in a gondola in Venice—her son had snapped the picture not long before he killed himself. I had taken them to Venice to cheer them up. We had a pretty good trip and it did cheer them up. Jill was looking up at the camera, at her son and me, with the sort of chaste composure some people perhaps can muster when facing a firing squad. Hers was the face of a woman who was playing the endgame and accepted the fact and was glad nonetheless to be in Venice. In a way I hated the picture—I often resolved to take it off my bookcase. And yet Jill had given it to me. To have put it away would have confirmed the cowardice of which she had so often accused me. So there it was, in front of my set of *The Golden Bough*, haunting me as Jill always had, whenever my eye chanced to fall on it.

"Her name was Jill Peel," I said. "She's dead. Her story's a sad story."

"Every time I hear about dead I wonder where Earl Dee is," T.R. said, moving closer to me.

"T.R., stop worrying," I said. "We'll go to Europe for a few months. He'll probably be back in jail before we return. Or he'll have forgotten he said he'd kill you."

"Earl Dee won't forget," she said. "Earl Dee keeps his promises. That's one thing I'll say for him."

"I'll hire more security guards then," I said, "just until we get our passports. I'll put one over at the highway with a walkie-talkie twenty-four hours a day. Earl Dee's not going to kill you. You need to stop worrying."

"Tell me about that woman," T.R. said.

"Well, it's not necessarily the best story to tell you while you're in this mood," I said, wishing I had put the picture away long ago.

"I want to know about her," T.R. said. "She looks like I feel, so let's try the hair of the dog."

"Well, okay," I said, as she snuggled close to me.

8

Jill Peel and I went back a long way, to my very first visit to Hollywood, just after my one novel was published. The novel had been optioned by a movie producer, and I had gone to Hollywood to discuss writing the script. I met Jill in the corridor of the old Columbia Studios on Gower Street; a departing boyfriend had just slapped her and she was standing in the corridor, crying.

288

I lived in San Francisco then. Sally, just pregnant with T.R., had left me and gone home to Texas. Jill and I fell in love and she came to San Francisco with me, but the love soon faltered. She was an animator then, and rather famous, having just won an Oscar for an animated short called *Mr. Molecule*. Her taste in all things—art, food, clothes, the design of rooms, furniture, directors, even daylight—was so much better than mine that I've often wondered since if I would even have managed to become an educated person if Jill Peel hadn't seen fit to take a few months out of her successful life to get me started.

"If she was so perfect, why didn't it work out?" T.R. asked, once I had explained that much.

"I didn't say she was perfect," I said. "She was far from perfect. For one thing, she had a terribly conflicted relationship with her son. But she did have impeccable taste."

"Vomit," T.R. said angrily.

"Pardon me?"

"I said vomit!" T.R. said. "Impeccable taste makes me want to throw up. Who gives a fuck, other than rich people? I hate impeccable taste. I guess I was just born tacky."

"If you're going to hate her because of things I tell you about her, why should I tell you about her?" I asked. "You don't have to compete with her, you know. She's dead."

"I guess I'm the one who knows who I have to compete with," T.R. said. "I don't think you

289

know anything other than how to have sick head-aches."

It was hard not to perceive that my daughter was mad at me; her body, which she had scooted next to mine, was stiff as a board. Decades of exposure to female anger had not made me indifferent to it, either. I have as much respect for it as white hunters are said to have for wounded lionesses. (I owned a large collection of white-hunter memoirs. I studied them in depth for a movie that never got made; the one thing I remember about those hunters is their respect for wounded lionesses.)

I stopped talking—I was watching the bushes, as it were. This tactic only made T.R. angrier.

"Are we just going to lay here?" she asked. "What happened after you two broke up?"

"I disappeared for a few years," I said. "I came to Texas to see if your mother would take me back, but she wouldn't."

"I don't blame her," T.R. said. "Why would she take you back if you'd been off fucking some-one with impeccable taste?"

"Oh, boy, are you mad at me!" I said. "You're extremely mad at me."

The comment amused her. I saw a trace of softening, even a smile.

"If you think this is extremely mad, you're gonna be surprised when you see me get extremely mad," she said. "I don't have to like that woman just because she had good taste."

"No, you don't," I admitted. "You just have to decide if you want to hear the rest of the story."

She gave a noncommittal shrug. "I guess," she said. "I want to find out if she got what she had coming to her."

I told her about the movie Jill directed: *Womanly Ways*, it was called, a low-budget, well-acted, beautifully directed film made in the sixties. It happened to catch the rising tide of feminist sentiment and did rather well. Jill won her second Oscar, this time for directing; for the next several months she was the hottest ticket in Hollywood. Her future seemed all opportunity; the film did well in Europe too, so, for a time, Jill was a member of the international A-list, right up there with Truffaut and Bertolucci.

Never lucky in her choice of lovers, she dissipated a certain amount of momentum in love affairs with a number of men, at best boring and at worst terrible, who had nothing in common except the fact that they were all jealous of her status. Then the years began to pass, and whatever remained of her momentum began to trickle away, as momentum will, in Hollywood. Development deal followed development deal, but somehow the pictures never got made. Jill had her standards and was not loath to defend them—she had those two Oscars, after all. She was seldom subtle, and never inclined to back down. Soon she had quarreled with every studio head in town. Most of those studio heads soon fell by the wayside, but Jill promptly quarreled with their replacements.

Then it was no longer studio heads she was quarreling with: *Womanly Ways* was seven or eight years back, a geological era in Hollywood terms. The executives Jill could get the meetings with were younger and younger, farther and farther from the seats of power.

Finally she got nothing made, and she was broke. She was offered deals to write scripts, deals to coproduce, jobs in production, but she turned them all down. Everyone who mentioned her mentioned her only to complain; she was difficult, she was impossible, she was finished.

During the years of her fame I carefully hid from Jill. Los Angeles is a big town; one can hide without confining oneself too closely. While she was running around with Bernardo and François, I was the humblest mole at Hanna-Barbera. I had no intention of embarrassing her by leaning over her table at Ma Maison to remind her of old times. In any case, I could not have got into Ma Maison, or afforded it even if I could have. I lived in the Valley. People in Beverly Hills speak of the Valley as if you have to have a passport to go to it. From my two-room apartment in the Toluca Cabana I could see the Hollywood hills, where Jill lived. I knew the road she lived on, but I never drove on it. I avoided her house, the hills, all of it. I lived in the Valley and read about Hollywood in the trades.

The years passed and I read less and less about Jill; for one thing, I couldn't always afford the trades. Once or twice a year I might pretend I was still going somewhere and splurge on a breakfast at the Sportsmen's Lounge, complete with the trades, but by that time I was drifting down the Valley; down the Valley and then out of the Valley and down the state, headed for my eventual exile in Blythe. Not until the pilot for "Al and Sal" was in preproduction, and fame but a tick away, did I return to Greater Los Angeles. I was in the Warner's commissary one day, having a bowl of chili, when I noticed a woman at the next table. The woman was Jill Peel. She was not actually crying, but she looked as if she'd feel better if she went on and cried.

"What's a commissary?" T.R. asked.

"Just a lunchroom," I said. "It's where the studios feed their slaves."

"What happened to her impeccable taste?" T.R. asked.

I ignored the question and went on with my story. Of course, the minute I noticed Jill, I began to pretend that I hadn't noticed her. I felt physically weak at the thought of trying to be part of Jill's life again. There was no reason to suppose she wanted me to be part of her life again, of course; but the thought that she might was enough to take away my appetite for the renowned Warner Brothers chili.

What I was suffering from was the sheepman's syndrome. As the sheepherder feels inferior to the cowboy, the television writer feels his peonage in comparison with a movie maker. Jill might not have been working much for the last decade, but she was still a movie maker; I was just a television writer.

But when the waitress brought Jill her check and she signed it, I panicked. I might be scared of her, but I couldn't bear to let her just walk away either. She had once been my dearest friend.

I almost knocked my table down, getting up so I could rush over to her.

"Howdy," I said.

"Congratulations," Jill said. "I thought for a while you weren't going to work up your nerve."

"I'm surprised I did," I admitted.

"Me, too, let's have dessert."

"Why do you look that way?" I asked. It was probably the most direct thing I'd asked a woman since she and I broke up. In my dealings with the female sex, what few there were, I had become as elaborately circumlocutional as Henry James. In general, I didn't want anyone, women particularly, to figure out what I meant too quickly, if indeed I meant anything.

Such tactics wouldn't cut it with Jill, though, any more than they would have with T.R. Every now and then, despite my caution, I seemed to end up with a blunt woman in my life.

"I look this way because Joe Percy died," Jill said.

"Oh, dear," I said. "When?"

"A month ago," Jill said. "I was the one who found him."

Joe Percy had been her oldest friend. Like myself he was a peon, a television writer. I had met

him only once or twice, but I knew that he worshiped Jill, adored her, loved her deeply. Probably
that's ill-put: he loved the woman, but worshiped
the talent. You'll see that a lot in Hollywood:
people with no talent or at best a half-talent in
love with someone who possesses the real thing.
Joe Percy had stood by Jill for as long as I could
remember. In the years when all I saw of her was
her picture in the trades, at various awards dinners
and fetes, Joe Percy, a portly man, was usually
her escort. Their relationship, from what I gathered, had never quite risen to passion, but it had
produced a rare devotion. It was hard to imagine
Jill without Joe Percy's devotion, yet there she
sat, alone.

"He died sitting in his chair," Jill said. "I got
back from Europe the night before and was too
tired to go see him. Now I wish I had."

Only the day before, someone in the studio had
told me they thought Jill had just directed a movie
in Europe—the first inkling I had that she was
working again.

"Did you make a picture?" I asked.

"I made a mess," she said.

We ordered some pie and stared at one another
warily while we poked at it. I guess we were both
wondering if the embers of our interesting friendship still had enough glow to be worth working
on. The ashes of a decade and a half were piled
on top of them, and neither of us had that easy a
touch with friendship.

"If it didn't work out the first time, why would it work out the second time?" T.R. asked.

Before I could answer, Jesse and Bo arrived at the door and looked in. They stared for a moment, picked up negative vibes from T.R., and went away.

"The first time, we were trying to be in love," I reminded my daughter. "This time we'd have both settled for someone to have a meal and a chat with now and then."

"I think you still wanted to fuck her," T.R. said. "Who wants to just sit around eating pie?"

"I wish you weren't so mad at me," I said.

"I don't think you ever tell the truth," she said. "Everything you say sounds wrong, so no wonder I'm mad. I guess it's your business if you want to spend your life eatin' pie with horrible women, but it makes me fuckin' mad."

"Why?" I asked.

"Just does," T.R. said, shrugging. "I ain't got impeccable taste, like all your girlfriends. I ain't got an impeccable brain, either. I ain't never even had a good job."

I gave up. I felt as if I were being squashed between the pains, the pain of thinking about Jill and the pain of T.R.'s bitter anger. Probably I deserved both pains, but it didn't make it any more pleasant to feel squashed.

"Oh, go on," T.R. said. "I give up."

"Give up?" I said. "Give up what? I'm just telling you about what happened to an old friend. Why do you need to give up?"

She shrugged again. "All you do is talk to women," she said. "You ought to understand why I give up."

"Well, I don't understand it!" I said. "You're twenty-two years old. You're healthy. You have two beautiful children. You even have a father now."

"Sort of," she said, shrugging again, the way the young shrug when they want you to know they feel hopeless.

"Not sort of," I protested. "There's nothing sort of about it. I love you very much. There's nothing I wouldn't try to help you with."

"I don't feel like no daughter," she said flatly. "It's more like I'm just one of your many girlfriends."

"T.R., you aren't just like one of my many girlfriends—and there aren't really that many, anyway," I said. "We've just known one another a few days. I can't make up for all that time in a few days. But I am determined to make up for it. Maybe in a year you'll know I mean it. Maybe then you'll feel like a daughter."

I was beginning to feel hopeless too, though. Her conviction was stronger than my conviction. At that point Muddy appeared in the door. Like the kids, he seemed merely to be checking the weather, and, like them, he immediately found it to be stormy.

"Go away, fuckhead!" T.R. yelled. "I'm talking to Daddy."

"Good lord," Muddy said ruefully, and walked away.

"Finish telling it," T.R. said. "Did you fuck her again or not?"

"No," I said. "We weren't really successful lovers even when we were lovers. I don't know why that would matter so much to you."

Again the shrug, which I was beginning to hate. Thinking of Jill was not easy for me, either, though I didn't try to explain that to T.R. The roiling surf of middle age had drowned Jill and me—at least it washed us apart. Our efforts to renew our friendship fell sadly flat. For one thing, "Al and Sal" took off. Within six months I was the new genius of television. The press could not get enough of me. No A-list party was complete without me, whereas, listwise, Jill had sunk so far down the alphabet as not to be countable at all. The town just forgot her. She became one of the hundreds of gifted, half-famous or once-famous people living out their days in Hollywood. Five years without really working is like a century in that town—Jill Peel's name, once one of the most respected in the movie community, became as exotic as Theda Bara's, or Francis X. Bushman's.

Jill quite rightly felt some bitterness about her own neglect, and, quite understandably, some resentment of my blinding success. She knew what I had once wanted to be—not a television writer. She remembered my old standards; indeed, she had helped me to form them and knew how far beneath them I was actually performing. Still, I *was* performing; I was never going to write *The Magic Mountain* but at least my energies hadn't failed. Those world-famous one hundred and ninety-eight episodes *did* get done.

I asked her to dinner a few times. We were polite to one another, but there was a deadness. The only live thing was Jill's resentment—sometimes she let a little of it out, stuck me with a small barb, but mostly I just heard about it from other people. Jill said this about you, I would hear. Jill said that about you. Little comments she had made or was said to have made got back to me.

It was sad. I could not see Jill without realizing that I cared about her, but I didn't know how to express the caring, really. Besides, I was busy; one can do episodic television or one can do life; it's impossible to do both adequately. Jill and I bumped into one another here and there for the next year or two; I sensed that she was a little sad about us too, more sad than angry, probably, but I didn't know what to do about it.

Then, to my great surprise, she called one day and asked a favor.

"I've found a script I want to do," she said. "It's really good, Danny—the first really good script to come my way in ten years. I want you to help me get it done."

"I'd love to," I said at once. "You want me to come by your house and get it?"

"Oh, you don't have to do that," she said, with a note of panic in her voice—the notion of me in her house was clearly not something she wished to entertain. "I'll just send it over."

"Send it over, I'll read it tonight," I said.

"I want you to be executive producer," she said. "The story's a little grim. But you're the emperor of television now. If you say you'll produce it it might get done."

"If it's as good as you say it is, there'll be no problem," I said.

Even as I hung up I realized I had said four fatal words. "There'll be no problem" is nothing one should ever say, or even think, in Hollywood. In those hills live nothing but problems.

The script came and indeed was wonderful, though grim. It was about teen-age suicide and was set in England. The setting was a problem in itself, but with this script I thought it might work in our favor. America wasn't going to want to see American teen-agers killing themselves; English teen-agers they just might accept. I made a few calls and got good responses, and, in the euphoria even a conditional yes can produce in Hollywood, Jill and I almost recovered our friendship. We set to work on the script, which had a few problems, and we worked well. Jill's mind had lost nothing—it was a needle, perfectly adapted to stitching up holes in scripts. That was not too surprising; what was surprising was that my mind had not lost much, either.

"It's not dead, it's just been sleeping," Jill said, in reference to my mind. For some three weeks we were almost our old selves, meeting in the late afternoon to eat and work on the script for an hour or two. We even laughed some. We cast and recast the film, and as we worked Jill's energy grew. She got her womanly shine back, too; guys began to look at her in restaurants, and her name once again began to pop up in the trades. We settled on a studio, arranged the workings of a skeleton of a deal; Jill went to England to find locations and audition British actors. I was going to follow her as soon as "Al and Sal" shut down for its hiatus.

I felt confident, and Jill did too. We talked transatlantically all the time; the production was beginning to take form. The day came when all that was needed was for the studio to say go, and instead, to my dismay, they said stop. It might have been predicted; *would* have been predicted if I had ever stopped to think clearly about the matter for five minutes. But I hadn't done that, of course. Drunk with the success that had already been mine for a few years because of "Al and Sal," I assumed they wouldn't dare stop one of my projects.

But they did.

It was a shock, though it shouldn't have been. Projects get to the starting line every day in Hollywood only to have the starter refuse to fire the gun. I knew that perfectly well, and so did Jill; we had seen it happen hundreds of times, and yet we had convinced ourselves that I was powerful enough that it wouldn't happen to us. That was merely hubris. Naturally I had taken the project to the studio where "Al and Sal" was being produced; the show had made the studio hundreds of millions, and even then, in its next-to-last season, was not doing badly. It was reasonable to assume they'd let somebody who'd made them hundreds of millions make a twelve-million-dollar movie.

Reasonable but wrong. They said no. At first I was polite. I reasoned with the studio head; then I went over him to the president of the giant multinational that owned the studio. Both were very polite, but the answer was still no. Jill's film was not going to happen; or at least it was not going to happen with that company.

"The emperor of television has no clothes," Jill said when I told her this news. "So what next, Emperor? Do I have to come home?"

"Don't you dare come home," I said. "Take a little holiday. Go to France for a few days. Go to Italy. This is not the only studio in town. I'll make us a deal somewhere."

Jill did as she was told and went to France. In the meantime, I went to Paramount, Fox, MGM-UA, Columbia, the lot of them. And the lot of them said no. I couldn't even engineer a trade-off: Jill's picture in return for some big PG comedy or something that they might want me to produce, direct, write. Plenty of PG comedies were available, but no one would touch Jill's picture. Finally I had to tell her to come home.

Because of that fiasco, what ground we had regained as friends was ultimately lost again. It wasn't my fault that the picture hadn't been made;

I did everything I could do and kept on doing it long after Jill herself had been given up. But the town didn't yield, and Jill and I fell out of synch again. It wasn't really that she blamed me for the failure of the project—she was a fair woman and never said a critical word to me about my handling of the matter.

In the process, though, another disappointment, and a big one, got attached to me. Once the film project failed to work we were faced again with the fact that *we* had sort of failed to work too. There were no more cheerful dinners. When I ran into Jill I always felt nervous, depressed, guilty. Her new glow had faded; she seemed dim and distracted. I would get worried and call her and then find that I had nothing much to say to her. When I asked her what she was doing, she said she was drawing again. Jill had always drawn beautifully; art, not film, had been her first calling.

"Ask me over sometime," I said. "I'd love to see what you're drawing."

"Well, maybe," she said.

"I think she knew you still wanted to fuck her and she wasn't interested," T.R. said. "If she said maybe, it really meant no."

"You didn't know her and you could be wrong," I said patiently. "Maybe Jill meant that she was thinking about it. If she meant no she'd have said no."

"Believe what you want to believe," T.R. said.

"You're too harsh," I said, wondering if young

people were always harder on their fellow humans than old people.

"Anyway, those were her last words to me," I said. "She was killed three days later."

"Uh-oh," T.R. said, looking scared suddenly.

"She was killed in her home," I said. "Bludgeoned to death, apparently by a burglar she'd surprised. Whoever did it took what money she had in her purse, and nothing else. The murder was never solved—or at least it hasn't been solved yet."

We sat in silence for a long time. I was remembering the shock I felt when I opened my *L.A. Times* and read that Jill was dead. As I was reading it, people began to call and tell me. I didn't really listen. Ahead of shock came anger, in this case. The story was at the very bottom of the first page: "below the fold," as newspapers say. That seemed horrible to me. Jill Peel had given as much of herself to motion pictures as anyone in town; *Womanly Ways* was one of the few distinguished American films of the sixties. Why was she below the fold?

I had never discussed death with Jill—even the major tragedy of her life, the suicide of her son, we'd never talked about. But the day after the funeral—her cameraman was there, her old, bereft parents, an old driver who had driven her limo during her brief heyday, a director or two, the old script girl who had been, I guess, her best friend, and a few others who looked as if they might have been from props, or makeup, a gaffer, a grip, who knows?—her lawyer called and informed me that she had made me her executor.

My own lawyer I could hire to deal with the tiresome legalities, but there was no getting around the fact that I would, at some point, have to go to her house and dispose of her effects, such as they were.

I put it off for a month, and then one day when I was feeling fairly strong, I drove up the little road into the brown hills, the very road I had avoided during the years of her fame and my obscurity; I took the key the lawyer gave me and went into the house. I began to tremble, I had to sit in a chair—all the love that was still there in me for Jill, the love that had never worked out— surged up and blinded me. It was a long time before I could stumble shakily around the house. If there had been anything to trip over I would have tripped over it, but Jill was a minimalist's minimalist; the house, looked at from the inside, was as spare as her life had seemed, looked at from the outside. She had a bed, a few chairs, a work table, a small bright studio room, a little art on the walls, a closetful of paintings that wouldn't fit on the walls, a few dishes, a pot to make tea in, a small pool, a few clothes, and two Oscars.

In her workroom were lots and lots of drawings, from every period of her life. In looking through them I felt like a sneak. Jill had always been very private—even when we were intimate she told me only what she wanted me to know—and about nothing was she so private as about her art. Still, sad as it was, I had to make some disposition of all those drawings; I had to look through them. And there were thousands. I felt as if I were peeking under Emily Dickinson's bed to discover those two thousand poems.

Perhaps Jill had not really been as great as Emily Dickinson, but it seemed to me that at least she stood at the edge of greatness. The longer I spent in the studio room, poking through drawer after drawer of drawings, the more my sense of Jill's life changed. She had put much into the effort to make motion pictures, but it seemed to me that she had put even more into this art—an art as lonely as Kafka, an art that almost no one had ever seen.

In one of the long drawers, mixed in with scores of sketches, I found a little portfolio—there were several in the studio, little groups of sketches Jill had wanted kept together. This one, though, had a title carefully blocked in: *Let the Stranger Consider.* I opened it; a little sheet of notepaper partially covered the first drawing. It said "For Danny"—nothing else. In the portfolio were twenty-two drawings, all self-portraits. Jill had looked in her bathroom mirror and sketched herself: in some she held a towel or a hairbrush, in others nothing; several were just her face, others were full length; in some she wore a bathrobe, in others she was nude; in all of them she was squarely facing the mirror, mostly at close range. In looking at the portraits I felt that I squarely faced her, too, in a sense: old friend and old love, a woman whose grace, like her sadness, had mostly remained unobserved, even by me, whom she might once have trusted with it. The last few portraits were spare to the point of incompleteness— one saw a feature but not the whole face or form; they were eerie drawings, made by a woman who seemed to be fading from her own view.

I did my duty as an executor; the house and the art were sold. Some of the money went to the Actors' Home, the rest to her parents, both of whom died within two years. Jill's drawings I gave to UCLA, where she had studied. The only thing I kept was *Let the Stranger Consider*—it seemed she had meant it for me.

Once or twice a year I looked through the album, hoping that in time I would understand what she wanted me to consider. Was it the fact that I had stayed a stranger, or was it she that I was to consider? She had been in her mid-forties when she drew those portraits; she didn't set out to flatter herself, but neither did she attempt to diminish her own appeal—her clarity, her frankness, her welcoming attitude. I never looked through the whole album consecutively; even just looking at two or three drawings at a time made me miss her too much. More often than not I just turned to the haunting drawings at the end, where Jill was recording her disappearance, her shrinkage.

In time I got to wondering about Jill. In the years when we were attempting to renew our friendship, I never asked her about her love life, and she never asked me about mine. I wasn't having a love life just then, and I doubt Jill was either. I knew several of her friends, and none of them ever mentioned a guy. But maybe there had been a guy; or maybe there was about to be one. She had been private but not exactly cautious; perhaps at the end she had welcomed the wrong man.

The woman was dead; it didn't really matter, and yet an old boyfriend's curiosity began to nag at me. Finally I called the detective who had investigated her death; he was bored at first, but he was also a big "Al and Sal" fan, and when he found out who I was, he obligingly looked up the file.

"She wasn't in the house but a moment when she was killed," he said. "Her keys were still in the door. She probably just ran afoul of some drifting dopehead."

I felt embarrassed for having asked. Why had I even supposed her death had to do with a boyfriend? What kind of worm was that, what kind of apple? Did I think the violence of love produced a more acceptable end than the violence of accident? I never resolved those questions, but I did regret calling the detective.

I finished my story by expressing that regret. T.R. sighed. All belligerence had left her. She looked very young and very sad.

"Do you know the Governor?" she asked, to my surprise.

"Oh, I've met him," I said. "I wouldn't say I know him. Why?"

"I used to read about you," T.R. said. "You know, little things in the paper, about you being at a party with the Governor."

"I have been at two or three parties with him," I said.

"Yeah, but you're famous, so you could get him on the phone, right?" she said. "You can call him up and ask him something if you want to, right?"

"I probably could," I agreed.

"Do it," T.R. said. "Ask him if Earl Dee's really out. If he's out I want to know it. I got two babies to raise. I don't want to end up like your friend. Just ask the Governor, Daddy. Call him right now."

When I put my arm around her she was shaking.

"I'll call him right now," I said.

For the first time I began to be a little worried about this dark man—Earl Dee.

9

I called the Governor and he gave me the name of the head of the prison board; the head of the prison board put me in touch with the warden of the Huntsville unit, who scratched his head a bit and said he'd have to call his Records department in order to locate Earl Dee.

The warden also turned out to be a fan of "Al and Sal"; he promptly called his Records department, and within thirty minutes a young lady in

Records called me back with some good news: Earl Dee was still in jail.

"Yep, he got in a fight and slammed a cell door on somebody's headbone," the girl said, in accents that bespoke East Texas. "The earliest we'd be letting him out is about two months from now."

"Thanks," I said. "That's a very big relief."

Just as I was putting down the phone I heard a terrible scream from T.R., who had decided to go swimming while I made my calls. The scream was so chilling I went into shock—my instinctive conclusion was that the young lady in Records had just told me a lie. Earl Dee *was* out, he had found us, and he was about to murder T.R. I managed to overcome my shock and scramble out the door. One glimpse of the pool was enough to show me my mistake. T.R.'s screams resulted from the fact that Godwin Lloyd-Jons was floating face down on the surface of the pool. The kids eyed his floating body with curiosity but little alarm.

"He's dead, he drowned!" T.R. said in a shaky voice. "Get him out, Daddy—maybe we can give him mouth-to-mouth."

"He's not dead," I assured her, wishing I could will the adrenaline that had squirted into me when T.R. screamed back into its ducts or glands or wherever adrenaline comes from.

"Get him out!" T.R. said. "I can't stand to touch dead things or I'd get him out myself."

"He's just doing his breath-control exercises—it's some kind of Eastern discipline he affects," I

310

said. "He's always floating on his face in the pool and scaring people like this."

T.R. stepped closer to the edge of the pool. Godwin seemed to be totally naked, as he often was when he chose to do his breath-control exercises.

"I don't know, Daddy," she said. "He sure looks dead to me."

Indeed, he did look dead. I would have thought so myself if I hadn't found him floating face down in the pool so many times only to see him suddenly start spurting like a porpoise, after which he would allow himself a few drags of air and then swim up and start being his obnoxious self.

Muddy came running out of the house with his AK-47 at the ready. He ran out and crouched beside the diving board.

"Where is he?" he asked, meaning Earl Dee.

"He's still in Huntsville," I said. "I just got the good news."

Just then Godwin began spurting like a porpoise. Until that moment, T.R. was highly skeptical of my opinion that he was alive.

"See, I told you," I said. "He loves to float face down in the pool."

When Godwin lazily swam to the edge of the pool, T.R. was waiting for him.

"What kind of little freak are you, going around scaring people like that?" she asked.

Godwin was largely deaf even when he didn't have water in his ears.

"My dear, apparently I forgot my trunks," he

said. "I do hope you'll forgive me. No offense was meant."

"Is that water cold or is that water warm?" T.R. asked. "I hate to jump off in a pool of cold water."

"I'm having a little difficulty hearing," Godwin admitted.

T.R. reached down and felt his arm, which was apparently warm enough to quell her fears about cold water.

"Swimming will feel a lot better now that I know Earl Dee's still in prison," she said. "How long did they say they'd keep him?"

"At least a couple of months," I said.

"Shoot, we can enjoy the summer then," she said, before plunging into the pool.

Muddy Box seemed a little disappointed that there was no Earl Dee to shoot at. "I guess if he'd come he'd have found out we wasn't no easy prey," he said.

The day that had started out so badly with my headache and T.R.'s anger and the sad story of Jill Peel turned into one of the most pleasant days the group of us had spent together. Godwin borrowed Jesse's towel and made himself presentable. Once presentable, he soon concocted a large quantity of Singapore Slings. Gladys brought out some guacamole and then decided to go swimming herself. Her archaic breast stroke so fascinated Jesse that T.R. and Muddy had to take turns ferrying her around the pool so she could watch Gladys.

"Don't look at me that way, Jesse—it's okay if cooks swim," Gladys said.

Buddy lumbered up to get Bo for their daily fishing trip. He took the news of Earl Dee's continued incarceration philosophically.

"Somebody'll slam his headbone, sooner or later," he said. "Don't matter how big and mean you are, there's always somebody bigger and meaner."

Anticipating the loss of his job due to this news, Buddy drank many Singapore Slings and various other things and got quite drunk. I informed him I had no intention of firing him; I wanted him to guard the house while we went to Europe.

"Which countries are in Europe?" T.R. asked. "Geography was my worst subject in school—I could never work up no interest in any place but Tyler."

"I guess I know what you worked up an interest in," Muddy said. He was not participating fully in the general good mood. Running out with his machine gun and finding no Earl Dee to shoot seemed to have left him feeling a little flat.

"How could you know, you grew up in Louisiana, you little birdbrain," T.R. said affectionately. "You never even heard of me until after I moved to Houston."

Godwin was having a hard time keeping his eyes off T.R., who wore a very skimpy bathing suit. In an effort to impress her, he rapidly named all the countries of Europe, starting with Iceland and working eastward until he came to Greece.

"What about Australia?" T.R. said. "You didn't name it. I thought Australia was over in

Europe somewhere. I've always wanted to see a kangaroo."

Once in a while, when excited, Godwin reverted to his old professorial mode. At such times he was inclined to spew out streams of erudition, much of it unrelated to any question that had been asked, or anything that a normal human might want to know. In this instance he began to talk about Ptolemy and Strabo. Soon we were left with no choice but to admit that we were dealing with a well-educated man. Godwin's spurts of erudition made me sulky, made T.R. sleepy, and didn't affect Muddy at all. While he was spurting, Pedro and Granny Lin came walking up from their hut. They went on into the house in search of beer.

"You started doing it when you was thirteen," Muddy said, apropos of nothing. "You told me you did that time when we went swimming in the ocean."

"So?" T.R. said. "What's it to you when I started? I didn't even know you then."

"Thirteen's pretty young to start," Muddy said resentfully. "I didn't even start till I was fifteen, and I'm a boy."

"There's no law saying girls can't start younger than boys," T.R. pointed out. A domestic argument seemed to be brewing. Godwin went on coughing up odd facts about Strabo and Ptolemy, oblivious to the fact that none of us was interested.

"And then there's Euclid," he said. "Quite an amazing mind, really."

"Muddy's got an amazing mind, too," T.R.

314

said cheerfully. "He keeps it in his dick. I've known two or three men whose only trace of brains are in their dicks."

"I guess you would know a few, if you started when you were thirteen," Muddy said resentfully.

"I didn't see no reason to wait," T.R. said, looking him in the eye. "If you wait, all that happens is that you get older. I've already got older but at least I had more fun than you did, along the way. Two years' more fun."

"Sometimes I wish I'd stayed in jail," Muddy said.

Ten minutes later they were smooching on the diving board. Shortly after that they disappeared for a while. Jesse brought a bucket of checkers out of the house, poured them into the pool, and watched them float. Bo had learned to swim under water and swam around and around, froglike—he was a good deal more pleasant as a grandchild when he was under water. Gladys napped on a towel as Godwin continued his lecture on Euclid.

"Godwin, I'm the only one listening," I pointed out. "Please don't tell me any more about Euclid. Don't tell me any more about Strabo or Ptolemy or Pliny or Herodotus or Martial or Catullus or Euripides or anyone. It's making my headache start up."

"T.R. is truly beautiful," Godwin said. "I could educate her in a year, perhaps less, were it not for the impediment of Muddy."

"Were it not for the impediment of Muddy, you'd be in over your head," I said.

"Nonsense, I'm convinced T.R. and I could make one another very happy," he said. "What a delicious irony it would be if I ended up your son-in-law."

"Godwin, if you try to fuck her I'll kill you," I said listlessly. I knew perfectly well he would try to fuck her if he got the slightest encouragement, or perhaps even if he didn't; I also knew I wouldn't kill him—at worst I would probably only exile him from Los Dolores, a trivial response at best. What I couldn't figure out was what difference it made, or what right I had to anything more than a simple opinion about T.R.'s choice of sexual partners. After all, she was grown, and I had made no attempt to influence her during her formative years. For all I knew she would be resentful if I even suggested that she pass up Godwin or anyone else; certainly all of my women friends would be resentful if I tried to get them to pass up anyone. They would see it as a violation of the tacit pact we had not to interfere with one another in that arena. Maybe T.R. had been right, earlier in the day, when she said she felt like one of my female friends rather than like my daughter. What was really involved in feeling like a father, or like a daughter? I didn't know, and I was beginning to feel gloomy at the thought that it might be something I could never learn—that my daughter would never feel that I was more than a friend. I already felt that *she* was more than a friend, and yet it was hard to be precise about the difference.

My spirits sank and Godwin noticed them sinking.

"Oh, piss," he said. "You're getting depressed again. Your daughter's perfectly wonderful. *Why* are you getting depressed?"

"Yeah, why?" Gladys said, sitting up. One of Gladys's more startling abilities was the ability to move instantly from deep sleep to full, even prickly, wakefulness. One minute she was snoring, the next minute she was insulting you.

"Because it's hard to know what all this means," I said. "I sort of like to have my thinking at least roughly aligned with my feeling. Neither of you would understand that because you never bother to think."

"That's because you're rich and we ain't," Gladys said. "You got so much money that you can think all you want to. I got to scramble, myself. If I sat around thinking, I'd never get nothing done."

"My point exactly," Godwin said smugly.

"Your point?" I said. "Why is it your point? You never do anything. You're a pampered guest. You enjoy total leisure. What makes you think you don't have time to think?"

Instead of answering, Godwin rolled into the water and began to float face down again. He often did that when confronted by his own illogic. It was a very irritating habit. I found myself wishing his breath-control tactics would fail him suddenly and that he'd just drown—or, if not actually drown, at least vomit for a few minutes.

I saw Pedro and Granny Lin walking across the hill, back to their hut. They were carrying a six-pack between them, each holding one of the little plastic loops that keep six-packs together. At a distance, at least, with the help of a lovely sunset, they seemed perfectly content. The sight of their contentment made me feel lonely and sad. I was already feeling sorry for myself because I didn't understand fatherhood; at the sight of two evidently contented old people I plunged even deeper into self-pity. Would I ever have anyone to walk across the downward slope of life with at sunset? Or would the sun always set with me alone, brooding and miserable, as it had so many times?

"They seem happy," I remarked to Gladys.

"Them two, they fight like tigers," Gladys said. She kicked Bo's beach ball into the water, hoping to hit Godwin with it, but she missed.

"I hate varicose veins," she added. "Every time I see my own legs I wish I'd never been born."

With that black comment she went into the house, leaving me to float in self-pity while Godwin floated in the pool. Pedro and Granny Lin fought like tigers? When did they fight like tigers? How did she know? What did they fight about? Of course, Gladys imagined things. In fact, she imagined hundreds of things. Perhaps she was imagining those tigerlike fights. Perhaps the old couple never fought; perhaps Gladys was confusing them with herself and Chuck. They certainly fought frequently, if more like humans than tigers.

I never liked fights, myself. The emotional benefits they were supposed to convey on healthy couples had always seemed overrated, at least insofar as I had ever been a part of a healthy couple, healthily fighting. The fights I had participated in, and there had been not a few, almost always signaled the demise of the couplehood as the two of us then knew it.

Now, though, I began to see the absence of fights in my life as yet one more sign of my extreme detachment. Here I sat at fifty-one, having lived, in theory at least, only about half my life, not even close enough to anyone even to have a fight with them, unless you counted Godwin and Gladys, with both of whom I had bitter fights practically every day. In that regard T.R.'s not-so-latent belligerence might prove a great blessing; she alone might be able to tug me back into a normally conflicted human relationship. She alone might reconnect me.

While I was contemplating that possibility, she and Muddy came racing across the patio, off the diving board, and into the pool. Both were naked. The shock waves of their dives sloshed Godwin around so vigorously that he was forced to abandon his breath-control exercises. For a moment he was rather confused, but when he saw that T.R. and Muddy were naked his eyes lit up. He immediately climbed out of the pool and began to take off his bathing trunks.

"Stop, what do you think you're doing?" T.R. asked. She looked rosy and very cheerful.

"You're skinny-dipping, I supposed I could, too," Godwin said.

"Forget it, if there's one thing I don't want to see, it's some old man's old dick," T.R. informed him merrily.

"My dear, what a harsh thing to say," Godwin replied.

"Not from her, that's almost a compliment," Muddy said. T.R. whirled, wrapped her arms around Muddy, and ducked him. The two of them sank from sight.

"What a remarkably pretty girl she is," Godwin said.

10

"When are we getting off to Europe?" T.R. asked the next morning. She and I and Godwin and Gladys were breakfasting on the patio. Jesse had been breakfasting too but had fallen asleep in her high chair in a puddle of Cheerios. Bo had gone off with Buddy to run the trotline they had set the night before.

"We have to apply for your passports," I said. "We could go to Fort Worth and get the applications today. Then we can send them up to the Senator I know. He can probably get them processed in two or three days. We could all go to Europe next week."

"A whole week's a long time to sit around out here on this hill thinking about how empty it is,"

T.R. said morosely. "Some days I miss the Mr. Burger. At least there were people around to talk to at the Mr. Burger. And there was places to go dancing at night."

Actually she and Muddy and Godwin had gone dancing the night before. They had driven all the way to Dallas, but failed to find a dance hall that came up to T.R.'s standards. Then they had come home and watched Fassbinder movies all night. Muddy was still inside, somewhere around the halfway point in *Berlin Alexanderplatz*. By all accounts—that is, by T.R.'s and Godwin's accounts—he was completely engrossed.

"Now he says he wants to go to Berlin," T.R. said. "The little fucker never even heard of Berlin until last night."

"That's good, though," I said. "It means he's got some curiosity."

I had stayed awake most of the night, too, buffeted by the high surf of a migraine. With morning, the surf had receded, though now and then I felt a departing wavelet. T.R. was not exactly sulky, but she was clearly restless.

"If it's merely a matter of picking up passport forms in Fort Worth, then there's obviously no need for everyone to go," Godwin said. He had on one of his seersucker suits. After so many years of seeing him naked at breakfast, it was definitely an irritant to have him looking like a colonial administrator. His ill-concealed designs on my daughter were also irritating.

"T.R. and I could accomplish that task quite

efficiently," Godwin said. "There's no reason for anyone else to be inconvenienced.' "

"It *is* just a matter of picking up passport forms, and if you're volunteering your services I accept them—you can do it perfectly well alone. Why would T.R. need to go?"

"Shoot, I'd go just to see some people," T.R. said, oblivious to the fact that I didn't want her to be alone with Godwin.

"I ain't workin' out as a country girl," she said without hostility. "I'm starting to miss Houston. I wouldn't even mind being in a traffic jam—at least there'd be other people around."

"A nice trip to Fort Worth would be better than nothing," Godwin said. "We wouldn't need to take the children, necessarily."

"Maybe I should call my friend the Senator," I said. "Senators have amazing powers. His staff might facilitate this for us—we could be in France by the weekend."

"Let's go someplace real crowded," T.R. said. "I'm getting itsy from sitting around here on this hill."

"There are some very nice beaches on the French Riviera," Godwin said. "Nudity is quite acceptable there."

"Who cares?" T.R. said. "If there's one thing I don't need to see, it's a bunch of dangling dicks. I've already told you that fifty times, so shut up about it. Jesse might hear you."

"That precious thing," Gladys said. "I'll miss

her so much I'll probably just sit around here and cry the whole time you're gone."

"No you won't, because you're coming," T.R. said. "I ain't dragging my kids around a bunch of foreign countries without some help."

The thought of Gladys in Europe had never occurred to me. Nor had it occurred to Godwin, or to Gladys herself. The thought was so novel that all three of us were paralyzed by it briefly.

"She's coming, ain't she, Daddy?" T.R. said firmly.

"Of course she can come if she wants to," I said gamely, trying to imagine what Gladys and France would make of one another.

"I might go," Gladys said tentatively. "On the other hand, what'll I do about Chuck? If I run off to Europe he'll head straight for that slut in Amarillo, and I'll have that preying on my mind the whole time I'm gone. Then when we get back, the first thing he'll do is ask for a divorce. That will be the end of that, and the kids will all blame me for running off to Europe and leaving Chuck to fend for himself. Not that he can't fend. He's probably off fending right now."

At that she burst into tears and buried her head in her arms. Gladys cried heartily. Godwin and I, inured to these cloudbursts, went calmly on with our breakfast.

"Well, you two are mighty cool," T.R. said. She herself seemed slightly awed by Gladys's sobs.

"They are, they don't never even stop eating

while I'm sitting here brokenhearted," Gladys said.

"If we didn't occasionally eat while you were crying we'd both starve," Godwin said. "Did it ever occur to you that you might be happier if you just divorced Chuck? After all, he's not exactly Errol Flynn."

The thought that Gladys's lot in life might be improved if she were married to Errol Flynn struck me as funny, and I laughed. T.R., who had probably never heard of Errol Flynn, thought this was inappropriate. She slammed her fist on the table.

"Shut up, you two!" she demanded. "You're just a couple of coldhearted old men. Gladys is having to get a divorce and you two sit there laughing."

"Right, I should never even have mentioned Errol Flynn," Godwin said. "Sorry, sorry, sorry."

His new habit of apologizing three times every time T.R. got the least bit testy was beginning to irritate me.

"One apology's enough, Godwin," I said.

"L.J., I hate the name Godwin!" T.R. yelled. Her mood was not improving. "How many times have I told you to call him L.J.? Every time I hear the name Godwin I want to throw up."

"Sorry, I'll learn," I said. "I've been calling him Godwin for many years, it's hard to switch overnight."

"It wouldn't be if you concentrated," T.R. insisted. "All he concentrates on is pussy, and all you do is make fun of Gladys. Now that I know Earl Dee is still in jail I'm beginning to wish I'd stayed in Houston. If it don't mean being murdered I'd rather be someplace where people kick up their heels once in a while."

"Of course, you do have to be photographed to get a passport," I said, desperately trying to come up with some diversions that might make T.R. less impatient. Passport photographs were the straw I grasped at. My impression was that T.R. checked few impulses. If she got much more discontented she might just go away, a thought I couldn't bear. I had quickly grown to love her so much that the thought of being without her again was intolerable. If I could get her to Fort Worth we could at least have a shopping spree, and that might divert her for a day or two until the passports came through and we could get safely off to France.

An hour later we were all crammed into the Cadillac, bound for Cowtown, as Fort Worth used to be called. Every inch of space in the car was thick with life, sound, smoke, cassettes, toys, bodies. Muddy and Godwin were quarrelsome and gloomy, Muddy because he hadn't wanted to go at all, and Godwin because another scheme to isolate T.R. and seduce her had been thwarted. I knew how skillfully Godwin preyed on female impatience, and was determined to give him no chance in this instance.

"Hi, hi, hi," Jesse said, many times. She stood by me, wildly excited to be going someplace. Bo had taken a dislike to Muddy; after trying to hit him in the face with a toy truck, he bit his wrist. Muddy grabbed him and shook him for a bit, and Bo burst into loud shrieks.

"Cut it out, that's child abuse, dickhead!" T.R. yelled over her shoulder. She wore huge yellow shades and was listening to one of Godwin's old Rolling Stones tapes. Gladys was chain-smoking furiously, intensely nervous at the thought of passport photographs, France divorce, estrangement from her children, and varicose veins, her latest obsession. She had begun to work varicose veins into almost every conversation.

"It's one thing that would be a problem for me on them nude beaches," she said. "Do them French women have varicose veins?"

"Please, the nude beaches are not for elderly people," Godwin said.

"Are you saying I'm elderly?" Gladys asked. "If I'm elderly, what does that make you?"

"Can't you drive faster?" Godwin asked, skirting the question. "We're merely creeping down the road."

Bo leaned over the seat and got a stranglehold on Jesse. He tried to pull her back over the seat so he could strangle her at his leisure. Jesse made strangling noises. T.R., inscrutable behind her shades, paid this atrocity no attention; neither did anyone else. I remembered how necessary it was to maintain a constant flow of oxygen to the brain and became a little panicky at the thought that Jesse's flow might be cut off. I tried to break Bo's hold with my free hand and almost smacked into the rear of a gravel truck. T.R., more tuned in to what was going on around her than she appeared to be, screamed.

"We'll all be killed, and I hope we are," Muddy said. "I wanted to stay home and watch that all-day movie. Having your picture made's a good way to get sent back to jail. They might get me and they might get you too."

"Buddy, would you sit on Bo?" T.R. asked.

Buddy was horrified at the thought of having to go to a foreign country—Fort Worth was foreign enough for him—but I had insisted that he come along in case we decided to take him to France as a kind of male nanny.

"Aw, he's just playing," Buddy said, carefully releasing Jesse, while Bo shrieked. Jesse immediately crawled down into the floorboards, under her mother's feet. She whimpered for a while.

We were several miles down the road before the import of Muddy's last remark hit me. He had said the authorities might get him, and they also might get T.R.

"Why would they get T.R.?" I asked. Fort Worth's modest skyline had just come into view.

"Because she's a big criminal," Muddy said. "Ain't you even told your daddy about your crimes, T.R.?"

T.R. remained inscrutable, deep behind her shades.

"A criminal, really?" Godwin said. The thought

327

that T.R. might be a criminal brought him out of his sulk. Criminals had always excited him.

"T.R., tell me what he means," I said. I felt wrong, asking such a question in front of a crowd, but I also felt anxious, suddenly. I had been rather complacently congratulating myself for handling the chaos in the car so casually—it seemed to me my ability to exist in close proximity to other humans was improving by leaps and bounds. But now, despite the proximity of a good many other humans, I became horribly anxious and couldn't contain my anxiety. I had to know what Muddy meant.

"Oh, T.R.'s a lot bigger criminal than me," Muddy said nastily. He was getting revenge for having been made to leave his movie.

I waited. I didn't want to ask T.R. again what Muddy meant. Up to that point in the drive I had been feeling rather good. I didn't have a headache and I was even rather calm, despite the presence of two children and six adults, including me, in the car. The mess and noise had not so far produced intolerable stress. Then Muddy dropped his bombshell, and intolerable stress made a comeback. There was a timpani roll in my temples as the blood vessels began to suck in blood. The mess and noise became immediately less tolerable. I felt as if I was in a riot rather than in a car; I wished I could just stop and ask everyone to step out except T.R. and Jesse. The latter, a refugee look in her eye, still sat on the floorboards, quietly chewing on a road map of Arkansas. The Little

Rock-Hot Springs area had already been badly mulched.

"She's eating Arkansas," I said, mainly to test my voice.

T.R. reached down and picked Jesse up. She faced me for a moment but didn't lower her shades.

"I been in a little trouble once or twice," she said.

"Little trouble," Muddy chortled. "Little trouble. I'd say that's a pretty good little understatement."

T.R. began to sing "Rockabye Baby" to Jesse. She did not elaborate.

11

Picking up passport applications took only two minutes, but getting the passport photographs almost destroyed us all. The thought of facing a photographer—even one as neutral as a passport photographer—caused an outbreak of vanity in both Buddy and Gladys. Buddy suddenly decided he wanted to look his best and went off to buy a necktie; Gladys decided she didn't like her eye shadow and went off in search of some she liked better.

"It's just a passport photograph," I pleaded.

"I hate the way I look on my driver's license," Gladys said. "This is my chance to do better."

Both left and both got lost. Fort Worth, a city

less than one hundred miles from where they had lived all their lives, was as foreign to them as São Paulo. An hour passed with no sign of either of them. T.R., Muddy, and the kids had long since been photographed. The photographer had to plead long and hard with T.R. before she would take off her sunglasses.

"They're going to want to see your eyes," he explained.

"I don't see why," T.R. said. "I guess I'm the one who decides who gets to see my eyes."

"Well, ma'am, not if you plan to go abroad," the photographer said.

"Just take off your dumb glasses," Muddy said.

"Fuck you," T.R. said. "And I'll tell you something else, Muddy—you're never gettin' to see nothin' else, ever."

"Why not?" Muddy asked, convinced—and also alarmed—by this threat.

"Because you can't keep your big mouth shut," T.R. said.

She eventually took off her sunglasses but still managed to look like an international terrorist in her pictures, as bitter and sullen-looking as any dues-paying member of the Bader-Meinhof gang.

Meanwhile, Bo suddenly developed a fever. Within minutes it was raging. T.R., from feeling his forehead, reckoned it to be in the vicinity of one hundred and four. Bo squirmed, whined, and abruptly vomited up a great many partially digested Crayolas.

Jesse immediately made friends with the photographer, a skinny, lonely-looking man, who informed her that he had a little girl just her age. Then he made the mistake of leaving her in his chair for a moment while he went to position a family of missionaries who were about to depart for Lesotho. Jesse reached for a lens cap, fell out of the chair, and split her forehead. Godwin, who reached her first, got a good deal of blood on his hands; as soon as he noticed the blood he became glassy-eyed, slumped against a wall, and fainted.

"Did L.J. just die?" T.R. asked, as Jesse shrieked and bled and Bo writhed and produced an occasional gobbet of Crayola.

"He's just one of those people who faint at the sight of blood," I said, fanning Godwin with a copy of *Newsweek*.

The missionary family looked as if they would be happy to leave us and get on with life in Lesotho.

Somehow T.R. and Muddy and I got the rest of us in the car, Jesse bleeding, Bo heaving, Godwin wobbling, and raced off to the emergency room. T.R. summoned her capacity for command and marched us past a dozen or so sufferers, most of whom looked so locked into the deep apathy of emergency rooms that they didn't seem to notice.

"If my babies die I'm suing you for millions," T.R. informed a perfectly nice doctor, who was so surprised by her vehemence that he did nothing but blink. Jesse shrieked so loudly when the doctor began to stitch up her gash that Muddy got a little faint himself and had to retreat to the waiting room to watch TV while T.R. and I held her down. Then the doctor, just to show T.R. that he was enthusiastic about his work, decided to pump Bo's stomach, in case he had consumed something more lethal than Crayolas. Bo fought so hard that I began to feel a little faint myself, but T.R. stoically chewed gum, held him down, and occasionally even grinned at me.

"How you doin' over there, Daddy?" she asked. "Real life's a lot more fun than writing TV shows, ain't it?"

"Sure," I said weakly. I was being careful not to make excessive claims.

A few minutes later, that part of our life over, we emerged into the sunlight of the hospital parking lot. Godwin, unfairly, it seemed to him, had been given no drugs, a fact that made him bitter.

"Fucking puritanical country," he complained. "If this had happened in Rangoon I could have had opium."

"Only you would think a thought like that," I said. "Fort Worth's very different from Rangoon."

"Yes, and more's the pity," Godwin said.

T.R. gave him some marijuana as soon as we got into the car, but it didn't lift his spirits very much. T.R.'s own spirits seemed to be bouncy, even rollicking, but she wasn't getting much support from the rest of us in the car. Bo was listless; it seemed they had sucked his aggression out with the contents of his stomach. Jesse, her head bandaged, looked like a tiny war victim; she immediately crept back to her position on the floorboards and sat staring into space. Although I knew she wasn't badly hurt, the sight of her staring into space, so small yet so forlorn, made me want to weep. Meanwhile, Muddy had sunk into a depression of his own. While in it he made the large mistake of saying once too often that he wished he'd stayed in jail.

T.R., who was driving, turned and gave him the finger. Then she whipped into a gas station, jumped out, got directions to the jail, and took us there. She slammed on the brakes right in front of it, startling two cops who had been leaning on their police cars, gossiping.

"Okay, Muddy, you're gettin' your wish," T.R. said. "Get out and turn yourself in. I imagine they'll take you back to Houston in a day or two."

"Aw, T.R., I never meant it," Muddy said. "I've just got this low feeling in me right now."

T.R. turned in her seat and scrutinized him for a moment. Her scrutiny seemed pitiless to me, and I believe Muddy also found it pitiless. He seemed to be about to obey her stern order when T.R. switched her pitiless look to the two cops, who immediately wilted under it and got into their respective cars.

T.R. winked at me.

"Perk up, Muddy, but just keep in mind that you're living on borrowed time," she said. "All of you gloom buckets are living on borrowed time.

Here we've got a pretty day and we're in town for a change and nobody's dead."

"We don't have many drugs, though," Godwin pointed out.

"Shut up, L.J.," T.R. said. "Here's the deal. If you think you can get yourselves to looking alive, then we'll go find Buddy and Gladys and go swimming out at that water wonderland we went to while Daddy was sick. If you can't cheer up I'm dumping you all out and you're on your own."

"On our own?" Muddy said, horrified. "What'll you be doin' while we're on our own?"

"I'll be gettin' laid if I can manage it," T.R. said merrily. "And if I can't manage the big number one I'll be dancin' or drinkin' tequila or cutting up as best I can. What I ain't gonna do is stay down in the dumps all day just to be one of the crowd."

"Swim," Jesse said distinctly, startling us all. Jesse had never said "swim" before.

"What did I just hear you say?" T.R. asked her daughter.

Such a direct question was too much for Jesse —she hid her face in her hands.

"Okay, if Jesse can learn a new word, the rest of you can cheer up," T.R. said.

We did cheer up, buoyed by her easy exuberance. Buddy and Gladys were soon found, sitting on a bus bench, Buddy wearing his new necktie, Gladys wearing an overabundance of eye shadow. Like Jesse, they too had a refugee look; they were so convinced we had abandoned them that it took them a while to accept their reversal of fortune.

Within an hour we were all at the water amusement park in Arlington, city of cul-de-sacs. There we disported ourselves like porpoises, all except Jesse, who had to content herself with wading in the tot's pool; I waded with her, under strict instructions not to let her get her bandage wet.

"Swim, swim, swim!" Jesse shrieked, proud of her new word.

T.R. and Muddy dived off every diving board and slid down every slide, only stopping occasionally to yell at one another or smooch. Muddy's spirits had risen like an elevator, and Buddy and Gladys weren't doing badly, either. They shot an artificial rapid in giant inner tubes and stayed in the pool at the bottom a long time, quietly bumping inner tubes and talking.

Godwin watched them ruefully.

He walked over to the kiddie pool. "Daniel, go make them get out before they fall in love," he said. He was still in a sulk because Fort Worth was so unlike Rangoon.

I thought it might be that Buddy and Gladys were falling in love, but I had no intention of interfering. Keeping Jesse from getting her bandage wet was a full-time job, anyway.

"Godwin, leave them alone," I said. "Why shouldn't they fall in love?" I said. "Maybe they'll find a little happiness."

"I can't bear your optimism," he said. "More likely they'll find despair, as I have. Besides, I can't bear the thought of them fucking. Shut your eyes and try to imagine those two bodies in flagrante."

"Godwin, they just have normal bodies," I said. "Not much worse than yours and mine—if any worse. I don't think you've found despair, either. I think you've had a lot of fun."

"I've found substantial desolation," he said. Then he noticed T.R. as she walked dripping out of the wave pool, and a light came into his eyes. Other eyes than ours were watching T.R. too. Her radiance at that moment cast a light that seemed to gladden all who saw it. Several couples who were lounging by the wave pool, some on towels and some in beach chairs, some skinny and some dumpy, all more or less sunburned, all looked at T.R. and smiled, but T.R. seemed oblivious to the aura her own beauty cast. She waited casually until Muddy caught up with her, and the two went off to get a hot dog.

"Swim, swim," Jesse said.

"What a magnificent girl," Godwin said. "My Aphrodite. I intend to propose soon."

"Propose what?" I inquired. "You better be careful what you propose to my daughter."

"Marriage, of course," Godwin said. "Sometimes sudden proposals work. In any case, I have nothing to lose."

I had bought Jesse a rubber duck. While I was trying to figure out if Godwin was serious, a little boy came over and tried to take Jesse's duck away from her. Jesse started to run away but instead

336

went plop in the water. Before I could intervene, the little boy jumped on top of her and grabbed the duck. Jesse squealed her terrible squeal; the little boy's mother took the duck away from him and gave it back to Jesse, but the damage was done: Jesse's bandage was very wet.

"Now we're in for it," Godwin said. "I may have to delay my proposal for a month or two because of your incompetence as a grandparent."

I was unnerved myself at the thought of what T.R. was going to say, but she was neither surprised nor critical.

"You can't really expect a little girl to go swimming and not get her bandage wet," she said. "Hand over some of those hundred-dollar bills you're so handy with and we'll just overlook this. Muddy and I want to go buy everything in sight."

Everything in sight turned out to be a car trunkful of heterogenous rubber pool animals for our own pool. The pièce de résistance was a hippo, but there were also several fish, a sea snake, and a large, inflatable floating mattress.

"What do you think we're gonna do on that inflatable mattress as soon as we get home, Muddy?" T.R. asked, as we were bearing down on Jacksboro at around ninety-five miles per hour. She was at the wheel, wearing one of the several new pairs of sunglasses she had bought. None of us had bothered to dress; the combination of packed bodies and wet bathing suits made the car smell like the inside of a washing machine.

337

"I couldn't guess in ten thousand years," Muddy said.

"Well, we are, anyway, even if you can't guess," T.R. said. "I can barely wait to try out that mattress."

"Don't the rest of you dare look, though," she said, sweeping the car with a sunglassed gaze.

"Aw, T.R.," Muddy said, abashed.

"We should have bought us a couple of them big inner tubes, Gladys," Buddy said. "It's good relaxation, floating around in inner tubes." He gave her a coltish look.

"They'd be too big for the pool," Gladys said. "We'd have to both get in one. One might fit in that pool."

Then, at the thought of what she'd just implied—the two of them sharing an inner tube—Gladys looked twice as embarrassed as Muddy and began to talk insane baby talk to Jesse, who wasn't impressed.

Neither was Godwin impressed. "I wish we'd brought more drugs," he said.

12

That night Muddy tried to watch the rest of *Berlin Alexanderplatz*. T.R. and I were watching it with him. But the two of them had spent much of the late afternoon in strictly enforced privacy on the new pool mattress, and whatever they did had left Muddy so exhausted that even his new idol, Fassbinder, couldn't keep him awake. As soon as it became clear that he was very soundly asleep T.R. turned off the TV.

"I guess I tuckered him out," T.R. said, stroking his hair. "Muddy's a pretty sweet little guy when all is said and done, 'specially done."

"I'm still worried about that trouble you were in," I said. She seemed contented, and I had been waiting for just such a moment of content to press my question. Even so, I pressed it casually, and as gently as possible.

"What trouble?" she asked.

"The trouble you said you got in once or twice."

"Oh, yeah," she said. "I got caught with one hundred and ten pounds of marijuana in the trunk of my car. I was hauling it for Big Pa."

"Your grandfather was a dope dealer?" I said, incredulous. "I thought he was some kind of minister before he became a car dealer."

"He'd stop and preach at the drop of a hat, all right," T.R. said. "It just got harder and harder to find churches that would let him preach. The minute they let him in the door he'd start gettin' people pregnant."

"I still never dreamed he was a dope dealer, though," I said.

T.R. gave me a light dig with her elbow, a gentle comment on my credulity.

"You shouldn't believe everything Mexican detectives tell you," she said. "Big Pa wasn't always a dope dealer, though. He only started selling dope after he got too old to make a good living stealing cars. Big Pa had just about a genius for stealing cars—least he did at one time. I bet half the cars that ever got stolen in Dallas he resold. That's how I met Earl Dee, or did I tell you that?"

"You haven't talked that much about Mr. Dee," I said.

"That's because of Muddy," T.R. whispered. "Muddy's about as jealous as you can get and he don't welcome *no* mention of E.D. Sound asleep as Muddy is, I still feel like I better whisper when I say that name."

"Did E.D. steal cars too?" I asked.

"Nope, E.D. wouldn't have been caught dead actually stealing a car," T.R. said. "Too tame for him. Earl Dee's happiest when he's pointin' guns at people. But he did drive for Big Pa for a while. If Big Pa had stolen a Cadillac he needed driven to Houston or San Antonio, sometimes Earl Dee could be bribed to do the job."

"Bribed with money?"

"Mostly Big Pa bribed him with dope," she said, watching Muddy closely to see if he showed any signs of waking. "But I was getting grown up by that time, and pretty soon Big Pa started bribing him with me."

Though I tried to keep my reactions neutral I'm sure I looked a little startled at this revelation.

"Shoot, I was happy to be the bribe," T.R. said, her eyes alight. Then Muddy twitched a few times and rolled on his side; T.R. watched him nervously. She leaned over and put her mouth

340

close to my ear—her breath smelled like chewing gum.

"Let's go outside," she said. "I get nervous as a cat talking about this around Muddy."

We stopped in the kitchen and mixed a pitcher of margaritas. Gladys and Buddy were watching TV and chatting. They stopped chatting as T.R. and I came through with our pitchers, but I heard them resume as we went out the door.

There was a full, white moon. I sipped a margarita, but T.R. drank most of the pitcher. She drank margaritas as if she were drinking Dr. Pepper, and then chewed the pulp of the limes we had squeezed into the tequila.

"How old were you when you got caught?" I asked.

"Oh, sixteen, the first time," T.R. said casually. "I wasn't hauling marijuana that time—that time it was just pills."

"Illegal pills?"

"Methamphetamines, 'bout four thousand of them," she said, cleaning out a lime. "All them truck drivers and roughnecks in East Texas got to have their pills or they'd fall asleep on the job and have wrecks and stuff. Big Ma worked in a pharmacy then. Big Pa just started dealing pills as a little sideline. Big Ma stole 'em by the thousands and Big Pa bribed his drivers with them. Earl Dee was a big pill-head or we might never have met."

She paused and looked at me thoughtfully.

"You sure you really wanta know all this stuff?"

she asked. "Maybe you oughtn't even to bother about knowing it. It's over now. If it's gonna upset you to know your little girl was a criminal, I just won't tell you."

"No, please tell me," I said. "Too much of your life's a blank to me. I think you're wonderful, no matter what you did. Please go on and fill in the blank."

T.R. laughed. "It wasn't no blank from my end," she said. "They let me off for the pills, I was just a juvenile and didn't have no record. I got a year suspended. It was really Earl Dee who was selling them pills, but I was so in love with him then I'd have gone to jail for life if he'd asked me to."

"Understandable," I said, but the word was just a form of punctuation. I couldn't remember having been in love so much that I would contemplate going to jail for life.

"Oh, yeah, we was hot as little pistols, me and Earl Dee back then," T.R. said. "Every single minute I wasn't with him I was thinking about him. To me it was ten times more exciting to run around being a criminal with Earl Dee than to date one of them rich boys that was always sniffing around me. Shoot, I'd get bored looking at a rich boy. But I sure didn't get bored with Earl Dee. All I could think about was helping him live his life of crime any way I could. He was supposed to haul that hundred and ten pounds of marijuana, but we'd been in our little trailer house screwing for three or four days, and he decided he'd rather stay home and watch TV. I barely got to the city limits before about fifty cops stopped me. Earl Dee found out it was happening and caught a ride to El Paso with a trucker. That was the last I seen of him till I got out of jail."

"He doesn't sound too gallant," I said.

T.R. shrugged. "Earl Dee wouldn't know what the word meant," she said. "I got caught and he didn't—that's the way criminals are."

"What happened with the law that time?" I asked.

"It wasn't no fun, that time," T.R. admitted. "I was looking at five to ten, because I wouldn't cooperate. All I could think about was how horny I'd get in five years if I didn't get no sack time with Earl Dee. But Big Pa bribed the assistant D.A. and I only got three years. I just served eight months, but it was still a good long time to do without."

T.R. paused, evidently a little depressed by her memories. "By the time I got out, Earl Dee had done so much cocaine he couldn't get it up anyway," she said. "Talk about disappointment. It was round about then that I met Muddy—we had the same probation officer."

"That sounds like a lucky encounter," I said. "I like Muddy."

T.R. didn't seem too impressed with her luck just at that moment.

"God, it's boring out here in the country," she said. "I'd go commit a crime right now if it wasn't so far to any place where you could commit crimes.

Looks like you'd go crazy sitting around out here with L.J. and Gladys. There's nothing to do out here but fuck, and you don't even have a girlfriend.

"At least you don't have one very handy that I can see," she said, suddenly diffident. She was fearful, I think, that she might have hurt my feelings.

"Nope, I don't have one handy," I said.

I felt she was watching me closely, and the thought made me a little nervous. She was my daughter—I wanted to be open with her, but at the same time I was frightened that she might ask me about my love life, or lack of it.

"Speak up, Daddy," T.R. said. "I told you about my criminal activities. It wouldn't hurt you to tell me about your girlfriends. I see their pictures on the wall, and I hear you talking to them on the phone, but they sure don't seem to hang around much."

"They're like you," I said. "City girls. They'd be bored to death around here."

"Well," T.R. said, a little restlessly, "you ain't nailed down, you know. If they won't come to you, you might just have to go to them once in a while."

"I do go see them," I said.

"I thought you said you hadn't even started your car for six months before you came to get me," she reminded me. "If you haven't started your car in six months, you must not be seeing your girlfriends too often."

344

"No, I haven't," I admitted cautiously.

T.R. scooted over beside me and put her arms around me. "I'm getting blue just from thinking what I'm thinking," she said.

"What are you thinking?"

"That you don't really have a girlfriend," she said.

"You're a smart girl," I said.

"How come you don't?"

"Beats me," I said.

"It's because you ain't tryin'," she said. "Of course it wouldn't hurt if you lost a little weight, but you're rich and famous—you could get a girlfriend.

"Besides, you're nice," she said, hugging me. Then she quietly started crying.

"Don't cry, sweetie," I said. "My lack of a girlfriend is not exactly a global tragedy."

"What ain't?" she gulped.

"That I don't have a girlfriend," I said. "Sometimes men my age just don't quite get around to having girlfriends."

"Bull!" T.R. said, jumping up. Her tears quickly turned to rage. "You just sit around on this stupid fuckin' hill, talkin' on the phone all day. No wonder nothing ever happens to you. Shoot, taking kids to the dentist beats living like you live. At least you get to hear somebody scream. I feel like I wanta scream right now."

"Well, you can," I said, horrified that I'd angered her.

"No, I can't scream, Jesse gets nightmares

when I scream, I have to learn to hold it down," she said.

"I've had quite a few girlfriends in my life," I assured her. "It's not that serious that I don't happen to have one right now."

"Let's go to France tomorrow," she said. "The only hope I see is if I get you moving right now."

"Honey, I haven't even sent in the passport applications yet," I said.

"I went to Mexico twice without no passport," T.R. said. "I bet France would let us in if we all just showed up in Paris, or wherever their airport is. Jesse and I can charm our way in just about anywhere."

She sat down beside me again and hugged me even tighter. I could feel her quivering. I held her as tightly as I could; she began to sob again, loud, gulping sobs.

"I knew I should have called you up sooner," she said. "I knew I ought never to have waited. I should have called you up last year. I let that fuckin' Muddy Box talk me out of it."

"Why would Muddy talk you out of it?" I asked, curious.

"Because he's a dickhead," T.R. said. "He was so in love he didn't want to share me with my own daddy. Now I waited too long, and you're all sad. I don't know what to do."

She was clinging to me, trembling, a look of tight pain on her young face. I held her and whispered "It's okay, it's okay," but suddenly I felt like crying myself, from confusion, from T.R.'s

346

half-formed accusation. I started to say, Don't be sad, I'm not doing anything—but even in my confusion I realized that the fact that I wasn't doing anything was why she *was* sad.

"I hate it, hate it, I hate it!" T.R. said. "I finally get my daddy, and now, look. It's all too late, everything's always been too late my whole life."

"No, it's not too late," I said. "Why would it be too late? We'll get the passports in a few days and head for France. I promise you I'll get a girl-friend right away. Maybe I'll get five or six."

T.R. just shook her head and shrugged hope-lessly.

"That ain't gonna happen," she said. "I'm on probation and Muddy's a jailbreaker. They'll look on their fuckin' computers and come and get us both. They'll catch us and handcuff us right there in the airport. They catch a lot of people in air-ports, that's why I'd rather go someplace we could just drive to."

The possibility of going someplace we could drive to had occurred to me also. I hadn't men-tioned it because I didn't want to make T.R. any more discouraged than she already was.

"It doesn't really have to be France," I said. "It could be Mexico or Canada. We could all just pile in the car and drive. It could be Colorado. It could be Minnesota. It could be New York or New Orleans."

"Okay," she said in the subdued, lifeless tone that a child uses when it gives up.

"Okay, Daddy," she said in the same tone.

"T.R., don't sound like that," I pleaded. I felt horrible—felt I had taken away her guts, or something.

"Don't sound like that," I repeated.

"Why can't I?" she asked. "It's how you sound. If you're gonna sound that way, so am I. Maybe it's the only way I can stay with you."

I was beginning to have a sense of *déjà vu*. Somewhere back along the road of my life I had had a similar, indeed an identical, conversation. Some other disappointed woman had vowed to stay with me by lowering her flame to my level, in effect. It might have been Jeanie—I couldn't be sure. But the sense of *déjà vu* was not pleasant; it was a pain in the breast, as if a lump of long-undigested love had risen to lodge once more in my throat. It was all I could do to breathe, and I knew that anything I said would be wrong, yet I also felt that I had to say something. Indeed, I knew even from my half-obscured memory of the analogous conversation from the past that whatever I found to say would be *precisely* wrong, would turn the woman's dull sadness into bitter anger or blistering contempt—and maybe that was the point.

"I don't know why you would even want to stay with me," I said.

T.R. looked stunned for a second and then whipped her elbow into my side as hard as she could—months later it was determined that the jab cracked a rib.

"Oh, get fucked!" she said, jumping up. "No wonder you don't have no girlfriend if you don't have no more feelings than to say a horrible thing like that. All I want to do is love you. Ain't you even gonna let me?"

"Of course, of course, I didn't mean to make you feel that way," I said. Even as I said it, I felt those same words echoing endlessly off the walls of the long tunnel of my past: I didn't mean to make you feel that way, Jill, I didn't mean to make you feel that way, Jeanie. I had never meant to make a single woman feel that way; and yet that way was exactly how I had made every one of them feel.

"You better just be careful!" T.R. said, her eyes blazing. "I ain't got impeccable taste, remember? I won't stand for just anything. You better start acting more like a daddy real quick or I'll take my babies and I'll be outa here—I won't be waitin' around for no passport, neither!"

Then, without giving me time to say anything else—if I had, it would have been even more precisely wrong, I have no doubt—she picked up the empty margarita pitcher and went into the house.

13

I spent the night wondering why in fifty years I had not gained even the most elemental sense of what to say—or what not to say—to women. The thing that stuck in my mind was that T.R. had threatened to leave, and I soon convinced myself that she *would* leave. The thought made me so depressed that I couldn't even get a migraine. A headache had been approaching, but it soon realized that it was going to be so far out-classed by my depression as to make the trip not worth it. I didn't have a trace of migraine, but my depression was world-class.

As soon as it became morning in New York, I called Jeanie, an early riser. I had already given her several reports on T.R., to all of which she listened avidly but not uncritically. Invariably I was asked to describe what T.R. was wearing on a particular occasion; then I would be interrogated in fine detail on emotional matters; what T.R. said, how she phrased it, what T.R. felt, and what I was doing about it. There was no doubt as to whose side Jeanie was on. From the first she made it clear that she was on T.R.'s side; if there was doubt about a particular line of action, T.R., not me, would get the benefit of that doubt.

This time I didn't so much wake her up as bring her to attention. She was sitting with her coffee looking out on Central Park. From the tone of her hello I could tell that it must not be the best of times, that her outlook for the day was not really an optimistic outlook; but at the sound of my voice she immediately rose from her drift and raised her antenna. Just thinking of her raising her antenna made me nervous and hesitant, because Jeanie's receiving equipment—her brain and her intuitive faculties—picked up far too much, even when she wasn't bothering to tune it, particularly. Even when she wasn't paying close attention she heard more than I really wanted her to hear, and when she *was* paying attention, as she was now, she not only heard more than I wanted her to hear, she heard more than I knew I was saying.

That was one reason I loved Jeanie so much: she would hear more than I knew I was saying, and she would be forgiving. There might be some snap and crackle before we got to the forgiveness, but the forgiveness always came.

"I've had a terrible fight with T.R.," I said at once.

"What did you do to her?" Jeanie asked.

"Nothing. I didn't do anything to her, it was just kind of a disagreement," I said. "Why would you assume I did something to her?"

"Because I can tell you're ashamed of yourself," Jeanie said—her receiver was obviously working well. "If you're ashamed of yourself it means you did something to your daughter."

"Well, I upset her but I didn't mean to," I said.

"What'd it start with?" Jeanie asked.

"I guess it started with the fact that I don't really have a girlfriend right now," I said.

Jeanie didn't say anything. A little silence grew into a big silence. Nothing made me nervous quicker than Jeanie falling silent on the phone.

"I wish you'd talk," I said. "Is it such a crime not to have a girlfriend?"

"That depends on why you don't have one and what you're planning to do about it," Jeanie said.

There was a pause. I was beginning to feel very disorganized mentally, and also very distraught.

"In certain circumstances, not having a girl-friend can be just about the worst of crimes," Jeanie said. "Not the absolute worst, but close."

"Well, I don't have any idea what circumstances you mean, in this case," I said.

"The circumstances would be if you had a perfectly nice woman available to you and you did absolutely nothing about it—how's that for being precise about the circumstances?" Jeanie said.

"I guess that's deadly precision," I admitted. "So now that I'm dead, what next?"

"Ordinarily there would be nothing next, but then we both know we'd rather be complicated than ordinary, so let's pass on that point," she said. "Just forget that I practiced my deadly precision and tell me everything you said when you upset T.R."

"Well, let's see," I began, trying to remember at what point in the conversation I realized I had upset her.

"Hey, don't start inventing it," Jeanie warned. "No invention. Truth is the only thing that's gonna save you. What did you say and what did she say?

"I'm gonna know immediately if you lie, remember," she added. "I'm gonna know it, so this one time you better not lie."

She sounded awfully alert, which meant there was no point in even attempting to lie. Sometimes when Jeanie was sleepy or distracted I could sneak a few small lies past her, although generally her intuition caught them and retained them somewhere in the great memory disk of her brain. A day or two later she'd call them up, examine them, and call to tell me exactly what I'd lied about.

This time I described our day and when I came to the evening and the conversation by the pool, I told her, as accurately as I could remember, every single word that T.R. and I had said to one another.

Retelling it upset me. I remembered how T.R.'s face had filled with pain. I felt terrible for having caused my daughter such pain. My voice, in recalling it, began to crack. I sniffed a few times and stopped talking. All of a sudden I began to cry. It seemed too sad; I regretted my emotional ineptness too much.

Jeanie waited me out, but this time I didn't feel any threat in the silence.

"I want to meet this girl," she said eventually. To my surprise her own voice was shaky and tearful.

"You can meet her, of course you can meet her," I said. "I'd love for you to meet her. I'm so proud of her I can hardly stand it."

"I'm glad you said that, Danny," Jeanie said. "You should be proud of her. She cracked the wall, and I never thought I'd live to see it cracked."

"What are you talking about?" I said. "What wall?"

"The one you built around you," Jeanie said. "Don't say it wasn't there. It was there. I tried to crack it but I didn't have the confidence, you know? What happened is, it cracked me, but that's okay, I'm working around my crack pretty well. But you were dying behind your wall, and you're lucky to have a daughter who had the guts to crack it. I hope she smashes it to fucking smithereens and you never have another peaceful day in your whole fucking life, Mr. Deck!"

Slam! went the phone.

I was horrified. What had gone wrong? I thought I'd better wait five minutes and call her back, but after about two minutes she called me back.

"I apologize for my outburst," she said, although she didn't sound remorseful, particularly.

"I don't know that it was an outburst exactly," I said.

"Right, it was only the trailer for an outburst," Jeanie said. "I'm putting the rest of the outburst in trust for you. The next time you provoke me I'll run the whole outburst for you, how do you think you'll like that?"

"I doubt that I'll like it much but I'm sure I'll deserve it," I said.

"Oh, fuck," Jeanie said. "When are you going to learn to stop pleading guilty? Your miserable little guilty pleas just make me angrier. There's never been any doubt about your guilt, so spare me your contrition."

"What if my contrition is all I have to offer?" I inquired.

"Offer it to somebody else," Jeanie said firmly. "It won't get you a peanut-butter sandwich at my

354

place. Stupid men and their stupid contrition are not my favorite things in life."

"I imagine T.R. feels the same way," I observed.

"Of course she feels the same way," Jeanie said. "She sounds a lot like me, only tougher."

"I hope she's not tougher," I said. "I hope no one's tougher. But if she is, how am I going to make up with her?"

"Not by talking," Jeanie said. "You may have to actually show some initiative. Women get tired of supplying all the initiative, you know. You said she likes to dance. Did you ever think of taking her dancing?"

"Jeanie, it's six in the morning," I reminded her. "It's kind of unusual to go dancing at six in the morning, and besides I really can't dance."

"Okay, spurn my suggestion," Jeanie said. "I'd be wildly happy if someone called me *right* now and offered to take me dancing *right* now, even if it is a little early. Who wants to look out the window and talk to stupid men on the phone every morning of their lives? I'd rather be dancing."

There was a very long silence.

"Hey, don't be sad," I said.

Jeanie didn't reply.

"I think you're a wonderful and beautiful genius," I said. "I think you've given me the perfect suggestion. I think I'll get my daughter up and take her dancing."

"Good, that would be a very advanced act,"

355

Jeanie said, but the clear note of sadness was in her voice.

"I wish we could end this conversation on an up note instead of a down note," I said. "You've helped me a lot. You always help me a lot."

"Bye, Danny," Jeanie said.

14

T.R. was sitting in the kitchen watching early-morning TV with Gladys on the midget television set Gladys kept on the kitchen table. They were both smoking. Jesse sat on the floor playing with an egg beater. I was surprised to see the egg beater. One whole side of the kitchen counter was covered with blenders; why would anyone in my house ever need to beat an egg?

"Where'd you get that egg beater?" I asked. "I haven't seen an egg beater in years."

Neither answered or even turned her head to look at me. The provenance of the egg beater held not the slightest interest for them, although Jesse had already learned to work it and was making the little blades go round and round.

Out the back window I could see Buddy and Bo cleaning fish.

"Hey, they caught some fish," I said. "Are we going to have fish for breakfast?"

"Swim," Jesse said immediately. Her brain had instantly connected fish-water-swim. She dropped the egg beater and began to take off her gown.

"Swim," she said again.

"No, we ain't goin' swimmin', keep your gown on, Jesse," T.R. said, in a monotone.

"Swim!" Jesse insisted—there was a threat of squeal in the way she said the word. She continued to undress. T.R. reached down and swatted her twice on her behind. Jesse looked stricken.

"I told you to keep your gown on," T.R. said.

For a moment Jesse tried not to cry, but the bitter injustice of life was too much for her; her face collapsed and she flung herself, sobbing, into Gladys's lap.

"Well, mind your momma, honey," Gladys said, picking Jesse up.

No one as yet had taken the slightest notice of me.

"Would anyone like to go dancing?" I asked, feeling profoundly silly. The prevailing mood in the kitchen did not suggest dancing.

T.R. finally looked at me. "Come again?" she said.

"I just wondered if anyone wanted to go dancing," I said. Repeating such a ridiculous suggestion made me feel even more foolish than I had felt the first time. Why had I let Jeanie talk me into doing something so absurd? Go dancing at six in the morning? I was not a man known for his dancing skills, either.

But T.R.'s face brightened as if I had turned on a light. She immediately stood up.

"Shoot, just let me put on my dancin' shoes," she said. "I'll be ready before you know it."

"I don't know where we'll find a place to dance at this hour," I said. The immediate success of my suggestion made me a little apprehensive.

"There's always Aunt Jimmie's," Gladys reminded me.

"Swim," Jesse gulped. I believe she was merely trying to reassert the reasonableness of her wish, but then the hopelessness of the situation overwhelmed her, and she burst into tears once more.

"Don't take it so hard, honey, it's temporary," Gladys said. She was looking out the backdoor, watching Buddy and Bo clean fish. It was not hard to tell she had her eye on Buddy.

Before I could reflect on what Glady's new interest might mean for the stability of the household, T.R. reappeared. Her energy level had risen so rapidly while she was dressing that my spacious kitchen seemed too small for her. Her eyes were already dancing; she radiated youth, health, mischief, sex. She had thrown on a skirt and a blouse, both red, and proceeded to dance her way around the kitchen table.

"Boy, I love to dance," she said.

At the sight of her beautiful mother dancing, Jesse forgot her woe. She gazed at her mom with forgiving wonder.

On the way to the highway we saw a small cloud of dust approaching, preceded by an ancient blue Volkswagen. It was Godwin, of course, returning from a nocturnal hitchhiker sweep of the surrounding countries. I pulled over to the side and stopped and waited.

"Good idea," T.R. said. "Let's take L.J. He ain't the world's best dancer, but he gets out there and tries."

Godwin was not in his teak-plantation mode this morning. He looked as if he had spent the night wallowing in fetid drains. He seemed half blind and kept peering at us through cupped hands, as if he were not quite sure who we were.

"We're going dancing," I said. "You can be invited if you want to."

Godwin considered his invitation for a few seconds, blinking. The delay was short, but even so, it was more than T.R. was in the mood to tolerate. She hit the horn and held it down for twenty seconds. Godwin, who probably had a fairly advanced hangover, held his ears and writhed as if he were being tortured.

"Get in if you're coming," T.R. said, when she let up on the horn. "And if you ain't going you might as well drive that little blue car off a cliff because I ain't never speaking to you again."

Godwin immediately ditched his Volkswagen and got in with us.

"Sorry, sorry, sorry," he said. "It's my eyes, you see."

"What'd you get in them, cum?" T.R. asked happily, offering him a stick of gum.

"Mace," Godwin said gloomily. "I really must make a point of avoiding Oklahoma. They Mace people at random up there."

"Who Maced you and why?" I asked.

"A service-station attendant Maced me for no

reason whatsoever," Godwin said. "I was merely chatting him up a bit; he was quite a good-looking young chap. He came over with a bottle of something and I thought perhaps he was going to clean my windshield. I was prepared to tip him lavishly, and what did he do but Mace me savagely.

"My dear, you look ravishing," he said to T.R., as we bumped on toward the highway. "You're as beautiful as Helen."

"Helen who?" T.R. asked. "Is she one of Daddy's so-called girlfriends?"

"Oh, no, Helen of Troy," Godwin said, and proceeded to try to explain the Trojan War. T.R., who couldn't have cared less, turned the stereo up as far as it would go and put in a heavy metal tape.

"Hers was the face that launched a thousand ships," Godwin screeched into the music.

"I don't want to hear about it, I get sick in boats," T.R. said.

It didn't take us long to reach Aunt Jimmie's Lounge, a weather-beaten county-line roadhouse with a large jukebox, a small dance floor, and a few tables where one could eat if one chose, or simply sit and drink beer and brood silently if that was one's mood—and it often *was* the mood of the roughnecks, cowboys, truckers, hay haulers, tool pushers and coyote trappers who frequented that lonely corner of the county. The roadhouse sat on the bleak gray prairies, and things were just as bleak inside as out. One felt that not a dime's worth of paint had been expended on the building since it was built, and it had been built in the thirties.

Not a dime's worth had been expended on Aunt Jimmie either; she sat by the cash register all day, smoking, reading the newspaper, and watching soap operas or whatever else offered on a blurry little black-and-white TV. People who had known Aunt Jimmie all their lives could not remember hearing her say anything. Service at the lounge was minimal. Her cooks—generally fortyish country women who were between marriages—never lasted long, but there was an endless supply of fortyish country women between marriages in that part of the country; Aunt Jimmie was rarely without a cook. Generally she also had a shaky, busted-up cowboy or retired roughneck as dishwasher, general factotum, and consort. Everyone had just called them boyfriends until Godwin came along, but he insisted that they were actually consorts. Efforts to make him explain the difference between a boyfriend and a consort proved fruitless. He may have known something none of the rest of us knew, though, for Aunt Jimmie seemed to like him and occasionally even let him clean up in her bathroom when he stumbled in from some particularly fetid roll in the drains.

T.R. marched right in, talked Aunt Jimmie out of a roll of quarters, and fed the roll hastily into the jukebox, punching in her selections as rapidly as if she were programming a computer.

I thought I might sit at a table, have a few cups of coffee, and contemplate dancing for a while, but T.R. would have none of that. She grabbed my hand and pulled me onto the dance floor immediately. Aunt Jimmie's jukebox was liberally sprinkled with golden oldies, but it was still a bit of a surprise to find myself, at that hour of the day, dancing to "The Tennessee Waltz," as sung by Tennessee Ernie Ford. I was a stumbling waltzer at best, but T.R. was a strong one and carried me with her. She put her head on my chest as we danced. I thought nothing of that until I felt a wetness seep through my shirt and realized she was crying.

"What's the matter?" I asked, alarmed. I tried to lift her chin but she dug her face tighter into my chest and kept on dancing.

We were, of course, the only couple on the dance floor. Godwin had gone into Aunt Jimmie's bathroom to clean up a bit. Aunt Jimmie was watching the morning news. There were three oil-field workers at one table, two dairy farmers at another table, and an old cowboy sitting in the corner, smoking and looking out at the gray land. No one seemed to think it odd that I was dancing with my glorious young daughter at six-thirty in the morning, or that she was hugging me and crying. There was something Balkan in the indifference of everyone in the bar to the fate of everyone else. The roughnecks looked bent, the dairy farmers defeated, the cowboy old and grizzled and sad. My troubles and T.R.'s didn't touch them; they were hard people in a hard place, so unconcerned about us that I didn't even feel embarrassed about my bad dancing. Aunt Jimmie's lounge might have been in Albania or some impoverished, rocky part of Greece for all the sympathy the customers showed for us or for one another.

"I wish I knew why you were crying," I whispered to T.R. She just hugged me and sniffed.

"It's okay, though," I assured her. "Cry if you want to."

The next song was by George Strait and was called "All My Exes Live in Texas."

"I'm glad that sad old waltz is over," T.R. said, flinging the last tear out of her eye as she picked up the beat. The beats got faster and faster as the songs she had chosen spun through the jukebox. I danced through six songs, by which time Godwin appeared, in his colonialist mode again, and danced several more with her, after which we all sat down and ate a huge breakfast. Then T.R. insisted on dancing again with me. The café was empty by then, all the customers having gone to work. Godwin sat at the counter and read Aunt Jimmie's paper while we danced.

"It's funny when you get your dream, ain't it?" T.R. said. "All through high school I'd watch other girls dancing with their daddies and I'd dream I'd dance with my own daddy some day."

"And now you have," I said.

T.R. looked me in the eye for a long time. Though she was dancing easily, her eyes seemed sad.

"Yep, now I have," she said.

"Don't you say nothin', Daddy," she added. "Please don't you say nothin'."

She didn't really have to warn me. One of the few things my strange life has taught me is not to try to talk away every sadness that a loved one shows you. I've tried that many times and only succeeded in driving the sadness deep as a nail into the loved one's heart.

With some effort I obeyed my daughter's injunction and kept silent. Song followed song, and we danced. T.R. soon put her face against my chest again—she danced and cried, cried and danced, through another whole roll of quarters, in Aunt Jimmie's empty café. Godwin finished his paper, got up, started to come out and cut in, took another look, thought better of it, and went to the car to take a nap. Aunt Jimmie sat at the counter, smoking and filing her nails. Old Walter Wafer, her current dishwasher and consort, took advantage of the morning lull to mop the floor. He tactfully mopped around us, and we danced. Wafer had scarcely finished when the early-lunch crowd began to file in, soon to be supplied with cheeseburgers, chicken-fried steaks, and beer. A little roughneck, tousleheaded and not yet resigned to Balkan disciplines, cast a glad eye at T.R. She caught the glance and marched right over to his table. Her spirits were definitely on the rise.

"Hey, how tall are you?" she asked.

The young roughneck was caught off guard by

the question; he looked shy and mumbled a measurement.

"That's tall enough, get up from there and dance with me," T.R. said. "I've just danced my poor old daddy to a frazzle."

I went to the bathroom. When I came out I saw that things were fine. The music was faster. T.R.'s skirt was whirling, her long legs were flashing, and even the stolidest dairy farmers were having trouble keeping their eyes on their steaks.

15

T.R. danced happily with the young roughneck until his deckmates finally dragged him out of the café to go back to work—he had to eat his cold cheeseburger on the fly. T.R. followed them out, flirting with the young man, whose name was Dexter, until the pickup drove away.

"What do you think, Daddy, is he cuter than Muddy or not?" T.R. asked.

"Now really," I said, "I hate to sound like a stern father but I hope you aren't seriously thinking of abandoning Muddy."

"You ain't a stern father and I think of abandoning Muddy every time I see something cuter," T.R. said. "Wake up, L.J., you're sleeping your life away."

"Who's speaking?" Godwin said groggily. He was often confused for a bit when he woke up from his naps.

T.R. just laughed and drove us home. Muddy was pacing up and down in front of the house, bristling with military equipment. Several trips to the Army-Navy store in Wichita Falls had allowed him to augment his arsenal; he now had binoculars, grenades, and a sniper's rifle with a starlight scope.

"Earl Dee's out," he informed us, as we stepped out of the car.

"Uh-oh," T.R. said. "We better be leaving then. How far away is he?"

"What I meant is, he's out of Huntsville," Muddy explained. "Right now they got him in jail in some place down the road. He shot up a laundrymat."

"A laundrymat?" T.R. said. "Why would he shoot up a laundrymat?"

"I don't know," Muddy said. "I guess one of the washing machines didn't behave."

"Maybe it's all a mistake," I said. T.R. had turned pale. She was looking at the car as if she wanted to get back in it and go.

"I was just told yesterday that he was still in Huntsville," I reminded them.

"Oh, them prisons make mistakes like that all the time," T.R. said. "Half the time they can't keep track of who they've got and who they haven't. I'm for getting out of here right now."

"You got a bunch of messages," Muddy informed me. "The sheriff of the place that's got him has been calling."

The house was in something of an uproar. Bo

was sitting on Jesse and beating her; Jesse was screaming and bleeding from the lip. T.R. immediately spanked Bo, who began to scream too. Neither Gladys nor Buddy was in evidence. While I was on the phone to the prison in Huntsville they emerged, sheepishly, from one of the bedrooms. Godwin, T.R., and Muddy began to smoke marijuana. Godwin had armed himself with a pistol of mine and kept cocking it and pointing it at the refrigerator while I talked on the phone.

"Godwin, don't shoot the icebox," I said.

It didn't take long to determine that the prison had indeed made a mistake; it was an Earl Dean who had mashed someone's head in with a cell door, not Earl Dee. I then called the sheriff of Palo Pinto county, who talked for ten minutes about how very much he and his family had loved "Al and Sal."

"We miss that show, Mr. Deck, I just can't tell you how much we miss that show," he said, several times. When it finally dawned on him that I was worried about Earl Dee, he seemed surprised.

"Why, you don't need to worry, Mr. Deck," the sheriff said. "You can just ease your mind off, right now. He's only been out three days and he's done violated his parole, plus he assaulted a washing machine with a deadly weapon. I'd say that'll get him at least another year. He ain't even supposed to have a deadly weapon, and the old lady whose washing machine he shot up is going to press charges. I'd say you and your family should just relax, because this Mr. Dee is looking at quite a bit of additional time."

"But are you sure there's no chance of his escaping?" I asked. "He's threatened my daughter several times and she's pretty worried."

The suggestion that a prisoner might escape from his jail took the sheriff by surprise.

"Oh, golly," he said. "He ain't gonna escape, we got this man under heavy guard. I been sheriff here sixteen years, nearly seventeen, and we ain't had no escapes. The only thing of an escape-type situation we had was one little thief who was stealing tools off oil rigs—we caught him and while we was bringing him back he rolled out of the dern patrol car, which was a bad technique, it turned out, because he busted his head on the pavement and we had to pay hospital bills on him for six weeks because the dern deputy hadn't made sure the car door was locked. With these courts like they are I've come to the conclusion it's best just to shoot people if they try to escape 'cause if they're dead there won't be that matter of the county getting stuck with no hospital bills."

The sheriff went on to assure me that Alcatraz itself was only slightly more secure than the Palo Pinto county jail. He then launched into a discussion of the episodes of "Al and Sal" that he and his family had admired the most. I listened politely; I definitely wanted the sheriff to stay on our side and do his best by us. Meanwhile, panic swirled around me. Jesse continued to scream intermittently, and Bo had a fit and banged his head on the floor. T.R., Muddy, Godwin, Gladys, and Buddy were all drinking margaritas. All except T.R. and Gladys were armed. T.R. sat with one foot in my lap, chewing lime pulps and listening to me talk to the garrulous sheriff. I rubbed her foot, which seemed to relax her. When the first foot was rubbed sufficiently she exchanged it for the other one, which I also rubbed.

"Well, he's in jail under heavy guard," I said, when I finally got off the phone. "I don't suppose we need to be too worried. They're planning to transport him right back to Huntsville as soon as the paperwork's done."

T.R. had calmed down a bit; she seemed thoughtful.

"How far away is this jail they have him in?" she asked.

"About sixty miles," I said, trying to remember exactly where Palo Pinto county was.

"Too close," T.R. concluded. "I ain't gonna get much sleep with Earl Dee less than a hundred miles away, I don't care what no sheriff says. You're always saying we can go anywhere we want to, any time we want to leave."

"We can, only excluding countries that require passports," I assured her.

"Fuck countries that require passports," T.R. said. "Let's go someplace that don't require nothing but money, and let's leave now."

"I can depart immediately," Godwin assured us.

"We're too many for one car," I pointed out. "Maybe we should go to Wichita and buy a van."

"Good idea," T.R. said. "We can fill it up with guns and take off. Call up the van store right now, Daddy."

I promptly called the biggest van dealership in the area and let the magic of my name and well-publicized fortune do the rest. I was promised the most expensive van in the place, fully serviced and ready to go in thirty minutes. Godwin and I left the rest of them to study a road atlas and went to get the van.

"I can depart immediately," Godwin repeated several times. I believe he was worried we might leave him behind to lead his own life, something he had given no thought to in several years.

"Godwin, we're all departing immediately," I said. "Shut up, you're making me nervous."

"I wonder how T.R. met this fellow Dee," Godwin said. "He must be rather a magnetic personality. It's been my experience that criminals often are."

Several times I'd been on the point of asking T.R. what attracted her to a man who would threaten her life, but at the last second I had always pulled back and left the question unasked. Attraction didn't have to mean, it only had to be. Why was I attracted to women so high-strung and brilliant that if you looked at them twice it would usually prompt a fit? Was it the brilliance that attracted me, or was it the fits, or was it the combination? Who knew? And if I could not answer

370

such a question for myself, there was no point in asking T.R. to try to explain what she had seen in Earl Dee.

"*De gustibus*," I said to Godwin as we raced toward Wichita Falls.

"I hate it when you resort to classical tags," Godwin said.

The van was ready as promised; Godwin insisted on taking the wheel at once, so he drove it and I followed him home in the Cadillac.

We arrived back at Los Dolores to find that panic had somewhat abated, sluiced away by several pitchers of margaritas. The whole gang was sitting around the kitchen table, armed to the teeth, and arguing over the road atlas. T.R. and Muddy were locked into a quiet but deadly debate over our immediate destination. T.R. wanted to go to Disneyland but Muddy had his heart set on Lake Louise.

"I seen it in a travelogue they showed us in jail," he said. "It's supposed to be the prettiest spot in the entire world. Buddy and Bo could sure get lots of fishing done."

"Baloney, let 'em fish in a ditch," T.R. said. "I want to go to Disneyland and then Hollywood. Maybe I'll be a movie star. Earl Dee wouldn't dare kill me if I was a movie star."

"But Lake Louise is a better hideout, just till they get him back in Huntsville," Muddy argued. "It wouldn't never dawn on him that we went to Lake Louise."

"Bull," T.R. said. "Nobody but Earl Dee

371

knows what might dawn on Earl Dee. A man that would empty his gun into a washing machine don't think like other people."

"I've heard Colorado's nice," Gladys offered.

"We could easily lose ourselves in the Yucatan," Godwin said.

"I've got an aunt in Saint Louis," Buddy said. "She might not mind puttin' us up for a while."

"Please, I can't stomach the Midwest," Godwin said. "So few nice asses there."

T.R. had been painting her fingernails while the debate raged. At some point she stopped in order to concentrate on her argument with Muddy, leaving the bottle of fingernail polish on the edge of the table. Jesse quietly appropriated the bottle and sat on the floor by the refrigerator, trying with poor success to paint her own fingernails. Finding the process tedious she had quietly dumped the remainder of the bottle on the floor and was spreading it around with her hands. T.R. and I noticed this at the same moment, and T.R. shrieked.

"Oh, my God, Jesse, what have you done now?" T.R. said.

Startled, Jesse held up her red hands. Realizing she had been caught in what might be considered a misdemeanor, she decided to try to charm her way out of trouble with her new word and a brilliant smile.

"Swim?" she said, hopefully.

"Oh, well, this means a trip to the store," T.R. said, not really angry with Jesse. "I sure ain't gonna show up in Hollywood with half my nails done and the other half not. Let's write up a list of things we need on the trip, and me and Muddy will go buy them."

"Go buy them yourself, I never agreed to go to Hollywood," Muddy said. "You're just a bully, T.R."

"In every little family somebody's got to be the boss, and in this little family it's me," T.R. informed him. She hugged his neck to show there were no hard feelings, but Muddy *had* hard feelings and went into one of his famous sulks. The rest of us quickly composed a list of dozens of items we might find useful on a trip to California.

"I bet we throw half of this stuff out, but that's okay, we'll buy it anyway," T.R. said. She had acquired a cowboy hat at some point and set it jauntily on her head as she got ready for the shopping trip. Then she grabbed me and insisted that we dance a few steps to her own rendition of "The Tennessee Waltz."

"When we get out there to L.A., we're gonna work on your dancing, Daddy," she said, giving me a little punch in the stomach. "You need to dance off some of that fat."

"Why don't you go shopping in the Cadillac while we load the van?" I suggested. "That way we'll get off quicker."

"These feet were made for dancin', Muddy," T.R. said, doing a suggestive dance around the kitchen in an effort to tempt him out of his sulk.

"If you're not careful they're gonna dance right over you."

"Couldn't we just stop by Lake Louise on the way to California?" Muddy said—he was holding firm in his sulk.

"Forget it," T.R. said, but she came closer—close enough to give him a juicy kiss.

"You don't never let nobody win," Muddy said, letting her pull him briefly into the dance.

"I got something else that's made for something else," T.R. said. "You don't wanta see Lake Louise bad enough to risk losing my something else, would you?"

"You wouldn't let me even if I wanted to," Muddy said, disengaging himself. "I'm gonna take a nap before we start on this stupid trip if we're really gonna go to L.A."

"Come on, L.J., you gotta help me buy things, this list has got a million things on it," T.R. said, snapping her fingers at me. The finger snap meant hand over the money, which I did, several hundred. At the last minute Buddy and Bo decided to go along to check out new fishing gear. As they left, Godwin was peering at the list, trying to determine if any essential delicacies had been left out.

I had every intention of getting on with the packing, but the excitements of the day had tired me a little, and before I could start I let myself be drawn into a checker game with Jesse, while Gladys busied herself getting fingernail polish off the floor. Jesse was in high spirits; she had invented a new checker strategy that pleased her even more than throwing my checkers on the floor. Every time I threatened to jump one of her men she simply put her finger on my checker and held it pinned to the board. I pretended that her finger was the finger of Superwoman; no effort of mine, strain though I might, could possibly move a checker once her finger was on it.

This tactic amused Jesse so that she soon became hysterical with laughter. Every time I started to jump her she popped a small finger on my checker and dissolved into helpless paroxyms of laughter.

"That little girl, I love to hear her laugh," Gladys said. She herself was exhibiting excellent spirits—post-coital euphoria, or so I assumed.

While Jesse and I were playing, Jesse subject to ever more prolonged fits of helpless giggling, the phone on the kitchen table rang and I picked it up.

"Mr. Deck, come quick, come quick," an unfamiliar young voice said. Jesse had just put her finger on a checker; impatient with the interruption of the game, she tried to pull my free hand toward the checkerboard.

"Come where, who are you?" I asked. Fear jammed into me like an arrow, almost closing my throat.

"I'm Jim at the filling station—come quick, Mr. Deck, he's killed them all!" the boy said. "He just drove up to the unleaded and pulled that gun and killed them all."

Still obeying Jesse, I concentrated enough to try and lift my checker, provoking another helpless gush of childish laughter. But Gladys, by the sink, looked at my face and paled. She had to grab the sink for support.

"Mr. Deck, come quick," the boy said again.

"Yes, I will," I said, hanging up.

"What?" Gladys said. "What?"

"The kid at the filling station in Thalia says he's killed them all," I said. My thin voice seemed to come from another person.

"Oh, no, Buddy was with them!" Gladys said, her face a knot of agony. "Buddy was with 'em! Here we just got in love and he was my last chance. Now I won't never have no other chance again as long as I live. Oh, no!"

Jesse, shocked and puzzled by the sudden changeability of adults, stopped giggling and put her small fist in her mouth.

16

It was only about seven minutes into Thalia. Muddy and I could see the crowd gathered at the filling station long before we got there. Hay trucks and cattle trucks and trucks with oil rigs on them were parked along the road almost to the city limits sign. With the exception of the local deputy, who looked pale and horrified at the responsibility that had been suddenly thrust upon him, the crowd around the bodies consisted mostly of truckers, cowboys, roughnecks, a few storekeepers, a stunned housewife or two.

The only person in the crowd who seemed to be acting with any presence of mind was Duane Moore, a local oilman I knew only slightly. Apart from Jim, the terrified gas station attendant, Duane had apparently been first on the scene, and what little he could do—call ambulances, for example—he had done.

As soon as we stepped out of the van Duane came over and tried to prepare us for what we would have to see. He told us that T.R. and Godwin were still alive, but his look was not reassuring.

"I'm not a doctor, but it looks pretty bad, Mr. Deck," he said. "Your English friend's shot to pieces and your daughter's been shot in the head."

"I should have come, I should have come," Muddy said; he could scarcely speak and was already descending into the deep pit of self-accusing remorse where he would dwell for years.

T.R. lay in the front seat of the Cadillac; she had been behind the wheel—Earl Dee had shot her in the head at point-blank range. Her eyes were closed and to me she looked much smaller and younger than she had looked only twenty minutes earlier. I couldn't see her wound, though there was blood on her forehead and blood on the seat. I wanted to sob but the arrow held my throat closed. Despite her shallow breathing, T.R. seemed gone: a dead bird, its flight over, small and limp on the ground.

Buddy lay between the gas pumps, quite dead; Godwin was stretched on the oily cement behind the car—though shot three times, he had managed to get Buddy's pistol and had fired several shots at Earl Dee before collapsing. He was fully conscious.

"I wish I'd killed that piece of pigshit," he said weakly, when I knelt beside him. "I did fire rather rapidly, perhaps I wounded him at least."

"Godwin, don't talk," I said. "The ambulance is coming."

"But I'm dying," Godwin said, recovering a bit of his strength. "I want to talk. Why should the dying be denied their last chance to speak? It's just a fucking literary convention. You find a dying man in a novel and the first thing the bloody author does is have someone tell him not to talk. What kind of behavior is that?

"I guess I shan't be buried beside the weedy Cam," he added wearily, as an afterthought.

"Godwin, talk, I'm sorry," I said. "I didn't realize what I was saying. It's just that if you shut up and save your strength you might not die."

"Where's Bo?" Muddy asked, remembering the child. "Bo was with them. Where's Bo?"

No one in the crowd had any idea, but he was not in the car and he was not in the crowd. The only logical inference was that Earl Dee had taken Bo with him, though no one could recall seeing this happen.

I left Godwin and went to kneel by the open car door, as close as I could get to T.R. She was

378

no different. I watched her face, hoping, hoping, hoping that she would open her eyes and look at me. Muddy crawled into the back seat, reached over, and took her limp hand. I'm sure he was hoping the same thing.

"She might come to," he said. "She might come to."

Then we heard the distant whirr of a helicopter.

"I called for the ambulance chopper," Duane said. "I figured, since it's this serious, you'd want to take them to Dallas."

"Thank you," I said.

Someone covered Buddy up. I thought of poor Gladys, terrified and desperate, at home with Jesse. The body of her last chance was lying dead between the leaded and the unleaded.

The helicopter eased down in the street, blowing dust over us all. Muddy and I tried to shield T.R. Then we had to stand aside while the young men of the ambulance crew expertly eased her out of the car and strapped her onto a stretcher. It took some time. The crowd around us had grown, but it was a silent crowd. The only ones who spoke were the ambulance men and Godwin, who did what he could to make theater out of this blood-soaked occasion. He chatted urbanely with the ambulance man, with me, with Duane Moore, in the best Gunga Din/Four Feathers tradition, as they got him onto a stretcher and lifted him into the helicopter. I resisted several impulses to tell him to shut up, though indeed I had never admired him more.

When the two were in the ambulance helicopter Muddy and I prepared to climb in with them but one of the young men stopped us.

"I'm sorry, we just have room for one," he informed us politely.

Muddy and I were startled. I didn't know what to say, but Muddy did.

"You go, you're her daddy," he said, with a look of desperate sadness on his thin face. "I got Jesse to take care of, anyway."

I got in, but I was not really convinced I was the one who should go. T.R. and Muddy were close; he was good to her. Perhaps he would be better than me at helping her rally, persuading her to live. I felt it was mostly a matter of persuasion, too. Once she opened her eyes, one of us would have to start persuading her. Better me, or better Muddy? I didn't know, and the sight of Muddy, standing in the dusty street, looking hopelessly at the helicopter that was about to carry his true love away, was almost too much to bear. I felt I should jump out and let him go, but I delayed my decision too long, and the young man shut the door and the helicopter rose. I sat numbly, looking at the upturned faces below us. Soon they blurred like images in a dream; then I couldn't see them at all.

Both of the young attendants were busy doing things to Godwin and T.R. They were giving them transfusions, attaching monitors—I don't know. I felt sick, partly from shock and partly from the conviction that I had erred in getting into the helicopter. Muddy was almost her husband; Muddy would probably have been more help; Muddy had a better right.

I sat blank for a moment or two, blank and sick; it was with difficulty that I could get Muddy's face out of my mind and bring my attention back to T.R.

"Uh-oh," I heard one of the ambulance men say. He looked at me in a curious way; he didn't elaborate. His look made me uneasy.

"What's the matter?" I asked. "How long will it take us to get to Dallas?"

"Oh, we'll be there pretty soon," the young man said softly. "We might get there in time to save the Englishman, if he'd just quit talking, but the bad news is we can't save your daughter, sir. Your daughter is dead."

"No," I said, trying to reject it. "No, she can't be—just hurry."

The young man sighed, took the seat beside me, and put his arm lightly around my shoulder.

"I remember you," he said. "You rode with us that day we came and got that little guy who blew up the oil tanks. That was him back at the filling station, wasn't it?"

"That was him," I said. I could see T.R.'s feet. They weren't moving. One of her sandals had fallen off, one foot was bare.

"Please check the monitor," I requested. "Please do that. It might be a mistake."

The young man stayed where he was, his arm around me. He said no more. I felt like leaping out of the helicopter. It would be a relief to plunge downward toward the brown plain. I would then be waiting for T.R. in the earth to which she would soon have to go. For a moment it seemed the only available loyal thing to do.

"Daniel, are you very distraught?" Godwin asked.

"Godwin, you really shouldn't talk," I said.

"I'm very distraught too," Godwin said.

_____ **17** _____

The young man had not been wrong—the years had come to T.R. That was how I thought about it when they gave up in the emergency room, when they told me again what the young man had told me in the helicopter. I couldn't say the accurate word, not over the phone to the grief-stricken Muddy or the anguished Gladys. I wanted it to be that something had come for my daughter— the years, or the wind, or the rain, or the earth, or the heavens or time itself—something had come for T.R. and taken her on.

Godwin was taken on too, but not at once. The emergency-room staff was amazed that he was alive, yet he babbled on for half an hour or more, though wounded in several major organs. The nurses kept trying to make him be quiet, but the young doctor in charge was in complete agreement with Godwin about the conversational rights of dying men.

"Of course, let him talk," he said. "Why not?"

Some of his babbling was regret at not having killed Earl Dee. For several minutes he was out of his head, but then his mind seemed to clear and he looked at me quite lucidly and said something in what I took to be Greek.

"Godwin, I'm sorry, I don't know a word of Greek," I said.

"*Iliad*, Sixth Book," Godwin said. "I always thought it rather florid. Odd it should occur to me now."

"I guess I've just forgotten the passage," I said, though I had never really read *The Iliad*.

"Daniel, would you mind putting together my book?" Godwin asked. "I'm afraid it's mainly a mass of notes at the moment, but some of the notes are rather good and I'd hate for them simply to be lost."

"Of course I'll put together your book," I said. "I'll try, anyway."

"I'm sure you can hire some bright young thing from Harvard to do the Greek for you," he said. "The only thing is, you mustn't let Gladys throw it all away. She's been trying to for years, you know."

"I won't let her throw it away, Godwin," I said.

"Poor old thing, she has a kind heart," Godwin said. "Is T.R. really dead?"

"Yes, she's gone," I said.

"What a magnificent girl," he said sadly. "I never got to fuck her."

I began to cry, but Godwin, always either a step

383

ahead of me or a step behind me, seemed quite lucid.

"She brought you her children just in time, didn't she?" he said. "What an admirable thing. You're sometimes a little slow in your perceptions, Daniel. I do hope you recognize what a great gift that was."

I didn't answer—couldn't. At that moment I recognized nothing. Godwin squeezed my hand. He began to talk in Greek again.

"It's really an odd comeuppance," he said. "I spent years with Euripides and now I can't remember a line of anything but Homer. It's rather a joke on me, isn't it?"

"Yes, I guess so," I said. He let go my hand. A minute or two later the young doctor came in and led me out. It occurred to me once I was in the hall that Godwin must be dead.

Near midnight that day, as I waited in Dallas for the bodies of my daughter and Godwin Lloyd-Jons to be released to me, Earl Dee shot a highway patrolman who had stopped him near Bartlesville, Oklahoma. A few minutes later he surrendered without a fight outside a convenience store in Pawhuska. Bo was with him. The patrolman he shot was only slightly injured.

IV

I never saw Earl Dee—didn't want to. My imagination was not interested in endowing him with any human traits; I did better if I simply thought of him as a dark force out of the Southern underclass, someone who might resemble Steve Cochran as he looked in *Storm Warning:* a sexy lout with a smirk. During the trial, when I happened to see a picture of him in a newspaper, he did have such a smirk. He received three life sentences.

When Bo was ten, he began to ask to visit his father. After giving it some thought, I let him, sending him to Texas with Hilton, a driver and man-of-all-work who had replaced Buddy in Bo's—though never in Gladys's—affections. We were living in California then, but Bo wanted to see his father, and I let it take place. Bo never reported on the visits; Bo never reported on anything. What he and his father said to one another, only they knew. Earl Dee was killed by an inmate when Bo was fourteen. After that, Bo disappeared for seven months, the first—but not the last—of his disappearances.

The first years, of course, were terrible for us all. Muddy Box and I spent three years endlessly trying to reverse the clock with our minds—to get back beyond the moment when T.R. danced out of the house and drove off to her death. Hundreds of times, privately and together, we reenacted her last half hour at Los Dolores, trying to rearrange events so that she didn't leave, and therefore didn't die. Muddy couldn't eat for a month; he shrank away to almost nothing. His particular torture was that he had let his stubborn desire to see Lake Louise separate him from T.R. at such a critical moment.

"But we didn't know what was going to happen," I told him, over and over. "We didn't know. Nobody could have known. She wasn't mad at you, either. She gave you a big kiss just before she left."

It didn't help.

"I knew he wasn't in Huntsville," Muddy said, over and over and over. "I knew he wasn't in Huntsville. I shouldn't have argued with her. I should have just done whatever she wanted, 'cause now I won't never have the chance."

My own tormented regret—amply justified when the facts came out—was that I had been lulled into a careless sense of security by the assurances of the sheriff of Palo Pinto county that Earl Dee was under heavy guard and could not possibly escape. How could I have been so ignorant of the conditions that actually prevail in small-town jails? My ignorance was every bit as inexcusable as Muddy's fixation on Lake Louise.

In fact, Earl Dee had already escaped when I

had my conversation with the sheriff—the sheriff just didn't know it. The "heavy guard" consisted of an inexperienced deputy who had been having sex with a fat teen-age shoplifter in the cell next to Earl Dee's when the jailbreak occurred. Earl Dee had made up to the girl and promised to take her with him if she'd help him get out—a promise he immediately broke. Whose idea it was to have sex, the girl's, the deputy's, or Earl Dee's, was never made clear, but a sex act occurred on the bunk in the girl's cell and the girl passed Earl Dee the deputy's gun and his keys. On the way out Earl Dee also took the deputy's hat, and drove away in the deputy's police car; he left the car and the hat in a town about forty miles north, stealing a Buick from behind a dentist's office.

I told myself that as a novelist and student of human behavior I should have predicted some such chain of events; but who really could have predicted that the fat teen-ager would get arrested for shoplifting just in time to succumb to the deputy's advances (if it *was* the deputy who made advances; he claimed he had been seduced, the teen-ager claimed that she gave in because the deputy promised to bring her a milkshake from the Dairy Queen across the street)—just in time to help Earl Dee escape?

Balzac himself could not have predicted that.

Later, there was a cry in the local paper for lawsuits. I was urged to sue Huntsville, the warden, the prison system, the probation officer, the sheriff of Palo Pinto county, the deputy, and even

389

the teen-age shoplifter; it was on her already hopeless young shoulders that the heaviest blame fell. It was only her second arrest for shoplifting, but the well-publicized knowledge that she screwed the deputy for a milkshake branded her as a hopelessly lost soul in local eyes.

Not in my eyes, though. The minute I saw their pictures in the paper—the skinny, bewildered deputy and the fat, sad girl—I was reminded that there were people worse off than me. Far from suing them, I got them both lawyers, good lawyers who eventually whittled the charges against them down to almost nothing. In time I came to feel sorrier for Melinda than for anyone in the whole grim affair. I guess the milkshake was the haunting detail, though Melinda told me it had really been a banana split and admitted that she had always had a crush on the deputy anyway and didn't mind being in jail if it meant she could be near him. She had done it for love, after all, and not for the banana split. His name was Dan.

I offered to put Melinda through college; she went for a semester and then got a job clerking in the drugstore where she had been caught shoplifting cosmetics. Two years later, shunned by almost everyone except one another, Melinda and Dan married, a one-day story in the local papers. I went to their sad little wedding, paid for their honeymoon to Lake Tahoe, and wept on the way home from the ceremony. I think they themselves never entirely got over the fact that their moment of indulgence, their tiny grab for pleasure, had played a part in ending my daughter's life. After the wedding I stopped keeping up with Melinda and Dan. I couldn't bear to keep up anymore—it was too sad.

The sheriff of Palo Pinto county was voted out in the next election. A year later he shot his wife and her lover, who happened to be the new sheriff. Then he tried to shoot himself, did a poor job, recovered, and served a term in Huntsville himself.

At that time, though, in the first months after the tragedy, I paid only fitful attention to the various trials. Every day was a plain that had to be crossed; every day Muddy and I played the hopeless game of trying to reverse time. Our minds would not stop trying to rearrange that last hour, or last afternoon, so as to make it all come out differently. Even when T.R. had begun to blur in both our minds, when painful dreams and hopeless fantasies had made us both half-crazy, we still spent far too many hours discussing Muddy's stubbornness about Lake Louise and my casual acceptance of the sheriff's assurances.

Then, to my amazement, almost to my dismay, Muddy began to recover. He edged out of his grief, leaving me more alone in mine than ever. Even on his worst days he was always infinitely good, infinitely patient with Bo and Jesse. He spent hours playing games with them; he took them camping, took them to Six Flags. When he began to recover he also began to read. The ten thousand books in my library, only so much furniture to him until then, began to interest him. I would wander out late at night to find him reading Engels, Karen Blixen, some nineteenth-century travel writer.

One day I asked Muddy if he would like to go to college and he said yes. That fall he started classes in Wichita Falls, finishing just as Jesse was ready for first grade. Cameras and mikes and all sorts of communications technology fascinated him. He decided he might like to go to graduate school in communications. We had just moved back to L.A. Muddy was dubious about the move at first, but he came with us and entered UCLA in the fall. He proved a superior student, popular with everyone. At the end of his second year, a Houston television station offered him a job as a weatherman. He did well as a weatherman, but greater things awaited him. One day the regular traffic reporter called in sick; traffic reporting is a vital position in Houston, where freeway gridlock is a constant threat. Muddy climbed into a helicopter and rose almost immediately into legend. Morning and afternoon he soared high over the teeming Houston freeways, looking for pockets of trouble. It soon became clear that Muddy Box had a genius for anticipating traffic problems and analyzing possible solutions. In the two years that he did traffic he saved millions of Texans many more millions of man-hours by redirecting them around problems that had only barely begun to develop. His morning and evening traffic reports drew 80 percent of the listening audience, an unheard-of rating, and one that quickly brought him offers from around the country. He could have gone anywhere—Manhattan, Chicago, L.A.—but Muddy remained loyal to Houston.

Perhaps it was not just Houston he was loyal to—perhaps it was also T.R. Though he became a successful man and appeared to have recovered, in his heart perhaps he hadn't. He took an apartment in the Lawndale area, not far from where he and T.R. had lived. When Jesse went there to visit—and Jesse went often—he took her to the same dance halls where he had once danced with her mother. If there were women in his life, they must have been minor—neither Jesse nor I were ever informed about any of them.

About midnight one November night, Muddy Box told a friend he was going to Lake Charles, for a few hours. Lake Charles was in Louisiana. On the way he had a flat on the bridge over the Old and Lost River. As he was changing it a passing horse trailer swayed a few inches into the emergency lane, and the bumper clipped him, killing him instantly. At the memorial service in Houston, three thousand people, remembering the hours his brilliant unsnarlings had saved them, gathered in the rain to show their respect. We buried him on the hill near Los Dolores, beside T.R. and Godwin. The next few months were the only time I feared for Jesse, for there was no measuring how deeply Jesse loved her dad.

2

As soon as she heard of the deaths, Jeanie came to Texas. The sight of me must have shocked her profoundly, though she never mentioned it. Almost at once my hair had turned white, and the weight that had led me to prefer caftans vanished; a human melt-down occurred so rapidly that soon I was even smaller than the small man I had once been. For a time I became hesitant and frail.

Jeanie immediately recognized that she could do little for the three adults, at that time mere stumbling globs of pain. For three weeks she devoted herself almost exclusively to the confused, frightened children. She took them on outings, picnics, shopping trips; sometimes she merely drove them around in the car, listening to music with them, getting them out of sight when our sorrow became too much. She colored and cut out collages with Jesse, bought mountains of play dough for Bo, and helped him sculpt an army of grotesque monsters. For three weeks she was able to focus all the love in her frustrated spirit on those two children; she sang to them and read them stories and taught them games she herself had never played. She employed all her energy, all her invention, all her brilliance to keep them in the light, not let them be engulfed by the darkness that shadowed the rest of the household.

At the time I hardly noticed this; I paid little

attention to what Jeanie was doing with the children. I was glad she was there, but too broken to really attend. Later, though, when it became clear that the children were healthy, even though saddled with three crushed adults, I came to feel that Jeanie had saved them. Even given that I'm partial to her, I think it's not an unfair opinion, though Jeanie herself won't allow it to be mentioned. For all her smarts, even Jeanie has her blind spots; she doesn't realize how easy it is to destroy a child.

After three weeks, though, I began to sense an uneasiness in her—a kind of traffic problem in her emotions. One morning I found her crying on the patio.

"What is it?" I asked.

"If I'm going, I'm going to have to go," she said.

"It's obvious that you have to go," I said, after a moment.

"Oh, Danny, don't say it's obvious," she said, wiping her eyes. "It isn't so obvious."

"It's obvious to me," I said. "We can't use no martyrs down here."

Jeanie sat and cried. My confidence was a straw at best, just then. I felt I had hurt the feelings of my one true friend. The others—Nema, Viveca, Marella, horrified that I had let myself become involved in a tragedy—began to float away. Grief was not their métier; movietown gossip and the colorful misdemeanors of their boyfriends could make no mark on it, and they were none of them women who could afford to make no mark.

"I was sort of trying to think of you," I said to Jeanie, who shrugged and went on crying.

At the end of the week, at my insistence, she made an escape, though a narrow one. Jesse clung to her and squealed more loudly than anyone had ever squealed throughout human history. Jeanie wept, I wept, Gladys wept, Muddy shut himself in his room, Bo banged his head on the floor. The world seemed to be ending for all of us. At the airport, during the interminable wait for her plane, our distress was writ so large that people shunned us as if we were lepers; the whole non-smoking section emptied; Jeanie and I sat in it alone, silent.

Yet, despite the agony of that parting—a necessary agony, I felt; I really *didn't* want her martyred, even for my grandchildren—the world didn't end for any of us. While I wandered around Los Dolores, deep in grief, Jeanie made three flops, an almost unredeemable situation for an aging actress. It seemed likely that she would soon be lucky to land a detergent commercial. In despair, she took the only role she could get, in an offbeat English film. She played a spinster who spends her days in the London Zoo, trying to cheer up the animals; by chance she meets the Prince of Wales at a ribbon-cutting and a tender passion develops, swelling until it almost shakes the throne. It all seemed wildly improbable; no one thought the picture had a chance; and yet the playground of art is littered with improbably successes. The little picture—*Love in the Monkey*

House—caught the heart of the world. It won best picture of the year in several countries, including the United States, and Jeanie won another Oscar. She took Jesse to the ceremony. That triumph bought her ten very active years, several more good roles, and another nomination.

The pain of those three weeks in Los Dolores altered our friendship a bit. Perhaps it was just that there was no longer enough left of me to keep the spark in it—I'm not sure. If so, my loss was Jesse's gain. Jeanie called Los Dolores often. We talked a bit, but it was not long before I realized she was really calling to talk to Jesse. When Jesse was three, Jeanie gave her a private line, making her one of the youngest regular long-distance customers in history. As soon as she was old enough to be entrusted to stewardesses, I began to send her to New York or L.A.—to wherever Jeanie was at the time—for week-long binges of shopping, theater, zoos, city life. Jeanie and Jesse's bond was deep, and never broken. It was Jeanie who hounded me into moving back to L.A. so the children could have good schools. "Danny, you have to wake up now," she said. "You can't just imprison those children there. You have to give them a chance."

When engaged, Jeanie could be a relentless, merciless nag, and in this case she was fully engaged. In some sense I was like an animal living at the bottom of the sea, an immense weight of water above me. To rise out of it to the top, through layers upon layers of inertia, was not easy, but Jeanie nagged, and I struggled upward, to somewhere near the surface. We moved to L.A. It made little difference to me or Bo, but an immense difference to Jesse and Jeanie, who became, in effect, big sister and little sister. Jeanie dressed Jesse, Jeanie formed her taste, Jeanie began to travel with her. Together they did the world: Paris, Egypt, China. Bo and I stayed home, mistrusting one another.

3

But four years passed before we left Los Dolores for Los Angeles, and in those dark years it was mainly Gladys who carried the daily load. She was right in the judgment she had made the moment she heard of Buddy's death: he had been her last chance. By accident, in her sadness she confessed to Chuck that she had slept with Buddy, whereupon Chuck beat her up, divorced her, and married the waitress in Amarillo.

Three of Gladys's five daughters got divorced in the same year. At various times all of them moved into Los Dolores to help Gladys with the housework, a succession of pale, distraught girls who lay around smoking and watching videos, leaving Gladys to care for their pale, watery babies, who seemed to be composed entirely of piss and tears.

Still, it meant there was life in the house; Bo

had children other than Jesse to beat up on and Jesse had several worshipful toddlers to command.

Poor Gladys, too, had her remorse; her mind, too, struggled with the need to rewrite the last day. Her references to what had gone on between her and Buddy that afternoon were cryptic to begin with, and always soon punctuated with crying jags, so that I was a long time understanding or locating the reason for her profound guilt.

"All the rest of my life I'll wish I'd let him," she said, one day, drying her eyes after a crying jag.

"But, Gladys, I thought you did let him," I said. "I thought that was why you were in the bedroom."

"Yeah, but he wanted to try for two," Gladys said sadly. "He wanted to try for two, and I wouldn't let him—I thought that would be rushing things a little."

"Oh, dear," I said.

"Yep," Gladys said, and began to cry again.

A few days later she confessed that she could barely remember Buddy—they had only known one another about two weeks. But the fact that she couldn't remember him did nothing to free her from the burden of remorse—she lived out her life believing that her silly reluctance to rush things had cost Buddy his life. Unfortunately she was right; if she'd kept him in the bedroom ten more minutes no one would have thought to take him on that fatal ride.

One day old Pedro came walking to the house

alone to get his beer. Gladys asked him why Granny Lin hadn't come with him—she had come to rely on Granny Lin.

"She forgot to wake up this morning," old Pedro said, opening a Coors.

A few months later he, too, forgot to wake up.

4

Then Gladys got sick. A cancer in her female organs began to consume her. I took her to Houston, to the great cancer hospital there, but Gladys hated the hospital, and in any case the cancer's appetite was not to be slowed.

Desperate, I managed to locate Elena and got her whole family—three sisters and a mother, six children in all—to move to Los Dolores to help us.

Gladys sat on the sunny patio, playing cards with Jesse, for the last month of her life.

"You ought to take these precious children and move," she said, one day—the very words I had been hearing from Jeanie.

"Well," I said noncommittally.

"This whole hill's becoming a graveyard," she said.

"That's one reason I stay," I admitted. "I like to be close to them."

"If you're that selfish, I'm sorry I wasted my life working for you," Gladys said. "Little children don't need to be playing on graves. Little children need some life around them."

"You're right, I give up, I'll move," I said.

"It's awful to be dying," Gladys said. "I'd rather be washing clothes, and I hate to wash clothes."

I was trying vaguely to keep my promise to Godwin vis à vis his book. I had several folders of his notes on the table before us.

"I never thought I'd be put in the same graveyard with L.J.," she said. "That comes as kind of a surprise."

"Gladys, you don't have to be," I said gently. "Other arrangements can be made."

"Naw, put me by him," Gladys said. "I was in love with him anyway, he just never took no notice. I guess I was too weird for him."

A few days later Jesse—used to death by this time—came stumbling into the kitchen one morning dragging a large stuffed turtle. She looked at me solemnly for a moment.

"I think Gladys kinda died," she said.

5

My one accomplishment the first year back in L.A. was to find a skinny graduate student of classics to help me locate the Greek references in Godwin's book notes. Her name was Clarissa, and besides locating Greek quotations she also taught Jesse French. Jeanie was already contemplating

401

lots of European travel for Jesse and herself and thought Jesse ought to acquire a language or two.

"Then I won't have to do all the talking," she allowed.

Fortunately Elena and her family moved to L.A. with us. Small Latin boyfriends eventually married all three sisters and took them away, but Elena, already equipped with two bouncing boys, rejected many suitors and seemed happy to stay with us.

Godwin's book, *Notes on Euripidean Elements in the Music of the Rolling Stones,* was published at my expense by a distinguished small press in Los Angeles. *The Times Literary Supplement* gave it a three-paragraph review.

That same year I gave two million dollars to establish a center and a hot line, in T.R.'s name, to inform women when men who had threatened them were being released from prison. In the first year the hot line received twenty-three thousand queries. Despite our efforts, four women lost their lives anyway, but I feel sure that some were saved, at least temporarily.

6

Once the modest duty of putting together Godwin's book was discharged, I had almost nothing to do. Day after day I sat on the top floor of our house in Santa Monica and looked out at the sea. I would really have preferred to be looking out at the plains, but the sea itself was a kind of plain. The sea would do.

I had no thought of writing again, but after four or five years I began to be visited by sentences. They collected and collided in my head. They were all sentences describing a girl much like T.R. The girl was growing up in a middle-sized town in East Texas, with criminal grandparents and even some criminal boyfriends. In my head, though not yet on paper, the sentences seemed like sentences that should be in a novel.

Fumblingly, after a year of thinking about it, I began to write the novel, which I called *Let the Stranger Consider*, borrowing the title from the haunting portfolio bequeathed me by Jill Peel. I thought that since Jill had given me the portfolio, perhaps her shade would not be offended if I stole the title.

I had been gone a long time from the country of prose, and had difficulty getting back across the border. My passport—the sentence—was never quite in order. The sentences I offered all lacked a certain stamp, or else they were dated or otherwise unusable. Several times I gave up and attempted to resign myself to a life spent in exile from prose, but resignation wouldn't come. I wanted to write a book, but I didn't know where to begin, and I had become an unwitting refugee from the English sentence.

For a time my nascent book had only one character, the girl who was much like T.R. But then the shadowy figure of an old man, a pious, Bible-thumping old criminal, began to emerge from the shadows. He was grandfather to the girl—the man T.R. had called Big Pa.

A month or so after she was killed I had had a letter from Big Pa. I had received a lot of mail from a lot of people then, and been touched by none of it; I could not remember that I had even read most of those letters, but I did remember getting one from Big Pa, though finding it again required a trip back to Los Dolores. There was an old trunk there, a Wells Fargo trunk, bought in Tucson, into which I had thrown thousands of letters, mostly fan mail, through the years. It seemed to me that, indifferent in my grief, I had thrown Big Pa's letter into the trunk. Five years had passed when I suddenly had a strong desire to read that letter.

And the letter was indeed there, written on tablet paper and mailed from an address in Lufkin, Texas. It was short:

DEAR MR. DECK—

It was on TV today that that evil monster has killed our Tyler Rose, she was a precious thing to me and to my late wife as well—I should have picked up a good cedar post and clubbed that black dog to death the day I met him, he was just a damn killer anyway. It's the Lord's kindness that my wife passed on last year as this heartbreak and tragedy would have been more than she could have stood. I am losing my eyesight and can barely see the

TV now anyway but my hearing's fair, I
never thought to hear such terrible news coming from the TV set—anyway we can be sure
he will sizzle in the burning lake of sulphur
throughout eternity and then some! But it
won't bring back our Tyler Rose.

LLOYD BYNUM

Lloyd Bynum was the man who had beaten me
up and chased me away the night T.R. was
born—helped by his wife, Big Ma. He had deflected me from my child, and I had hated him
for years, though of course it was my fault, not
his, that I had accepted the deflection.

Lufkin was not that far. On the spur of the
moment I decided to go see if the old man was
still alive.

Not only was he alive, but he was at the address
on the letter, a small frame house in the poor white
part of Lufkin. When I knocked at the screen door
an amiable young black woman appeared and
asked me what I wanted.

"I was wondering if Mr. Bynum was in," I said.
"My name is Deck."

"Deck?" she asked, her face brightening. "Are
you the one who wrote the TV show?"

"I'm the one," I said.

"Yeah, he's in," she said, unlatching the door.
"He's always in, except when I take him for his
walks. He talks about you all the time."

"About me?" I asked, surprised.

"You, if you're the one wrote the TV show,"

405

she said. "He says you was part of his family. He don't have much to be proud of these days, but he's real proud of you."

At one point the irony of such a remark would have caused me to turn and leave, but I was older and had often drunk the dark milk of irony. I followed the girl out to a small screened-in porch at the back of the house, where a gaunt old man wearing khakis and an undershirt sat on a faded couch, holding a flyswatter.

"Here, gimme that flyswatter," the girl said. "What you think you're doing? You can't see to swat no flies anyway."

"Aw, let me keep it, I might get one of them accidentally," the old man said. "I need something to do with my hands."

"You got company," the girl said.

"Hope it's female company, I could use some female company," the old man said, attempting a toothless leer. His false teeth sat on a small table beside the couch.

"It's that man who wrote the TV show—you know, your son-in-law," the girl said.

"Danny Deck, Mr. Bynum," I said.

"Well, I swear," the old man said, attempting to stand up. He made it to his feet but wobbled so badly that he had to sit back down almost at once, and he sat so heavily that he knocked his false teeth off the table. It was clear that he couldn't see me at all, but he was waving his big old hand for me to shake, and I finally managed to catch it and shake it.

"Gosh, I'm glad you came, Dan," he said at once. "I'm feeble but at least I ain't got the Alzheimer's. Want to hear what I think would make a good story for the TV?"

It was not the opening I had expected—though I don't know why not. Virtually everyone alive has a story they think would be perfect for TV.

"See, I knew them all," the old man said. "I could tell you things about them that ain't never got in the papers. I could tell it and you could write it and we could make a show that wouldn't quit."

I had no idea what he was talking about.

"Who was it you knew, Mr. Bynum?" I asked. "I'm confused."

"Why, the oilmen," he said. "The wildcatters. I knew Hunt. I knew Getty. I knew Dad Joiner. Hunt owes me money to this day, although I'll never collect it. I beat him in a poker game and it made Getty jealous, because Getty could rarely even take a hand from Hunt."

"Goodness," I said. "I bet you do know some stories."

"Dad Joiner was the best," the old man said. "Hunt was plenty smart, and the first smart thing he did was latch onto Dad Joiner and stick to him like a tick. Hunt found Dad Joiner, and Dad Joiner found the oil."

The amiable young black girl brought us both glasses of lemonade. The old man quaffed his in two swallows, eager to get on with his stories about the great days of the East Texas oil fields, when

407

legends on the order of Hunt and Getty walked the earth. He was perfectly friendly and also perfectly selfish. All he wanted was to get his oil-boom stories on TV and make a fortune—a common dream.

As he talked I began to grow sad. This was the man my daughter had grown up with—no monster, just a normally selfish old man; a child of the boom who had nonetheless missed the boom and turned to a life of petty crime instead. He had known the great ones, but he himself was not great. I had hoped, I suppose, to hear him talk about T.R., to gain a sense of what her childhood had been like; but he never mentioned T.R. He had raised her, but she was gone, and he had forgotten her; she didn't haunt him as she haunted me. I couldn't hate him, and I had found out nothing from him. The trip had been a miss.

Abruptly he began to tire.

"Lord, it's tiresome not to be able to see," he said. "I can't even see that nigger gal. I don't even know if she's pretty or not."

"She's pretty and she's also nice," I assured him.

"I think I'll take a little nap, Dan," he said, swinging his long legs onto the couch. "I'll just keep this flyswatter. Let me know when you do the show."

"You oughta hear him snore," the young woman said, as I was leaving. "That old man sure do snore."

I took three years to write the novel. I thought it would be about my daughter—about T.R. Perhaps I thought that in writing it I would discover some of the things about her that I didn't know; perhaps I thought the book would bring some of her back to me. By truthful imaginings I would find my daughter.

I worked hard and in time regained a certain art, but the art refused to be used as I had hoped to use it. It took its own path, and the path led not to T.R. but to the old man. It became a book about a lecherous, criminal old preacher who seduced half the wives in his congregation and sold dope out of his parsonage. The girl, his granddaughter, figured in the story only slightly; Lloyd Bynum had deflected me once again.

The book was a modest success.

From time to time Lloyd Bynum called, to see how our show was progressing, and to ramble on about Hunt, Getty, and Dad Joiner. Once or twice I sent him money. The nice black woman, Amy, called the day after he died to ask for a job. I needed someone to look after Los Dolores, so I hired her; she lives there with me still. Her husband, Otis, comes and goes, but Amy stayed and raised a fine family. I helped send all her kids to college. Her oldest boy, Robert, was one of the few people Bo could be said to like.

I tried with Bo, Gladys tried with him, Muddy tried with him, Elena tried with him, Amy tried with him, Hilton tried with him, but it's fair to say that with the exception of his mother, his sister, and Buddy, nobody ever really liked Bo. We all lived with a kind of low-grade anxiety when Bo was around, never really knowing what he might do. When he was five or six, I had to banish all firearms from the house because Bo managed to load a shotgun and killed Elena's cat.

"I don't like old cats," he said, without remorse, when asked to explain.

Over the years Bo broke hundreds of objects: dishes, glasses, toys, TVs, lawn mowers, fishing equipment. The objects he destroyed got larger and more expensive as he got older, but the pattern of destruction hardly varied. One day, when we were in town, he carried out six hundred videos and threw them in the swimming pool, apparently just so he could watch them float. When he was big enough to mow the lawn, he set Jesse's favorite doll on the grass and sliced it to shreds with the mower.

I thought maybe Buddy had the right idea when he got him interested in fishing, so I took him fishing a few times. Unfortunately I was a terrible fisherman; only turtles took my bait.

"You can't catch anything but turtles," Bo said

disgustedly. He walked back to the house. I don't think he ever took me seriously again.

If there was a good Bo, Jesse was the only person who saw it. She saw plenty of the bad Bo too—throughout their childhood he was constantly punching her, knocking her down, sitting on her, trying to run over her with tricycles or bikes, trying to drown her in the pool; he disrupted her birthday parties and immediately broke most of her favorite toys. Thanks to him, Jesse had a more-or-less permanent fat lip. But Jesse, though she wept, squealed, grieved over decapitated dolls and disemboweled stuffed animals, was not one to hold grudges. Occasionally she would even manage to engage her brother in peaceful pursuits for a few hours—coloring, secret clubhouses, or (as they got older) listening to records. When he got expelled from schools, as he did frequently, Jesse would immediately insist on being withdrawn too; often she was able to secure him another chance. When he got arrested in Pacific Palisades for stealing stereos out of cars, Jesse did tireless liaison work, pleading with his probation officer to overlook his constant infractions and give him one more chance. When he disappeared, it was Jesse he called when he needed money; when he reappeared it was in her apartments near the various campuses where she studied that he chose to crash. Twice he stole her boyfriends' cars, one of which he totaled, but Jesse managed to persuade the boyfriends not to press charges.

When Bo was sixteen I finally did something

411

for him that worked—which was to get him flying lessons. My motive was partly selfish. As I became more and more reclusive, I developed a horror of airports: of the noise, the waiting, the crowds. I would begin to hyperventilate at the mere thought of an airport; having to mix with masses of people made me shaky. For days before a trip I would get headaches far more intense than my normal headaches. Once or twice, for minor trips, I chartered planes, at vast expense, just to avoid airports.

It occurred to me that if Bo could become a pilot I could buy a small plane and he could fly me home to Texas whenever I needed to go. Flying lessons proved to be the one thing I ever suggested that Bo was enthusiastic about. He soon became an adept small-plane pilot. I bought him a nice Cessna and he flew me to Texas in it exactly once. Then he flew away in the Cessna and essentially never came back. Jesse told me he was working at a flying school in Mexico somewhere. I didn't hear from him for two years; then he called, needing money for some repairs to the plane. I sent the money. It was the last time he ever asked for money. It was also the last time I heard from him. Presumably he was still working for the mysterious flying school in Mexico. Sometimes he flew into whatever city Jesse was studying in at the time and stayed with his sister for a few days. I assumed he was flying dope, but I made no effort to confirm my assumption. When asked about her brother, Jesse became uncharacteristically vague.

412

Mostly I don't think about Bo, but when I do think about him I feel guilty. When he was not yet three, T.R. had expressed the hope that he would not become a criminal; I raised him and he became a criminal. It was not a triumph. I wished, for T.R.'s sake, that I had known how to do a better job.

9

Six years after T.R.'s death, Jeanie Vertus got married. Her husband was a director named Eric Roth. Eric, a few years younger than Jeanie, was gifted, lively, appealing, nice. The marriage was unusually happy. Once you saw the two of them together it became hard to imagine how they could have lived apart.

I seldom again heard the tragic note in Jeanie's voice—the note that had defined her for so long both as a woman and an actress. One might have thought that that note was the mark of her greatness, but it wasn't true. She worked just as well happy as she had worked unhappy, and, in some cases, better.

I got fewer and fewer calls from Jeanie, as the years passed. At first, when she did call, she would be guiltstricken; it would occur to her that she hadn't called me in a month, or two months, or more. Fortunately some quirk allowed me to take a comic approach to Jeanie's inadvertent desertion on these occasions. I made little comedies of the

413

mishaps I might have sustained during her periods of inattention; my comedies were so successful, such brilliant inventions in their own right, that Jeanie always hung up relieved, convinced that I was holding my own without her.

It was neither entirely true nor entirely a lie. I missed Jeanie deeply, yet I was glad she had got lucky, and I didn't really expect her to call that often. The rules of happiness are as strict as the rules of sorrow; indeed, perhaps more strict. The two states have different densities, I've come to think. The lives of happy people are dense with their own doings—crowded, active, thick—urban, I would almost say.

But the sorrowing are nomads, on a plain with few landmarks and no boundaries; sorrow's horizons are vague and its demands few. Jeanie and I had not become strangers; it was just that she lived in the city and I lived on the plain.

10

When Jesse was ready for college—it seemed to take her only a few years to grow up—I left L.A. for good and went back home to Texas. I settled back in at Los Dolores, replaced the ocean with the plain. I made reading lists for Amy's very bright children; I used my still-considerable influence to get them into good schools. Occasionally I drove to Houston, to attend a benefit, see a show at a museum.

Always, when in Houston, I drifted over to the Lawndale area, an Asian barrio by this time. The Mr. Burger was gone, replaced by a spiffy little restaurant called The Wok.

Sometimes I visited Sue Lin; she and her husband owned a computer store, staffed mainly by their lively children.

I tried to find Dew, but no one was sure where Dew had gone.

Apart from having a larger Asian barrio, Houston had not changed much. The dance halls along Telephone Road and over by the ship channel were as sleazy as they had been in T.R.'s time or in my own youth. The city still had its funkiness, its odors, its beautiful clouds. Sometimes I drifted aimlessly in the older parts of town—the Heights, the Third Ward. Always I dreamed of my lost daughter, who had so loved to kick up her heels in just such places.

Sometimes I drove on down to Galveston and walked by the sea, dreaming of T.R. My mind continued to be tormented by the lost years; it wouldn't just let them go; it picked at them. They had become an obsession with me.

In my obsession I remembered the name of the nice girl who had been killed in the wreck—Annie Elgin, T.R.'s high school friend. She was dead, but her mother was alive. I went again to East Texas and found Mrs. Elgin living in the same lovely, well-kept house the detective had sent me pictures of. She was a pleasant, courteous woman, but so plainly horrified by my appearance—I looked pretty weird by this time, I guess—that I excused myself after fifteen minutes and never bothered her again. I learned as little about T.R. from her as I had learned from Lloyd Bynum. Accepting this lesson at last, I never went to East Texas again.

The last source that might have told me something about T.R.'s youth was the man who killed her, Earl Dee. Several times, before he himself was killed, I contemplated visiting him in prison. But if Lloyd Bynum and Annie Elgin's mother weren't really interested, could I expect better of Earl Dee? After all, she was just an old girlfriend to him, and a treacherous one at that. Probably he had forgotten her two weeks after he killed her. A visit with him might just make matters worse; in the end I let it go, and with it the hope of knowing very much about T.R.'s early years.

I remained obsessed, but my obsession was sterile; I never learned any of the things I wanted to know about T.R. It was as if she had risen unexpectedly from the dark sea of time, walked with me on the beach for a few bright moments, and had then gone quietly back to the long waters. But a critical human ability—the ability to let the lost be lost, the dead be dead—was another of the several I turned out not to have; not, at least, in any healthy measure. To this day I spend a lot of time just staring out the window, hoping to see a girl who isn't there.

11

Into the rubble of this broken life stepped Jesse. Never as beautiful as her mother, never as brash, never as vivid, Jesse had in full T.R.'s dauntless-ness, her absolute resolution. Only twenty months old when T.R. was killed, she forgot her mother quickly and set about making the most of what she had—in her case a rough brother and three crushed adults.

In my blackest days, when all I could really do was sit on the bed and look out the window, Jesse sat with me. She would push a chair over to the bed and climb up. Then for an hour or two she would be up and down, assembling doll families, stuffed animals, coloring books, scissors. Once she had everything she needed, she would stay on the bed with me for hours, coloring, cutting, dis-cussing weighty matters with her doll families, reprimanding the stuffed animals. When I napped, Jesse napped with me; when I fell silent, Jesse talked.

And talked and talked and talked: to me, to Gladys, to her father. She padded through the house tirelessly, ever hopeful; she wouldn't let any of us alone. Rearranging furniture was her passion from the age of three on—we were soon predicting a great future for Jesse in interior design. Any piece of furniture small enough for her to lift or push would soon be traveling from room to room, being frequently repositioned. Jesse made up her mind quickly and changed it just as quickly.

She was six when we moved to Santa Monica and had a whole new house to furnish. Jeanie came out for a week. She and Jesse disappeared; a day or two later, truckfuls of furniture began to arrive.

Interior decoration was not Jesse's only passion, however. As she grew older a month scarcely passed without her plunging into a new enthusiasm: architecture, movies, vintage clothes, surfboarding, dancing, hang-gliding, photography, girlfriends, boyfriends, anthropology, Mexico, the world. Guided by excellent teachers in excellent schools, often accompanied on her various journeys by Jeanie—one of the few people as hard to keep up with as Jesse—it soon seemed Jesse was everywhere, doing everything. I began to worry; I gave her lectures on the necessity of discipline and focus; I warned her solemnly of the danger of spreading herself too thin.

Jesse ignored my lectures and kept spreading, but by the time she was seventeen and a freshman at UCLA it seemed that either filmmaking or anthropology was most likely to capture her. She helped out a bit one summer on a commercial some friends were making; then she and a boyfriend took off for Nepal and made a film about the honey-hunters—old men who harvest honey from beehives up on the cliffs. It was called *High Honey* and got a lot of notice from both documentarians and anthropologists.

I watched with pleasure, with amazement, and

finally with joy as my granddaughter's mind expanded. Six months after returning from Nepal, not yet eighteen, she decided that what she needed was more education. In rapid succession she left UCLA for Berkeley, Berkeley for the University of Chicago, Chicago for Columbia, Columbia for the Sorbonne. I visited her occasionally in several of her schools, marveling at the way she took what she wanted from each of the available brain pools; the great universities were like intellectual furniture warehouses to Jesse. She rushed through them with bright eyes open, made her selection in a few weeks, and went on to the next warehouse. After one look at Jesse, or one talk, many great brains made themselves available, more or less, for whatever Jesse had in mind.

She soon had boyfriends of all ages, and, it sometimes seemed, in all places. When men saw Jesse coming, their hopes immediately rose. She was pretty, she was hopeful, almost anything interesting or almost anyone friendly delighted her; but, most of all, Jesse was welcoming. She had no trouble sharing herself, and she possessed the rare knack of passing on without hurting those she was leaving. Jesse left, but her men stayed loyal—remarkably loyal, for men—and in time the whole North American continent seemed to be crowded with Jesse's boyfriends, past, present, and would-be.

"They're getting kinda thick," she said to me with a quick, soft grin—the grin that never failed to remind me of all the fat lips she had sported as a little girl growing up with Bo.

We were in Texas, drinking beer on the patio; Jesse had just bought her ticket for France.

"Maybe the kindest thing to do is just skip the country," she said. "What do you think, Grandpa?"

"Why not, sweetie?" I said. "Take a trip."

"Yeah," Jesse said. "I think I'll just put a long tape on my message machine and skip the country."

Jesse usually managed to do the kindest thing. Next morning she gave me a nice kiss and a long hug and skipped the country. The long tape on her message machine was exhausted in only a couple of days.

Next thing I knew Jesse had a Hungarian boyfriend and was in Budapest. Then she had an Italian boyfriend and was in Positano. It was six months before she settled in Paris, but she did finally settle in Paris, to sit at the feet of people who had sat at the feet of Sartre or Roman Jakobson, Lacan and Lévi-Strauss, and Ladurie, Barthes and Foucault.

Almost immediately she and one of her film professors embarked on a little movie about Madame Riccoboni. As it happened, I knew a little bit about Riccoboni—I had learned it nearly forty years earlier while doing a script about the Duchess of Dino. I was able to be slightly helpful.

Jesse called often, sometimes two or three times a week, to talk to me about the latest book, the latest film, the latest professor, Jeanie and Eric's latest visit, or the latest boyfriend. Most of her calls were from her tiny apartment in Montparnasse, but Jesse loved to take trips and had no foolish inhibitions about spending money. She also shared my fondness for grande luxe hotels. Jesse and her new guy might be at the Villa Hassler, the Gritti Palace, the Hotel du Cap Eden Roc. One of her ongoing subjects was to improve my creaky French, so that when I finally came over and we did the Dordogne or the Camargue or the Loire valley Jesse wouldn't have to do all the talking.

I expect she just didn't want to see her famous grandfather embarrassed, but I knew perfectly well that was exactly what would happen when I did finally go, for the French language and I had never been on close or easy terms. One reason among many why I stuck close to the Mediterranean when in Europe was that conversational standards in the warm south were somewhat less severe than they were apt to be in the frosty north.

Jesse called and called; she called and called, talking and talking in her quick, slangy French, as I sat at my window looking out on the Texas plain. I watched the graceful hawks soaring above the hill south of Los Dolores; I saw the dawn's colors to the east, where Jesse was, and the sunset's colors fading in the west. Jesse called and called; she called and called; she was not about to let her grandfather go.

Sometimes if she called in the morning, before

I managed to emerge from sleep or migraine, I would get a little confused, be unable to follow the reasoning of some Godardian auteurist or poststructuralist semiotician. More and more often I tended to let the meaning go and merely let myself be lifted by the breeze of Jesse's young voice, as the hawks on my hills were lifted by the south wind.

She was not only my breeze, she was—to borrow the immortal phrase of Governor Jimmy Davis—my sunshine, her love the only radiance likely to pierce the clouds of age and confusion beneath which I lived.

Jesse called and called; she called and called. Less and less could I follow what she was telling me—France had made her precise just as age was making me vague—but as her smart French poured it into my ear, I began to float back in memory; in my granddaughter's voice I began to hear the lovely echo of the voices of all those fabulous European girls I had had such fun with so long ago, the stars and the starlets—Pier, Senta, Françoise Dorléac, the glorious Romy Schneider. Their voices, like Jesse's now, had once all whistled the brainy, sexual whistle of youth and health, tunes that those who once could whistle too lose but never forget.

A note on the text
Large print edition designed by
Genevieve A. Connell
of G.K. Hall & Co.

ACB